Harriet Beecher Stowe

We and Our Neighbors

Or, the records of an unfashionable street

Harriet Beecher Stowe

We and Our Neighbors
Or, the records of an unfashionable street

ISBN/EAN: 9783337042103

Printed in Europe, USA, Canada, Australia, Japan

Cover: Foto ©Andreas Hilbeck / pixelio.de

More available books at **www.hansebooks.com**

NEW NEIGHBORS.

*"Who can have taken the Ferguses' house, sister?" said a brisk little
old lady, peeping through the window blinds.*—p. 7.

WE AND OUR NEIGHBORS:

OR,

THE RECORDS OF AN UNFASHIONABLE STREET.

(Sequel to " My Wife and I.")

A NOVEL.

By HARRIET BEECHER STOWE.

Author of "Uncle Tom's Cabin," "My Wife and I," etc.

With Illustrations.

NEW YORK:

J. B. FORD & COMPANY.

CONTENTS.

LIST OF ILLUSTRATIONS.

WE AND OUR NEIGHBORS.

CHAPTER I.

THE OTHER SIDE OF THE STREET.

"WHO can have taken the Ferguses' house, sister?" said a brisk little old lady, peeping through the window blinds. "It's taken! Just come here and look! There's a cart at the door."

"You don't say so!" said Miss Dorcas, her elder sister, flying across the room to the window blinds, behind which Mrs. Betsey sat discreetly ensconced with her knitting work. "Where? Jack, get down, sir!" This last remark was addressed to a rough-coated Dandie Dinmont terrier, who had been winking in a half doze on a cushion at Miss Dorcas's feet. On the first suggestion that there was something to be looked at across the street, Jack had ticked briskly across the room, and now stood on his hind legs on an old embroidered chair, peering through the slats as industriously as if his opinion had been requested. "Get down, sir!" persisted Miss Dorcas. But Jack only winked contumaciously at Mrs. Betsey, whom he justly considered in the light of an ally, planted his toe nails more firmly in the embroidered chair-bottom, and stuck his nose further between the slats, while Mrs. Betsey took up for him, as he knew she would.

"Do let the dog alone, Dorcas! *He* wants to see as much as anybody."

"Now, Betsey, how am I ever to teach Jack not to

jump on these chairs if you will always take his part?
Besides, next we shall know, he'll be barking through
the window blinds," said Miss Dorcas.

Mrs. Betsey replied to the expostulation by making a
sudden diversion of subject. "Oh, look, look!" she
called, "that must be *she*," as a face with radiant, dark
eyes, framed in an aureole of bright golden hair, appeared in the doorway of the house across the street.
"She's a pretty creature, anyway—much prettier than
poor dear Mrs. Fergus."

"Henderson, you say the name is?" said Miss Dorcas.

"Yes. Simons, the provision man at the corner, told
me that the house had been bought by a young editor, or
something of that sort, named Henderson—somebody
that writes for the papers. He married Van Arsdel's
daughter."

"What, the Van Arsdels that failed last spring? One
of our mushroom New York aristocracy—up to-day and
down to-morrow!" commented Miss Dorcas, with an air
of superiority. "Poor things!"

"A very imprudent marriage, I don't doubt," sighed
Mrs. Betsey. "These upstart modern families never
bring up their girls to do anything."

"She seems to be putting her hand to the plough,
though," said Miss Dorcas. "See, she actually is lifting
out that package herself! Upon my word, a very pretty
creature. I think we must take her up."

"The Ferguses were nice," said Mrs. Betsey, "though
he was only a newspaper man, and she was a nobody;
but she really did quite answer the purpose for a neighbor—not, of course, one of our sort exactly, but a very
respectable, lady-like little body."

"Well," said Miss Dorcas, reflectively, "I always said
it doesn't do to carry exclusiveness too far. Poor dear
Papa was quite a democrat. He often said that he had

seen quite good manners and real refinement in people of the most ordinary origin."

"And, to be sure," said Mrs. Betsey, "if one is to be too particular, one doesn't get anybody to associate with. The fact is, the good old families we used to visit have either died off or moved off up into the new streets, and one does like to have *somebody* to speak to."

"Look there, Betsey, do you suppose that's Mr. Henderson that's coming down the street?" said Miss Dorcas.

"Dear me!" said Mrs. Betsey, in an anxious flutter. "Why, there are *two* of them—they are both taking hold to lift out that bureau—see there! Now *she's* put her head out of the chamber window there, and is speaking to them. What a pretty color her hair is!"

At this moment the horse on the other side of the street started prematurely, for some reason best known to himself, and the bureau came down with a thud; and Jack, who considered his opinion as now called for, barked frantically through the blinds.

Miss Dorcas seized his muzzle energetically and endeavored to hold his jaws together, but he still barked in a smothered and convulsive manner; whereat the good lady swept him, *vi et armis*, from his perch, and disciplined him vigorously, forcing him to retire to his cushion in a distant corner, where he still persistently barked.

"Oh, poor doggie!" sighed Mrs. Betsey. "Dorcas, how can you?"

"How can I?" said Miss Dorcas, in martial tones. "Betsey Ann Benthusen, this dog would grow up a perfect pest of this neighborhood if I left him to you. He *must* learn not to get up and bark through those blinds. It isn't so much matter now the windows are shut, but the *habit* is the thing. Who wants to have a dog firing a fusillade when your visitors come up the front steps—

barking-enough-to-split-one's-head-open," added Miss Dorcas, turning upon the culprit, with a severe staccato designed to tell upon his conscience.

Jack bowed his head and rolled his great soft eyes at her through a silvery thicket of hair.

"You are a *very* naughty dog," she added, impressively.

Jack sat up on his haunches and waved his front paws in a deprecating manner to Miss Dorcas, and the good lady laughed and said, cheerily, "Well, well, Jacky, be a good dog now, and we'll be friends."

And Jacky wagged his tail in the most demonstrative manner, and frisked with triumphant assurance of restored favor. It was the usual end of disciplinary struggles with him. Miss Dorcas sat down to a bit of worsted work on which she had been busy when her attention was first called to the window.

Mrs. Betsey, however, with her nose close to the window blinds, continued to announce the state of things over the way in short jets of communication.

"There! the gentlemen are both gone in—and there! the cart has driven off. Now, they've shut the front door," etc.

After this came a pause of a few moments, in which both sisters worked in silence.

"I wonder, now, *which* of those two was the husband," said Mrs. Betsey at last, in a slow reflective tone, as if she had been maturely considering the subject.

In the mean time it had occurred to Miss Dorcas that this species of minute inquisition into the affairs of neighbors over the way was rather a compromising of her dignity, and she broke out suddenly from a high moral perch on her unconscious sister.

"Betsey," she said, with severe gravity, "I really suppose it's no concern of ours *what* goes on over at the other house. Poor dear Papa used to say if there was anything that was unworthy a true lady it was a disposition to gossip. Our neighbors' affairs are nothing to us. I think it is Mrs. Chapone who says, 'A well-regulated mind will repress curiosity.' Perhaps, Betsey, it would be well to go on with our daily reading."

Mrs. Betsey, as a younger sister, had been accustomed to these sudden pullings-up of the moral check-rein from Miss Dorcas, and received them as meekly as a well-bitted pony. She rose immediately, and, laying down her knitting work, turned to the book-case. It appears that the good souls were diversifying their leisure hours by reading for the fifth or sixth time that enlivening poem, Young's *Night Thoughts.* So, taking down a volume from the book-shelves and opening to a mark, Mrs. Betsey commenced a sonorous expostulation to Alonzo on the value of time. The good lady's manner of rendering poetry was in a high-pitched falsetto, with inflections of a marvelous nature, rising in the earnest parts almost to a howl. In her youth she had been held to possess a talent for elocution, and had been much commended by the amateurs of her times as a reader of almost professional merit. The decay of her vocal organs had been so gradual and gentle that neither sister had perceived the change of quality in her voice, or the nervous tricks of manner which had grown upon her, till her rendering of poetry resembled a preternatural hoot. Miss Dorcas beat time with her needle and listened complacently to the mournful adjurations, while Jack, crouching himself with his nose on his forepaws, winked very hard and surveyed Miss Betsey with an uneasy excitement, giving from time to time low growls as her voice rose in emphatic places; and finally, as if even a dog's patience could stand it no longer, he chorused a startling point with a sharp yelp!

" There !" said Mrs. Betsey, throwing down the book. " What *is* the reason Jack *never* likes me to read poetry ? "

Jack sprang forward as the book was thrown down, and running to Mrs. Betsey, jumped into her lap and endeavored to kiss her in a most tumultuous and excited manner, as an expression of his immense relief.

" There! there! Jacky, good fellow—down, down ! Why, how odd it is! I can't think what excites him so in my reading," said Mrs. Betsey. . " It must be something that he notices in my intonations," she added, innocently.

The two sisters we have been looking in upon are worthy of a word of introduction. There are in every growing city old houses that stand as breakwaters in the tide of modern improvement, and may be held as fortresses in which the past entrenches itself against the never-ceasing encroachments of the present. The house in which the conversation just recorded has taken place was one of these. It was a fragment of ancient primitive New York known as the old Vanderheyden house, only waiting the death of old Miss Dorcas Vanderheyden and her sister, Mrs. Betsey Benthusen, to be pulled down and made into city lots and squares.

Time was when the Vanderheyden house was the country seat of old Jacob Vanderheyden, a thriving Dutch merchant, who lived there with somewhat foreign ideas of style and stateliness.

Parks and gardens and waving trees had encircled it, but the city limits had gained upon it through three generations; squares and streets had been opened through its grounds, till now the house itself and the garden-patch in the rear was all that remained of the ancient domain. Innumerable schemes of land speculators had attacked the old place; offers had been insidiously made to the proprietors which would have put them in possession of dazzling wealth, but they gallantly maintained their position. It is true their income in ready money was but scanty, and their taxes had, year by year, grown higher as the value of the land increased. Modern New York, so to speak, foamed and chafed like a great red dragon before the old house, waiting to make a mouthful of it, but the ancient princesses within bravely held their own and refused to parley or capitulate.

Their life was wholly in the past, with a generation whose bones had long rested under respectable tombstones. Their grandfather on their mother's side had been a signer of the Declaration of Independence; their grandfather on the paternal side was a Dutch merchant of some standing in early New York, a friend and correspondent of Alexander Hamilton's and a co-worker with him in those financial schemes by which the treasury of the young republic of America was first placed on a solid basis. Old Jacob did good service in negotiating loans in Holland, and did not omit to avail himself of the golden opportunities which the handling of a nation's wealth presents. He grew rich and great in the land, and was implicitly revered in his own family as being one of the nurses and founders of the American Republic. In the ancient Dutch secretary which stood in the corner of the sitting-room where our old ladies spent their time were many letters from noted names of a century or so back—papers yellow with age, but whose contents were all alive with the foam and fresh turbulence of what was then the existing life of the period.

Mrs. Betsey Benthusen was a younger sister and a widow. She had been a beauty in her girlhood, and so much younger than her sister that Miss Dorcas felt all the pride and interest of a mother in her success, in her lovers, in her marriage; and when that marriage proved a

miserable failure, uniting her to a man who wasted her
fortune and neglected her person, and broke her heart,
Miss Dorcas received her back to her strong arms and
made a home and a refuge where the poor woman could
gather up and piece together, in some broken fashion,
the remains of her life as one mends a broken Sèvres
china tea cup.

Miss Dorcas was by nature of a fiery, energetic temperament, intense and original—precisely the one to be a
contemner of customs and proprieties; but a very severe
and rigid education had imposed on her every yoke of
the most ancient and straitest-laced decorum. She had
been nurtured only in such savory treatises as Dr. Greg-
ory's *Legacy to his Daughters*, Mrs. Chapone's *Letters*,
Miss Hannah More's *Cœlebs in Search of a Wife*, Watts
On the Mind, and other good books by which our great
grandmothers had their lives all laid out for them in
exact squares and parallelograms, and were taught exactly what to think and do in all possible emergencies.

But, as often happens, the original nature of Miss
Dorcas was apt to break out here and there, all the more
vivaciously for repression, in a sort of natural geyser:
and so, though rigidly proper in the main, she was apt to
fall into delightful spasms of naturalness.

Notwithstanding all the remarks of Mrs. Chapone
and Dr. Watts about gossip, she still had a hearty and
innocent interest in the pretty young housekeeper that
was building a nest opposite to her, and a little quite
harmless curiosity in what was going on over the way.

A great deal of good sermonizing, by the by, is expended on gossip, which is denounced as one of the
seven deadly sins of society; but, after all, gossip has its
better side: if not a Christian grace, it certainly is one
of those weeds which show a good warm soil.

The kindly heart, that really cares for everything hu-

man it meets, inclines toward gossip, in a good way.
Just as a morning glory throws out tendrils, and climbs
up and peeps cheerily into your window, so a kindly
gossip can't help watching the opening and shutting of
your blinds and the curling smoke from your chimney.
And so, too, after all the high morality of Miss Dorcas,
the energetic turning of her sister to the paths of propriety, and the passage from Young's *Night Thoughts*, with
its ponderous solemnity, she was at heart kindly musing
upon the possible fortunes of the pretty young creature
across the street, and was as fresh and ready to take up
the next bit of information about her house as a brisk
hen is to discuss the latest bit of crumb thrown from a
window.

Miss Dorcas had been brought up by her father in
diligent study of the old approved English classics. The
book-case of the sitting-room presented in gilded order
old editions of the *Rambler*, the *Tattler*, and the *Spectator*,
the poems of Pope, and Dryden, and Milton, and Shakespeare, and Miss Dorcas and her sister were well versed
in them all. And in view of the whole of our modern
literature, we must say that their studies might have been
much worse directed.

Their father had unfortunately been born too early to
enjoy Walter Scott. There is an age when a man cannot
receive a new author or a new idea. Like a lilac bush
which has made its terminal buds, he has grown all he
can in this life, and there is no use in trying to force him
into a new growth. Jacob Vanderheyden died considering Scott's novels as the flimsy trash of the modern
school, while his daughters hid them under their pillows,
and found them all the more delightful from the vague
sensation of sinfulness which was connected with their
admiration. Walter Scott was their most modern land-
mark; youth and bloom and heedlessness and impropri-

ety were all delightfully mixed up with their reminiscences of him—and now, here they were still living in an age which has shelved Walter Scott among the classics, and reads Dickens and Thackeray and Anthony Trollope.

Miss Dorcas had been stranded, now and then, on one of these "trashy moderns"—had sat up all night surreptitiously reading *Nicholas Nickleby*, and had hidden the book from Mrs. Betsey lest her young mind should be carried away, until she discovered, by an accidental remark, that Mrs. Betsey had committed the same delightful impropriety while off on a visit to a distant relative. When the discovery became mutual, from time to time other works of the same author crept into the house in cheap pamphlet editions, and the perusal of them was apologized for by Miss Dorcas to Mrs. Betsey, as being well enough, now and then, to see what people were reading in these trashy times. Ah, what is fame! Are not Dickens and Thackeray and Trollope on their inevitable way to the same dusty high shelf in the library, where they will be praised and not read by the forthcoming *jeunesse* of the future?

If the minds of the ancient sisters were a museum of by-gone ideas, and literature, and tastes, the old Vanderheyden house was no less a museum of by-gone furniture. The very smell of the house was ghostly with past suggestion. Every article of household gear in it had grown old together with all the rest, standing always in the same spot, subjected to the same minute daily dusting and the same semi-annual house-cleaning.

Carlyle has a dissertation on the "talent for annihilating rubbish." This was a talent that the respectable Miss Dorcas had none of. Carlyle thinks it a fine thing to have; but we think the lack of it may come from very respectable qualities. In Miss Dorcas it came from a vivid imagination of the possible future uses to which every decayed or broken household article might be put. The pitcher without nose or handle was fine china, and might yet be exactly the thing for something, and so it went carefully on some high perch of preservation, dismembered; the half of a broken pair of snuffers certainly looked too good to throw away—possibly it might be the exact thing needed to perfect some invention. Miss Dorcas vaguely remembered legends of inventors who had laid hold on such chance adaptations at the very critical point of their contrivances, and so the half snuffers waited years for their opportunity. The upper shelves of the closets in the Vanderheyden house were a perfect crowded mustering ground for the incurables and incapables of household belongings. One might fancy them a Hotel des Invalides of things wounded and fractured in the general battle of life. There were blades of knives without handles, and handles without blades; there were ancient tea-pots that leaked—but might be mended, and doubtless would be of some good in a future day; there were cracked plates and tea-cups; there were china dishcovers without dishes to match; a coffee-mill that wouldn't grind, and shears that wouldn't cut, and snuffers that wouldn't snuff—in short, every species of decayed utility.

Miss Dorcas had in the days of her youth been blest with a brother of an active, inventive turn of mind; the secret crypts and recesses of the closets bore marks of his unfinished projections. There were all the wheels and weights and other internal confusions of a clock, which he had pulled to pieces with a view of introducing an improvement into the machinery, which never was introduced; but the wheels and weights were treasured up with pious care, waiting for *somebody* to put them together again. All this array of litter was fated to come down from its secret recesses, its deep, dark closets, its high

shelves and perches, on two solemn days of the year devoted to house-cleaning, when Miss Dorcas, like a good
general, looked them over and reviewed them, expatiated
on their probable capabilities, and resisted gallantly any
suggestions of Black Dinah, the cook and maid of all
work, or Mrs. Betsey, that some order ought to be taken
to rid the house of them.

"Dear me, Dorcas," Mrs. Betsey would say, "what is
the use of keeping such a clutter and litter of things that
nothing can be done with and that never can be used?"

"Betsey Ann Benthusen," would be the reply, "you
always were a careless little thing. You never understood any more about housekeeping than a canary bird
—not a bit." In Miss Dorcas's view, Mrs. Betsey, with
her snow white curls and her caps, was still a frivolous
young creature, not fit to be trusted with a serious opinion on the nicer points of household management.
"Now, who knows, Betsey, but some time we may meet
some poor worthy young man who may be struggling
along as an inventor and may like to have these wheels
and weights! I'm sure brother Dick said they were
wonderfully well made."

"Well, but, Dorcas, all those cracked cups and broken
pitchers; I do think they are dreadful!"

"Now, Betsey, hush up! I've heard of a kind of
new cement that they are manufacturing in London, that
makes old china better than new; and when they get it
over here I'm going to mend these all up. You wouldn't
have me throw away *family* china, would you?"

The word "*family* china" was a settler, for both Mrs.
Betsey and Miss Dorcas and old Dinah were united in
one fundamental article of faith: that "the *Family*" was
a solemn, venerable and awe-inspiring reality. What, or
why, or how it was, no mortal could say.

Old Jacob Vanderheyden, the grandfather, had been

in his day busy among famous and influential men, and had even been to Europe as a sort of attaché to the first American diplomatic corps. He had been also a thriving merchant, and got to himself houses, and lands, and gold and silver. Jacob Vanderheyden, the father, had inherited substance and kept up the good name of the family, and increased and strengthened its connections. But his son and heir, Dick Vanderheyden, Miss Dorcas's elder brother, had seemed to have no gifts but those of dispersing; and had muddled away the family fortune in all sorts of speculations and adventures as fast as his father and grandfather had made it. The sisters had been left with an income much abridged by the imprudence of the brother and the spendthrift dissipation of Mrs. Betsey's husband; they were forsaken by the retreating waves of rank and fashion; their house, instead of being a center of good society, was encompassed by those ordinary buildings devoted to purposes of trade whose presence is deemed incompatible with genteel residence. And yet, through it all, their confidence in the rank and position of their family continued unabated. The old house, with every bit of old queer furniture in it, the old window curtains, the old tea-cups and saucers, the old bedspreads and towels, all had a sacredness such as pertained to no modern things. Like the daughter of Zion in sacred song, Miss Dorcas "took pleasure in their dust and favored the stones thereof." The old blue willow-patterned china, with mandarins standing in impossible places, and bridges and pagodas growing up, as the world was made, out of nothing, was to Miss Dorcas consecrated porcelain—even its broken fragments were impregnated with the sacred flavor of ancient gentility.

Miss Dorcas's own private and personal closets, drawers, and baskets were squirrel's-nests of all sorts of memorials of the past. There were pieces of every

gown she had ever worn, of all her sister's gowns, and
of the mortal habiliments of many and many a one
beside who had long passed beyond the need of earthly
garments. Bits of wedding robes of brides who had
long been turned to dust; fragments of tarnished gold
lace from old court dresses; faded, crumpled, artificial
flowers, once worn on the head of beauty; gauzes and
tissues, old and wrinkled, that had once set off the triumphs of the gay—all mingled in her crypts and drawers
and trunks, and each had its story. Each, held in her
withered hand, brought back to memory the thread of
some romance warm with the color and flavor of a life
long passed away.

Then there were collections, saving and medicinal;
for Miss Dorcas had in great force that divine instinct
of womanhood that makes her perceptive of the healing
power inherent in all things. Never an orange or an
apple was pared on her premises when the peeling was
not carefully garnered—dried on newspaper, and neatly
stored away in paper bags for sick-room uses.

There were closets smelling of elderblow, catnip,
feverfew, and dried rose leaves, which grew in a bit of
old garden soil back of the house; a spot sorely retrenched and cut down from the ample proportions it
used to have, as little by little had been sold off, but still
retaining a few growing things, in which Miss Dorcas
delighted. The lilacs that once were bushes there had
grown gaunt and high, and looked in at the chamber
windows with an antique and grandfatherly air, quite of
a piece with everything else about the old Vanderheyden
house.

The ancient sisters had few outlets into the society
of modern New York. Now and then, a stray visit came
from some elderly person who still remembered the Van-
derheydens, and perhaps about once a year they went to

the expense of a carriage to return the call, and rolled up into the new part of the town like shadows of the past. But generally their path of life led within the narrow limits of the house. Old Dinah, the sole black servant remaining, was the last remnant of a former retinue of negro servants held by old Jacob when New York was a slave State and a tribe of black retainers was one of the ostentations of wealth. All were gone now, and only Dinah remained, devoted to the relics of the old family, clinging with a cat-like attachment to the old place.

She was like many of her race, a jolly-hearted, pig-headed, giggling, faithful old creature, who said "Yes'm" to Miss Dorcas and took her own way about most matters; and Miss Dorcas, satisfied that her way was not on the whole a bad one in the ultimate results, winked at her free handling of orders, and consented to accept her, as we do Nature, for what could be got out of her.

"They are going to have mince-pie and broiled chicken for dinner over there," said Mrs. Betsey, when the two ladies were seated at their own dinner-table that day.

"How in the world did you know that?" asked Miss Dorcas.

"Well! Dinah met their girl in at the provision store and struck up an acquaintance, and went in to help her put up a bedstead, and so she stopped a while in the kitchen. The tall gentleman with black hair *is* the husband—I thought all the while he was," said Mrs. Betsey. "The other one is a Mr. Fellows, a great friend of theirs, Mary says——"

"Mary!—who is Mary?" said Miss Dorcas.

"Why, Mary McArthur, their girl—they only keep one, but she has a little daughter about eight years old to help. I wish we had a little girl, or something that one might train for a waiter to answer door-bells and do little things."

"Our door-bells don't call for much attention, and a little girl is nothing but a plague," interposed Miss Dorcas.

"Dinah has quite fallen in love with Mrs. Henderson," said Mrs. Betsey; "she says that she is the handsomest, pleasantest-spoken lady she's seen for a great while."

"We'll call upon her when they get well settled," said Miss Dorcas, definitively.

Miss Dorcas settled this with the air of a princess. She felt that such a meritorious little person as the one over the way ought to be encouraged by people of good old families.

Our readers will observe that Miss Dorcas listened without remonstrance and with some appearance of interest to the items about minced pie and broiled chicken; but high moral propriety, as we all know, is a very cold, windy height, and if a person is planted on it once or twice a day, it is as much as ought to be demanded of human weakness.

For the rest of the time one should be allowed, like Miss Dorcas, to repose upon one's laurels. And, after all, it is interesting, when life is moving in a very stagnant current, even to know what your neighbor has for dinner!

CHAPTER II.

HOW WE BEGIN LIFE.

(Letter from Eva Henderson to Isabelle Courtney.)

MY DEAR BELLE: Well, here we are, Harry and I, all settled down to housekeeping quite like old folks. All is about done but the *last things*,—those little touches, and improvements, and alterations that go off into airy perspective. I believe it was Carlyle that talked about an "infinite shoe-black" whom all the world could not quite satisfy so but that there would always be a next thing in the distance. Well, perhaps it's going to be so in housekeeping, and I shall turn out an infinite housekeeper; for I find this little, low-studded, unfashionable home of ours, far off in a tabooed street, has kept all my energies brisk and busy for a month past, and still there are more worlds to conquer. Visions of certain brackets and lambrequins that are to adorn my spare chamber visit my pillow nightly, while Harry is placidly sleeping the sleep of the just. I have been unable to attain to them because I have been so busy with my parlor ivies and my Ward's case of ferns, and some perfectly seraphic hanging baskets, gorgeous with flowering nasturtiums that are now blooming in my windows. There is a dear little Quaker dove of a woman living in the next house to ours who is a perfect witch at gardening—a good kind of witch, you understand, one who could make a broomstick bud and blossom if she undertook it —and she has been my teacher and exemplar in these matters. Her parlor is a perfect bower, a drab dove's nest wreathed round with vines and all a-bloom with geraniums; and mine is coming on to look just like it. So you see all this has kept me ever so busy.

Then there are the family accounts to keep. You may think that isn't much for our little concern, but you would be amazed to find how much there is in it. You see, I have all my life concerned myself only with figures of speech and never gave a thought about figures of arithmetic or troubled my head as to where money came from, or went to; and when I married Harry I had a general idea that we were going to live with delightful economy. But it is astonishing how much all our simplicity costs, after all. My account-book is giving me a world of new ideas, and some pretty serious ones too.

Harry, you see, leaves every thing to me. He has to be off to his office by seven o'clock every morning, and I am head marshal of the commisariat department—committee of one on supplies, and all that—and it takes up a good deal of my time.

You would laugh, Belle, to see me with my matronly airs and graces going my daily walk to the provision-store at the corner, which is kept by a tall, black-browed lugubrious man, with rough hair and a stiff stubby beard, who surveys me with a severe gravity over the counter, as if he wasn't sure that my designs were quite honest.

"Mr. Quackenboss," I say, with my sweetest smile, "have you any nice butter?"

He looks out of the window, drums on the counter, and answers "Yes," in a tone of great reserve.

"I should like to look at some," I say, undiscouraged.

"It's down cellar," he replies, gloomily chewing a bit of chip and casting sinister glances at me.

"Well," I say, cheerfully, "shall I go down there and look at it?"

"How much do you want?" he asks, suspiciously.

"That depends on how well I like it," say I.

"I s'pose I *could* get up a cask," he says in a ruminating tone; and now he calls his partner, a cheerful, fat, roly-poly little cockney Englishman, who flings his h's round in the most generous and reckless style. His alert manner seems to say that he would get up forty casks a minute and throw them all at my feet, if it would give me any pleasure.

So the butter-cask is got up and opened, and my severe friend stands looking down on it and me as if he would say, "This also is vanity."

"I should like to taste it," I say, "if I had something to try it with."

He scoops up a portion on his dirty thumbnail and seems to hold it reflectively, as if a doubt was arising in his mind of the propriety of this mode of offering it to me.

And now my cockney friend interposes with a clean knife. I taste the butter and find it excellent, and give a generous order which delights his honest soul; and as he weighs it out he throws in, gratis, the information that his little woman has tried it, and he was sure I would like it, for she is the *tidiest* little woman and the *best* judge of butter; that they came from Yorkshire, where the pastures round were so sweet with a-many violets and cowslips—in fact, my little cockney friend strays off into a kind of pastoral that makes the little grocery store quite poetic.

I call my two grocers familiarly Tragedy and Comedy, and make Harry a good deal of fun by recounting my adventures with them. I have many speculations about Tragedy. He is a married man, as I learn, and I can't help wondering what Mrs. Quackenboss thinks of him. Does he ever shave—or does she kiss him in the rough—or has she given up kissing him at all? How did he act when he was in love?—if ever he was in love —and what *did* he say to the lady to induce her to marry

B

him? How did he look when he did it? It really makes
me shudder to think of such a mournful ghoul coming
back to the domestic circle at night. I should think the
little "Quacks" would all run and hide. But a truce to
scandalizing my neighbor—he may be better than I am,
after all!

I ought to tell you that some of my essays in provis-
ioning my garrison might justly excite his contempt—they
have been rather appalling to my good Mary McArthur.
You know I had been used to seeing about a ten-pound
sirloin of beef on Papa's table, and the first day I went
into the shop I assumed an air of easy wisdom as if I had
been a housekeeper all my life, and ordered just such a
cut as I had seen Mamma get, with all sorts of vegetables
to match, and walked home with composed dignity.
When Mary saw it she threw up her hands and gave
an exclamation of horror—"Miss Eva!" she said, "when
will we get all this eaten up?" And verily that beef
pursued us through the week most like a ghost. We had
it hot, and we had it cold; we had it stewed and hashed,
and made soup of it; we sliced it and we minced it, and
I ate a great deal more than was good for me on purpose
to "save it." Towards the close of the week Harry civil-
ly suggested (he never finds fault with anything I do, but
he merely *suggested*) whether it wouldn't be better to
have a little variety in our table arrangements; and then
I came out with the whole story, and we had a good
laugh together about it. Since then I have come down
to taking lessons of Mary, and I say to her, "How much
of this, and that, had I better get?" and between us we
make it go quite nicely.

Speaking of neighbors, my dear blessed Aunt Maria,
whom I suppose you remember, has almost broken
her heart about Papa's failing and my marrying Harry
and, finally, our coming to live on an unfashionable street

—which in her view is equal to falling out of heaven into some very suspicious region of limbo. She almost quarreled with us both because, having got married contrary to her will, we would also insist on going to housekeeping and having a whole house to ourselves on a back street instead of having one little, stuffy room on the back side of a fashionable boarding house. Well, I made all up with her at last. If you *will* have your own way, and persist in it, people *have to* make up with you. You thus get to be like the sun and moon which, though they often behave very inconveniently, you have to make the best of; and so Aunt Maria has concluded to make the best of Harry and me. It came about in this wise: I went and sat with her the last time she had a sick headache, and kissed her, and bathed her head, and told her I wanted to be a good girl and did really love her, though I couldn't always take her advice now I was a married woman; and so we made it up.

But the trouble is that now she wants to show me how to run this poor little unfashionable boat so as to make a good show with the rest of them, and I don't want to learn. It's easier to keep out of the regatta. My card-receiver is full of most desirable names of people who have come in their fashionable carriages and coupés, and they have "oh'd" and "ah'd" in my little parlors, and declared they were "quite sweet," and "so odd," and "*so* different, you know;" but, for all that, I don't think I shall try to keep up all this gay circle of acquaintances. Carriage-hire costs money; and when paid for by the hour, one asks whether the acquaintances are worth it. But there are some real noble-hearted people that I mean to keep. The Van Astrachans, for instance. Mrs. Van Astrachan is a solid lump of goodness and motherliness, and that sweet Mrs. Harry Endicott is most lovable. You remember Harry Endicott, I

suppose, and what a trump card he was thought to be
among the girls, one time when you were visiting us, and
afterwards all that scandal about him and that pretty
little Mrs. John Seymour? She is dead now, I hear, and
he has married this pretty Rose Ferguson, a friend of
hers; and since his *wife* has taken him in hand, he has
turned out to be a noble fellow. They live up on Mad-
ison avenue quite handsomely. They are among the "*real
folks*" Mrs. Whitney tells about, and I think I must keep
them. The Elmores I don't care much for. They are a
frivolous, fast set, and what's the use? Sophie and her
husband, my old friend Wat Sydney, I keep mainly because she won't give me up. She is one of the clinging
sort, and is devoted to me. They have a perfect palace
up by the park—it is quite a show-house, and is, I understand, to be furnished by Harter. So, you see, it's like
a friendship between princess and peasant.

Now, I foresee future conflicts with Aunt Maria in all
these possibilities. She is a nice woman, and bent on
securing what she thinks my interest, but I can't help
seeing that she is somewhat

> "A shade that follows wealth and fame."

The success of my card-receiver delights her, and
not to improve such opportunities would be, in her view,
to bury one's talent in a napkin. Yet, after all, I differ.
I can't help seeing that intimacies between people with a
hundred thousand a year and people of our modest
means will be full of perplexities.

And then I say, Why not try to find all the neighbor-
liness I can on my own street? In a country village, one
finds a deal in one's neighbors, simply because one must.
They are there; they are all one has, and human nature
is always interesting, if one takes it right side out. Next
door is the gentle Quakeress I told you of. She is

nobody in the gay world, but as full of sweetness and loving kindness as heart could desire. Then right across the way are two antiquated old ladies, very old, very precise, and very funny, who have come in state and called on me; bringing with them the most lovely, tyrannical little terrier, who behaved like a small-sized fiend and shocked them dreadfully. I spy worlds of interest in their company if once I can rub the stiffness out of our acquaintance, and then I hope to get the run of the delightfully queer old house.

Then there are our set—Jim Fellows, and Bolton, and my sister Alice, and the girls—in and out all the time. We sha'n't want for society. So if Aunt Maria puts me up for a career in the gay world I shall hang heavy on her hands.

I haven't much independence *myself*, but it is no longer *I*, it is *We*. Eva Van Arsdel alone was anybody's property; Mamma talked her one way, her sister Ida another way, and Aunt Maria a third; and among them all her own little way was hard to find. But now Harry and I have formed a firm and compact *We*, which is a fortress into which we retreat from all the world. I tell them all, *We* don't think so, and *We* don't do so. Isn't that nice? When will you come and see us?

Ever your loving   EVA.

CHAPTER III.

FROM the foregoing letter our readers may have con-
jectured that the natural self-appointed ruler of the
fortunes of the Van Arsdel family was "Aunt Maria," or
Mrs. Maria Wouvermans.

That is to say, this lady had always considered such
to be her mission, and had acted upon this supposition
up to the time that Mr. Van Arsdel's failure made shipwreck of the fortunes of the family.

Aunt Maria had, so to speak, reveled in the fortune
and position of the Van Arsdels. She had dictated the
expenditures of their princely income; she had projected
parties and entertainments; she had supervised lists of
guests to be invited; she had ordered dresses and carriages and equipages, and hired and dismissed servants at
her sovereign will and pleasure. Nominally, to be sure,
Mrs. Van Arsdel attended to all these matters; but really
Aunt Maria was the power behind the throne. Mrs. Van
Arsdel was a pretty, graceful, self-indulgent woman, who
loved ease and hated trouble—a natural climbing plant
who took kindly to any bean-pole in her neighborhood,
and Aunt Maria was her bean-pole. Mrs. Van Arsdel's
wealth, her station, her éclat, her blooming daughters, all
climbed up, so to speak, on Aunt Maria, and hung their
flowery clusters around her, to her praise and glory. Besides all this, there were very solid and appreciable
advantages in the wealth and station of the Van Arsdel
family as related to the worldly enjoyment of Mrs. Maria
Wouvermans. Being a widow, connected with an old

rich family, and with but a small fortune of her own
and many necessities of society upon her, Mrs. Wouvermans had found her own means in several ways
supplemented and carried out by the redundant means of
her sister. Mrs. Wouvermans lived in a moderate house
on Murray Hill, within comfortable proximity to the
more showy palaces of the New York nobility. She had
old furniture, old silver, camel's hair shawls and jewelry
sufficient to content her heart, but her yearly income was
far below her soul's desires, and necessitated more economy than she liked. While the Van Arsdels were in full
tide of success she felt less the confinement of these
limits. What need for her to keep a carriage when a
carriage and horses were always at her command for the
asking—and even without asking, as not infrequently
came to be the case? Then, the Van Arsdel parties and
hospitalities relieved her from all expensive obligations of
society. She returned the civilities of her friends by invitations to her sister's parties and receptions; and it is an
exceedingly convenient thing to have all the glory of
hospitality and none of the trouble—to have convenient
friends to entertain for you any person or persons with
whom you may be desirous of keeping up amicable relations. On the whole, Mrs Wouvermans was probably
sincere in the professions, to which Mr. Van Arsdel used
to listen with a quiet amused smile, that "she really enjoyed Nelly's fortune more than if it were her own."

"Haven't a doubt of it," he used to say, with a twinkle
of his eye which he never further explained.

Mr. Van Arsdel's failure had nearly broken Aunt
Maria's heart. In fact, the dear lady took the matter
more sorely than the good man himself.

Mr. Van Arsdel was, in a small dry way, something of
a philosopher. He was a silent man for the most part,
but had his own shrewd comments on the essential worth

of men and things—particularly of men in the feminine gender.   He had never checked his pretty wife in any of her aspirations, which he secretly valued at about their real value; he had never quarreled with Aunt Maria or interfered with her sway in his family within certain limits, because he had sense enough to see that she was the stronger of the two women, and that his wife could no more help yielding to her influence than a needle can help sticking to a magnet.

But the race of fashionable life, its outlays of health and strength, its expenditures for parties, and for dress and equipage, its rivalries, its gossip, its eager frivolities, were all matters of which he took quiet note, and which caused him often to ponder the words of the wise man of old, "What profit hath a man of all his labor and the vexation of his heart, wherein he hath labored under the sun?"

To Mr. Van Arsdel's eye the only profit of his labor and travail seemed to be the making of his wife frivolous, filling her with useless worries, training his daughters to be idle and self-indulgent, and his sons to be careless and reckless of expenditure.   So when at last the crash came, there was a certain sense of relief in finding himself once more an honest man at the bottom of the hill, and he quietly resolved in his inmost soul that he never would climb again.   He had settled up his affairs with a manly exactness that won the respect of all his creditors, and they had put him into a salaried position which insured a competence, and with this he resolved to be contented; his wife returned to the economical habits and virtues of her early life; his sons developed an amount of manliness and energy which was more than enough to compensate for what they had lost in worldly prospects. He enjoyed his small, quiet house and his reduced establishment as he never had done a more brilliant one, for

he felt that it was founded upon certainties and involved
no risks. Mrs. Van Arsdel was a sweet-tempered, kindly
woman, and his daughters had each and every one met
the reverse in a way that showed the sterling quality
which is often latent under gay and apparently thoughtless young womanhood.

Aunt Maria, however, settled it in her own mind, with
the decision with which she usually settled her relatives'
affairs, that this state of things would be only temporary.

"Of course," she said to her numerous acquaintances,
"of course, Mr. Van Arsdel will go into business again—
he is only waiting for a good opening—he 'll be up again
in a few years where he was before."

And to Mrs. Van Arsdel she said, "Nelly, you must
keep him up—you mustn't hear of his sinking down and
doing nothing "—*doing nothing* being his living contentedly on a comfortable salary and going without the
"pomps and vanities." "Your husband, of course, will
go into some operations to retrieve his fortunes, you
know," she said. "What is he thinking of?"

"Well, really, Maria, I don't see as he has the least
intention—he seems perfectly satisfied to live as we do."

"You must put him up to it, Nelly—depend upon it,
he's in danger of sinking down and giving up; and he
has splendid business talents. He should go to operating
in stocks, you see. Why, men make fortunes in that way.
Look at the Bubbleums, and the Flashes, they were all
down two years ago, and now they're up higher than ever,
and they did it all in stocks. Your husband would find
plenty of men ready to go in with him and advance
money to begin on. No man is more trusted. Why,
Nelly, that man might die a millionaire as well as not,
and you ought to put him up to it; it's a wife's business
to keep her husband up."

"I *have* tried to, Maria; I have been just as cheerful

as I knew how to be, and I've retrenched and economized everywhere, as all the girls do—they are wonderful, those girls! To see them take hold so cheerfully and help about household matters, you never would dream that they had not been brought up to it; and they are so prudent about their clothes—so careful and saving. And then the boys are getting on so well. Tom has gone into surveying with a will, and is going out with Smithson's party to the Rocky Mountains, and Hal has just got a good situation in Boston ——"

"Oh, yes, that is all very well; but, Nelly, that isn't what I mean. You know that when men fail in business they are apt to get blue and discouraged and give up enterprise, and so gradually sink down and lose their faculties. That's the way old Mr. Snodgrass did when he failed."

"But I don't think, Maria, that there is the least danger of my husband's losing his mind—or sinking down, as you call it. I never saw him more cheerful and seem to take more comfort of his life. Mr. Van Arsdel never did care for style—except as he thought it pleased me—and I believe he really likes the way we live now better than the way we did before; he says he has less care."

"And you are willing to sink down and be a nobody, and have no carriage, and rub round in omnibuses, and have to go to little mean private country board instead of going to Newport, when you might just as well get back the position that you had. Why, it's downright stupidity, Nelly!"

"As to mean country board," pleaded Mrs. Van Arsdel, "I don't know what you mean, Maria. We kept our old homestead up there in Vermont, and it's a very respectable place to spend our summer in."

"Yes, and what chances have the girls up there—

where nobody sees them but oxen? The girls ought to be considered. For their sakes you ought to put your husband up to do something. It's cruel to them, brought up with the expectations they have had, to have to give all up just as they are coming out. If there is any time that a mother *must* feel the want of money it is when she has daughters just beginning to go into society; and it is cruel towards young girls not to give them the means of dressing and doing a little as others do; and dress does cost so abominably, now-a-days; it's perfectly frightful—people cannot live creditably on what they used to."

"Yes, certainly, it is frightful to think of the requirements of society in these matters," said Mrs. Van Arsdel. "Now, when you and I were girls, Maria, you know we managed to appear well on a very little. We embroidered our own capes and collars, and wore white a good deal, and cleaned our own gloves, and cut and fitted our own dresses; but, then dress was not what it is now. Why, making a dress now is like rigging a man-of-war—it's so complicated—there are so many parts, and so much trimming."

"Oh, it's perfectly fearful," said Aunt Maria; "but, then, what is one to do? If one goes into society with people who have so much of all these things, why one must, at least, make some little approach to decent appearance. We must keep within sight of them. All I ask," she added, meekly, "is to be *decent*. I never expect to run into the extremes those Elmores do—the waste and the extravagance that there must be in that family! And there's Mrs. Wat Sydney coming out with the whole new set of her Paris dresses. I should like to know, for curiosity's sake, just what that woman has spent on her dresses!"

"Yes," said Mrs. Van Arsdel, warming with the subject, "you know she had all her wardrobe from Worth,

and Worth's dresses come to something. Why, Polly
told me that the lace alone on some of those dresses
would be a fortune."

"And just to think that Eva might have married Wat
Sydney," said Aunt Maria. "It does seem as if things
in this world fell out on purpose to try us!"

"Well, I suppose they do, and we ought to try and
improve by them," said Mrs. Van Arsdel, who had some
weak, gentle ideas of a moral purpose in existence, to
which even the losses and trials of lace and embroidery
might be made subservient. "After all," she added, "I
don't know but we ought to be contented with Eva's
position. Eva always was a peculiar child. Under all
her sweetness and softness she has quite a will of her
own; and, indeed, Harry is a good fellow, and doing
well in his line. He makes a very good income, for a
beginning, and he is rising every day in the literary
world, and I don't see but that they have as good an
opportunity to make their way in society as the Sydneys
with all their money."

"Sophie Sydney is perfectly devoted to Eva," said
Aunt Maria.

"And well she may be," answered Mrs. Van Arsdel,
"in fact, Eva made that match; she actually turned him
over to her. You remember how she gave her that prize
croquet-pin that Sydney gave her, and how she talked to
Sydney, and set him to thinking of Sophie—oh, pshaw!
Sydney never would have married that girl in the world
if it had not been for Eva."

"Well," said Aunt Maria, "it's as well to cultivate
that intimacy. It will be a grand summer visiting place
at their house in Newport, and we want visiting places
for the girls. I have put two or three anchors out to the
windward, in that respect. I am going to have the
Stephenson girls at my house this winter, and your girls

must help show them New York, and cultivate them, and then there will be a nice visiting place for them at Judge Stephenson's next summer. You see the Judge lives within an easy drive of Newport, so that they can get over there, and see and be seen."

"I'm sure, Maria, it's good in you to be putting yourself out for my girls."

"Pshaw, Nelly, just as if your girls were not mine—they are all I have to live for. I can't stop any longer now, because I must catch the omnibus to go down to Eva's; I am going to spend the day with her."

"How nicely Eva gets along," said Mrs. Van Arsdel, with a little pardonable motherly pride; "that girl takes to housekeeping as if it came natural to her."

"Yes," said Aunt Maria; "you know I have had Eva a great deal under my own eye, first and last, and it shows that early training will tell." Aunt Maria picked up this crumb of self-glorification with an easy matter-of-fact air which was peculiarly aggravating to her sister.

In her own mind Mrs. Van Arsdel thought it a little too bad. "Maria always did take the credit of everything that turned out well in my family," she said to herself, "and blamed me for all that went wrong."

But she was too wary to murmur out loud, and bent her head to the yoke in silence.

"Eva needs a little showing and cautioning," said Aunt Maria; "that Mary of hers ought to be watched, and I shall tell her so—she mustn't leave everything to Mary."

"Oh, Mary lived years with me, and is the most devoted, faithful creature," said Mrs. Van Arsdel.

"Never mind—she needs watching. She's getting old now, and don't work as she used to, and if Eva don't look out she won't get half a woman's work out of her—these old servants always take liberties. I shall look into things there. Eva is my girl; I sha'n't let anyone get around her;" and Aunt Maria arose to go forth. But if anybody supposes that two women engaged in a morning talk are going to stop when one of them rises to go, he knows very little of the ways of womankind. When they have risen, drawn up their shawls, and got ready to start, then is the time to call a new subject, and accordingly Aunt Maria, as she was going out the door, turned round and said : " Oh ! there now ! I almost forgot what I came for :—What *are* you going to do about the girls' party dresses ?"

" Well, we shall get a dressmaker in the house. If we can get Silkriggs, we shall try her."

" Now, Nelly, look here, I have found a real treasure —the nicest little dressmaker, just set up, and who works cheap. Maria Meade told me about her. She showed me a suit that she had had made there in imitation of a Paris dress, with ever so much trimming, cross-folds bound on both edges, and twenty or thirty bows, all cut on the bias and bound, and box-plaiting with double quilling on each side all round the bottom, and going up the front—graduated, you know. There was waist, and overskirt, and a little sacque, and, will you believe me, she only asked fifteen dollars for making it all."

" You don't say so !"

" It's a fact. Why, it must have been a good week's work to make that dress, even with her sewing machine. Maria told me of her as a great secret, because she really works so well that if folks knew it she would be swamped with work, and then go to raising her price—that's what they all do when they can get a chance—but I've been to her and engaged her for you."

" I'm sure, Maria, I don't know what we should do if you were not always looking out for us."

" I don't know—I'm getting to be an old woman,"

said Aunt Maria. "I'm not what I was. But I consider your family as my appointed field of labor—just as our rector said last Sunday, we must do the duty next us. But tell the girls not to talk about this dressmaker. We shall want all she can do, and make pretty much our own terms with her. It's nice and convenient for Eva that she lives somewhere down in those out-of-the-way regions where she has chosen to set up. Well, good morning;" and Aunt Maria opened the house-door and stood upon the top of the steps, when a second postscript struck her mind.

"There now!" said she, "I was meaning to tell you that it is getting to be reported everywhere that Alice and Jim Fellows are engaged."

"Oh, well, of course there's nothing in it," said Mrs. Van Arsdel. "I don't think Alice would think of him for a moment. She likes him as a friend, that's all."

"I don't know, Nelly; you can't be too much on your guard. Alice is a splendid girl, and might have almost anybody. Between you and me—now, Nelly, you must be sure not to mention it—but Mr. Delafield has been very much struck with her."

"Oh, Maria, how can you? Why, his wife hasn't been dead a year!"

"Oh, pshaw! these widowers don't always govern their eyes by the almanac," said Aunt Maria, with a laugh. "Of course, John Delafield will marry again. I always knew that; and Alice would be a splendid woman to be at the head of his establishment. At any rate, at the little company the other night at his sister's, Mrs. Singleton's, you know, he was perfectly devoted to her, and I thought Mrs. Singleton seemed to like it."

"It would certainly be a fine position, if Alice can fancy him," said Mrs. Van Arsdel. "Seems to me he is rather querulous and dyspeptic, is n't he?"

"Oh, well, yes; his health is delicate; he needs a wife to take care of him."

"He's so yellow!" ruminated Mrs. Van Arsdel, ingenuously. "I never could bear thin, yellow men."

"Oh, come, don't you begin, Nelly—it's bad enough to have girls with their fancies. What we ought to look at are the solid excellences. What a pity that the marrying age always comes when girls have the least sense! John Delafield is a solid man, and if he should take a fancy to Alice, it would be a great piece of good luck. Alice ought to be careful, and not have these reports around, about her and Jim Fellows; it just keeps off advantageous offers. I shall talk to Alice the first time I get a chance."

"Oh, pray don't, Maria—I don't think it would do any good. Alice is very set in her way, and it might put her up to make something of it more than there is."

"Oh, never fear me," said Aunt Maria, nodding her head; "I understand Alice, and know just what needs to be said. I sha'n't do her any harm, you may be sure," and Aunt Maria, espying her omnibus afar, ran briskly down the steps, thus concluding the conference.

Now it happened that adjoining the parlor where this conversation had taken place was a little writing-cabinet which Mr. Van Arsdel often used for the purposes of letter-writing. On this morning, when his wife supposed him out as usual at his office, he had retired there to attend to some correspondence. The entrance was concealed by drapery, and so he had been an unintentional and unsuspected but much amused listener to Aunt Maria's adjurations to his wife on his behalf.

All through his subsequent labors of the pen, he might have been observed to pause from time to time and laugh to himself. The idea of lying as a quiet dead weight on the wheels of the progress of his energetic relation was something vastly pleasing to the dry and secretive turn of his humor—and he rather liked it than otherwise.

"We shall see whether I am losing my faculties," he said to himself, as he gathered up his letters and departed.

CHAPTER IV.

MY DEAR MOTHER: Harry says I must do all the writing to you and keep you advised of all our affairs, because he is so driven with his editing and proof-reading that letter-writing is often the most fatiguing thing he can do. It is like trying to run after one has become quite out of breath.

The fact is, dear mother, the demands of this New York newspaper life are terribly exhausting. It's a sort of red-hot atmosphere of hurry and competition. Maga-zines and newspapers jostle each other, and run races, neck and neck, and everybody connected with them is kept up to the very top of his speed, or he is thrown out of the course. You see, Bolton and Harry have between them the oversight of three papers—a monthly magazine for the grown folk, another for the children, and a weekly paper. Of course there are sub-editors, but they have the general responsibility, and so you see they are on the *qui vive* all the time to keep up; for there are other papers and magazines running against them, and the price of success seems to be eternal vigilance. What is exacted of an editor now-a-days seems to be a sort of general omniscience. He must keep the run of everything,—politics, science, religion, art, agriculture, general literature; the world is alive and moving everywhere, and he must know just what's going on and be able to have an opinion ready made and ready to go to press at any moment. He must tell to a T just what they are doing in Ashantee and Dahomey, and what they don't do and ought to do in New York. He must be wise and instructive about currency and taxes and tariffs, and able to guide Congress; and then he must take care of the Church, — know just what the Old Catholics are up to, the last new kink of the Ritualists, and the right and wrong of all the free fights in the different denominations. It really makes my little head spin just to hear what they are getting up articles about. Bolton and Harry are kept on the chase, looking up men whose specialties lie in these lines to write for them. They have now in tow a Jewish Rabbi, who is going to do something about the Talmud, or Targums, or something of that sort; and a returned missionary from the Gaboon River, who entertained Du Chaillu and can speak authentically about the gorilla; and a lively young doctor who is devoting his life to the study of the brain and nervous system. Then there are all sorts of writing men and women sending pecks and bushels of articles to be printed, and getting furious if they are not printed, though the greater part of them are such hopeless trash that you only need to read four lines to know that they are good for nothing; but they all expect them to be re-mailed with explanations and criticisms, and the ladies sometimes write letters of wrath to Harry that are perfectly fearful.

Altogether there is a good deal of an imbroglio, and you see with it all how he comes to be glad that I have a turn for letter-writing and can keep you informed of how we of the interior go on. My business in it all is to keep a quiet, peaceable, restful home, where he shall always have the enjoyment of seeing beautiful things and find everything going on nicely without having to think why, or how, or wherefore; and, besides this, to do every

little odd and end for him that he is too tired or too
busy to do; in short, I suppose some of the ambitious
lady leaders of our time would call it playing second
fiddle.   Yes, that is it; but there must be second fiddles
in an orchestra, and it's fortunate that I have precisely
the talent for playing one, and my doctrine is that the
second fiddle *well* played is quite as good as the first.
What would the first be without it?

After all, in this great fuss about the men's sphere and
the women's, isn't the women's ordinary work just as important and great in its way?   For, you see, it's what the
men with all their greatness can't do, for the life of them.
I can go a good deal further in Harry's sphere than he
can in mine.   I can judge about the merits of a transla-
tion from the French, or criticise an article or story, a
great deal better than he can settle the difference between
the effect of tucking and inserting in a dress, or of cherry
and solferino in curtains.   Harry appreciates a room
prettily got up as well as any man, but how to get it up
—all the shades of color and niceties of arrangement, the
thousand little differences and agreements that go to it—
he can't comprehend.   So this man and woman question
is just like the quarrel between the mountain and the
squirrel in Emerson's poem, where " Bun " talks to the
mountain :

> " If I am not so big as you,
>   You're not so small as I,
>   And not half so spry.
>   If I cannot carry forests on my back,
>   Neither can you crack a nut."

I am quite satisfied that, first and last, I shall crack a
good many nuts for Harry.   Not that I am satisfied with
a mere culinary or housekeeping excellence, or even an
artistic and poetic skill in making home lovely ; I do want
a sense of something noble and sacred in life—something

to satisfy a certain feeling of the heroic that always made me unhappy and disgusted with my aimless fashionable girl career. I always sympathized with Ida, and admired her because she had force enough to do something that she thought was going to make the world better. It is better to try and fail with such a purpose as hers than never to try at all; and in that point of view I sympathize with the whole woman movement, though I see no place for myself in it. But my religion, poor as it is, has always given this excitement to me: I never could see how one could profess to be a Christian at all and not live a heroic life—though I know I never have. When I hear in church of the "glorious company of the apostles," the "goodly fellowship of the prophets," the "noble army of martyrs," I have often such an uplift—and the tears come to my eyes, and then my life seems so poor and petty, so frittered away in trifles. Then the communion service of our church always impresses me as something so serious, so profound, that I have wondered how I dared go through with it; and it always made me melancholy and dissatisfied with myself. To offer one's soul and body and spirit to God a living sacrifice surely ought to mean something that should make one's life noble and heroic, yet somehow it didn't do so with mine.

It was one thing that drew me to Harry, that he seemed to me an earnest, religious man, and I told him when we were first engaged that he must be my guide; but he said no, we must go hand in hand, and guide each other, and together we would try to find the better way. Harry is very good to me in being willing to go with me to my church. I told him I was weak in religion at any rate, and all my associations with good and holy things were with my church, and I really felt afraid to trust myself without them. I have tried going to his sort of services with him, but these extemporaneous prayers

don't often help me. I find myself weighing and considering in my own mind whether that is what I really do
feel or ask ; and if one is judging or deciding one can't be
praying at the same time. Now and then I hear a good
man who so wraps me up in his sympathies, and breathes
such a spirit of prayer as carries me without effort, and
that is lovely ; but it is so rare a gift ! In general I long
for the dear old prayers of my church, where my poor
little naughty heart has learned the way and can go on
with full consent without stopping to think.

So Harry and I have settled on attending an Episcopal mission church in our part of the city. Its worshipers
are mostly among the poor, and Harry thinks we might
do good by going there. Our rector is a young Mr. St.
John, a man as devoted as any of the primitive Christians.
I never saw anybody go into work for others with more
entire self-sacrifice. He has some property, and he supports himself and pays about half the expenses of the
mission besides. All this excites Harry's respect, and he
is willing to do himself and have me do all we can to
help him. Both Alice and I, and my younger sisters,
Angelique and Marie, have taken classes in his mission
school, and the girls help every week in a sewing-school,
and, so far as practical work is concerned, everything
moves beautifully. But then, Mr. St. John is very high
church and very stringent in his notions, and Harry,
who is ultra-liberal, says he is good, but narrow ; and
so when they are together I am quite nervous about
them. I want Mr. St. John to appear well to Harry,
and I want Harry to please Mr. St. John. Harry is
æsthetic and likes the church services, and is ready
to go as far as anybody could ask in the way of interesting and beautiful rites and ceremonies, and he likes
antiquities and all that, and so to a certain extent they
get on nicely ; but come to the question of church

authority, and Lloyd Garrison and all the radicals are not more untamable. He gets quite wild, and frightens me lest dear Mr. St. John should think him an infidel. And, in fact, Harry has such a sort of latitudinarian way of hearing what all sorts of people have to say, and admitting bits of truth here and there in it, as sometimes makes me rather uneasy. He talks with these Darwinians and scientific men who have an easy sort of matter-of-course way of assuming that the Bible is nothing but an old curiosity-shop of by-gone literature, and is so tolerant in hearing all they have to say, that I quite burn to testify and stand up for my faith—if I knew enough to do it; but I really feel afraid to ask Mr. St. John to help me, because he is so set and solemn, and confines himself to announcing that thus and so is the voice of the church; and you see that don't help me to keep up my end with people that don't care for the church.

But, Mother dear, isn't there some end to toleration; ought we Christians to sit by and hear all that is dearest and most sacred to us spoken of as a by-gone superstition, and smile assent on the ground that everybody must be free to express his opinions in good society? Now, for instance, there is this young Dr. Campbell, whom Harry is in treaty with for articles on the brain and nervous system—a nice, charming, agreeable fellow, and a perfect enthusiast in science, and has got so far that love or hatred or inspiration or heroism or religion is nothing in his view but what he calls "cerebration"—he is so lost and absorbed in cerebration and molecules, and all that sort of thing, that you feel all the time he is observing you to get facts about some of his theories as they do the poor mice and butterflies they experiment with.

The other day he was talking, in his taking-for-granted, rapid way, about the absurdity of believing in prayer, when I stopped him squarely, and told him that he ought not to talk in that way; that to destroy faith in prayer was taking away about all the comfort that poor, sorrowful, oppressed people had. I said it was just like going through a hospital and pulling all the pillows from under the sick people's heads because there might be a more perfect scientific invention by and by, and that I thought it was cruel and hard-hearted to do it. He looked really astonished, and asked me if I believed in prayer. I told him our Saviour had said, "Ask, and ye shall receive," and I believed it. He seemed quite astonished at my zeal, and said he didn't suppose any really cultivated people now-a-days believed those things. I told him I believed everything that Jesus Christ said, and thought he knew more than all the philosophers, and that he said we had a Father that loved us and cared for us, even to the hairs of our heads, and that I shouldn't have courage to live if I didn't believe that. Harry says I did right to speak up as I did. Dr. Campbell don't seem to be offended with me, for he comes here more than ever.. He is an interesting fellow, full of life and enthusiasm in his profession, and I like to hear him talk.

But here I am, right in the debatable land between faith and no faith. On the part of a great many of the intelligent, good men whom Harry, for one reason or other, invites to our house, and wants me to be agreeable to, are all shades of opinion, of half faith, and no faith, and I don't wish to hush free conversation, or to be treated like a baby who will cry if they make too much noise; and then on the other hand is Mr. St. John—whom I regard with reverence on account of his holy, self-denying life—who stands so definitely entrenched within the limits of the church, and does not in his own mind ever admit a doubt of anything which the church has settled; and between them and Harry and all I don't know just what I ought to do.

I am sure, if there is a man in the world who means in all things to live the Christian life, it's Harry. There is no difference between him and Mr. St. John there. He is ready for any amount of self-sacrifice, and goes with Mr. St. John to the extent of his ability in his efforts to do good; and yet he really does not believe a great many things that Mr. St. John thinks are Christian doctrines. He says he believes only in the wheat, and not in the chaff, and that it is only the chaff that will be blown away in these modern discussions. With all this, I feel nervous and anxious, and sometimes wish I could go right into some good, safe, dark church, and pull down all the blinds, and shut all the doors, and keep out all the bustle of modern thinking, and pray, and meditate, and have a lovely, quiet time.

Mr. St. John lends me from time to time some of his ritualistic books; and they are so refined and scholarly, and yet so devout, that Harry and I are quite charmed with their tone; but I can't help seeing that, as Harry says, they lead right back into the Romish church—and by a way that seems enticingly beautiful. Sometimes I think it would be quite delightful to have a spiritual director who would save you all the trouble of deciding, and take your case in hand, and tell you exactly what to do at every step. Mr. St. John, I know, would be just the person to assume such a position. He is a natural school-master, and likes to control people, and, although he is so very gentle, I always feel that he is very stringent, and that if I once allowed him ascendancy he would make no allowances. I can feel the "*main de fer*" through the perfect gentlemanly polish of his exterior; but you see I *know* Harry never would go completely under his influence, and I shrink from anything that would divide me from my husband, and so I don't make any move in that direction.

C

You see, I write to *you* all about these matters, for my mamma is a sweet, good little woman who never troubles her head with anything in this line, and my god-mother, Aunt Maria, is a dear worldly old soul, whose heart is grieved within her because I care so little for the pomps and vanities. She takes it to heart that Harry and I have definitely resolved to give up party-going, and all that useless round of calling and dressing and visiting that is called "going into society," and she sometimes complicates matters by trying her forces to get me into those old grooves I was so tired of running in. I never pretend to talk to her of the deeper wants or reasons of my life, for it would be ludicrously impossible to make her understand. She is a person over whose mind never came the shadow of a doubt that she was right in her views of life ; and I am not the person to evangelize her.

Well now, dear Mother, imagine a further complication. Harry is very anxious that we should have an evening once a week to receive our friends—an informal, quiet, sociable, talking evening, on a sort of ideal plan of his, in which everybody is to be made easy and at home, and to spend just such a quiet, social hour as at one's own chimney-corner. But fancy my cares, with all the menagerie of our very miscellaneous acquaintances! I should be like the man in the puzzle that had to get the fox and geese and corn over in one boat without their eating each other. Fancy Jim Fellows and Mr. St. John! Dr. Campbell, with his molecules and cerebration, talking to my little Quaker dove, with her white wings and simple faith, or Aunt Maria and mamma conversing with a Jewish Rabbi! I believe our family have a vague impression that Jews are disreputable, however gentlemanly and learned ; and I don't know but Mr. St. John would feel shocked at him. Nevertheless, our Rabbi is a very excellent German gentleman, and one of the most interesting talkers I have heard. Oh! then there are our rococo antiquities across the street, Miss Dorcas Vander-heyden and her sister. What shall I do with them all? Harry has such boundless confidence in my powers of doing the agreeable that he seems to think I can, out of this material, make a most piquant and original combination. I have an awful respect for the art *de tenir salon*, and don't wonder that among our artistic French neighbors it got to be a perfect science. But am I the woman born to do it in New York?

Well, there's no way to get through the world but to keep doing, and to attack every emergency with courage. I shall do my possible, and let you know of my success.

Your daughter,

EVA.

CHAPTER V.

A TEMPEST IN A TEAPOT.

THE housekeeping establishment of Eva Henderson, *née* Van Arsdel, was in its way a model of taste, order, and comfort. There was that bright, attractive, cosy air about it that spoke of refined tastes and hospitable feelings—it was such a creation as only the genius of a thorough home-artist could originate. There are artists who work in clay and marble, there are artists in water-colors, and artists in oils, whose works are on exhibition through galleries and museums: but there are also, in thousands of obscure homes, domestic artists, who contrive out of the humblest material to produce in daily life the sense of the beautiful; to cast a veil over its prosaic details and give it something of the charm of a poem.

Eva was one of these, and everybody that entered her house felt her power at once in the atmosphere of grace and enjoyment which seemed to pervade her rooms.

But there was underneath all this an unseen, humble operator, without whom one step in the direction of poetry would have been impossible; one whose sudden withdrawal would have been like the entrance of a black frost into a flower-garden, leaving desolation and unsightliness around: and this strong pivot on which the order and beauty of all the fairy contrivances of the little mistress turned was no other than the Irish Mary McArthur, cook, chambermaid, laundress, and general operator and adviser of the whole.

Mary was a specimen of the best class of those women whom the old country sends to our shores. She belonged to the family of a respectable Irish farmer, and had been carefully trained in all household economics and sanctities. A school kept on the estate of their landlord had been the means of instructing her in the elements of a plain English education. She wrote a good hand, was versed in accounts, and had been instructed in all branches of needle-work with a care and particularity from which our American schools for girls might take a lesson. A strong sense of character pervaded her family life—a sense of the decorous, the becoming, the true and honest, such as often gives dignity to the cottage of the laboring man of the old world. But the golden stories of wealth to be gotten in America had induced her parents to allow Mary with her elder brother to try their fortunes on these unknown shores. Mary had been fortunate in falling into the Van Arsdel family; for Mrs. Van Arsdel, though without the energy or the patience which would have been necessary to control or train an inexperienced and unsteady subject, was, on the whole, appreciative of the sterling good qualities of Mary, and liberal and generous in her dealings with her.

In fact, the Van Arsdels were in all things a free, careless, good natured, merry set, and Mary reciprocated their kindliness to her with all the warmth of her Irish heart. Eva had been her particular pet and darling. She was a pretty, engaging child at the time she first came into the family. Mary had mended her clothes, tidied her room, studied her fancies and tastes, and petted her generally with a whole-souled devotion. "When you get a husband, Miss Eva," she would say, "I will come and live with *you*." But before that event had come to pass, Mary had given her whole heart to an idle, handsome, worthless fellow, whom she appeared to love in direct proportion to his good-for-nothingness. Two daughters were the offspring of this marriage, and then Mary became a widow, and had come with her youngest child under the shadow of " Miss Eva's " roof-tree.

Thus much to give back-ground to the scenery on which Aunt Maria entered, on the morning when she took the omnibus at Mrs. Van Arsdel's door.

Eva was gone out when the door-bell of the little house rang. Mary looking from the chamber window saw Mrs. Wouvermans standing at the door step. Now against this good lady Mary had always cherished a secret antagonism. Nothing so awakens the animosity of her class as the entrance of a third power into the family, between the regnant mistress and the servants ; and Aunt Maria's intrusions and dictations had more than once been discussed in the full parliament of Mrs. Van Arsdel's servants. Consequently the arrival of a police officer armed with a search warrant could not have been more disagreeable or alarming. In an instant Mary's mental eye ran over all her own demesne and premises— for when one woman is both chambermaid, cook and laundress, it may well be that each part of these different departments cannot be at all times in a state of absolute perfection. There was a cellar table that she had been intending this very morning to revise ; there were various short-comings in pantry and closet which she had intended to set in order.

But the course of Mrs. Wouvermans was straight and unflinching as justice. A brisk interrogation to the awe-struck little maiden who opened the door showed her that Eva was out, and the field was all before her. So she marched into the parlor, and, laying aside her things, proceeded to review the situation. From the parlor to the little dining-room was the work of a moment ; thence

to the china closet, where she opened cupboards and
drawers and took note of their contents; thence to the
kitchen and kitchen pantry, where she looked into the
flour barrel, the sugar barrel, the safe, the cake box, and
took notes.

When Mary had finished her chamber work and came
down to the kitchen, she found her ancient adversary
emerging from the cellar with several leaves of cabbage
in her hands which she had gathered off from the offend-
ing table. In her haste to make a salad for a sudden
access of company, the day before, Mary had left these
witnesses, and she saw that her sin had found her out.

"Good morning, Mary," said Mrs. Wouvermans, in
the curt, dry tone that she used in speaking to servants,
"I brought up these cabbage leaves to show you. Nothing is more dangerous, Mary, than to leave any refuse
vegetables in a cellar; if girls are careless about such
matters they get thrown down on the floor and rot and
send up a poisonous exhalation that breeds fevers. I
have known whole families poisoned by the neglect of
girls in these little matters."

"Mrs. Wouvermans, I was intending this very morning to come down and attend to that matter, and all the
other matters about the house," said Mary. "There has
been company here this week, and I have had a deal to
do."

"And Mary, you ought to be very careful never to
leave the lid of your cake box up—it dries the cake. I
am very particular about mine."

"And so am I, ma'am; and if my cake box was open
it is because somebody has been to it since I shut it. It
may be that Mrs. Henderson has taken something
out."

"I noticed, Mary, a broom in the parlor closet not
hung up; it ruins brooms to set them down in that way."

By this time the hot, combative blood of Ireland rose in Mary's cheek, and she turned and stood at bay.

"Mrs. Wouvermans, *you* are not my mistress, and this is not *your* house; and I am not going to answer to you, but to Mrs. Henderson, about my matters."

"Mary, don't you speak to me in that way," said Mrs. Wouvermans, drawing herself up.

"I *shall* speak in just that way to anybody who comes meddling with what they have no business with. If you was my mistress, I'd tell you to suit yourself to a better girl; and I shall ask Mrs. Henderson if I am to be over-looked in this way. No *lady* would ever do it," said Mary, with a hot emphasis on the word *lady*, and tears of wrath in her eyes.

"There's no use in being impertinent, Mary," said Mrs. Wouvermans, with stately superiority, as she turned and sailed up stairs, leaving Mary in a tempest of impotent anger.

Just about this time Eva returned from her walk with a basket full of cut flowers, and came singing into the kitchen and began arranging flower vases; not having looked into the parlor on her way, she did not detect the traces of Aunt Maria's presence.

"Well, Mary," she called, in her usual cheerful tone, "come and look at my flowers."

But Mary came not, although Eva perceived her with her back turned in the pantry.

"Why, Mary, what is the matter?" said Eva, following her there and seeing her crying. "Why, you dear soul, what has happened? Are you sick?"

"Your Aunt Maria has been here."

"Oh, the horrors, Mary. Poor Aunt Maria! you mustn't mind a word she says. Don't worry, now—*don't* —you know Aunt Maria is always saying things to us girls, but *we* don't mind it, and you mustn't; we know she *means* well, and we just let it pass for what it's worth.".

"Yes; you are young ladies, and I am only a poor woman, and it comes hard on me. She's been round looking into every crack and corner, and picked up those old cabbage leaves, and talked to me about keeping a cellar that would give you all a fever—it's too bad. You know yesterday I hurried and cut up that cabbage to help make out the dinner when those gentlemen came in and we had only the cold mutton, and I was going to clear them away this very morning."

"I know it, Mary; and you do the impossible for us all twenty times a day, if you did drop cabbage leaves once; and Aunt Maria has no business to be poking about my house and prying into our management; but, you see, Mary, she's my aunt, and I can't quarrel with her. I'm sorry, but we must just bear it as well as we can—now promise not to mind it—for my sake."

"Well, for your sake, Miss Eva," said Mary, wiping her eyes.

"You know we all think you are a perfect jewel, Mary, and couldn't get along a minute without you. As to Aunt Maria, she's old, and set in her way, and the best way is not to mind her."

And Mary was consoled, and went on her way with courage, and with about as much charity for Mrs. Wouvermans as an average good Christian under equal provocation.

Eva went on singing and making up her vases, and carried them into the parlor, and was absorbed in managing their respective positions, when Aunt Maria came down from her tour in the chambers.

"Seems to me, Eva, that your hired girl's room is furnished up for a princess," she began, after the morning greetings had been exchanged.

"What, Mary's? Well, Mary has a great deal of neatness and taste, and always took particular pride in her room when she lived at mamma's, and so I have arranged hers with special care. Harry got her those pictures of the Madonna and infant Jesus, and I gave the *bénitier* for holy water, over her bed. We matted the floor nicely, and I made that toilet table, and draped her looking-glass out of an old muslin dress of mine. The pleasure Mary takes in it all makes it really worth while to gratify her."

"I never pet servants," said Mrs. Wouvermans, briefly. "Depend on it, Eva, when you've lived as long as I have, you'll find it isn't the way. It makes them presumptuous and exacting. Why, at first, when I blundered into Mary's room, I thought it must be yours—it had such an air."

"Well, as to the air, it's mostly due to Mary's perfect neatness and carefulness. I'm sorry to say you wouldn't always find my room as trimly arranged as hers, for I am a sad hand to throw things about when I am in a hurry. I love order, but I like somebody else to keep it."

"I'm afraid," said Aunt Maria, returning with persistence to her subject, "that you are beginning wrong with Mary, and you'll have trouble in the end. Now I saw she had white sugar in the kitchen sugar-bowl, and there was the tea caddy for her to go to. It's abominable to have servants feel that they must use such tea as we do."

"Oh, well, aunty, you know Mary has been in the family so long I don't feel as if she were a servant; she seems like a friend, and I treat her like one. I believe Mary really loves us."

"It don't do to mix sentiment and business," said Aunt Maria, with sententious emphasis. "I never do. I don't want my servants to love me—that is *not* what I have them for. I want them to *do my work*, and take their wages. They understand that there are to be no favors—everything is specifically set down in the bargain I make with them; their work is all marked out. I never talk with them, or encourage them to talk to me, and that is the way we get along."

"Dear me, Aunt Maria, that may be all very well for such an energetic, capable housekeeper as you are, who always know exactly how to manage, but such a poor little thing as I am can't set up in that way. Now I think it's a great mercy and favor to have a trained girl that knows more about how to get on than I do, and that is fond of me. Why, I know rich people that would be only too glad to give Mary double what we give, just to have somebody to depend on.

"But, Eva, child, you're beginning wrong—you ought not to leave things to Mary as you do. You ought to attend to everything yourself. I always do."

"But you see, aunty, the case is very different with you and me. You are so very capable and smart, and know so exactly how everything ought to be done, you can make your own terms with everybody. And, now I think of it, how lucky that you came in! I want you to give me your judgment as to two pieces of linen that I've just had sent in. You know, Aunty, I am such a perfect ignoramus about these matters."

And Eva tripped up stairs, congratulating herself on turning the subject, and putting her aunt's busy advising faculties to some harmless and innocent use. So, when she came down with her two pieces of linen, Aunt Maria tested and pulled them this way and that, in the approved style of a domestic expert, and gave judgment at last with an authoritative air.

" *This* is the best, Eva—you see it has a round thread, and very little dressing."

"And *why* is the round thread the best, Aunty?"

"Oh, because it always is—everybody knows _that_, child; all good judges will tell you to buy the round threaded linen, that's perfectly well understood."

Eva did not pursue the inquiry farther, and we must all confess that Mrs. Wouverman's reply was about as satisfactory as those one gets to most philosophical inquiries as to why and wherefore. If our reader doubts that, let him listen to the course of modern arguments on some of the most profound problems; so far as can be seen, they consist of inflections of Aunt Maria's style of statement—as, "Oh, of course everybody knows _that_, now;" or, negatively, "Oh, nobody believes _that_, now-a-days." Surely, a mode of argument which very wise persons apply fearlessly to subjects like death, judgment and eternity, may answer for a piece of linen.

"Oh, by-the-by, Eva, I see you have cards there for Mrs. Wat Sydney's receptions this winter," said Aunt Maria, turning her attention to the card plate. "They are going to be very brilliant, I'm told. They say nothing like their new house is to be seen in this country."

"Yes," said Eva, "Sophie has been down here urging me to come up and see her rooms, and says they depend on me for their receptions, and I'm going up some day to lunch with her, in a quiet way; but Harry and I have about made up our minds that _we_ sha'n't go to parties. You know, Aunty, we are going in for economy, and this sort of thing costs so much."

"But, bless your soul, child, what is money for?" said Aunt Maria, innocently. "If you have _any_ thing you ought to improve your advantages of getting on in society. It's important to Harry in his profession to be seen and heard of, and to push his way among the notables, and, with due care and thought and economy, a person with your air and style, and your taste, can appear as well as anybody. I came down here, among other things, to look over your dresses, and see what can be done with them."

"Oh, thank you a thousand times, Aunty dear, but what do you think all my little wedding finery would do for me in an assemblage of Worth's spick-and-span new toilettes? In our own little social circles I am quite a leader of the mode, but I should look like an old last night's bouquet among all their fresh finery!"

"Well, now, Eva, child, you talk of economy and all that, and then go spending on knick-knacks and mere fancies what would enable you to make a very creditable figure in society."

"Really, Aunty, is it possible now, when I thought we were being *so* prudent?"

"Well, there's your wood fire, for instance; very cheerful, I admit, but it's a downright piece of extravagance. I know that the very richest and most elegant people, that have everything they can think of, have fallen back on the fancy of having open wood fires in their parlors, just for a sort of ornament to their rooms, but you don't really need it—your furnace keeps you warm enough."

"But, Aunty, it looks so bright and cheerful, and Harry is so fond of it! We only have it evenings, when he comes home tired, and he says the very sight of it rests him."

"There you go, now, Eva—with wood at fifteen dollars a cord!—going in for a mere luxury just because it pleases your fancy, and you can't go into society because it's so expensive. Eva, child, that's just like you. And there are twenty other little things that I see about here," said Aunt Maria, glancing round, "pretty enough, but each costs a little. There, for instance, those cut flowers in the vases cost something."

"But, Aunty, I got them of a poor little man just set-

ting up a green-house, and Harry and I have made up
our minds that it's our duty to patronize him. I'm
going up to Sophie's to get her to take flowers for her
parties of him."

"It's well enough to get Sophie to do it, but you
oughtn't to afford it," said Aunt Maria; "nor need you
buy a new matting and pictures for your servant's room."

"Oh, Aunty, mattings are so cheap; and those pictures didn't cost much, and they make Mary so happy!"

"Oh, she'd be happy enough any way. You ought to
look out a little for yourself, child."

"Well, I do. Now, just look at the expense of going
to parties. To begin with, it annihilates all your dresses, at one fell swoop. If I make up my mind, for instance, not to go to parties this winter, I have dresses
enough and pretty enough for all my occasions. The
minute I decide I must go, I have *nothing*, absolutely
nothing, to wear. There must be an immediate outlay.
A hundred dollars would be a small estimate for all the
additions necessary to make me appear with credit.
Even if I take my old dresses as the foundation, and use
my unparalleled good taste, there are trimmings, and
dressmaker's bills, and gloves, and slippers, and fifty
things; and then a carriage for the evening, at five dollars a night, and all for what? What *does* anybody get
at a great buzzing party, to pay for all this? Then Harry
has to use all his time, and all his nerves, and all his
strength on his work. He is driven hard all the time
with writing, making up the paper, and overseeing at
the office. And you know parties don't begin till near
ten o'clock, and if he is out till twelve he doesn't rest
well, nor I either—it's just so much taken out of our
life—and we don't either of us enjoy it. Now, why
should we put out our wood fire that we *do* enjoy, and
scrimp in our flowers, and scrimp in our home comforts,

and in our servant's comforts, just to get what we don't want after all?"

"Oh, well, I suppose you are like other new married folks, you want to play Darby and Joan in your chimney-corner," said Aunt Maria, "but, for all that, I think there are duties to society. One cannot go out of the world, you know; it don't do, Eva."

"I don't know about that," said Eva. "We are going to try it."

"What! living without society?"

"Oh, as to that, we shall see our friends other ways. I can see Sophie a great deal better in a quiet morning-call than an evening reception; for the fact is, whoever else you see at a party you don't see your hostess—she hasn't a word for you. Then, I'm going to have an evening here."

"*You* an evening?"

"Yes; why not? See if I don't, and we'll have good times, too."

"Why, who do you propose to invite?"

"Oh, all our folks, and Bolton and Jim Fellows; then there are a good many interesting, intelligent men that write for the magazine, and besides, our acquaintances on this street."

"In this street? Why, there isn't a creature here," said Aunt Maria.

"Yes, there are those old ladies across the way."

"What! old Miss Dorcas Vanderheyden and that Mrs. Benthusen? Well, they belong to an ancient New York family, to be sure; but they are old as Methusaleh."

"So much the better, Aunty. Old things, you know, are all the rage just now; and then there's my little Quaker neighbor."

"Why, how odd! They are nice enough, I suppose,

and well enough to have for neighbors; but he's nothing but a watchmaker. He actually works for Tiffany!"

"Yes; but he is a very modest, intelligent young man, and very well informed on certain subjects. Harry says he has learned a great deal from him."

"Well, well, child, I suppose you must take your own way," said Aunt Maria.

"I suppose we must," said Eva, shaking her head with much gravity. "You see, Aunty, dear, a wife must accommodate herself to her husband, and if Harry thinks this is the best way, you know—and he does think so, very strongly—and isn't it lucky that I think just as he does? You wouldn't have me fall in with those strong-minded Bloomer women, would you, and sail the ship on my own account, independently of my husband?"

Now, the merest allusion to modern strong-mindedness in woman was to Aunt Maria like a red rag to a bull; it aroused all her combativeness.

"No; I am sure I wouldn't," she said, with emphasis. "If there's anything, Eva, where I see the use of all my instructions to you, it is the good sense with which you resist all such new-fangled, abominable notions about the rights and sphere of women. No; I've always said that the head of the woman is the man; and it's a wife's duty to live to please her husband. She may try to influence him—she ought to do that—but she never ought to do it *openly.* I never used to oppose Mr. Wouvermans. I was always careful to let him suppose he was having his own way; but I generally managed to get mine," and Aunt Maria plumed herself and nodded archly, as an aged priestess who is communicating to a young neophyte secrets of wisdom.

In her own private mind, Eva thought this the most terrible sort of hypocrisy; but her aunt was so settled

and contented in all her own practical views, that there
was not the least use in arguing the case. However,
she couldn't help saying, innocently,

"But, Aunty, I should be afraid sometimes he would
have found me out, and then he'd be angry."

"Oh, no; trust me for that," said Aunt Maria, complacently. "I never managed so bunglingly as that.
Somehow or other, he didn't exactly know how, he found
things coming round my way; but I never opposed him
openly—I never got his back up. You see, Eva, these
men, if they *do* get their backs up, are terrible, but *any*
of them can be led by the nose—so I'm glad to find that
you begin the right way. Now, there's your mother—
I've been telling her this morning that it's her duty to
make your father go back into business and retrieve his
fortunes. He's got a good position, to be sure—a respectable salary; but there's no sort of reason why he
shouldn't die worth his two or three millions as well as
half the other men who fail, and are up again in two or
three years. But Nellie wants force. She is no manager. If I were your father's wife, I should set him on
his feet again pretty soon. Nellie is such a little dependent body. She was saying this morning how would she
ever have got along with her family without me! But
there are some things that even I can't do—nobody but
a wife could, and Nelly isn't up to it."

"Poor, dear little mamma," said Eva. "But are you
quite sure, Aunt Maria, that her ways are not better
adapted to papa than any one's else could be? Papa is
very positive, though so very quiet. He is devoted to
mamma. Then, again, Aunty, there is a good deal of
risk in going into speculations and enterprises at papa's
age. Of course, you know I don't know anything about
business or that sort of thing; but it seems to me like a
great sea where you are up on the wave to-day and down

to-morrow. So if papa really *won't* go into these things, perhaps it's all for the best."

"But, Eva, it is so important now for the girls, poor things, just going into society—for you know they can't keep out of it, even if you do. It will affect all their chances of settlement in life—and that puts me in mind, Eva, something or other must be done about Alice and Jim Fellows. Everybody is saying if they're not engaged they ought to be."

"Oh, Aunty, how exasperating the world is! Can't a man and woman have a plain, honest friendship? Jim has shown himself a true friend to our family. He came to us just in all the confusion of the failure, and helped us heart and hand in the manliest way—and we *all* like him. Alice likes him, and I don't wonder at it."

"Well, are they engaged?" said Aunt Maria, with an air of statistical accuracy.

"How should I know? I never thought of asking. I'm not a police detective, and I always think that if my friends have anything they want me to know, they'll tell me; and if they don't want me to know, why should I ask them?"

"But, Eva, one is responsible for one's relations. The fact is, such an intimacy stands right in the way of a girl's having good offers—it keeps other parties off. Now, I tell you, as a great secret, there is a very fine man, immensely rich, and every way desirable, who is evidently pleased with Alice."

"Dear me, Aunty! how you excite my curiosity. Pray who is it?" said Eva.

"Well, I'm not at liberty to tell you more particularly; but I *know* he's thinking about her; and this report about her and Jim would operate very prejudicially. Now shall I have a talk with Alice, or will you?"

"Oh, Aunty dear, don't, for pity's sake, say a word to

Alice. Young girls are so sensitive about such things. If it *must* be talked of, let me talk with Alice."

"I really thought, if I had a good chance, I'd say something to the young man himself," said Aunt Maria, reflectively.

"Oh, good heavens! Aunty, don't *think* of it. You don't know Jim Fellows."

"Oh, you needn't be afraid of me," said Aunt Maria. "I am a great deal older and more experienced than you, and if I do do anything, you may rest assured it will be in the most discreet way. I've managed cases of this kind before you were born."

"But Jim is the most peculiar"—

"Oh, I know all about him. Do you suppose I've seen him in and out in the family all this time without understanding him perfectly?"

"But I don't really think that there is the least of anything serious between him and Alice."

"Very likely. He would not be at all the desirable match for Alice. He has very little property, and is rather a wild, rattling fellow; and I don't like newspaper men generally."

"Oh, Aunty, that's severe now. You forget Harry."

"Oh, well, your husband is an exception; but, as a general rule, I don't like 'em—unprincipled lot *I* believe," said Aunt Maria, with a decisive nod of her head. "At any rate, Alice can do better, and she ought to."

The ringing of the lunch bell interrupted the conversation, much to the relief of Eva, who discovered with real alarm the course her respected relative's thoughts were taking.

Of old she had learned that the only result of arguing a point with her was to make her more set in her own way, and she therefore bent all her forces of agreeableness to produce a diversion of mind to other topics. On the principle that doctors apply mustard to the feet, to divert the too abundant blood from the head, Eva started a brisk controversy with Aunt Maria on another topic, in hopes, by exhausting her energies there, to put this out of her mind. With what success her strategy was crowned, it will remain to be seen.

CHAPTER VI

THE SETTLING OF THE WATERS.

IT will not be doubted by those who know the ways of family dictators that Mrs. Maria Wouvermans left Eva's house after her day's visit in a state of the most balmy self-satisfaction, as one who has done a good day's work.

"Well, I 've been up at Eva's," she said to her sister, as she looked in on returning, "and really it was well I went in. That Mary of hers is getting careless and negligent, just as all old servants do, and I just went over the whole house, and had a plain talk with Mary. She flew up about it, and was impertinent, of course; but I put her down, and I talked plainly to Eva about the way she 's beginning with her servants. She 's just like you, Nellie, slack and good-natured, and needs somebody to keep her up. I told her the way she is beginning—of petting Mary, and fussing up her room with carpet and pictures, and everything, just like any other—would n't work. Servants must be kept in their places."

Now, Mrs. Van Arsdel had a spirit of her own; and the off-hand, matter-of-fact manner in which her sister was accustomed to speak of her as no manager touched a vital point. What housekeeper likes to have her capacity to guide a house assailed? Is not that the spot where her glory dwells, if she has any? And it is all the more provoking when such charges are thrown out in perfect good nature, not as designed to offend, but thrown in *par parenthèse*, as something everybody would acknowl-

edge, and too evident to require discussion. While proceeding in the main part of a discourse Mrs. Wouvermans
was quite in the habit of these frank side disclosures of
her opinion of her sister's management, and for the most
part they were submitted to in acquiescent silence, rather
than to provoke a controversy; but to be called "slack"
to her face without protest or rejoinder was more than
she could bear; so Mrs. Van Arsdel spoke up with spirit:

"Maria, you are always talking as if I don't know
how to manage servants. All I know is that you are
always changing, and I keep mine years and years."

"That's because you let them have their own way,"
said her sister. "You can keep servants if you don't
follow them up, and insist on it that they shall do their
duty. Let them run all over you and live like mistresses,
and you can keep them. For my part, I like to change
—new brooms always sweep clean."

"Well, it's a different thing, Maria—you with your
small family, and mine with so many. I'd rather bear anything than change."

"Oh, well, yes; I suppose there's no help for it,
Nellie. Of course I wasn't blaming you, so don't fire
up about it. I know you can't make yourself over,"
said Aunt Maria. This was the tone with which she
usually settled discussions with those who differed from
her on modes and measures. After all, they could not
be like her, so where was the use of talking?

Aunt Maria also had the advantage in all such encounters of a confessed reputation as an excellent manager. Her house was always elegant, always in order.
She herself was gifted with a head for details that never
failed to keep in mind the smallest item, and a wiry,
compact constitution that never knew fatigue. She held
the keys of everything in her house, and always turned
every key at the right moment. She knew the precise

weight, quantity, and quality of everything she had in possession, where it was and what it might be used for; and, as she said, could go to anything in her house without a candle in the darkest night. If her servants did not love, they feared her, and had such a sense of her ever vigilant inspection that they never even tried to evade her. For the least shadow of disobedience she was ready to send them away at a moment's warning, and then go to the intelligence office and enter her name for another, and come home, put on apron and gloves, and manfully and thoroughly sustain the department till they came.

Mrs. Wouvermans, therefore, was celebrated and lauded by all her acquaintances as a perfect housekeeper, and this added sanction and terror to her *pronunciamentos* when she walked the rounds as a police inspector in the houses of her relations.

It is rather amusing to a general looker-on in this odd world of ours to contrast the serene, cheerful good faith with which these constitutionally active individuals go about criticising, and suggesting, and directing right and left, with the dismay and confusion of mind they leave behind them wherever they operate.

They are often what the world calls well-meaning people, animated by a most benevolent spirit, and have no more intention of giving offense than a nettle has of stinging. A large, vigorous, well-growing nettle has no consciousness of the stings it leaves in the delicate hands that have been in contact with it; it has simply acted out its innocent and respectable nature as a nettle. But a nettle armed with the power of locomotion on an ambulatory tour, is something the results of which may be fearful to contemplate.

So, after the departure of Aunt Maria our little housekeeper, Eva, was left in a state of considerable

nervousness and anxiety, feeling that she had been
weighed in the balance of perfection and found wofully
wanting.   She was conscious, to begin with, that her
characteristic virtues as a housekeeper, if she had any,
were not entirely in the style of her good relative.   She
was not by nature statistical, nor given to accounts and
figures.   She was not sharp and keen in bargains; she
was, she felt in her inmost, trembling soul, a poor little
mollusk, without a bit of a shell, hiding in a cowardly
way under a rock and ready at any time to be eaten up
by big fishes.   She had felt so happy in her unlimited
trust in Mary, who knew more than she did about housekeeping—but she had been convicted by her aunt's cross-
questions of having resigned the very signet ring and
scepter of her house into her hands.   Did she let Mary
go all over the house?   Did she put away the washing?
Did Eva allow her to open her drawers?   Did n't she
count her towels and sheets every week, and also her
tea-spoons, and keep every drawer and cupboard locked?
She ought to.   To all these inquiries Eva had no satisfactory response, and began to doubt within herself
whether she had begun aright.   With sensitive, conscientious people there is always a residuum of self-distrust
after discussions of the nature we have indicated, however vigorously and skillfully they may have defended
their courses at the time.

Eva went over and over in her own mind her self-
justifications—she told herself that she and her aunt were
essentially different people, incapable of understanding
each other sympathetically or acting in each other's ways,
and that the well-meant, positive dicta of her relative
were to be let go for what they were worth, and no more.

Still she looked eagerly and anxiously for the return of her husband, that she might reinforce herself
by talking it over with him.   Hers was a nature so

TALKING IT OVER.

" Come now, Puss, out with it. Why that anxious brow? What domestic catastrophe ? ' — p. 73.

transparent that, before he had been five minutes in the house, he felt that something had gone wrong; but, the dinner-bell ringing, he retired at once to make his toilet, and did not open the subject till they were fairly seated at table.

"Well, come now, Puss—out with it! Why that anxious brow? What domestic catastrophe? Anything gone wrong with the ivies?"

"Oh, no; the ivies are all right, growing beautifully —it isn't that—"

"Well, then, what is it? It seems there is something."

"Oh, nothing, Harry; only Aunt Maria has been spending the day here."

Eva said this with such a perplexed and woful face that Harry leaned back in his chair and laughed.

"What a blessing it is to have relations," he said; "but I thought, Eva, that you had made up your mind not to care for anything Aunt Maria says?"

"Well, she has been all over the house, surveying and reviewing as if she owned us, and she has lectured Mary and got her into hysterics, and talked to me till I am almost bewildered—wondering at everything we mean to do, and wanting us to take her ways and not ours."

"My dearest child, why need you care? Take it as a rain-storm, when you've been caught out without your umbrella. That's all. Or why can't you simply and firmly tell her that she must not go over your house or direct your servants?"

"Well, you see, that would never do. She would feel so injured and abused. I've only just made up and brought things to going smoothly, and got her pacified about our marriage. There would be another fuss if I should talk that way. Aunt Maria always considered

D

me her girl, and maintains that she is a sort of special guardian to me, and I think it very disagreeable
to quarrel with your relations, and get on unpleasant
terms with them."

"Well, *I* shall speak to her, Eva, pretty decidedly, if
you don't."

"Oh, do n't, do n't, Harry! She 'd never forgive
you. No. Let me manage her. I have been managing
her all day to keep the peace, to keep her satisfied and
pleased; to *let* her advise me to her heart's content,
about things where I can take advice. Aunt Maria is
a capital judge of linens and cottons, and all sorts of
household stuffs, and can tell to a certainty just how
much of a thing you 'd want, and the price you ought
to pay, and the exact place to get it; and I have been
contriving to get her opinion on a dozen points where
I mean to take it; and I think she has left, on the
whole, highly satisfied with her visit, though in the main
I did n't give in to her a bit about our plans."

"Then why so tragic and tired-looking?"

"Oh, well, after all, when Aunt Maria talks, she says
a great many things that have such a degree of sense
in them that it worries me. Now, there 's a good deal
of sense in what she said about trusting too much to
servants, and being too indulgent. I know mamma's
girls used to get spoiled so that they would be perfect
tyrants. And yet I cannot for the life of me like Aunt
Maria's hard, ungracious way of living with servants,
as if they were machines.

"Ah, well, Eva, it 's always so. Hard, worldly people
always have a good deal of what looks like practical
sense on their side, and kindness and unselfishness certainly have their weak points; there 's no doubt of that.
The Sermon on the Mount is open to a great deal of
good hard worldly criticism, and so is every attempt

to live up to it practically; but, never mind. We all know that the generous way is the strong way, and the best way, in the long run."

"And then you know, Harry, I have n't the least talent for being hard and sharp," said Eva, "and so I may as well take the advantages of my sort of nature."

"Certainly you may; people never succeed out of their own line."

" Then there 's another trouble. I 'm afraid Aunt Maria is going to interfere with Alice, as she tried to do with me. She said that everybody was talking about her intimacy with Jim, and that if *I* did n't speak to Alice *she* must."

"Confound that woman," said Harry; "she 's an un-mitigated old fool! She 's as bad as a runaway steam engine; somebody ought to seize and lock her up."

"Come, sir, keep a civil tongue about my relations," said Eva, laughing.

"Well, I must let off a little to you, just to lower steam to the limits of Christian moderation."

"Alice is n't as fond of Aunt Maria as I am, and has a high spirit of her own, and I 'm afraid it will make a terrible scene if Aunt Maria attacks her, so I suppose I must talk to her myself; but what do you think of Jim, Harry? Is there anything in it, on his part?"

"How can I say? you know just as much as I do and no more, and you are a better judge of human nature than I am."

"Well, would you like it to have Alice take Jim— supposing there were anything."

"Why, yes, very well, if she wants him."

"But Jim is such a volatile creature—would you want to trust him?"

"He is constant in his affections, which is the main thing. I 'm sure his conduct when your father failed showed that; and a sensible, dignified woman like Alice might make a man of him."

"It's odd," said Eva, "that Alice, who is so prudent, and has such a high sense of propriety, seems so very indulgent to Jim. None of his escapades seem to offend her."

"It's the doctrine of counterparts," said Harry; "the steady sensible nature admires the brilliancy and variety of the volatile one."

"For my part," said Eva, "I can't conceive of Jim's saying anything in serious earnest. The very idea of his being sentimental seems funny—and how can anybody be in love without being sentimental?"

"There are diversities of operation," said Harry. "Jim must make love in his own way, and it will probably be an original one."

"But, really now, do you know," persisted Eva, "I think Alice might be mated with a man of much higher class than Jim. He is amiable, and bright, and funny, and agreeable. Yet I don't deny but Alice might do better."

"So she might, but the perversity of fate is that the superior man isn't around and Jim *is;* and, ten to one, if the superior man were in the field, Alice would be perverse enough to choose Jim. And, after all, you must confess, give Jim Fellows a fortune of a million or two, a place in Newport, and another on the North River, and even you would call it a brilliant match, and think it a fortunate thing for Alice."

"Oh, dear me, Harry, that's the truth, to be sure. Am I so worldly?"

"No; but ideal heroes are not plentiful, and there are few gems that don't need rich setting. The first questions as to a man are, is he safe, has he no bad habits, is he kind and affectionate in his disposition and capable

of constant affection? and, secondly, does the woman feel
that sort of love that makes her prefer him even to men
that are quite superior? Now, whether Alice feels in
that way toward Jim is what remains to be seen. I'm
sure I can't tell. Neither can I tell whether Jim has any
serious intentions in regard to her. If they were only let
alone, and not watched and interfered with, I 've no doubt
the thing would adjust itself in the natural course of
things.

"But see here, I must be going to my club, and,
now I think of it, I 've brought some Paris letters from
the girls for you, to pass the evening with."

" You have? Letters from Ida and Caroline? You
naughty creature, why did n't you give them to me before ? "

" Well, your grave face when I first came in put everything else out of my head; and then came on all this
talk : but it 's just as well, you 'll have them to read while
I 'm gone."

" Do n't stay late, Harry."

" No; you may be sure I 've no temptation. I 'd
much rather be here with you watching our own back-
log. But then I shall see several fellows about articles
for the magazine, and get all the late news, and, in short,
take an observation of our latitude and longitude; so,
au revoir ! "

CHAPTER VII.

LETTERS AND AIR-CASTLES.

AFTER Harry went out, Eva arranged the fire, dropped the curtains over the window, drew up an easy chair into a warm corner under the gas-light, and began looking over the outside of her Parisian letters with that sort of luxurious enjoyment of delay with which one examines the post-marks and direction of letters that are valued as a great acquisition. There was one from her sister Ida and one from Harry's cousin Caroline. Ida's was opened first. It was dated from a boarding-house in the Rue de Clichy, giving a sort of journalised view of their studies, their medical instructors, their walks and duties in the hospital, all told with an evident and vigorous sense of enjoyment. Eva felt throughout what a strong, cheerful, self-sustained being her sister was, and how fit it was that a person so sufficient to herself, so equable, so healthfully balanced and poised in all her mental and physical conformation, should have undertaken the pioneer work of opening a new profession for women. "I never could do as she does, in the world," was her mental comment, "but I am thankful that she can." And then she cut the envelope of Caroline's letter.

To a certain extent there were the same details in it —Caroline was evidently associated in the same studies, the same plans, but there was missing in the letter the professional enthusiasm, the firmness, the self-poise, and calm clearness. There were more bursts of feeling on the pictures in the Louvre than on scientific discoveries; more sensibility to the various æsthetic wonders which Paris opens to an uninitiated guest than to the treasures of anatomy and surgery. With the letter were sent two or three poems, contributions to the Magazine—poems full of color and life, of a subdued fire, but with that undertone of sadness which is so common in all female poets. A portion of the letter may explain this :

" You were right, my dear Eva, in saying, in our last interview, that it did not seem to you that I had the kind of character that was adapted to the profession I have chosen. I don't think I have. I am more certain of it from comparing myself from day to day with Ida, who certainly is born and made for it, if ever a woman was. My choice of it has been simply and only for the reason that I must choose something as a means of self-support, and more than that, as a refuge from morbid distresses of mind which made the still monotony of my New England country life intolerable to me. This course presented itself to me as something feasible. I thought it, too, a good and worthy career—one in which one might do one's share of good for the world. But, Eva, I can feel that there is one essential difference between Ida and myself: she is peculiarly self-sustained and sufficient to herself, and I am just the reverse. I am full of vague unrest; I am chased by seasons of high excitement, alternating with deadly languor. Ida has hard work to know what to do with me. You were right in supposing, as you intimate in your letter, that a certain common friend has something to do with this unrest, but you cannot, unless you know my whole history, know how much. There was a time when he and I were all the world to each other—when shall I ever forget that time! I was but seventeen ; a young girl, so ignorant of life! I never had seen one like him; he was a whole new revelation to

me; he woke up everything there was in me, never to go
to sleep again; and then to think of having all this tide
and current of feeling checked—frozen. My father overwhelmed him with accusations; every baseness was laid
to his charge. I was woman enough to have stood for
him against the world if he had come to me. I would
have left all and gone to the ends of the earth with him
if he had asked me, but he did not. There was only
one farewell, self-accusing letter, and even that fell into
my father's hands and never came to me till after his
death. For years I thought myself wantonly trifled with
by a man of whose attentions I ought to be ashamed. I
was indignant at myself for the love that might have been
my glory, for it is my solemn belief that if we had been
let alone he would have been saved all those wretched
falls, those blind struggles that have marred a life whose
purpose is yet so noble.

"When the fates brought us together again in New
York, I saw at a glance that whatever may have been the
proud, morbid conscientiousness that dictated his long
silence, he loved me still;—a woman knows that by an
unmistakable instinct. She can *feel* the reality through
all disguises. *I know* that man loves me, and yet he does
not now in word or deed make the least profession beyond the boundaries of friendship. He is my friend;
with entire devotion he is willing to spend and be spent
for me—but he will accept nothing from me. I, who
would give my life to him willingly—I must do nothing
for him!

"Well, it's no use writing. You see now that I am a
very unworthy disciple of your sister. She is so calm
and philosophical that I cannot tell her all this; but you,
dear little Eva, you know the heart of woman, and you
have a magic key which unlocks everybody's heart in
confidence to you. I seem to see you, in fancy, with

good Cousin Harry, sitting cosily in your chimney-corner; your ivies and nasturtiums growing round your sunny windows, and an everlasting summer in your pretty parlors, while the December winds whistle without. Such a life as you two lead, such a home as your home, is worth a thousand 'careers' that dazzle ambition. Send us more letters, journals, of all your pretty, lovely home life, and let me warm myself in the glow of your fireside. Your Cousin, CARRY."

Eva finished this letter, and then folding it up sat with it in her lap, gazing into the fire, and pondering its contents. If the truth must be told, she was revolving in her young, busy brain a scheme for restoring Caroline to her lover, and setting them up comfortably at housekeeping on a contiguous street, where she had seen a house to let. In five minutes she had gone through the whole programme—seen the bride at the altar, engaged the house, bought the furniture, and had before her a vision of parlors, of snuggeries and cosy nooks, where Caroline was to preside, and where Bolton was to lounge at his ease, while she and Caroline compared housekeeping accounts. Happy young wives develop an aptitude for match-making as naturally as flowers spring in a meadow, and Eva was losing herself in this vision of Alnaschar, when a loud, imperative, sharp bark of a dog at the front door of the house called her back to life and the world.

Now there are as many varieties to dog-barks as to man-talks. There is the common bow-wow, which means nothing, only that it is a dog speaking; there is the tumultuous angry bark, which means attack; the conversational bark, which, of a moonlight night, means gossip; and the imperative staccato bark which means immediate business. The bark at the front door was of

this kind: it was loud and sharp, and with a sort of indignant imperativeness about it, as of one accustomed
to be attended to immediately.

Eva flew to the front door and opened it, and there
sat Jack, the spoiled darling of Miss Dorcas Vanderheyden and her sister, over the way.

"Why, Jacky! where did you come from?" said Eva.
Jacky sat up on his haunches and waved his forepaws in
a vigorous manner, as was his way when he desired to
be specially ingratiating.

Eva seized him in her arms and carried him into the
parlor, thinking that as he had accidentally been shut
out for the night she would domesticate him for a while,
and return him to his owners on the morrow. So she
placed him on the ottoman in the corner and attempted
to caress him, but evidently that was not the purpose he
had in view. He sprang down, ran to the door and
snuffed, and to the front windows and barked imperi-
ously.

"Why, Jack, what do you want?"

He sprang into a chair and barked out at the Vanderheyden house.

Eva looked at the mantel clock—it wanted a few
minutes of ten—without, it was a bright moonlight night.

"I 'll run across with him, and see what it is," she
said. She was young enough to enjoy something like
an adventure. She opened the front door and Jack
rushed out, and then stopped to see if she would follow;
as she stood a moment he laid hold on the skirt of her
dress, as if to pull her along.

"Well, Jacky, I 'll go," said Eva. Thereat the creature bounded across the street and up the steps of the
opposite house, where he stood waiting. She went up
and rang the door-bell, which appeared to be what he
wanted, as he sat down quite contented on the doorstep.

Nobody came. Eva looked up and down the street. "Jacky, we shall have to go back, they are all asleep," she said. But Jacky barked contradiction, sprang nearer to the door, and insisted on being let in.

"Well, if you say so, Jacky, I must ring again," she said, and with that she pulled the door-bell louder, and Jack barked with all his might, and the two succeeded after a few moments in causing a perceptible stir within.

Slowly the door unclosed, and a vision of Miss Dorcas in an old-fashioned broad-frilled night-cap peeped out. She was attired in a black water-proof cloak, donned hastily over her night gear.

"Oh, Jack, you naughty boy!" she exclaimed, stooping eagerly to the prodigal, who sprung tumultuously into her arms and began licking her face.

"I 'm so much obliged to you, Mrs. Henderson," she said to Eva. "We went down in the omnibus this afternoon, and we suddenly missed him, the naughty fellow," she said, endeavoring to throw severity into her tones.

Eva related Jack's ruse.

"Did you ever!" said Miss Dorcas; "the creature knew that we slept in the back of the house, and he got you to ring our door-bell. Jacky, what a naughty fellow you are!"

Mrs. Betsey now appeared on the staircase in an equal state of dishabille:

"Oh dear, Mrs. Henderson, we are *so* shocked!"

"Dear me, never speak of it. I think it was a cunning trick of Jack. He knew you were gone to bed, and saw I was up and so got me to ring his door-bell for him. I do n't doubt he rode up town in the omnibus. Well, good-night!"

And Eva closed the door and flew back to her own little nest just in time to let in Harry.

The first few moments after they were fairly by the

fireside were devoted to a recital of the adventure, with dramatic representations of Jack and his mistresses.

"It's a capital move on Jack's part. It got me into the very interior of the fortress. Only think of seeing them in their night-caps! That is carrying all the out-works of ceremony at a move."

"To say nothing of their eternal gratitude," said Harry.

"Oh, that of course. They were ready to weep on my neck with joy that I had brought the dear little plague back to them, and I do n't doubt are rejoicing over him at this moment. But, oh, Harry, you must hear the girls' Paris letters."

"Are they very long?" said Harry.

"Fie now, Harry; you ought to be interested in the girls."

"Why, of course I am," said Harry, pulling out his watch, "only—what time is it?"

"Only half-past ten—not a bit late," said Eva. As she began to read Ida's letter, Harry settled back in the embrace of a luxurious chair, with his feet stretched out towards the fire, and gradually the details of Paris life mingled pleasingly with a dream—a fact of which Eva was made aware as she asked him suddenly what he thought of Ida's views on a certain point.

"Now, Harry—you have n't been asleep?"

"Just a moment. The very least in the world," said Harry, looking anxiously alert and sitting up very straight.

Then Eva read Caroline's letter.

"Now, is n't it too bad?" she said, with eagerness, as she finished.

"Yes, it is," said Harry, very gravely. "But, Eva dear, it's one of those things that you and I can do nothing to help—it is ἀνάγκη."

"What 's ananke?"

"The name the old Greeks gave to that perverse Something that brought ruin and misery in spite of and out of the best human efforts."

"But I want to bring these two together."

"Be careful how you try, darling. Who knows what the results may be? It 's a subject Bolton never speaks of, where he has his own purposes and conclusions; and it 's the best thing for Caroline to be where she has as many allurements and distractions as she has in Paris, and such a wise, calm, strong friend as your sister.

"And now, dear, may n't I go to bed?" he added, with pathos, "You 've no idea, dear, how sleepy I am."

"Oh, certainly, you poor boy," said Eva, bustling about and putting up the chairs and books preparatory to leaving the parlor.

' You see," she said, going up stairs, "he was so imperious that I really had to go with him."

"He! Who?"

"Why, Jack, to be sure, he did all but speak," said Eva, brush in hand, and letting down her curls before the glass. "You see I was in a reverie over those letters when the barking roused me—I don't think you ever heard such a barking; and when I got him in, he wouldn't be contented—kept insisting on my going over with him —was n't it strange?

Harry, by this time composed for the night and half asleep, said it was.

In a few moments he was aroused by Eva's saying, suddenly,

"Harry, I really think I ought to bring them together. Now, could n't I do something?"

"With Jack?" said Harry, drowsily.

"Jack!—oh, you sleepy-head! Well, never mind. Good night."

CHAPTER VIII

THE VANDERHEYDEN FORTRESS TAKEN.

"NOW, Harry, I 'll tell you what I 'm going to do this morning," said Eva, with the air of a little general, as she poured his morning coffee.

"And what are you going to do?" replied he, in the proper tone of inquiry.

"Well, I 'm going to take the old fortress over the way by storm, this very morning. I 'm going to rush through the breach that Jack has opened into the very interior and see what there is there. I 'm perfectly dying to get the run of that funny old house; why, Harry, it 's just like a novel, and I should n't wonder if I could get enough out of it for you to make an article of."

"Thank you, dear; you enter into the spirit of article-hunting like one to the manner born."

"That I do; I 'm always keeping my eyes open when I go about New York for bits and hints that you can work up, and I 'm sure you ought to do something with this old Vanderheyden house. I know there must be ghosts in it; I 'm perfectly certain."

"But you would n't meet them in a morning call," said Harry, "that 's contrary to all ghostly etiquette."

"Never mind, I 'll get track of them. I 'll become intimate with old Miss Dorcas and get her to relate her history, and if there is a ghost-chamber I 'll be into it."

"Well, success to you," said Harry; "but to me it looks like a formidable undertaking. Those old ladies are so padded and wadded in buckram."

"Oh, pshaw! there 's just what Jack has done for me,

he has made a breach in the padding and buckram.
Only think of my seeing them at midnight in their night-
caps! And such funny night-caps! Why, it's an occasion long to be remembered, and I would be willing to
wager anything they are talking it over at this minute;
and, of course, you see, it's extremely proper and quite
a part of the play that I should come in this morning to
inquire after the wanderer, and to hope they did n't catch
cold, and to talk over the matter generally. Now, I *like*
that old Miss Dorcas; there seems to me to be an immense amount of character behind all her starch and
stiffness, and I think she's quite worth knowing. She'll
be an acquisition if one can only get at her."

"Well, as I said, success and prosperity go with you!"
said Harry, as he rose and gathered his papers to go to
his morning work.

"I'll go right out with you," said Eva, and she
snatched from the hat-tree a shawl and a little morsel of
white, fleecy worsted, which the initiated surname "a
cloud," and tied it over her head. "I'm going right in
upon them now," she said.

It was a brisk, frosty morning, and she went out with
Harry and darted across from the door. He saw her in
the distance, as he went down the street, laughing and
kissing her hand to him on the door-step of the Vanderheyden house.

Just then the sound of the door-bell—unheard of in
that hour in the morning—caused an excitement in the
back breakfast-parlor, where Miss Dorcas and Mrs. Betsey were at a late breakfast, with old Dinah standing
behind Miss Dorcas' chair to get her morning orders,
giggling and disputing them inch by inch, as was her
ordinary wont.

The old door-bell had a rustling, harsh, rusty sound,
as if cross with a chronic rheumatism of disuse.

"Who under the sun!" said Miss Dorcas. "Jack, be still!"

But Jack wouldn't be still, but ran and snuffed at the door, and barked as if he smelt a legion of burglars.

Eva heard, within the house, the dining-room door open, and then Jack's barking came like a fire of artillery at the crack of the front door, where she was standing. It was slowly opened, and old Dinah's giggling countenance appeared. "Laws bless your soul, Mis' Henderson," she said, flinging the door wide open, "is that you? Jack, be still, sir!"

But Eva had caught Jack up in her arms, and walked with him to the door of the breakfast room.

"Do pray excuse me," she said, "but I thought I'd just run over and see that you hadn't taken any cold."

The scene within was not uninviting. There was a cheerful wood fire burning on the hearth behind a pair of gigantic old-fashioned brass fire-irons. The little breakfast-table, with its bright old silver and India china, was drawn comfortably up in front. Miss Dorcas had her chair on one side, and Miss Betsey on the other, and between them there was a chair drawn up for Jack, where he had been sitting at the time the door-bell rang.

"We are ashamed of our late hours," said Miss Dorcas, when she had made Eva sit down in an old-fashioned claw-footed arm-chair in the warmest corner; "we don't usually breakfast so late, but, the fact is, Betsey was quite done up by the adventure last night."

"Perhaps," said Eva, "I had better have tried keeping Jack till morning."

"Oh no, indeed, Mrs. Henderson," said Mrs. Betsey, with energy; "I know it's silly, but I shouldn't have slept a wink all night if Jack hadn't come home. You know he sleeps with me," she added.

Eva did not know it before, but she said "Yes" all the same, and the good lady rushed on:

"Yes; Dorcas thinks it's rather silly, but I do let Jack sleep on the foot of my bed. I spread his blanket for him every night, and I always wash his feet and wipe them clean before he goes to bed, and when you brought him back you really ought to have seen him run right up stairs to where I keep his bowl and towel; and he stood there, just as sensible, waiting for me to come and wash him. I wish you could have seen how dirty he was! I can't think where ever that dog gets his paws so greasy."

"'Cause he will eat out o' swill-pails!" interposed Dinah, with a chuckle. "Greatest dog after swill-pails I ever see. That's what he's off after."

"Well, I don't know why. It's very bad of him when we always feed him and take such pains with him," said Mrs. Betsey, in accents of lamentation.

"Dogs is allers jest so," said Dinah; "they's arter nastiness and carron. You can't make a Christian out o' a dog, no matter what you do."

Old Dinah was the very impersonation of that coarse, hard literalness which forces actual unpalatable facts upon unwilling ears. There was no disputing that she spoke most melancholy truths, that even the most infatuated dog-lovers could not always shut their eyes to. But Mrs. Betsey chose wholly to ignore her facts and treat her communication as if it had no existence, so she turned her back to Dinah and went on.

"I don't know what makes Jack have these turns of running away. Sometimes I think it's our system of dieting him. Perhaps it may be because we don't allow him all the meat he wants; but then they say if you do give these pet dogs meat they become so gross that it is quite shocking."

Miss Dorcas rapped her snuff-box, sat back in her chair, and took snuff with an air of antique dignity that seemed to call heaven and earth to witness that she only tolerated such fooleries on account of her sister, and not at all in the way of personal approbation.

The nurture and admonition of Jack was the point where the two sisters had a chronic controversy, Miss Dorcas inclining to the side of strict discipline and vigorous repression.

In fact, Miss Dorcas soothed her violated notions of dignity and propriety by always speaking of Jack as "Betsey's dog"—he was one of the permitted toys and amusements of Betsey's more juvenile years; but she felt called upon to keep some limits of discipline to prevent Jack's paw from ruling too absolutely in the family councils.

"You see," said Mrs. Betsey, going on with her reminiscences of yesterday, "we had taken Jack down town with us because we wanted to get his photographs; we'd had him taken last week, and they were not ready till yesterday."

"Dear me, do show them to me," said Eva, entering cheerfully into the humor of the thing; and Mrs. Betsey trotted up stairs to get them.

"You see how very absurd we are," said Miss Dorcas; "but the fact is, Mrs. Henderson, Betsey has had her troubles, poor child, and I'm glad to have her have anything that can be any sort of a comfort to her."

Betsey came back with her photographs, which she exhibited with the most artless innocence.

"You see," said Miss Dorcas, "just how it is. If people set out to treat a dog as a child, they have to take the consequences. That dog rules this whole family, and of course he behaves like spoiled children generally. Here, now, this morning; Betsey and I both have bad colds because we were got out of bed last night with that creature."

Here Jack, seeming to understand that he was the subject-matter of some criticism, rose up suddenly on his haunches before Miss Dorcas and waved his paws in a supplicatory manner at her. Jack understood this to be his only strong point, and brought it out as a trump card on all occasions when he felt himself to be out of favor. Miss Dorcas laughed, as she generally did, and Jack seemed delighted, and sprang into her lap and offered to kiss her with the most brazen assurance.

"Oh, well, Mrs. Henderson, I suppose you see that we are two old fools about that dog," she said. "I do n't know but I am almost as silly as Betsey is, but the fact is one must have *something*, and a dog is not so much risk as a boy, after all. Yes, Jack," she said, tapping his shaggy head patronizingly, "after all you 're no more impudent than puppies in general."

"I never quarrel with anyone for loving dogs," said Eva. "For my part I think no family is complete without one. I tell Harry we must 'set up' our dog as soon as we get a little more settled. When *we* get one, we 'll compare notes."

"Well," said Miss Dorcas, "I always comfort myself with thinking that dear Sir Walter, with all his genius, went as far in dog-petting as any of us. You remember Washington Irving's visit to Abbotsford?"

Eva did not remember it, and Miss Dorcas said she must get it for her at once; she ought to read it. And away she went to look it up in the book-case in the next room.

"The fact is," said Mrs. Betsey, mysteriously, "though Dorcas has so much strength of mind, she is to the full as silly about Jack as I am. When I was gone to Newburg, if you 'll believe me, *she* let Jack sleep on her bed. Dinah knows it, does n't she?"

Dinah confirmed this fact by a loud explosing, in which there was a singular mixture of snort and giggle; and to cover her paroxysm she seized violently on the remains of the breakfast and bore them out into the kitchen, and was heard giggling and gurgling in a rill of laughter all along the way.

Mrs. Betsey began gathering up and arranging the cups, and filling a lacquered bowl of Japanese fabric with hot water, she proceeded to wash the china and silver.

" What *lovely* china," said Eva, with the air of a connoisseur.

" Yes," said Mrs. Betsey, " this china has been in the family for three generations, and we never suffer a servant to touch it."

" Please let *me* help you," said Eva, taking up the napkin sociably, " I do so love old china."

And pretty soon one might have seen a gay morning party—Mrs. Betsey washing, Eva wiping, and Miss Dorcas the while reading scraps out of *Abbotsford* about Maida, and Finette, and Hamlet, and Camp, and Percy, and others of Walter Scott's four-footed friends. The ice of ceremony and stiffness was not only broken by this bit of morning domesticity, but floated gaily downstream never to be formed again.

You may go further into the hearts of your neighbors by one-half hour of undressed rehearsal behind the scenes than a century of ceremonious posing before the footlights.

Real people, with anything like heart and tastes and emotions, do not *enjoy* being shut up behind barricades, and conversing with their neighbors only through loopholes. If any warm-hearted adventurer gets in at the back door of the heart, the stiffest and most formal are often the most thankful for the deliverance.

The advent of this pretty young creature, with her air of joy and gaiety, into the shadowed and mossy precincts of the old Vanderheyden house was an event to be dated from, as the era of a new life. She was to them a flower, a picture, a poem; and a thousand dear remembrances and new capabilities stirred in the withered old hearts to meet her.

Her sincere artlessness and naïf curiosity, her genuine interest in the old time-worn furniture, relics and belongings of the house gave them a new sense of possession. We seem to acquire our things over again when stimulated by the admiration of a new spectator.

"Dear me," said Eva, as she put down a tea-cup she was wiping, "what a pity I have n't some nice old china to begin on! but all my things are spick and span new; I do n't think it 's a bit interesting. I do love to see things that look as if they had a history."

"Ah! my dear child, you are making history fast enough," said Miss Dorcas, with that kind of half sigh with which people at eighty look down on the aspirants of twenty; "do n't try to hurry things."

"But I think *old* things are so nice," said Eva. "They get so many associations. Things just out of Tiffany's or Collamore's have n't associations—there 's no poetry in them. Now, everything in your house has its story. It 's just like the old villas I used to see in Italy where the fountains were all mossy."

"We are mossy enough, dear knows," said Miss Dorcas, laughing, "Betsey and I."

"I 'm so glad I 've got acquainted with you," said Eva, looking up with clear, honest eyes into Miss Dorcas's face; "it 's so lonesome not to know one's neighbors, and I 'm an inexperienced beginner, you know. There are a thousand questions I might ask, where your experience could help me."

"Well, do n't hesitate, dear Mrs. Henderson," said Mrs. Betsey; "do use us if you can. Dorcas is really quite a doctor, and if you should be ill any time, do n't fail to let us know. *We* never have a doctor. Dorcas always knows just what to do. You ought to see her herb closet—there 's a little of everything in it; and she is wonderful for strengthening-mixtures."

And so Eva was taken to see the herbal, and thence, by natural progression, through the chambers, where she admired the old furniture. Then cabinets were unlocked, old curiosities brought out, snatches and bits of history followed, and, in fact, lunch time came in the old Vanderheyden house before any of them perceived whither the tide of social enthusiasm had carried them. Eva stayed to lunch. Such a thing had not happened for years to the desolate old couple, and it really seemed as if the roses of youth and joy, the flowers of years past, all bloomed and breathed around her, and it was late in the day before she returned to her own home to look back on the Vanderheyden fortress as taken. Two stiff, ceremonious strangers had become two warm-hearted, admiring friends—a fortress locked and barred by constraint had become an open door of friendship. Was it not a good morning's work?

CHAPTER IX.

JIM AND ALICE.

THE recent discussions of the marriage question, betokening unrest and dissatisfaction with the immutable claims of this institution, are founded, no doubt, on the various distresses and inconveniences of ill-assorted marriages.

In times when the human being was little developed, the elements of agreement and disagreement were simpler, and marriages were proportionately more tranquil. But modern civilized man has a thousand points of possible discord in an immutable near relation where there was one in the primitive ages.

The wail, and woe, and struggle to undo marriage bonds, in our day, comes from this dissonance of more developed and more widely varying natures, and it shows that a large proportion of marriages have been contracted without any advised and rational effort to ascertain whether there was a reasonable foundation for a close and life-long intimacy.

It would seem as if the arrangements and customs of modern society did everything that could be done to render such a previous knowledge impossible.

Good sense would say that if men and women are to single each other out, and bind themselves by a solemn oath, forsaking all others to cleave to each other as long as life should last, there ought to be, before taking vows of such gravity, the very best opportunity to become minutely acquainted with each other's dispositions, and habits, and modes of thought and action. It would seem to be the dictate of reason that a long and intimate friendship ought to be allowed, in which, without any bias or commitment, young people might have full opportunity to study each other's character and disposition, being under no obligation, expressed or implied, on account of such intimacy to commit themselves to the irrevocable union.

Such a kind of friendship is the instinctive desire of both the parties that make up society. Both young men and young women, as we observe, would greatly enjoy a more intimate and friendly intercourse, if the very fact of that initiatory acquaintance were not immediately seized upon by busy A, B, and C, and reported as an engagement. The flower that might possibly blossom into the rose of love is withered and blackened by the busy efforts of gossips to pick it open before the time.

Our young friend, Alice Van Arsdel, was what in modern estimation would be called just the "nicest kind of a girl." She had a warm heart, a high sense of justice and honor, she was devout in her religious profession, conscientious in the discharge of the duties of family life. Naturally, Alice was of a temperament which might have inclined her to worldly ambition. She had that keen sense of the advantages of wealth and station which even the most sensible person may have, and, had her father's prosperity continued, might have run the gay career of flirtation and conquest supposed to be proper to a rich young belle.

The failure of her father not only cut off all these prospects, but roused the deeper and better part of her nature to comfort and support her parents, and to assist in all ways in trimming the family vessel to the new navigation. Her self-esteem took a different form. Had she been enthroned in wealth and station, it would have taken pleasure in reigning; thrown from that position, it became her pride to adapt herself entirely to the proprieties of her different circumstances. Up to that hour, she had counted Jim Fellows simply as a tassel on her fan, or any other appendage to her glittering life. When the crash came, she expected no more of him than of a last summer's bird, and it was with somewhat of pleased surprise that, on the first public tidings of the news, she received from Jim an expensive hot-house bouquet of a kind that he had never thought of giving in prosperous days.

"The extravagant boy!" she said. Yet she said it with tears in her eyes, and she put the bouquet into water, and changed it every day while it lasted. The flowers and the friends of adversity have a value all their own.

Then Jim came, came daily, with downright unsentimental offers of help, and made so much fun and gaiety for them in the days of their breaking up as almost shocked Aunt Maria, who felt that a period of weeping and wailing would have been more appropriate. Jim became recognized in the family as a sort of factotum, always alert and ready to advise or to do, and generally knowing where every body or thing which was wanted in New York was to be found. But, as Alice was by no means the only daughter, as Marie and Angelique were each in their way as lively and desirable young candidates for admiration, it would have appeared that here was the best possible chance for a young man to have a friendship whose buds even the gossips would not pick open to find if there were love inside of them. As a young neophyte of the all-powerful press, Jim had the dispensation of many favors, in the form of tickets to operas, concerts, and other public entertainments, which were means of conferring enjoyment and variety, and dispensed impartially among the sisters. Eva's house, in all the history of its finding, inception, and construc-

E

tion, had been a ground for many a familiar meeting
from whence had grown up a pleasant feeling of com-
radeship and intimacy.

The things that specialized this intimacy, as relating
to Alice more than to the other sisters, were things as indefinite and indefinable as the shade mark between two
tints of the rainbow; and yet there undoubtedly was
a peculiar intimacy, and since the misfortunes of the
family it had been of a graver kind than before, though
neither of them cared to put it into words. Between a
young man and a young woman of marriageable age a
friendship of this kind, if let alone, generally comes to its
bud and blossom in its own season; and there is something unutterably vexatious and revolting to every fibre
of a girl's nature to have any well-meaning interference
to force this denouement.

Alice enjoyed the unspoken devotion of Jim, which
she perceived by that acute sort of divination of which
women are possessed; she felt quietly sure that she had
more influence over him, could do more with him, than
any other woman; and this consciousness of power over
a man is something most agreeable to girls of Alice's degree of self-esteem. She assumed to be a sort of mentor;
she curbed the wild sallies of his wit, rebuking him if he
travestied a hymn, or made a smart, funny application of
a text of Scripture. But, as she generally laughed, the
culprit was not really overborne by the censure. She
had induced him to go with her to Mr. St. John's church,
and even to take a class in the Sunday-school, where he
presided with the unction of an apostle over a class of
street "*gamins,*" who certainly never found a more entertaining teacher.

Now, although Marie and Angelique were also teachers in the same school, it somehow always happened that
Jim and Alice walked to the scene of their duties in com-

pany. It was one of those quiet, unobserved arrangements of particles which are the result of laws of chemical affinity. These street *tête-à-têtes* gave Alice admirable opportunity for those graceful admonitions which are so very effective on young gentlemen when coming from handsome, agreeable monitors. On a certain Sunday morning in our history, as Alice was on her way to the mission school with Jim, she had been enjoining upon him to moderate his extreme liveliness to suit the duties of the place and scene.

"It's all very well, Alice," he said to her, "so long as I don't have to be too much with that St. John. But I declare that fellow stirs me up awfully: he looks so meek and so fearfully pious that it's all I can do to keep from ripping out an oath, just to see him jump!"

"Jim, you bad fellow! How can you talk so?"

"Well, it's a serious fact now. Ministers ought n't to *look* so pious! It's too much a temptation. Why, last Sunday, when he came trailing by so soft and meek and asked me what books we wanted, I perfectly longed to rip out an oath and say, 'Why in thunder can't you speak louder.' It's a temptation of the devil, I know; but you must n't let St. John and me run too much together, or I shall blow out."

"Oh, Jim, you must n't talk so. Why, you really shock me—you grieve me."

"Well, you see, I've given up swearing for ever so long, but some kinds of people do tempt me fearfully, and he's one of 'em, and then I think that he must think I'm a wolf in sheep's clothing. But then, you see, a wolf understands those cubs better than a sheep. You ought to hear how I put gospel into them. I make 'em come out on the responses like little Trojans. I've promised every boy who is 'sharp up' on his Collect next Sunday a new pop-gun."

"O Jim, you creature!" said Alice, laughing.

"By George, Alice, it's the best way. You don't know anything about these little heathen. You've got to take 'em where they live. They put up with the Collect for the sake of the pop-gun, you see."

"But, Jim, I really was in hopes that you would look on this thing seriously," said Alice, endeavoring to draw on a face of protest.

"Why, Alice, I am serious; didn't I go round to the highways and hedges, drumming up those little varmints? Not a soul of them would have put his head inside a Sunday-school room if it hadn't been for me. I tell you I ought to be encouraged now. I'm not appreciated."

"Oh Jim, you *have* done beautifully."

"I should think I had. I keep a long face while they are there, and don't swear at Mr. St. John, and sing like a church robin. So I think you ought to let me let out a little to you going home. That eases my mind; it's the confessional—Mr. St. John believes in that. I *didn't* swear, mind you. I only felt like it; maybe that 'll wear off, by-and-by. So don't give me up, yet."

"Oh, I don't; and I'm perfectly sure, Jim, that you are the very person that can do good to these wild boys. Of course the free experience of life which young men have, enables them to know how to deal with such cases better than we girls can."

"Yes, you ought to hear me expound the commandments, and put it into them about stealing and lying. You see Jim knows a thing or two, and is up to their tricks. They don't come it round Jim, I tell you. Any boy that don't toe the crack gets it. I give 'em C sharp with the key up."

"O Jim, you certainly are original in your ways! But I dare say you're right," said Alice. "You know how to get on with them."

"Indeed I do. I tell you I know what's what for these boys, though I don't know, and don't care about, what the old coves did in the first two centuries, and all that. Don't you think, Alice, St. John is a little prosy on that chapter?"

"Mr. St. John is such a good man that I receive everything he says on subjects where he knows more than I do," said Alice, virtuously.

"Oh pshaw, Alice! if a fellow has to swallow every good man's hobby-horses, hoofs, tail and all, why he'll have a good deal to digest. I tell you St. John is too 'other-worldly,' as Charles Lamb used to say. He ought to get in love, and get married. I think, now, that if our little Angie would take him in hand she would bring him into mortal spheres, make a nice fellow of him."

"Oh, Mr. St. John never will marry," said Alice, solemnly; "he is devoted to the church. He has published a tract on holy virginity that is beautiful."

"Holy grandmother!" said Jim; "that's all bosh, Ally. Now you are too sensible a girl to talk that way. That's going to Rome on a high canter."

"I don't think so," said Alice, stoutly. "For my part, I think if a man, for the sake of devoting himself to the church, gives up family cares, I reverence him. I like to feel that my rector is something sacred to the altar. The very idea of a clergyman in any other than sacred relations is disagreeable to me."

"Go it, now! so long as I'm not the clergyman!"

"You sauce-box!"

"Well, now, mark my words. St. John is a man, after all, and not a Fra Angelico angel, with a long neck and a lily in his hand, and, I tell you, when Angie sits there at the head of her class, working and fussing over those girls, she looks confoundedly pretty, and if St. John finds it out I shall think the better of him, and *I* think he will."

"Pshaw, Jim, he never looks at her."

"Don't he? he does though. I've seen him go round and round, and look at her as if she was an electrical battery, or something that he was afraid might go off and kill him. But he *does* look at her. I tell you, Jim knows the signs of the sky."

With which edifying preparation of mind, Alice found herself at the door of the Sunday-school room, where the pair were graciously received by Mr. St. John.

CHAPTER X

MR. ST. JOHN.

THAT good man, in the calm innocence of his heart, was ignorant of the temptations to which he exposed his tumultuous young disciple. He was serenely gratified with the sight of Jim's handsome face and alert, active figure, as he was enacting good shepherd over his unruly flock. Had he known the exact nature of the motives which he presented to lead them to walk in the ways of piety, he might have searched a good while in primitive records before finding a churchly precedent

Arthur St. John was by nature a poet and idealist He was as pure as a chrysolite, as refined as a flower; and, being thus, had been, by the irony of fate, born on one of the bleakest hillsides of New Hampshire, where there was a literal famine of any esthetic food. His childhood had been fed on the dry husks of doctrinal catechism; he had sat wearily on hard high-backed seats and dangled his little legs hopelessly through sermons on the difference between justification and sanctification. His ultra-morbid conscientiousness had been wrought into agonized convulsions by stringent endeavors to carry him through certain prescribed formulæ of conviction of sin and conversion; efforts which, grating against natures of a certain delicate fiber, produce wounds and abrasions which no after-life can heal. To such a one the cool shades of the Episcopal Church, with its orderly ways, its poetic liturgy, its artistic ceremonies, were as the shadow of a great rock in a weary land. No converts are so disposed to be ultra as converts by reaction; and persons of a poetic and imaginative temperament are peculiarly liable to these extremes.

Wearied with the intense and noisy clangor of modern thought, it was not strange if he should come to think free inquiry an evil, look longingly back on the ages of simple credulity, and believe that the dark ages of intellect were the bright ones of faith. Without really going over to the Romish Church, he proposed to walk that path, fine as the blade that Mahomet fabled as the Bridge of Paradise, in which he might secure all the powers and influences and advantages of tnat old system without its defects and corruptions.

So he had established his mission in one of the least hopeful neighborhoods of New York. The chapel was a marvel of beauty and taste at small expense, for St. John was in a certain way an ecclesiastical architect and artist. He could illuminate neatly, and had at command a good store of the beautiful forms of the past to choose from. He worked at diaphanous windows which had all the effect of painted glass, and emblazoned texts and legends, and painted in polychrome, till the little chapel dazzled the eyes of street vagabonds, who never before had been made welcome to so pretty a place in their lives. Then, when he impressed it on the minds of these poor people that this lovely, pretty little church was their Father's house, freely open to them every day, and that prayers and psalms might be heard there morning and evening, and the holy communion of Christ's love every Sunday, it is no marvel if many were drawn in and impressed. Beauty of form and attractiveness of color in the church arrangements of the rich may cease to be means of grace and become wantonness of luxury—but for the very poor they are an education, they are means of quickening the artistic sense, which is twin brother to the spiritual. The rich do not need these things, and the poor do.

St. John, like many men of seemingly gentle temperament, had the organizing talent of the schoolmaster. No one could be with him and not *feel* him; and the intense purpose with which he labored, in season and out of season, carried all before it. He marshaled his forces like an army; his eye was everywhere and on everyone. He trained his choir of singing boys for processional singing; he instructed his teachers, he superintended and catechised his school. In the life of incessant devotion to the church which he led, woman had no place except as an obedient instrument. He valued the young and fair who flocked to his standard, simply and only for what they could do in his work, and apparently had no worldly change with which to carry on commerce of society.

Yet it was true, as Jim said, that his eye had in some way or other been caught by Angelique; yet, at first, it was in the way of doubt and inquiry, rather than approval.

Angelique was gifted by nature with a certain air of piquant vivacity, which gave to her pretty person the effect of a French picture. In heart and character she was a perfect little self-denying saint, infinitely humble in her own opinion, devoted to doing good wherever her hand could find it, and ready at any time to work her pretty fingers to the bone in a good cause. But yet undeniably she had a certain style and air of fashion not a bit like "St. Jerome's love" or any of the mediæval saints. She could not help it. It was not her fault that everything about her had a sort of facility for sliding into trimly fanciful arrangement—that her little hats would sit so jauntily on her pretty head, that her foot and ankle had such a provoking neatness, and that her daintily gloved hands had a hundred little graceful move-

ments in a moment. Then her hair had numberless mu-
tinous little curly-wurlies, and flew of itself into the golden
mists of modern fashion; and her almond-shaped hazel
eyes had a trick of glancing like a bird's, and she looked
always as if a smile might break out at any moment, even
on solemn occasions;—all which were traits to inspire
doubt in the mind of an earnest young clergyman, in whose
study the pictures of holy women were always lean, long-
favored, with eyes rolled up, and looking as if they never
had heard of a French hat or a pair of gaiter-boots. He
watched her the first Sunday that she sat at the head of
her class, looking for all the world like a serious-minded
canary bird, and wondered whether so evidently airy and
worldly a little creature would adapt herself to the earnest
work before her; but she did succeed in holding a set of
unpromising street-girls in a sort of enchanted state while
she chippered to them in various little persuasive intonations, made them say catechism after her, and then told
them stories that were not in any prayer-book. After a
little observation, he was convinced that she would "do."
But the habit of watchfulness continued!

On this day, as Jim had suggested the subject,
Alice somehow was moved to remark the frequent direction of Mr. St. John's eyes.

On this Sunday Angelique had had the misfortune to
don for the first time a blue suit, with a blue velvet hat
that gave a brilliant effect to her golden hair. In front
of this hat, nodding with every motion of her head, was
a blue and gold humming bird. She wore a cape of ermine, and her class seemed quite dazzled by her appearance. Now Mr. St. John had worked vigorously to get
up his little chapel in blue and gold, gorgeous to behold;
but a blue and gold teacher was something that there
was no churchly precedent for—although if we look into
the philosophy of the thing there may be the same sort of

influence exercised over street barbarians by a prettily-dressed teacher as by a prettily-dressed church. But as Mr. St. John gazed at Angelique, and wondered whether it was quite the thing for her to look so striking, he saw a little incident that touched his heart. There was a poor, pinched, wan-visaged little girl, the smallest in the class, whose face was deformed by the scar of a fearful burn. She seemed to be in a trembling ecstacy at Angie's finery, and while she was busy with her lesson stealthily laid her thin little hand upon the ermine cape. Immediately she was sharply reproved by a coarse, strong, older sister, who had her in charge, and her hand rudely twitched back.

Angie turned with bright, astonished eyes, and seeing the little creature cowering with shame, beamed down on her a lovely smile, stooped and kissed her.

"You like it, dear?" she said frankly. "Sit up and rest your cheek on it, if you like," and Angie gathered her up to her side and went on telling of the Good Shepherd.

Arthur St. John took the whole meaning of the incident. It carried him back beyond the catacombs to something more authentic, even to HIM who said, "Suffer little children to come unto me," and he felt a strange, new throb under his surplice.

The throb alarmed him to the degree that he did not look in that direction again through all the services, though he certainly did remark certain clear, bird-like tones in the chants with a singular feeling of nearness.

Just about this time, St. John, unconsciously to himself, was dealing with forces of which no previous experience of life had given him a conception. He passed out of his vestry and walked to his solitary study in a kind of maze of vague reverie, in which golden hair and hazel eyes seemed strangely blent with moral enthusiasms. "What a lovely spirit!" he thought; and he felt as if he would far rather have followed her out of the door than to have come to the cold, solitary sanctities of his own room.

Mr. St. John's study was not the sanctum of a self-indulgent, petted clergyman, but rather that of one who took life in very serious earnest. His first experience of pastoral life having been among the poor, the sight of the disabilities, wants, and dangers, the actual terrible facts of human existence, had produced the effect on him that they often do on persons of extreme sensibility and conscientiousness. He could not think of retaining for himself an indulgence or a luxury while wants so terrible stared him in the face; and his study, consequently, was furnished in the ascetic rather than the esthetic style. Its only ornaments were devotional pictures of a severe mediæval type and the books of a well-assorted library. There was no carpet; there were no lounging chairs or sofas of ease. In place was a *prie dieu* of approved antique pattern, on which stood two wax candles and lay his prayer-book. A crucifix of beautiful Italian workmanship stood upon it, and it was scrupulously draped with the appropriate churchly color of the season.

As we have said, this room seemed strangely lonely as he entered it. He was tired with work which had begun early in the morning, with scarce an interval of repose, and a perversely shocking idea presented itself to his mind—how pleasant it would be to be met on returning from his labors by just such a smile as he had seen beaming down on the poor little girl.

When he found himself out, and discovered that this was where his thoughts were running to, he organized a manly resistance; and recited aloud, with unction and emphasis, Moore's exquisite version of St. Jerome's opinion of what the woman should be whom a true priest might love.

> " Who is the maid my spirit seeks,
> Through cold reproof and slander's blight ?

Has *she* Love's roses on her cheeks?
  Is *her's* an eye of this world's light?
No—wan and sunk with midnight prayer
  Are the pale looks of her I love;
Or if at times a light be there,
  Its beam is kindled from above.

I choose not her, my heart's elect,
  From those who seek their Maker's shrine
In gems and garlands proudly deck'd
  As if themselves were things divine.
No—Heaven but faintly warms the breast
  That beats beneath a broider'd vail;
And she who comes in glitt'ring vest
  To mourn her frailty, still is frail.

Not so the faded form I prize
  And love, because its bloom is gone;
The glory in those sainted eyes
  Is all the grace *her* brow puts on.
And ne'er was Beauty's dawn so bright,
  So touching, as that form's decay
Which, like the altar's trembling light,
  In holy luster wastes away."

"Certainly, not in the least like *her*," he thought, and he resolved to dismiss the little hat with the humming bird, the golden mist of hair, and the glancing eyes, into the limbo of vain thoughts.

Mr. St. John, like many another ardent and sincere young clergyman, had undertaken to be shepherd and bishop of souls, with more knowledge on every possible subject than the nature of the men and women he was to guide.

A fastidious taste, scholarly habits, and great sensitiveness, had kept him out of society during all his collegiate days. His life had been that of a devout recluse. He knew little of mankind, except the sick and decrepid old women, whom he freely visited, and who had for nothing the vision of his handsome face and the charm

of his melodious voice amid the dirt and discomforts of
their sordid poverty.   But fashionable young women, the
gay daughters of ease and luxury, were to him rather objects of suspicion and apprehension than of attraction.
If they flocked to his church, and seemed eager to enlist
in church work under his leadership, he was determined
that there should be no sham in it.   In sermon after sermon, he denounced in stringent terms the folly and guilt
of the sentimental religion which makes playthings of
the solemn rituals of the church, which wears the cross
as a glittering bauble on the outside, and shrinks from
every form of the real self-denial which it symbolizes.

Angelique, by nature the most conscientious of beings, had listened to this eloquence with awful self-
condemnation.   She felt herself a dreadfully sinful little
girl, that she had lived so unprofitable a life hitherto, and
she undertook her Sunday-school labors with an intense
ardor.   When she came to visit in the poor dwellings
from whence her pupils were drawn, and to see how devoid their life was of everything which she had been
taught to call comfort, she felt wicked and selfish for enjoying even the moderate luxuries allowed by her father's
reduced position.   The allowance that had been given her
for her winter wardrobe seemed to be more than she had a
right to keep for herself in face of the terrible destitutions
she saw.   Secretly she set herself to see how much she
could save from it.   She had the gift of a quick eye and
of deft fingers; and so, after running through the fashionable shops of dresses and millinery to catch the ideal of
the hour, she went to work for herself.   A faded merino
was ripped, dyed, and, by the aid of clever patterns and
skillful hands, transformed into the stylish blue suit.
The little blue velvet hat had been gathered from the
trimmings of an old dress.   The humming bird had
been a necessary appendage, to cover the piecing of the

velvet; and thus the outfit which had called up so many alarmed scruples in Mr. St. John's mind was as completely a work of self-denial and renunciation as if she had come out in the black robe of a Sister of Charity.

The balance saved was, in her own happy thought, devoted to a Christmas outfit for some of the poorest of her scholars, whose mothers struggled hard and sat up late washing and mending to make them decent to be seen in Sunday-school.

But how should Mr. St. John know this, which Angie had not even told to her own mother and sisters? To say the truth, she feared that perhaps she might be laughed at as Quixotic, or wanting in good sense, in going so much beyond the usual standard in thoughtfulness for others, and, at any rate, kept her own little counsel. Mr. St. John knew nothing about women in that class of society, their works and ways, where or how they got their dresses; but he had a general impression that fashionable women were in heathen darkness, and spent on dress fabulous amounts that might be given to the poor. He had certain floating views in his mind, when further advanced in his ministry, of instituting a holy sisterhood, who should wear gray cloaks, and spend all their money and time in deeds of charity.

On the present occasion, he could see only the very patent fact that Angelique's dress was stylish and becoming to an alarming degree; that, taken in connection with her bright cheeks, her golden hair, and glancing hazel eyes, she was to the full as worldly an object as a blue-bird, or an oriole, or any of those brilliant creatures with which it has pleased the Maker of all to distract our attention in our pilgrimage through this sinful and dying world.

Angie was so far from assuming to herself any merit

in this sacrifice that her only thought was how little it
would do.   Had it been possible and proper, she would
have willingly given her ermine cape to the poor, wan
little child, to whom the mere touch of it was such a
strange, bewildering luxury; but she had within herself
a spice of practical common sense which showed her
that our most sacred impulses are not always to be literally obeyed.

Yet, while the little scarred cheek was resting on her
ermine in such apparent bliss, there mingled in with the
thread of her instructions to the children a determina-
tion next day to appraise cheap furs, and see if she
could not bless the little one with a cape of her very own.

Angie's quiet common sense always stood her in
good stead in moderating her enthusiasms, and even
carried her at times to the length of differing with the
rector, to whom she looked up as an angel guide.   For
example, when he had expatiated on the propriety and
superior sanctity of còming fasting to the holy communion, sensible Angie had demurred.

"I must teach my class," she pleaded with herself,
"and if I should go all that long way up to church
without my breakfast, I should have such a sick-headache that I couldn't do anything properly for them. I'm
always cross and stupid when that comes on."

Thus Angie concluded by her own little light, in
her own separate way, that "to do good was better than
sacrifice."   Nevertheless, she supposed all this was because she was so low down in the moral scale, for did
not Mr. St. John fast?—doubtless it gave him headache,
but he was so good he went on just as well with a headache as without—and Angie felt how far she must rise to
be like that.

*   *   *   *   *   *   *   *

"'There now," said Jim Fellows, triumphantly, to

Alice, as they were coming home, "didn't you see your
angel of the churches looking in a certain direction this
morning?"

Alice had, as a last resort, a fund of reserved dignity
which she could draw upon whenever she was really
and deeply in earnest.

"Jim," she said, without a smile, and in a grave tone,
"I have confidence that you are a true friend to us all."

"Well, I hope so," said Jim, wonderingly.

"And you are too kind-hearted and considerate to
wish to give real pain."

"Certainly I am."

"Well, then, promise me never to make remarks of
that nature again, to me or anybody else, about Angie
and Mr. St. John. It would be more distressing and
annoying to *her* than anything you could do; and the
dear child is now perfectly simple-hearted and uncon-
strained, and cheerful as a bird in her work. The
least intimation of this kind might make her conscious
and uncomfortable, and spoil it all. So promise me
now."

Jim eyed his fair monitress with the kind of wicked
twinkle a naughty boy gives to his mother, to ascertain
if she is really in earnest, but Alice maintained a brow
of "sweet, austere composure," and looked as if she expected to be obeyed.

"Well, I perfectly long for a hit at St. John," he said,
"but if you say so, so it must be."

"You promise on your honor?" insisted Alice.

"Yes, I promise on my honor; so there!" said Jim.
"I wont even wink an eyelid in that direction. I'll
make a perfect stock and stone of myself. But," he
added, "Jim can have his thoughts for all that."

Alice was not exactly satisfied with the position assumed by her disciple, she therefore proceeded to fortify

him in grace by some farther observations, delivered in a very serious tone.

"For my part," she said, "I think nothing is in such bad taste, to say the least, as the foolish way in which some young people will allow themselves to talk and think about an unmarried young clergyman, while he is absorbed in duties so serious and has feelings so far above their comprehension. The very idea or suggestion of a flirtation between a clergyman and one of his flock is utterly repulsive and disagreeable."

Here Jim, with a meek gravity of face, simply interposed the question :

"What is flirtation?"

"You know, now, as well as I do," said Alice, with heightened color. "You need n't pretend you do n't."

"Oh," said Jim. "Well, then, I suppose I do." And the two walked on in silence, for some way; Jim with an air of serious humility, as if in a deep study, and Alice with cheeks getting redder and redder with vexation.

"Now, Jim," she said at last, "you are very provoking."

"I 'm sure I give in to everything you say," said Jim, in an injured tone.

"But you act just as if you were making fun all the time; and you know you are."

"Upon my word I do n't know what you mean. I have assented to every word you said—given up to you hook and line—and now you're not pleased. I tell you it 's rough on a fellow."

"Oh, come," said Alice, laughing at the absurdity of the quarrel; "there 's no use in scolding you."

Jim laughed too, and felt triumphant; and just then they turned a corner and met Aunt Maria coming from church.

CHAPTER XI.

WHEN Mrs. Wouvermans met our young friends, she was just returning home after performing her morning devotions in one of the most time-honored churches in New York. She was as thorough and faithful in her notions of religion as of housekeeping. She adhered strictly to *her own* church, in which undeniably none but ancient and respectable families worshiped, and where she was perfectly sure that whatever of dress or deportment she saw was certain to be the correct thing.

It was a church of eminent propriety. It was large and lofty, with long-drawn aisles and excellent sleeping accommodations, where the worshipers were assisted to dream of heaven by every appliance of sweet music, and not rudely shaken in their slumbers by any obtrusiveness on the part of the rector.

In fact, everything about the services of this church was thoroughly toned down by good breeding. The responses of the worshipers were given in decorous whispers that scarcely disturbed the solemn stillness; for when a congregation of the best-fed and best-bred people of New York on their knees declare themselves "miserable sinners," it is a matter of delicacy to make as little disturbance about it as possible. A well-paid choir of the finest professional singers took the whole responsibility of praising God into their own hands, so that the respectable audience were relieved from any necessity of exertion in that department. As the most brilliant

lights of the opera were from time to time engaged to
render the more solemn parts of the service, flocks of
sinners who otherwise would never have entered a church
crowded to hear these " morning stars sing together;"
let us hope, to their great edification. The sermons of
the rector, delivered in the dim perspective, had a
plaintive, far-off sound, as a voice of one " crying in the
wilderness," and crying at a very great distance. This
was in part owing to the fact that the church, having
been built after an old English ecclesiastical model in
days when English churches were used only for processional services, was entirely unadapted for any purposes
of public speaking, so that a man's voice had about as
good chance of effect in it as if he spoke anywhere in
the thoroughfares of New York.

The rector, the Rev. Dr. Cushing, was a good, amiable man; middle-aged, adipose, discreet, devoted to " our
excellent liturgy," and from his heart opposed to anything which made trouble.

From the remote distances whence his short Sunday
cry was uttered, he appeared moved to send protests
against two things : first, the tendency to philosophical
speculation and the skeptical humanitarian theories of
the age ; and second, against Romanizing tendencies in
the church. The young missionary, St. John, who got
up to early services at conventual hours, and had prayers
every morning and evening, and communion every Sunday and every Saint's day; who fasted on all the Ember
Days, and called on other people to fast, and seemed
literally to pray without ceasing; appeared to him a
bristling impersonation of the Romanizing tendencies of
the age, and one of those who troubled Israel. The
fact that many of the young ladies of the old established
church over which the good Doctor ministered were
drawn to flock up to the services of this disturber gave

to him a realizing sense of the danger to which the whole church was thereby exposed.

On this particular morning he had selected that well-worn text, "Are not Abana and Pharpar, rivers of Damascus, better than all the waters of Jordan? May I not wash in them and be clean?"

Of course, like everybody who preaches on this text, he assumed that Jordan was the true faith as *he* preached it, and that the rivers of Damascus were any and every faith that diverged from his own.

These improper and profane rivers were various. There was, of course, modern skepticism with profuse allusions to Darwin; there were all sorts of modern humanitarian and social reforms; and there was in the bosom of the very church herself, he regretted to state, a disposition to go off after the Abana and Pharpar of Romish abominations. All these were to be avoided, and people were to walk in those quiet paths of godliness in which they had been brought up to walk, and, in short, do pretty much as they had been doing, undisturbed by new notions, or movements, or ideas, whether out of the church or in.

And as he plaintively recited these exhortations, his voice coming in a solemn and spectral tone adown the far-off aisles, it seemed to give a dreamy and unreal effect even to the brisk modern controversies and disturbances which formed his theme. The gorgeous, many-colored lights streamed silently the while through the stained windows, turning the bald head of one ancient church-warden yellow, and of another green, and another purple, while the white feathers on Mrs. Demas's bonnet passed gradually through successive tints of the rainbow; and the audience dosed off at intervals, and awakened again to find the rector at another head, and talking about something else; and so on till the closing ascription

to the Trinity, when everybody rose with a solemn sense
that something or other was over. The greater part of
the audience in the intervals of somnolency congratulated
themselves that *they* were in no danger of running after
new ideas, and thanked God that they never speculated
about philosophy. As to turning out to daily morning
and evening prayers, or fasting on any days whatsoever,
or going into any extravagant excesses of devotion and
self-sacrifice, they were only too happy to find that it was
their duty to resist the very suggestion as tending directly to Romanism.

The true Jordan, they were happy to find, ran directly
through their own particular church, and they had only
to continue their stated Sunday naps on its borders as
before.

Mrs. Wouvermans, however, was not of a dozing or
dreamy nature. Her mind, such as it was, was always
wide awake and cognizant of what she was about. She
was not susceptible of a dreamy state : to use an idiom-
atic phrase, she was always up and dressed ; everything
in her mental vision was clear cut and exact. The sermon was intensified in its effect upon her by the state of
the Van Arsdel pew, of which she was on this Sunday
the only occupant. The fact was, that the ancient and
respectable church in which she worshiped had just been
through a contest, in which Mr. Simons, a young assistant rector, had been attempting to introduce some of
the very practices hinted at in the discourse. This fer-
vid young man, full of fire and enthusiasm, had incautiously been made associate rector for this church, at the
time when Dr. Cushing had been sent to Europe to re-
cover from a bronchial attack. He was young, earnest
and eloquent, and possessed with the idea that all those
burning words and phrases in the prayer-book, which had
dropped like precious gems dyed with the heart's blood of

saints and martyrs, ought to mean something more than
they seemed to do for modern Christians. Without introducing any new ritual, he set himself to make vivid
and imperative every doctrine and direction of the
prayer-book, and to bring the drowsy company of pew-
holders somewhere up within sight of the plane of the
glorious company of apostles and the noble army of
martyrs with whose blood it was sealed. He labored
and preached, and strove and prayed, tugging at the
drowsy old church, like Pegasus harnessed to a stone
cart. He set up morning and evening prayers, had communion every Sunday, and annoyed old rich saints by
suggesting that it was their duty to build mission chapels
and carry on mission works, after the pattern of St. Paul
and other irrelevant and excessive worthies, who in their
time were accused of turning the world upside down.
Of course there was resistance and conflict, and more
life in the old church than it had known for years; but
the conflict became at last so wearisome that, on Mr.
Cushing's return from Europe, the young angel spread
his wings and fled away to a more congenial parish in a
neighboring city.

But many in whom his labors had wakened a craving
for something real and earnest in religion strayed off to
other churches, and notably the younger members of the
Van Arsdel family, to the no small scandal of Aunt Maria.

The Van Arsdel pew was a perfect fort and intrench-
ment of respectability. It was a great high, square wall-
pew, well cushioned and ample, with an imposing array of
prayer-books; there was room in it for a regiment of
saints, and here Aunt Maria sat on this pleasant Sunday
listening to the dangers of the church, all alone. She
felt, in a measure, like Elijah the Tishbite, as if she
only were left to stand up for the altars of her faith.

Mrs. Wouvermans was not a person to let an evil run

on very far without a protest. "While she was musing the fire burned," and when she had again mounted guard in the pew at afternoon service, and still found herself alone, she resolved to clear her conscience; and so she walked straight up to Nellie's, to see why none of them were at church.

"It's a shame, Nellie, a perfect shame! There wasn't a creature but myself in our pew to-day, and good Dr. Cushing giving such a sermon this morning!"

This to Mrs. Van Arsdel, whom she found luxuriously ensconced on a sofa drawn up before the fire in her bedroom.

"Ah, well, the fact is, Maria, I had such a headache this morning," replied she, plaintively.

"Well, then, you ought to have made your husband and family go; somebody ought to be there! It positively isn't respectable."

"Ah, well, Maria, my husband, poor man, gets so tired and worn out with his week's work, I haven't a heart to get him up early enough for morning service. Mr. Van Arsdel isn't feeling quite well lately; he hasn't been out at all to-day."

"Well, there are the girls, Alice and Angelique and Marie, where are they? All going up to that old Popish, ritualistic chapel, I suppose. It's too bad. Now, that's all the result of Mr. Simons's imprudences. I told you, in the time of it, just what it would lead to. It leads straight to Rome, just as I said. Mr. Simons set them a-going, and now he is gone and they go where they have *lighted* candles on the altar every Sunday, and Mr. St. John prays with his back to them, and has processions, and wears all sorts of heathenish robes; and your daughters go there, Nellie."

The very plumes in Aunt Maria's hat nodded with warning energy as she spoke

"Are you *sure* the candles are *lighted?*" said Mrs.
Van Arsdel, sitting up with a weak show of protest, and
looking gravely into the fire. "I was up there once, and
there were candles on the altar, to be sure, but they were
not lighted."

"They *are* lighted," said Mrs. Wouvermans, with
awful precision. "I've been up there myself and seen
them. Now, how *can* you let your children run at loose
ends so, Nellie? I only wish you had heard the sermon
this morning. He showed the danger of running into
Popery; and it really was enough to make one's blood run
cold to hear how those infidels are attacking the church,
carrying all before them; and then to think that the
only true church should be all getting divided and
mixed up and running after Romanism! It's perfectly
awful."

"Well, I don't know what we can do," said Mrs. Van
Arsdel, helplessly.

"And we've got both kinds of trouble in our family.
Eva's husband is reading all What's-his-name's works—
that evolution man, and all that; and then Eva and the
girls going after this St. John—and he's leading them
as straight to Rome as they can go."

Poor Mrs. Van Arsdel was somewhat fluttered by
this alarming view of the case, and clasped her pretty,
fat, white hands, that glittered with rings like lilies with
dew-drops, and looked the image of gentle, incapable
perplexity.

"I don't believe Harry is an infidel," she said at last.
"He has to read Darwin and all those things, because
he has to talk about them in the magazine; and as to
Mr. St. John—you know Eva is delicate and can't walk
so far as our church, and this is right round the corner
from her; and Mr. St. John is a good man. He does
ever so much for the poor, and almost supports a mission

F

there; and the Bishop doesn't forbid him, and if the
Bishop thought there was any danger, he would."

"Well, I can't think, for my part, what our Bishop can
be thinking of," said Aunt Maria, who was braced up to
an extraordinary degree by the sermon of the morning.
"I don't see how he can let them go on so—with candles,
and processions, and heathen robes, and all that. I'd
process 'em out of the church in quick time. If I were
he, I'd have all that sort of trumpery cleaned out at
once; for just see where it leads to! I may not be as
good a Christian as I ought to be—we all have our short-
comings—but one thing I know, *I do hate the Catholics*
and all that belongs to them; and I'd no more have such
goings on in *my* diocese than I'd have moths in my carpet! I'd sweep 'em right out!" said Aunt Maria, with a
gesture as if she held the besom of destruction.

Mrs. Wouvermans belonged to a not uncommon class
of Christians, whose evidences of piety are more vigorous
in hating than in loving. There is no manner of doubt
that she would have made good her word, had she been a
bishop.

"Oh, well, Maria," said Mrs. Van Arsdel, drawing
her knit zephyr shawl about her with a sort of consolatory movement, and settling herself cosily back on her
sofa, "it's evident that the Bishop doesn't see just as
you do, and I am content to allow what he does. As to
the girls, they are old enough to judge for themselves,
and, besides, I think they are doing some good by teaching in that mission school. I hope so, at least. Anyway, I couldn't help it if I would. But, do tell me, *did*
Mrs. Demas have on her new bonnet?"

"Yes, she did," said Aunt Maria, with vigor; "and
I can tell you it's a perfect fright, if it did come from
Paris. Another thing I saw—*fringes have come round
again!* Mrs. Lamar's new cloak was trimmed with fringe."

"You don't say so," said Mrs. Van Arsdel, contemplating all the possible consequences of this change. "There was another reason why I couldn't go out this morning," she added, rather irrelevantly—"I had no bonnet. Adrienne couldn't get the kind of ruche necessary to finish it till next week, and the old one is too shabby. Were the Stuyvesants out?"

"Oh, yes, in full force. She has the same bonnet she wore last year, done over with a new feather."

"Oh, well, the Stuyvesants can do as they please," said Mrs. Van Arsdel; "everybody knows who they are, let them wear what they will."

"Emma Stuyvesant had a new Paris hat and a sacque trimmed with bullion fringe," continued Aunt Maria. "I thought I'd tell you, because you can use what was on your velvet dress over again; it's just as good as ever."

"So I can"—and for a moment the great advantage of going punctually to church appeared to Mrs. Van Arsdel. "Did you see Sophie Sidney?"

"Yes. She was gorgeous in a mauve suit with hat to match; but she has gone off terribly in her looks—yellow as a lemon."

"Who else did you see?" said Mrs. Van Arsdel, who liked this topic of conversation better than the dangers of the church.

"Oh, well, the Davenports were there, and the Livingstones, and of course Polly Elmore, with her tribe, looking like birds of Paradise. The amount of time and money and thought that family gives to dress is enormous! John Davenport stopped and spoke to me coming out of church. He says, 'Seems to me, Mrs. Wouvermans, your young ladies have deserted us; you mustn't suffer them to stray from the fold,' says he. I saw he had his eye on our pew when he first came into church."

"I think, Maria, you really are quite absurd in your suspicions about that man," said Mrs. Van Arsdel. "I don't think there's anything in it."

"Well, just wait now and see. I know more about it than you do. If only Alice manages her cards right, she can get that man."

"Alice will never manage cards for any purpose. She is too proud for that. She hasn't a bit of policy."

"And there was that Jim Fellows waiting on her home. I met him this morning, just as I turned the corner."

"Well, Alice tries to exert a good influence over Jim, and has got him to teach in Mr. St. John's Sunday-school."

"Fiddlesticks! What does he care for Sunday-school?"

"Well, the girls all say that he does nicely. He has more influence over that class of boys than anybody else would."

"Likely! Set a rogue to catch a rogue," said Aunt Maria. "It's his being seen so much with Alice that I'm thinking of. You may depend upon it, it has a bad effect."

Mrs. Van Arsdel dreaded the setting of her sister's mind in this direction, so by way of effecting a diversion she rang and inquired when tea would be ready. As the door opened, the sound of very merry singing came up stairs. Angelique was seated at the piano and playing tunes out of one of the Sunday-school manuals, and the whole set were singing with might and main. Jim's tenor could be heard above all the rest.

"Why, is that fellow here?" said Aunt Maria.

"Yes," said Mrs. Van Arsdel; "he very often stays to tea with us Sunday nights, and he and the girls sing hymns together."

"Hymns!" said Aunt Maria. "I should call that a regular jollification that they are having down there."

"Oh, well, Maria, they are singing children's tunes out of one of the little Sunday-school manuals. You know children's tunes are so different from old-fashioned psalm tunes!"

Just then the choir below struck up

"Forward, Christian soldier,"

with a marching energy and a vivacity that was positively startling, and, to be sure, not in the least like the old, long-drawn, dolorous strains once supposed to be peculiar to devotion. In fact, one of the greatest signs of progress in our modern tunes is the bursting forth of religious thought and feeling in childhood and youth in strains gay and airy as hope and happiness—melodies that might have been learned of those bright little "fowls of the air," of whom the Master bade us take lessons, so that a company of wholesome, healthy, right-minded young people can now get together and express themselves in songs of joy, and hope, and energy, such as childhood and youth ought to be full of.

Let those who will talk of the decay of Christian faith in our day; so long as songs about Jesus and his love are bursting forth on every hand, thick as violets and apple blossoms in June, so long as the little Sunday-school song books sell by thousands and by millions, and spring forth every year in increasing numbers, so long will it appear that faith is ever fresh-springing and vital. It was the little children in the temple who cried, "Hosanna to the Son of David," when chief priests and scribes were scowling and saying, "Master, forbid them," and doubtless the same dear Master loves to hear these child-songs now as then.

At all events, our little party were having a gay and

festive time over two or three new collections of Clarion, Golden Chain, Golden Shower, or what not, of which Jim had brought a pocketful for the girls to try, and certainly the melodies as they came up were bright and lively and pretty enough to stir one's blood pleasantly. In fact, both Aunt Maria and Mrs. Van Arsdel were content for a season to leave the door open and listen.

"You see," said Mrs. Van Arsdel, "Jim is such a pleasant, convenient, obliging fellow, and has done so many civil turns for the family, that we quite make him at home here; we don't mind him at all. It's a pleasant thing, too, and a convenience, now the boys are gone, to have some young man that one feels perfectly free with to wait on the girls; and where there are so many of them, there's less danger of anything particular. There's no earthly danger of Alice's being specially interested in Jim. He isn't at all the person she would ever think seriously of, though she likes him as a friend."

Mrs. Wouvermans apparently acquiesced for the time in this reasoning, but secretly resolved to watch appearances narrowly this evening, and if she saw what warranted the movement to take the responsibility of the case into her own hands forthwith. Her perfect immutable and tranquil certainty that she was the proper person to manage anything within the sphere of her vision gave her courage to go forward in spite of the fears and remonstrances of any who might have claimed that they were parties concerned.

Mr. Jim Fellows was one of those persons in whom a sense of humor operates as a subtle lubricating oil through all the internal machinery of the mind, causing all which might otherwise have jarred or grated to slide easily. Many things which would be a torture to more earnest people were to him a source of amusement. In fact, humor was so far a leading faculty that it was difficult to keep him within limits of propriety and decorum, and prevent him from racing off at unsuitable periods like a kitten after a pin-ball, skipping over all solemnities of etiquette and decorum. He had not been so long intimate in the family without perfectly taking the measure of so very active and forth-putting a member as Aunt Maria. He knew exactly—as well as if she had told him—how she regarded him, for his knowledge of character was not the result of study, but that sort of clear sight which in persons of quick perceptive organs seems like a second sense. He saw into persons without an effort, and what he saw for the most part only amused him.

He perceived immediately on sitting down to tea that he was under the glance of Mrs. Wouverman's watchful and critical eye, and the result was that he became full and ready to boil over with wicked drollery. With an apparently grave face, without passing the limits of the most ceremonious politeness and decorum, he contrived, by a thousand fleeting indescribable turns and sliding intonations and adroit movements to get all the girls into a tempest of suppressed gaiety. There are wicked rogues known to us all who have this magical power of making those around them burst out into indiscreet sallies of laughter, while they retain the most edifying and innocent air of gravity. Seated next to Aunt Maria, Jim managed, by most devoted attention and reverential listening, to draw from her a zealous analysis of the morning sermon, which she gave with the more heat and vigor, hoping thereby to reprove the stray sheep who had thus broken boundaries.

Her views of the danger of modern speculation, and her hearty measures for its repression, were given with an earnestness that was from the heart.

"I can't understand what anybody wants to have

these controversies for, and listen to these infidel philosophers. I never doubt. I never have doubted. I do n't
think I have altered an iota of my religious faith since I
was seven years old; and if I had the control of things,
I 'd put a stop to all this sort of fuss."

"You then would side with his Holiness, the Pope,"
said Jim. "That's precisely the ground of his last allo-
cution."

"No, indeed, I shouldn't. I think Popery is worse
yet—it's terrible! Dr. Cushing showed *that* this morning, and it's the greatest danger of our day; and I think
that Mr. St. John of yours is nothing more than a decoy
duck to lead you all to Rome. I went up there once and
saw 'em genuflecting, and turning to the east, and burning candles, and that's all I want to know about them."

"But the east is a perfectly harmless point of the compass," said Jim, with suavity; " and though I don't want
candles in the daytime myself, yet I don't see what harm
it does anybody to burn them."

" Why, that's just what the Catholics do," said Mrs.
Wouvermans.

" Oh, that 's it, is it!" said Jim, with a submissive air.
"Must n't we do *any* thing that Catholics do ?"

"No, indeed," said Aunt Maria, falling into the open
trap with affecting naïveté.

"Then we must n't pray at all," said Jim.

"Oh, pshaw! of course I did n't mean that. You know
what I mean."

" Certainly, ma'am. I think I understand," said Jim,
while Alice, who had been looking reprovingly at him,
led off the subject into another strain.

But Mrs. Wouvermans was more gracious to Jim that
evening than usual, and when she rose to go home that
young gentleman offered his attendance, and was accepted with complacency.

Mrs. Wouvermans, in a general way, believed in what is called Providence. That is to say, when any little matter fell out in a manner exactly apposite to any of her schemes, she called it providential. On the present occasion, when she found herself walking in the streets of New York alone, in the evening, with a young man who treated her with flattering deference, it could not but strike her as a providential opportunity not to be neglected of fulfilling her long-cherished intentions and giving a sort of wholesome check and caution to the youth. So she began with infinite adroitness to prepare the way. Jim, the while, who saw perfectly what she was aiming at, assisting her in the most obliging manner.

After passing through sundry truisms about the necessity of caution and regarding appearances, and thinking what people will say to this and that, she proceeded to inform him that the report was in circulation that he was engaged to Alice.

"The report does me entirely too much honor," said Jim. "But of course if Miss Alice isn't disposed to deny it, I am not."

"Of course Miss Alice's friends will deny it," said Aunt Maria, decisively. "I merely mentioned it to you that you may see the need of caution. You know, of course, Mr. Fellows, that such reports stand in the way of *others* who might be disposed—well, you understand."

"Oh, perfectly, exactly, quite so," said Jim, who could be profuse of his phrases on occasion, "and I'm extremely obliged to you for this suggestion; undoubtedly your great experience and knowledge of the ways of society will show you the exact way to deal with such things."

"You see," pursued Mrs. Wouvermans, in a confidential tone, "there is at present a person every way admirable and desirable, who is thinking very seriously

of Alice; it 's quite confidential, you know; but you must
be aware—of the danger."

"I perceive—a blight of the poor fellow's budding
hopes and early affections," said Jim, fluently; "well,
though of course the very suggestion of such a report in
regard to me is flattery far beyond my deserts, so that I
can 't be annoyed by it, still I should be profoundly sorry
to have it occasion any trouble to Miss Alice."

"I felt sure that you would n't be offended with me
for speaking so very plainly. I hope you 'll keep it entirely private."

"Oh, certainly," said Jim, with the most cheerful
goodwill. "When ladies with your tact and skill in human nature talk to us young fellows you *never* give offense.
We take your frankness as a favor.".

Mrs. Wouvermans smiled with honest pride. Had
she not been warned against talking to this youth as
something that was going to be of most explosive tendency? How little could Nellie, or Eva, or any of them,
appreciate her masterly skill! She really felt in her heart
disposed to regret that so docile a pupil, one so appreciative of her superior abilities, was not a desirable
matrimonial *parti*. Had Jim been a youth of fortune
she felt that she could have held up both hands for him.

"He really *is* agreeable," was her thought, as she shut
the door upon him.

THE DOMESTIC ARTIST.

" A spray of ivy that was stretching towards the window had been drawn
back, and forced to wreathe itself around a picture."—p. 131.

CHAPTER XII

WHY CAN'T THEY LET US ALONE?

HARRY went out to his office, and Eva commenced the morning labors of a young housekeeper.

What are they? Something in their way as airy and pleasant as the light touches and arrangements which Eve gave to her bower in Paradise—gathering up stray rose-leaves, tying up a lily that the rain has bent, looping a honeysuckle in a more graceful festoon, and meditating the while whether she shall have oranges and figs and grapes, or guavas and pineapples, for her first course at dinner.

Such, according to Father Milton, were the ornamental duties of the first wife, while her husband went out to his office in some distant part of Eden.

But Eden still exists whenever two young lovers set up housekeeping, even in prosaic New York; only our modern Eves wear jaunty little morning caps and fascinating wrappers and slippers, with coquettish butterfly bows. Eva's morning duties consisted in asking Mary what they had better have for dinner, giving here and there a peep into the pantry, re-arranging the flower vases, and flecking the dust from her pictures and statuettes with a gay and glancing brush of peacock's feathers. Sometimes the morning arrangements included quite a change; as, this particular day, when, on mature consideration, a spray of ivy that was stretching towards the window had been drawn back and forced to wreathe itself around a picture, and a spray of nasturtium, gemmed

with half-opened golden buds, had been trained in its
place in the window.

One may think this a very simple matter, but whoever
knows all the resistance which the forces of matter and
the laws of gravitation make to the simplest improvement
in one's parlor, will know better.

It required a scaffolding made of a chair and an ottoman to reach the top of the pictures, and a tack-hammer
and little tacks. Then the precise air of arrangement
and exact position had to be studied from below, after
the tacks were driven, and that necessitated two or three
descents from the perch to review, and the tumbling of
the ottoman to the floor, and the calling of Mary in to
help, and to hold the ottoman firm while the persevering
little artist finished her work. It is by ups and downs
like these, by daily labor of modern Eves, each in their
little paradises, O ye Adams! that your houses have that
"just right" look that makes you think of them all day,
and long to come back to them at night.

"Somehow or other," you say, "I do n't know how it
is, my wife's things have a certain air; her vines grow
just as they ought to, her flowers blossom in just the
right places, and her parlors always look pleasant."
You do n't know how many periods of grave consideration, how many climbings on chairs and ottomans, how
many doings and undoings and shiftings and changes
produce the appearance that charms you. Most people
think that flower vases are very simple affairs; but the
keeping of parlors dressed with flowers is daily work for
an hour or two for any woman. Nor is it work in vain.
No altar is holier than the home altar, and the flowers
that adorn it are sacred.

Eva was sitting, a little tired with her strenuous exer-
tions, contemplating her finished arrangement with satisfaction, when the door-bell rang, and Alice came in.

"Why, Allie, dear, how nice of you to be down here so early! I was just wanting somebody to show my changes to. Look there. See how I 've looped that ivy round mother's picture; is n't it sweet?" and Eva caressingly arranged a leaf or two to suit her.

"Charming!" said Alice, but with rather an abstracted, preoccupied tone.

"And look at this nasturtium; it 's full of buds. See, the yellow is beginning to show. I 've fastened it in a wreath around the window, so that the sun will shine through the blossoms."

"It 's beautiful," said Alice, still absently and nervously playing with her bonnet strings.

"Why, darling, what 's the matter?" said Eva, suddenly noticing signs of some unusual feeling. "What ails you?"

"Well," said Alice, hastily untying her bonnet strings and throwing it down on the sofa, "I 've come up to talk with you. I hope," she said, flushing crimson with vexation, "that Aunt Maria is satisfied now; she is the most exasperating woman I ever knew or heard of!"

"Dear me, Allie, what has she done now?"

"Well, what do you think? Last Sunday she came to our house to tea, drawn up in martial array and ready to attack us all for not going to the old church—that stupid, dead old church, where people do nothing but doze and wake up to criticise each other's bonnets—but you really would think to hear Aunt Maria talk that there was a second Babylonian captivity or something of that sort coming on, and we were getting it up. You see, Dr. Cushing has got excited because some of the girls are going up to the mission church, and it 's led him to an unwonted exertion; and Aunt Maria quite waked up and considers herself an apostle and prophet. I wish you could have heard her talk. It 's enough to make any

cause ridiculous to have one defend it as she did.
You ought to have heard that witch of a Jim Fellows arguing with her and respectfully leading her into all sorts
of contradictions and absurdities till I stopped him.   I
really wouldn't let him lead her to make such a fool of
herself."

"Oh, well, if that's all, Allie, I don't think you need
to trouble your head," said Eva.   "Aunt Maria, of
course, will hold on to her old notions, and her style of
argument never was very consecutive."

"But that isn't all.   Oh, you may be sure I didn't
care for what she said about the church.   I can have my
opinion and she hers, on that point."

"Well, then, what is the matter?"

"Well, if you'll believe me, she has actually undertaken to tutor Jim Fellows in relation to his intimacy
with me."

"Oh, Allie," groaned Eva, "has she done that?   I
begged and implored her to let that matter alone."

"Then she's been talking with you, too! and I wonder how many more," said Alice in tones of disgust.

"Yes, she did talk with me in her usual busy, imperative way, and told me all that Mrs. Thus-and-so and
Mr. This-and-that said—but people are always saying
things, and if they don't say one thing they will another.
I tried to persuade her to let it alone, but she seemed to
think you must be talked with; so I finally told her that
if she'd leave it to me I would say all that was necessary.   I did mean to say something, but I didn't want to
trouble you.   I thought there was no hurry."

"Well, you see," said Alice, "Jim went home with
her that night, and I suppose she thought the opportunity too good to be neglected.   I don't know just what
she said to him, but I know it was about me."

"How do you know?   Did Jim tell you?"

"No, indeed; catch him telling me! He knows too much for that. Aunt Maria let it out herself."

"Let it out herself?"

"Yes; she blundered into it before she knew what she was saying, and betrayed herself; and then, when I questioned her, she had to tell me."

"How came she to commit herself so?"

"It was just this. You know the little party Aunt Maria had Tuesday evening,—the one you could n't come to on account of that Stephens engagement."

"Yes; what of it?"

"I really suspect that was all got up in the interest of one of Aunt Maria's schemes to bring me and that John Davenport together. At any rate, there he was, and his sister; and really, Eva, his treatment of me was so marked that it was quite disagreeable. Why, the man seemed really infatuated. His manner was so that everybody remarked it; and the colder and more distant I grew, the more it increased. Aunt Maria was delighted. She plumed herself and rushed round in the most satisfied way, while I was only provoked. I saw he was going to ask to wait on me home, and so I fell back on a standing engagement that I have with Jim, to go with me whenever anybody asks that I do n't want to go with. Jim and I have always had that understanding in dancing and at parties, so that we can keep clear of disagreeable partners and people. I was determined I would n't walk home with that man, and I told Jim privately that he was to be on duty, and he took the hint in a minute. So when Mr. Davenport wound up his attentions by asking if he should have the pleasure of seeing me home, I told him with great satisfaction that I was engaged, and off I walked with Jim. The girls were in a perfect state of giggle, to see Aunt Maria's indignation."

"And so really you don't like this Mr. Davenport?"

"Like him! Indeeed I don't. In the first place, it isn't a year yet since his wife died; and everybody was pitying him. He could hardly be kept alive, and fainted away, and had to have hot bottles at his feet, and all that. All the old ladies were rolling up their eyes; such a sighing and sympathizing for John Davenport; and now, here he is!"

"Poor man!" said Eva, "I suppose he is lonesome."

"Yes. I suppose, as Irving says, the greatest compliment he can pay to his former wife is to display an eagerness for another; but his attentions are simply disagreeable to me."

"After all, the worst crime you allege seems to be that he is too sensitive to your attractions."

"Yes; and shows it in a very silly way—making me an object of remark! He may be very nice and very worthy, and all that; but in any such relation as that he is so unpleasant to me! I can't *bear* him, and I'm not going to be talked or maneuvered into anything that might commit me to even consider him. I remember the trouble you had for being persuaded to let Wat Sydney dangle after you. I will not have anything of the kind. I am a decided young woman, and know my own mind."

"Well, how did you learn about Aunt Maria and Jim?"

"How? Oh, well, the next day comes Aunt Maria to talk with Mamma, who wasn't there, by the bye; Papa hates so to go out that she has got to staying at home with him. But the next day came an exaggerated picture of my triumphs to Mamma and a lecture to me on my bad behavior. The worst of all, she said, was the very marked thing of my going home with Jim; and in her heat she let out that she had spoken to him and warned him of what folks would think and say of such appearances. I *was* angry then, and I expressed my mind freely to Aunt Maria, and we had a downright quarrel. I said things I ought not to say, just as one always does, and—now isn't it disagreeable? Isn't it *dreadful?*" said Alice, with the earnestness of a young girl whose whole nature goes into her first trouble. "Nothing could be nicer and more just what a thing ought to be than my friendship with Jim. I have influence over him and I can do him good, and I enjoy his society, and the kind of easy, frank understanding that there is between us, that we can say *any* thing to each other; and what business is it of anybody's? It's our own affair, and no one's else."

"Certainly it is," said Eva, sympathizingly.

"And Aunt Maria said that folks were saying that if we were n't engaged we ought to be. What a hateful thing to say! As if there were any impropriety in a friendship between a gentleman and a lady. Why may not a gentleman and a lady have a special friendship as well one lady with another, or one gentleman with another? I don't see."

"Neither do I," said Eva, responsively.

"Now," said Alice, "the suggestion of marriage and all that is disagreeable to me. I'm thinking of nothing of the kind. I like Jim. Well, I don't mind saying to you, Eva, who can understand me, that I *love* him, in a sort of way. I am interested for him. I know his good points and I know his faults, and I'm at liberty to speak to him with perfect freedom, and I think there is nothing so good for a young man as such a friendship. We girls, you know, dear, can do a great deal for young men if we try. We are not tempted as they are; we have not their hard places and trials to walk through, and we can make allowances, and they will receive things from us that they would n't from any one else, and they show us just the best side of their nature, which is the truest side of everybody."

"Certainly, Alice. Harry was saying only a little while ago that your influence would make a man of Jim; and I certainly think he has wonderfully improved of late—he seems more serious."

"We've learned to know him better; that's all," said Alice. "Young men rattle and talk idly to girls when they don't feel acquainted and haven't real confidence in their friendship, just as a sort of blind. They don't dare to express their real, deepest feelings."

"Well, I didn't know that Jim had any," said Eva, incautiously.

"Why, Eva, how unjust you are to Jim!" said Alice, with flushing cheeks. "I shouldn't have thought it of you; so many kind things as Jim has done for us all!"

"My darling, I beg Jim's pardon with all my heart," said Eva, laughing to herself at this earnest championship. "I didn't mean quite what I said, but you know, Alice, his sort of wild rattling way of talking over all subjects, so that you can't tell which is jest and which is earnest."

"Oh! *I* can always tell," said Alice. "I always can make him come down to the earnest part of him, and Jim has, after all, really good, sensible ideas of life and aspirations after what is right and true. He has the temptation of having been a sort of spoiled child. People do so like a laugh that they set him on and encourage him in saying all sorts of things he ought not. People have very little principle about that. So that anyone amuses them, they never consider whether he does right to talk as he does; they'll set Jim up to talk because it amuses them, and then go away and say what a rattle he is, and that he has no real principle or feeling. They just make a buffoon of him, and they know nothing about the best part of him."

"Well, Alice, I dare say you do see more of Jim's real nature than any of us."

"Oh! indeed I do; and I know how to appeal to it. Even when I can't help laughing at things he ought not to say—and sometimes they are so droll I can't help it —afterwards I have *my* say and tell him really and soberly just what I think, and you've no idea how beautifully he takes it. Oh, Jim really is good at heart, there's no doubt about that."

"Do you think Aunt Maria's meddling will make trouble between you?"

"No! only that it's an awkward, disagreeable thing to speak of; but I shall speak to Jim about it and let him understand, if he doesn't now, just what Aunt Maria is, and that he mustn't mind anything she says. I feel rather better, now I've relieved my mind to you, and perhaps shall have more charity for Aunt Maria."

"After all, poor soul," said Eva, "it's her love for us that leads her to vex us in all these ways. She can't help planning and fussing and lying awake nights for us. She failed in getting a splendid marriage for me, and now she's like Bruce's spider, up and at her web again weaving a destiny for you. It's in her to be active; she has no children; her house don't half satisfy her as a field of enterprise, and she, of course, is taking care of Mamma and our family. If Mamma had not been just the gentle, lovely, yielding woman she is, Aunt Maria never would have got such headway in the family and taken such airs about us."

"She perfectly tyrannizes over Mamma," said Alice. "She's always coming up to lecture her for not doing this, that, or the other thing. Now all this talk about our going to Mr. St. John's church;—poor, dear, little

Mamma is as willing to let us do as we please as the
flowers are to blossom, and then Aunt Maria talks as if
she were abetting a conspiracy against the church.   I
know that we are all living more serious, earnest lives
for Mr. St. John's influence.   It may be that he is
going too far in certain directions; it may be that in the
long run such things tend to dangerous extremes, but
I do n't see any real harm in them so far, and I find real
good."

"Well, you know, dear, that Harry is n't of our
church—he is a Congregationalist—but his theory is
that Christian people should join with any other Christian people who they see are really working in earnest to
do good.   This church is near by us, where we can conveniently go, and as I have my house to attend to and
am not strong you know, that is quite a consideration.
I know Harry do n't agree with Mr. St. John at all about
his ideas of the church, and he thinks he carries some
of his ceremonies too far; but, on the whole, he really
is doing a great deal of practical good, and Harry is
willing to help him.   I think it 's just lovely in Harry to
do so.   It is real liberality."

"I wish," said Alice, "that Mr. St. John were a little
freer in his way.   There is a sort of solemnity about him
that is depressing, and it seems to set Jim off in a spirit
of contradiction.   He says Mr. St. John stirs up the evil
within him, and makes him long to break over bounds
and say something wicked, just to shock him."

"I 've had that desire to shock very proper people
in the days of my youth," said Eva.   "I do n't know
what it comes from."

"I think," said Alice, "that, to be sure, this is an
irreverent age, and New York is an irreverent place; but
yet I think people may carry the outside air of reverence too far.   Do n't you?   They impose a sort of con-

straint on everybody around them that keeps them from knowing the people they associate with. Mr. St. John, for instance, knows nothing about Jim, he never acts himself out before him."

"Oh, dear me," said Eva, "fancy what he would think if he should see Jim in one of his frolics."

"And yet, Jim, in his queer way, appreciates Mr. St. John," said Alice. "He says he's 'a brick' after all, by which he means that he does good, honest work; and Jim has been enough around among the poor of New York, in his quality of newspaper writer, to know when a man does good among them. If Mr. St. John only could learn to be indulgent to other people's natures he might do a great deal for Jim."

"I rather think Jim will be your peculiar parish for some time to come," said Eva with a smile, "but Harry and I are projecting schemes to draw Mr. St. John into more general society. That's one of the things we are going to try to do in our 'evenings.' I don't believe he has ever been into general society at all; he ought to hear the talk of his day—he talks and feels and thinks more in the past than the present; he's all the while trying to restore an ideal age of reverence and devotion, but he ought to know the real age he lives in. If we could get him to coming to our house every week, and meeting real live men, women and girls of to-day and entering a little into their life, it would do him good."

"I suppose he'd be afraid of any indulgence!"

"We must not put it to him as an indulgence, but a good hard duty," said Eva; "we should never catch him with an indulgence."

"When are you going to begin?"

"I've been talking with Mary about it, and I rather think I shall take next Thursday for the first. I shall depend on you and the girls to help me keep the thing

balanced, and going on just right. Jim must be moderated, and kept from coming out too strong, and everybody must be made to have a good time, so that they 'll
want to come again. You see we want to get them to
coming every week, so that they will all know one another by-and-by, and get a sort of home feeling about
our rooms; such a thing is possible, I think."

The conversation now meandered off into domestic
details, not further traceable in this chapter.

CHAPTER XIII

OUR "EVENING" PROJECTED.

"WELL, Harry," said Eva, when they were seated at dinner, "Alice was up at lunch with me this morning, in such a state! It seems, after all, Aunt Maria could not contain her zeal for management, and has been having an admonitory talk with Jim Fellows about his intimacy with Alice."

"Now, I declare that goes beyond me," said Harry, laying down his knife and fork. "That woman's impertinence is really stupendous. It amounts to the sublime."

"Does n't it? Alice was in such a state about it; but we talked the matter down into calmness. Still, Harry, I 'm pretty certain that Alice is more seriously interested in Jim than she knows of. Of course she thinks it 's all friendship, but she is so sensitive about him, and if you make even the shadow of a criticism she flames up and defends him. You ought to see."

"Grave symptoms," said Harry.

"But as she says she is not thinking nor wanting to think of marriage—"

"Any more than a certain other young lady was, with whom I cultivated a friendship some time ago," said Harry, laughing.

"Just so," said Eva; "I plume myself on my forbearance in listening gravely to Alice and not putting in any remarks; but I remembered old times and had my suspicions. *We* thought it was friendship, did n't we, Harry? And I used to be downright angry if anybody suggested anything else. Now I think Allie's friendship for Jim is getting to be of the same kind. Oh, she knows him *so* well! and she understands him so perfectly! and she has *so* much influence over him! and they have such perfect comprehension of each other! and as to his faults, oh, she understands all about them! But, mind you, nobody must criticise him but herself—that's quite evident. I did make a blundering remark or so; but I found it was n't at all the thing, and I had to beat a rapid retreat, I assure you."

"Well, poor girl! I hope you managed to console her."

"Oh, I was sympathetic and indignant, and after she had poured out her griefs she felt better; and then I put in a soothing word for Aunt Maria, poor woman, who is only monomaniac on managing our affairs."

"Yes," said Harry, "forgiveness of enemies used to be the *ultima thule* of virtue; but I rather think it will have to be forgiveness of friends. I call the man a perfect Christian that can always forgive his friends."

"The fact is, Aunt Maria ought to have had a great family of her own—twelve or thirteen, to say the least. If Providence had vouchsafed her eight or nine ramping, roaring boys, and a sprinkling of girls, she would have been a splendid woman and we should have had better times."

"She puts me in mind of the story of the persistent broomstick that would fetch water," said Harry; "we are likely to be drowned out by her."

"Well, we can accept her for a whetstone to sharpen up our Christian graces on," said Eva. "So, let her go. I was talking over our projected evening with Alice, and we spent some time discussing that."

"When are you going to begin?" said Henry. "'Well begun is half done,' you know."

Said Eva, "I've been thinking over what day is best,

and talking about it with Mary. Now, we can't have it
Monday, there's the washing, you know; and Tuesday
and Wednesday come baking and ironing."

"Well, then, what happens Thursday?"

"Well, then, it's precisely Thursday that Mary and I
agreed on. We both made up our minds that it was the
right day. One would n't want it on Friday, you know,
and Saturday is too late; besides, Mr. St. John never
goes out Saturday evenings."

"But what's the objection to Friday?"

"Oh, the unlucky day. Mary would n't hear of beginning anything on Friday, you know. Then, besides,
Mr. St. John, I suspect, fasts every Friday. He never
told me so, of course, but they say he does; at all events,
I'm sure he would n't come of a Friday evening, and I
want to be sure and have *him*, of all people. Now, you
see, I've planned it all beautifully. I'm going to have a
nice, pretty little tea-table in one corner, with a vase of
flowers on it, and I shall sit and make tea. That breaks
the stiffness, you know. People talk first about the tea
and the china, and whether they take cream and sugar,
and so on, and the gentlemen help the ladies. Then
Mary will make those delicate little biscuits of hers
and her charming sponge-cake. It's going to be perfectly quiet, you see—from half-past seven till eleven—
early hours and simple fare, 'feast of reason and flow
of soul.'"

"Quite pastoral and Arcadian," said Harry. "When
we get it going it will be the ideal of social life. No
fuss, no noise; all the quiet of home life with all the
variety of company; people seeing each other till they
get really intimate and have a genuine interest in meeting each other; not a mere outside, wild beast show, as
it is when people go to parties to gaze at other people
and see how they look in war-paint."

G

"I feel a little nervous at first," said Eva; "getting people together that are so diametrically opposed to each other as Dr. Campbell and Mr. St. John, for instance. I'm afraid Dr. Campbell will come out with some of his terribly free speaking, and then Mr. St. John will be so shocked and distressed."

"Then Mr. St. John must get over being shocked and distressed. Mr. St. John needs Dr. Campbell," said Harry. "He is precisely the man he ought to meet, and Dr. Campbell needs Mr. St. John. The two men are intended to help each other: each has what the other wants, and they ought to be intimate."

"But you see, Dr. Campbell is such a dreadful unbeliever!"

"In a certain way he is no more an unbeliever than Mr. St. John. Dr. Campbell is utterly ignorant of the higher facts of moral consciousness—of prayer and communion with God—and therefore he doesn't believe in them. St. John is equally ignorant of some of the most important facts of the body he inhabits. He does not believe in them—ignores them."

"Oh, but now, Harry, I didn't think that of you—that you could put the truths of the body on a level with the truths of the soul."

"Bless you, darling, since the Maker has been pleased to make the soul so dependent on the body, how can I help it? Why, just see here; come to this very problem of saving a soul, which is a minister's work. I insist there are cases where Dr. Campbell can do more towards it than Mr. St. John. He was quoting to me only yesterday a passage from Dr. Wigan, where he says, 'I firmly believe I have more than once changed the moral character of a boy by leeches applied to the inside of his nose.'"

"Why, Harry, that sounds almost shocking."

" Yet it's a fact—a physiological fact—that some of the worst vices come through a disordered body, and can be cured only by curing the body. So long as we are in this mortal state, our souls have got to be saved *in* our bodies and by the laws of our bodies; and a doctor who understands them will do more than a minister who doesn't. Why, just look at poor Bolton. The trouble that he dreads, the fear that blasts his life, that makes him afraid to marry, is a disease of the body. Fasting, prayer, sacraments, couldn't keep off an acute attack of dipsomania; but a doctor might."

"Oh, Harry, do you think so? Well, I must say I do think Mr. St. John is as ignorant as a child about such matters, if I may judge from the way he goes on about his own health. He ignores his body entirely, and seems determined to work as if he were a spirit and could live on prayer and fasting."

" Which, as he isn't a spirit, won't do," said Harry. " It may end in making a spirit of him before the time."

" But don't you think the disinterestedness he shows is perfectly heroic?" said Eva.

" Oh, certainly!" said Harry. " The fact is, I should despair of St. John if he hadn't set himself at mission work. He is naturally so ideal, and so fastidious, and so fond of rules, and limits, and order, that if he hadn't this practical common-sense problem of working among the poor on his hands, I should think he wouldn't be good for much. But drunken men and sorrowful wives, ragged children, sickness, pain, poverty, teach a man the common-sense of religion faster than anything else, and I can see St. John is learning sense for everybody but himself. If he only don't run his own body down, he'll make something yet."

" I think, Harry," said Eva, " he is a little doubtful

of whether you really go with him or not. I do n't think he knows how much you like him."

"Go with him! of course I do. I stand up for St. John and defend him. So long as a man is giving his whole life to hard work among the poor and neglected he may burn forty candles, if he wants to, for all I care. He may turn to any point of the compass he likes, east, west, north, or south, and wear all the colors of the rainbow if it suits him, and I won't complain. In fact, I like processions, and chantings, and ceremonies, if you do n't get too many of them. I think, generally speaking, there's too little of that sort of thing in our American life. In the main, St. John preaches good sermons; that is, good, manly, honest talks to people about what they need to know. But then his mind is tending to a monomania of veneration. You see he has a mystical, poetic element in it that may lead him back into the old idolatries of past ages, and lead weak minds there after him; that's why I want to get him acquainted with such fellows as Campbell. He needs to learn the common sense of life. I think he is capable of it, and one of the first things he has got to learn is not to be shocked at hearing things said from other people's points of view. If these two men could only like each other, so as to listen tolerantly and dispassionately to what each has to say, they might be everything to each other."

"Well, how to get a mordant to unite these two opposing colors," said Eva.

"That's what you women are for—at least such women as you. It's your mission to interpret differing natures—to bind, and blend, and unite."

"But how shall we get them to like each other?" said Eva. "Both are so very intense and so opposite. I suppose Dr. Campbell would consider most of Mr. St. John's ideas stuff and nonsense; and I know, as well as

I know anything, that if Mr. St. John should hear Dr. Campbell talking as he talks to you, he would shut up like a flower—he would retire into himself and not come here any more."

"Oh, Eva, that's making the man too ridiculous and unmanly. Good gracious! Can't a man who thinks he has God's truth—and *such* truth!—listen to opposing views without going into fits? It's like a soldier who cannot face guns and wants to stay inside of a clean, nice fort, making pretty stacks of bayonets and piling cannon balls in lovely little triangles."

"Well, Harry, I know Mr. St. John isn't like that. I don't think he's cowardly or unmanly, but he is very reverent, and, Harry, you are *very* free. You do let Dr. Campbell go on so, over everything. It quite shocks me."

"Just because my faith is so strong that I can afford it. I can see when he is mistaken; but he is a genuine, active, benevolent man, following truth when he sees it, and getting a good deal of it, and most important truth, too. We've got to get truth as we can in this world, just as miners dig gold out of the mine with all the quartz, and dirt, and dross; but it pays."

"Well, now, I shall try my skill, and do my best to dispose these two refractory chemicals to a union," said Eva. "I'll tell you how let's do. I'll interest Dr. Campbell in Mr. St. John's health. I'll ask him to study him and see if he can't take care of him. I'm sure he needs taking care of."

"And," said Harry, "why not interest Mr. St. John in Dr. Campbell's soul? Why shouldn't he try to convert him from the error of his ways?"

"That would be capital," said Eva. "Let each convert the other. If we could put Dr. Campbell and Mr. St. John together, what a splendid man we could make of them!"

"Try your best, my dear; but meanwhile I have three or four hours' writing to do this evening."

"Well, then, settle yourself down, and I will run over and expound my plans to the good old ladies over the way. I am getting up quite an intimacy over there; Miss Dorcas is really vastly entertaining. It's like living in a past age to hear her talk."

"You really have established a fashion of rushing in upon them at all sorts of hours," said Harry.

"Yes, but they like it. You have no idea what nice things they say to me. Even old Dinah quivers and giggles with delight the minute she sees me—poor old soul! You see they're shut up all alone in that musty old house, like enchanted princesses, and gone to sleep there; and I am the predestined fairy to wake them up!"

Eva said this as she was winding a cloud of fleecy worsted around her head, and Harry was settling himself at his writing-table in a little alcove curtained off from the parlor.

"Don't keep the old ladies up too late," said Harry.

"Never you fear," said Eva. "Perhaps I shall stay to see Jack's feet washed and blanket spread. Those are solemn and impressive ceremonies that I have heard described, but never witnessed."

It was a bright, keen, frosty, starlight evening, and when Eva had rung the door-bell on the opposite side, she turned and looked at the play of shadow and firelight on her own window-curtains.

Suddenly she noticed a dark form of a woman coming from an alley back of the house, and standing irresolute, looking at the windows. Then she drew near the house, and seemed trying to read the name on the door-plate.

There was something that piqued Eva's curiosity

about these movements, and just as the door was opening behind her into the Vanderheyden house, the strange woman turned away, and as she turned, the light of the street-lamp flashed strongly on her face. Its expression of haggard pain and misery was something that struck to Eva's heart, though it was but a momentary glimpse, as she turned to go into the house; for, after all, the woman was nothing to her, and the glimpse of her face was purely an accident, such as occurs to one hundreds of times in the streets of a city.

Still, like the sound of a sob or a cry from one unknown, the misery of those dark eyes struck painfully to Eva's heart; as if to *her*, young, beloved, gay and happy, some of the ever-present but hidden anguish of life —the great invisible mass of sorrow—had made an appeal.

But she went in and shut the door, gave one sigh and dismissed it.

CHAPTER XIV.

MR. ST. JOHN IS OUT-ARGUED.

A WOMAN has two vernal seasons in her life. One is the fresh, sweet-brier, apple-blossom spring of girlhood—dewy, bird-singing, joyous and transient. The other is the spring of young marriage, before the austere labors and severe strains of real life commence.

It is the spring of wedding presents, of first house-keeping, of incipient, undeveloped matronage. If the young girl is charming, with her dawning airs of woman-hood, her inexperienced naïve assumptions, her grave, ignorant wisdom, at which elders smile indulgently—so is the new-made wife with her little matronly graces, her pretty sense of responsibility in her new world of power.

In the first period, the young girl herself is the object of attention and devotion. She is the permitted center of all eyes, the leading star of her own little drama of life. But with marriage the center changes. Self begins to melt away into something higher. The girl recognizes that it is no longer her individuality that is the chief thing, but that she is the priestess and minister of a family state. The *home* becomes her center, and to her home passes the charm that once was thrown around her person. The pride that she may have had in self becomes a pride in her home. Her home is the new impersona-tion of herself; it is her throne, her empire. How often do we see the young wife more sensitive to the adorn-ment of her house than the adornment of her person, willing even to retrench and deny in the last, that her home may become more cheerful and attractive! A pretty set of china for her tea-table goes farther with her than a gay robe for herself. She will sacrifice ribbons and laces for means to adorn the sacred recesses which have become to her an expansion of her own being.

The freshness of a new life invests every detail of the freshly arranged *ménage*. Her china, her bronzes, her pictures, her silver, her table cloths and napkins, her closets and pantries, all speak to her of a new sense of possession—a new and different hold on life. Once she was only a girl, moving among things that belonged to mamma and papa; now she is a matron, surrounded everywhere by things that are her own—a princess in her own little kingdom. Nor is the chaim lessened that she no longer uses the possessive singular, but says *our*. And behind those pronouns, *we* and *our*, what pleasant security! What innocent pharisaism of self-complacency, as each congratulates the other on "our" ways, "our" plans, "our" arrangements; each, the while, sure that they two are the fortunate among mankind, and that all who are not blest as they are proper subjects for indulgent pity. "After all, my dear," says he, "what can you expect of poor Snooks?—a bachelor, poor fellow. If he only had a wife like you, now," etc., etc. Or, "I can't really blame Cynthia with that husband of hers, Harry dear. If I were married to such a man, I should act like a little fiend. If she had only such a husband as you, now!" This secret, respectable, mutual admiration society of married life, of how much courage and hope is it the parent! For, do not our failures and mistakes often come from discouragement? Does not every human being need a believing second self, whose support and approbation shall reinforce one's failing courage? The saddest hours of life are when we doubt ourselves. To sensitive, excitable people, who expend nervous energy freely, must come many such low tides. "Am I really a miserable failure—a poor, good-for-nothing, abortive attempt?" In such crises we need another self to restore our equilibrium.

Our young friends were just in the second spring of life's new year. They were as fond and proud of their little house as a prince of his palace—possibly a good deal more so. They were proud of each other. Eva felt sure that Harry was destined to the high places of the literary world. She read his editorials with sincere admiration, hid his poems away in her heart, and pasted them carefully in her scrap-book. Fame and success she felt sure ought to come to him, and would. He was "such a faithful, noble-hearted fellow, and worked so steadily." And he, with what pride he spoke the words "my wife"! With what exultation repressed under an air of playful indifference he brought this and that associate in to dine, and enjoyed the admiration of her and her pretty home, and graceful, captivating ways. He liked to see the effect of her gay, sparkling conversation, her easy grace, on these new subjects; for Eva was, in truth, a charming woman. The mixture of innocent shrewdness, of sprightly insight, of bright and airy fancy about her, made her society a thing to be longed after, as people long for a pleasant stimulant. Like all bright, earnest young men, Harry wanted to "lend a hand" to make the world around him brighter and better, and had his ideas of what a charming, attractive home might do as a center to many hearts in promoting mutual brotherhood and good fellowship. He had not a doubt of their little social venture in society, nor that Eva was precisely the person to make of their house a pleasant resort, to be in herself the blending and interpreting medium through whom differing and even discordant natures should be brought to understand the good that was in one another.

As a preparation for the first experiment, Eva had commenced by inviting Mr. St. John to dinner, that she might enlist his approbation of her scheme and have time to set it before him in that charming fireside hour, when spirits, like flowers, open to catch the dews of influence. After dinner Harry had an engagement at the printing-office, and left Eva the field all to herself; and she managed her cards admirably. Mr. St. John had been little accustomed to the society of cultured, attractive women; but he had in his own refined nature every sensibility to respond agreeably to its influences; and already this fireside had come to be a place where he loved to linger. 'And so, when she had him comfortably niched in his corner, she opened the first parallel of her siege.

"Now, Mr. St. John, you have been preaching to us about self-denial, and putting us all up to deeds of self-sacrifice—I have some self-denying work to propose to you."

Mr. St. John opened his blue eyes wide at this exordium, and looked an interrogation.

"Well, Mr. St. John," pursued Eva, "we are going to have little social reunions at our house every Thursday, from seven till ten, for the purpose of promoting good feeling and fellowship, and we want our rector to be one of us and help us."

"Indeed, Mrs. Henderson, I have not the least social tact. My sphere does n't lie at all in that direction," said Mr. St. John, nervously. "I have no taste for general society."

"Yes, but I think you told us last Sunday we were not to consult our tastes. You told us that if we felt a strong distaste for any particular course, it might pos-

sibly show that just here the true path of Christian heroism lay."

"You turn my words upon me, Mrs. Henderson. I
was thinking then of the distaste that people usually feel
for visiting the poor and making themselves practically
familiar with the unlovely side of life."

"Well, but may it not apply the other way? You
are perfectly familiar and at home among the poor, but
you have always avoided society among cultured persons
of your own class. May not the real self-denial for you
lie there? You have a fastidious shrinking from strangers. May it not be your duty to overcome it? There
are a great many I know in our circle who might be the
better for knowing you. Have you a right to shrink
back·from them?"

Mr. St. John moved uneasily in his chair.

"Now," pursued Eva, "there's a young Dr. Campbell
that I want you to know. To be sure, he is n't a believer
in the church—not a believer at all, I fear; but still a
charming, benevolent, kindly, open-hearted man, and I
want him to know you, and come under good influences."

"I do n't believe I 'm at all adapted," said Mr. St.
John, hesitatingly.

"Well, dear sir, what do you say to us when we say
the same about mission work? Do n't you tell us that
if we honestly try we shall learn to adapt ourselves?"

"That is true," said St. John, frankly.

"Besides," said Eva, "Mr. St. John, Dr. Campbell
might do *you* good. All your friends feel that you are
too careless of your health. Indeed, we all feel great
concern about it, and you might learn something of Dr.
Campbell in this."

Thus Eva pursued her advantage with that fluent
ability with which a pretty young woman at her own

fireside always gets the best of the argument. Mr. St.
John, attacked on the weak side of conscientiousness,
was obliged at last to admit that to spend an evening
with agreeable, cultivated, well-dressed people might be
occasionally as much a shepherd's duty as to sit in the
close, ill-smelling rooms of poverty and listen to the
croonings and maunderings of the ill-educated, improvi-
dent, and foolish, who make so large a proportion of the
less fortunate classes of society. It had been suggested to
him that a highly-educated, agreeable young doctor, who
talked materialism and dissented from the thirty-nine
articles, might as properly be borne with as a drinking
young mechanic who talked unbelief of a lower and less
respectable order.

Now it so happened, by one of those unexpected co-
incidences that fall out in the eternal order of things,
that Eva was reinforced in her course of argument by
a silent and subtle influence, of which she was herself
scarcely aware. The day seldom passed that one or
other of her sisters did not form a part of her family
circle, and on this day of all others the fates had willed
that Angelique should come up to work on her Christmas presents by Eva's fireside.

Imagine, therefore, as the scene of this conversation,
a fire-lighted room, the evening flicker of the blaze falling in flecks and flashes over books and pictures, and
Mr. St. John in a dark, sheltered corner, surveying without being surveyed, listening to Eva's animated logic,
and yet watching a very pretty tableau in the opposite
corner.

There sat Angelique, listening to the conversation,
with the fire-light falling in flashes on her golden hair
and her lap full of worsteds—rosy, pink, blue, lilac, and
yellow. Her little hands were busy in some fleecy wonder, designed to adorn the Christmas-tree for the mis-

sion school of his church; and she knit and turned and
twisted the rosy mystery with an air of grave interest,
the while giving an attentive ear to the conversation.

Mr. St. John was not aware that he was looking at
her; in fact, he supposed he was listening to Eva, who
was eloquently setting forth to him all the good points
in Dr. Campbell's character, and the reasons why it was
his duty to seek and cultivate his acquaintance; but
while she spoke and while he replied he saw the little
hands moving, and a sort of fairy web weaving, and the
face changing as, without speaking a word, she followed
with bright, innocent sympathy the course of the conversation.

When Eva, with a becoming air of matronly gravity,
lectured him for his reckless treatment of his own health,
and his want of a proper guide on that subject, Angelique's eyes seemed to say the same; and sometimes,
when Eva turned just the faintest light of satire on the
ascetic notions to which he was prone, those same eyes
sparkled with that frank gaiety that her dimpled face
seemed made to express. Now the kitten catches at her
thread, and she stops, and bends over and dangles the
ball, and laughs softly to herself, and St. John from his
dark corner watches the play. There is something of
the kitten in her, he thinks. Even her gravest words
have suggested the air of a kitten on good behavior, and
perhaps she may be a naughty, wicked kitten—who
knows? A kitten lying in wait to catch unwary birds
and mice! But she looked so artless—so innocent!—her
little head bent on one side like a flower, and her eyes
sparkling as if she were repressing a laugh!—a nervous
idea shot through the conversation to Mr. St. John's
heart. What if this girl *should* laugh at him? St. Jerome himself might have been vulnerable to a poisoned
arrow like this. What if he really were getting absurd

notions and ways in the owl-like recesses and retirements
of his study—growing rusty, unfit for civilized life?
Clearly it was his duty to "come forth into the light of
things," and before he left that evening he gave his
pledge to Eva that he would be one of the patrons of her
new social enterprise.

It is to be confessed that as he went home that night
he felt that duty had never worn an aspect so agreeable.
It was certainly his place as a good fisher of men to study
the habits of the cultured, refined, and influential portion
of society, as well as of its undeveloped children. Then,
he did n't say it to himself, but the scene where these
investigations were to be pursued rose before him insensibly as one where Angelique was to be one of the
entertainers. It would give him a better opportunity of
studying the genus and habits of that variety of the
church militant who train in the uniform of fashionable
girls, and to decide the yet doubtful question whether
they had any genuine capacity for church work. Angelique's evident success with her class was a puzzle to
him, and he thought he would like to know her better,
and see if real, earnest, serious purposes could exist under that gay exterior.

Somehow, he could not fancy those laughing eyes and
that willful, curly, golden hair under the stiff cap of a
Sister of Charity; and he even doubted whether a gray
cloak would seem as appropriate as the blue robe and
ermine cape where the poor little child had rested her
scarred cheek. He liked to think of her just as she
looked then and there. And why should n't he get acquainted with her? If he was ever going to form a sisterhood of good works, certainly it was his duty to
understand the sisters. Clearly it was!

CHAPTER XV

"HAVING company" is one of those incidents of life which in all circles, high or low, cause more or less searchings of heart.

Even the moderate "tea-fight" of good old times necessitated not only anxious thought in the hostess herself, but also a mustering and review of best "bibs and tuckers," through the neighborhood.

But to undertake a "serial sociable" in New York, in this day of serials, was something even graver, causing many thoughts and words in many houses.

Witness the following specimens:

"I confess, Nellie, *I* can't understand Eva's ways," said Aunt Maria, the morning of the first Thursday. "She don't come to *me* for advice; but I confess I don't understand her."

Aunt Maria was in a gloomy, severe state of mind, owing to the contumacy and base ingratitude of Alice in rejecting her interposition and care, and she came down this morning to signify her displeasure to Nellie at the way she had been treated.

"I don't know what you mean, sister," said Mrs. Van Arsdel, deprecatingly. "I'm sure I don't know of anything that Eva's been doing lately."

"Why, these evenings of hers; I don't understand them. Setting out to have receptions in that little out-of-the-way shell of hers! Why, who'll go? Nobody wants to ramble off up there, and not get to anything after all. It's going to be a sort of mixed-up affair—

newspaper men, and people that nobody knows—all well enough in their way, perhaps; but *I* shan't be mixed up in it." Aunt Maria nodded her head gloomily, and the bows and feathers on her hat quivered protestingly.

"Oh, they are going to be just unpretending sociable little gatherings," said Mrs. Van Arsdel. "Just the family and a few friends; and *I* think they are going to be pleasant. I wish you would go, Maria. Eva will be disappointed."

"No, she won't. It's evident, Nelly, that your girls don't any of them care about me, or regard anything I say. Well, I only hope they mayn't live to repent it; that's all."

Aunt Maria said this with that menacing sniff with which people in a bad humor usually dispense Christian charity. The dark awfulness of the hope expressed really chilled poor little Mrs. Van Arsdel's blood. From long habits of dependence upon her sister, she had come to regard her displeasure as one of the severer evils of life. To keep the peace with Maria, as far as she herself was concerned, would have been easy. Contention was fatiguing to her. It was a trouble to have the responsibility of making up her own mind; and she was quite willing that Maria should carry her through the journey of life, buy her tickets, choose her hotels, and settle with her cabmen. But, complicated with a husband, and a family of bright, independent daughters, each endowed with a separate will of her own, Mrs. Van Arsdel led on the whole a hard life. People who hate trouble generally get a good deal of it. It's all very well for a gentle acquiescent spirit to be carried through life by *one* bearer. But when half a dozen bearers quarrel and insist on carrying one opposite ways, the more facile the spirit, the greater the trouble.

Mrs. Van Arsdel, in fact, passed a good deal of her

life in being talked over to one course of conduct by
Aunt Maria, and talked back again by her girls. She
resembled a weak, peaceable hamlet on the border-land
between France and Germany, taken and retaken with
much wear and tear of spirit, and heartily wishing peace
at any price.

"I don't see how Eva is going to afford all this,"
continued Aunt Maria gloomily.

"Oh! there's to be no evening entertainment, nothing but a little tea, and biscuit, and sponge cake, in the
most social way," pleaded Mrs. Van Arsdel.

"But all this, every week, in time comes to a good
deal," said Aunt Maria. " Now, if Eva would put all the
extra trouble and expense of these evenings into *one good
handsome party* of select people and have it over with,
why *that* would be something worth while, and I would
help her get it up. Such a party stands for something.
But she doesn't come to *me* for advice. I'm a superannu-
ated old woman, I suppose," and Aunt Maria sighed in
a way heart-breaking to her peace-loving sister.

"Indeed, Maria, you are wrong. You are provoked
now. You don't mean so."

"I'm—*not* provoked. Do you suppose I care? I
don't! but I can *see*, I suppose! I'm not *quite* blind yet,
I hope, and I sha'n't go where I'm not wanted. And
now, if you'll give me those samples, Nellie, I'll go to
Arnold's and Stewart's and look up that dress for you,
and then I'll take your laces to the mender's. It's a
good morning's work to go up to that dark alley where
she rooms; but I'll do it, now I'm about it. I'm not so
worn out yet but what I am acceptable to do errands for
you," said Aunt Maria, with gloomy satisfaction.

"Oh, Maria, how can you talk so!" said little Mrs.
Van Arsdel, with tears in her eyes. "You really are
unjust."

"There's no use in discussing matters, Nellie. Give me the patterns and the laces," said Aunt Maria, obdurately. "Here! I'll sort 'em out. You never have anything ready," she said, opening her sister's drawer, and taking right and left such articles as she deemed proper, with as much composure as if her sister had been a seven-year-old child. "There!" she said, shutting the drawer, "now I'm ready. Good morning!"—and away she sailed, leaving her sister abased in spirit, and vaguely contrite for she couldn't tell what.

Aunt Maria had the most disagreeable habit of venting her indignation on her sister, by going to most uncomfortable extremes of fatiguing devotion to her service. With a brow of gloom and an air of martyrdom, she would explore shops, tear up and down stair-cases, perform fatiguing pilgrimages for Nellie and the girls; piling all these coals of fire on their heads, and looking all the while so miserably abused and heart-broken that it required stronger discrimination than poor Mrs. Van Arsdel was gifted with not to feel herself a culprit.

"Only think, your Aunt Maria says she won't go this evening," she said in a perplexed and apprehensive tone to her girls.

"Glad of it," said Alice, and the words were echoed by Angelique.

"Oh, girls, you oughtn't to feel so about your aunt!"

"We don't," said Alice, "but as long as she feels so about us, it's just as well not to have her there. We girls are all going to do our best to make the first evening a success, so that everybody shall have a good time and want to come again; and if Aunt Maria goes in her present pet, she would be as bad as Edgar Poe's raven."

"Just fancy our having her on our hands, saying '*nevermore*' at stated intervals," said Angelique, laughing; "why, it would upset everything!"

"Angelique, you oughtn't to make fun of your aunt," said Mrs. Van Arsdel, with an attempt at reproving gravity.

"I'm sure it's the nicest thing we *can* make of her, Mammy dear," said Angelique; "it's better to laugh than to cry any time. Oh, Aunt Maria will *keep*, never fear. She'll clear off by-and-by, like a northeast rain-storm, and then we shall like her well as ever; sha'n't we, girls?"

"Oh, yes; she always comes round after a while," said Alice.

"Well, now I'm going up to help Eva get the rooms ready," said Angelique, and out she fluttered, like a flossy bit of thistle-down.

Angelique belonged to the corps of the laughing saints—a department not always recognized by the straiter sort in the church militant, but infinitely effective and to the purpose in the battle of life. Her heart was a tender but a gay one—perhaps the lovingness of it kept it bright; for love is a happy divinity, and Angelique loved everybody, and saw the best side of everything; besides, just now she was barely seventeen, and thought the world a very nice place. She was the very life of the household, the one who loved to run and wait and tend; who could stop gaps and fill spaces, and liked to do it: and so, this day, she devoted herself to Eva's service in the hundred somethings that pertain to getting a house in order for an evening reception.

*　　*　　*　　*　　*　　*　　*　　*

On the opposite side of the way, the projected hospitalities awoke various conflicting emotions.

"Dinah, I don't really know whether I shall go to that company to-night or not," said Mrs. Betsey confidentially to Dinah over her ironing-table.

"Land sakes, Mis' Betsey," said Dinah, with her accustomed giggle, "how you talk! What you 'feard on?"

Mrs. Betsey had retreated to the kitchen, to indulge herself with Dinah in tremors and changes of emotion which had worn out the patience of Miss Dorcas in the parlor. That good lady, having made up her mind definitively to go and take Betsey with her, was indisposed to repeat every half hour the course of argument by which she had demonstrated to her that it was the proper thing to do.

But the fact was, that poor Mrs. Betsey was terribly fluttered by the idea of going into company again. Years had passed in that old dim house, with the solemn clock tick-tocking in the corner, and the sunbeam streaming duskily at given hours through the same windows, with no sound of coming or going footsteps. There the two ancient sisters had been working, reading, talking, round and round on the same unvarying track, for weeks, months and years, and now, suddenly, had come a change. The pretty, gay, little housekeeper across the way had fluttered in with a whole troop of invisible elves of persuasion in the very folds of her garments, and had cajoled and charmed them into a promise to be supporters of her "evenings," and Miss Dorcas was determined to go. But all ye of womankind know that after every such determination comes a review of the wherewithal, and many tremors.

Now Miss Dorcas was self-sufficing, and self-sustained. She knew herself to be Miss Dorcas Vanderheyden, in the first place; and she had a general confidence, by right of her family and position, that all her belongings were the right things. They might be out of fashion—so much the worse for the fashion; Miss Dorcas wore them with a cheerful courage. Yet, as she fre-

quently remarked, "sooner or later, if you let things lie,
fashion always comes round to them." They had come
round to her many times in the course of her life, and
always found her ready for them. But Mrs. Betsey was
timorous, and had a large allowance of what the phre-
nologists call "approbativeness." In her youth she had
been a fashionable young belle, and now she had as many
flutters and tremors about her gray curls and her caps as
in the days when she sat up all night in an arm-chair
with her hair dressed and powdered for a ball. In fact,
an old lady's cap is undeniably a tender point. One
might imagine it to be a sort of shrine or last retreat in
which all her youthful love of dress finds asylum; and,
in estimating her fitness for any scene of festivity, the
cap is the first consideration. So, when Dinah chuckled,
"What ye 'feard on, honey?" Mrs. Betsey came out
with it :

"Dinah, I don't know which of my caps to wear."

"Lor' sakes, Mis' Betsey, wear yer new one. What's
to hender?"

"Well, you see, it's trimmed with lilac ribbons, and
the shade don't go with my new brown gown ; they look
horridly together. Dorcas never does notice such things,
but they don't go well together. I tried to tell Dorcas
about it, but she shut me up, saying I was always
fussy."

"Well, laws ! then, honey, wear your other cap—it's a
right nice un now," said Dinah in a coaxing tone.

"Trimmed with white ribbon—" said Mrs. Betsey,
ruminating; "but you see, Dinah, that ribbon has really
got quite yellow; and there's a spot on one of the
strings," she added, in a tone of poignant emotion.

"Well, now, I tell ye what to do," said Dinah; "you
jest wear your new cap with them laylock ribbins, and
wear your black silk : that are looks illegant now."

"But my black silk is so old; it's pieced under the arm, and beginning to fray in the gathers."

"Land sake, Mis' Betsey! who's agoin' to look under your arm?" said Dinah. "They a'n't agoin' to set you up under one o' them sterry scopes to be looked at, be they? You'll do to pass now, I tell ye; now don't go to gettin' fluttered and 'steriky, Mis' Betsey. Why don't ye go right along, like Mis' Dorcas? She don't have no megrims and tantrums 'bout what she's goin' to wear."

Dinah's tolerant spirit in admitting this discussion was, however, a real relief to Mrs. Betsey. Like various liquors which are under a necessity of working them-selves clear, Mrs. Betsey found a certain amount of *talk* necessary to clear her mind when proceeding to act in any emergency, and for this purpose a listener was essen-tial; but Dorcas was so entirely above such fluctuations as hers—so positive and definite in all her judgments and conclusions—that she could not enjoy in her society the unlimited amount of discussion necessary to clarify her mental vision.

It was now about the fifth or sixth time that all the possibilities with regard to her wardrobe had been up for consideration that day; till Miss Dorcas, who had borne with her heroically for a season, had finally closed the discussion by recommending a chapter in *Watts on the Mind* which said a great many unpleasant things about people who occupy themselves too much with tri-fles, and thus Mrs. Betsey was driven to unbosom her-self to Dinah.

"Then, again, there's Jack," she added; "I'm sure I don't know what he'll think of our both being out; there never such a thing happened before."

"Land sake, Mis' Betsey, jest as if Jack cared! Why, he'll stay with me. I'll see arter *him*—I will."

"Well, you must be good to him, Dinah," said Mrs. Betsey, apprehensively.

"Ain't I allers good to him?   I don't set him up for a graven image and fall down and washup him, to be sure; but Jack has good times with me, if I *do* make him mind."

The fact was, that Dinah often seconded the disciplinary views of Miss Dorcas with the strong arm, pulling Jack backward by the tail, and correcting him with vigorous thumps of the broomstick when he fell into those furors of barking which were his principal weakness.

Dinah had all the sociable instincts of her race; and it moved her indignation that the few acquaintances who found their way to the forsaken old house should be terrified and repelled by such distracted tumults as Jack generally created when the door-bell rang.   Hence her attitude toward him had so often been belligerent that poor Mrs. Betsey felt small confidence in leaving him to the trying separation of the evening under Dinah's care.

"Well, Dinah, you won't whip Jack if he does bark? I dare say he'll be lonesome.   You must make allowances for him."

"Oh, laws, yes, honey, I'll make 'lowance, never you fear."

"And you really think the black dress will do?"

"Jest as sartin as I be that I'm here a ironin' this 'ere pillow-bier.   Why, honey, you'll look like a pictur, you will."

"Oh, Dinah, I'm an old-woman."

"Well, honey, what if you be?   Land sakes, don't I remember when you was the belle of New York *city?* Lord love ye!   Them *was* days!   When 'twas all comin' and goin', hosses a-prancin', house full, and fellers fairly a-tumblin' over each other jest to get a look at ye. Laws, honey, ye was wuth lookin' at in dem days."

"Oh, Dinah, you silly old soul, what nonsense you talk!"

"Well, honey, you know you was de handsomest gal goin'. Now you knows you was," said Dinah, chuckling and shaking her portly sides.

"I suppose I wasn't bad looking," said Mrs. Betsey, laughing in turn; and the color flushed in her delicate, faded cheeks, and her pretty bright eyes grew misty with a thought of all the little triumphs, prides, and regrets of years ago.

To say the truth, Mrs. Betsey, though past the noon-time of attraction, was a very pretty old woman. Her hands were still delicate and white, her skin was of lily fairness, and her hair like fine-spun silver; and she retained still all the nice instincts and habits of the woman who has known herself charming. She still felt the discord of a shade in her ribbons like a false note in music, and was annoyed by the slightest imperfection of her dress, however concealed, to a degree which seemed at times wearisome and irrational to her stronger minded sister.

But Miss Dorcas, who had carried her in her arms, a heart-broken wreck snatched from the waves of a defeated life, bore with her as heroically as we ever can bear with another whose nature is wholly of a different make and texture from our own.

In general, she made up her mind with a considerable share of good sense as to what it was best for Betsey to do, and then made her do it, by that power which a strong and steady nature exercises over a weaker one.

Miss Dorcas had made up her mind that more society, and some little change in her modes of life, would be a

H

benefit to her sister; she had taken a strong fancy to Eva, and really looked forward to her evenings as something to give a new variety and interest in life.

*   *   *   *   *   *   *   *

"Now, Jim," said Alice, in a monitory tone, "you know we all depend on you to manage this thing just right to-night. You mustn't be too lively and frighten the serious folks; but you must keep things moving, just as you know how."

"Well, are you going to have 'our rector?'" said Jim.

"Certainly. Mr. St. John will be there."

"And of course, our little Angie," said Jim.

"Certainly. Angie, and Mamma, and Papa, and I, shall all be there," said Alice, with dignity. "Now, Jim!"

The exclamation was addressed not to anything which this young gentleman had said, but to a certain wicked sparkle in his eye which Alice thought predicted coming mischief.

"What's the matter now?" said Jim.

"I know just what you're thinking," said Alice; "and now, Jim, you mustn't *look* that way to-night."

"Look *what* way!"

"Well, you mustn't in *any* way—look, sign, gesture or word—direct anybody's attention to Mr. St. John and Angie. Of course there's nothing there; it's all a fancy of your own—a *very* absurd one; but I've known people made very uncomfortable by such absurd suggestions."

"Well, am I to wear green spectacles to keep my eyes from looking?"

"You are to do just right, Jim, and nobody knows how that is to be done better than you do. You know that you have the gift of entertaining, and there isn't a mortal creature that you can't please, if you try; and you mustn't talk to those you like best to-night, but bestow yourself wherever a hand is needed. You must entertain those old ladies over the way, and get acquainted with Mr. St. John, and talk to the pretty Quaker woman; in short, make yourself generally useful."

"O. K.," said Jim. "I'll be on hand. I'll make love to all the old ladies, and let the parson admonish me, as meek as Moses; and I'll look right the other way, if I see him looking at Angie. Anything more?"

"No, that'll do," said Alice, laughing. "Only do your best, and it will be good enough."

*   *   *   *   *   *   *   *

Eva was busy about her preparations, when Dr. Campbell came in to borrow a book.

"Now, Dr. Campbell," said she, "you're just the man I wanted to see. I must tell you that one grand reason why I want to be sure and secure you for our evenings, and this one in particular, is I have caught our rector and got his promise to come, and I want you to study him critically, for I'm afraid he's in the way to get to heaven long before we do, if he isn't looked after. He's not in the least conscious of it, but he does need attention."

Dr. Campbell was a hale young man of twenty-five; blonde, vigorous, high-strung, active, and self-confident, and as keen set after medical and scientific facts as a race-horse for the goal. As a general thing, he had no special fancy for clergymen; but a clergyman as a physical study, a possible verification of some of his theories, was an object of interest, and he readily promised Eva that he would spare no pains in making Mr. St. John's acquaintance.

"Now, drolly enough," said Eva, "we're going to have a Quaker preacher here. I went in to invite Ruth and her husband; and lo, they have got a celebrated minister staying with them, one Sibyl Selwyn. She is as lovely as an angel in a pressed crape cap and dove-colored gown; but what Mr. St. John will think about her I don't know."

"Oh, Mrs. Henderson, there'll be trouble there, depend on it," said Dr. Campbell. "He won't recognize her ordination, and very likely she won't recognize his. You see, I was brought up among the Friends. I know all about them. If your friend Sibyl should have a 'concern' laid on her for your Mr. St. John, she would tell him some wholesome truths."

"Dear me," said Eva. "I hope she won't have a 'concern' the very first evening. It would be embarrassing."

"Oh, no; to tell the truth, these Quaker preachers are generally delightful women," said Dr. Campbell. "I'm sure I ought to say so, for my good aunt that brought me up was one of them, and I don't doubt that Sibyl Selwyn will prove quite an addition to your circle."

Well, the evening came, and so did all the folks. But what they said and did, must be told in another chapter.

CHAPTER XVI.

MR. ST. JOHN was sitting in his lonely study, contemplating with some apprehension the possibilities of the evening.

Perhaps few women know how much of an ordeal general society is to many men. Women are naturally social and gregarious, and have very little experience of the kind of shyness that is the outer bark of many manly natures, in which they fortify all the more sensitive part of their being against the rude shocks of the world.

As we said, Mr. St. John's life had been that of a recluse and scholar, up to the time of his ordination as a priest. He was, by birth and education, a New England Puritan, with all those habits of reticence and self-control which a New England education enforces. His religious experiences, being those of reaction from a sterile and severe system of intellectual dogmatism, still carried with them a tinge of the precision and narrowness of his early life. His was a nature like some of the streams of his native mountains, inclining to cut for itself straight, deep, narrow currents; and all his religious reading and thinking had run in one channel. As to social life, he first began to find it among his inferiors; among those to whom he came, not as a brother man, but as an authoritative teacher—a master, divinely appointed, set apart from the ordinary ways of men. In his rôle of priest he felt strong. In the belief of his divine and sacred calling, he moved among the poor and ignorant with a conscious superiority, as a being of a higher sphere.   There was something in this which was a protection to his natural diffidence; he seemed among his parishioners to feel surrounded by a certain sacred atmosphere that shielded him from criticism. But to mingle in society as man with man, to lay aside the priest and be only the gentleman, appeared on near approach a severe undertaking.   As a priest at the altar he was a privileged being, protected by a kind of divine aureole, like that around a saint.   In general society he was but a man, to make his way only as other men; and, as a man, St. John distrusted and undervalued himself. As he thought it over, he inly assented to the truth of what Eva had so artfully stated—that this ordeal of society was indeed, for him, the true test of self-sacrifice. Like many other men of refined natures, he was nervously sensitive to personal influences.   The social sphere of those around him affected him, through sympathy, almost as immediately as the rays of the sun impress the daguerreotype plate; but he felt it his duty to subject himself to the ordeal the more because he dreaded it. "After all," he said to himself, "what is my faith worth, if I cannot carry it among men?   Do I hold a lamp with so little oil in it that the first wind will blow it out?"

It was with such thoughts as these that he started out on his usual afternoon tour of visiting and ministration in one of the poorest alleys of his neighborhood.

As he was making his way along, a little piping voice was heard at his elbow:

"Mr. St. Don; Mr. St. Don."

He looked hastily down and around, to meet the gaze of a pair of dark childish eyes looking forth from a thin, sharp little face.   Gradually, he recognized in the thin, barefoot child, the little girl whom he had seen in Angie's class, leaning on her.

"What do you want, my child?"

"Mother's took bad, and Poll's gone to wash for her. They told me to watch till you came round, and call you. Mother wants to see you."

"Well, show me the way," said Mr. St. John, affably, taking the thin, skinny little hand.

The child took him under an alley-way, into a dark, back passage, up one or two rickety staircases, into an attic, where lay a woman on a poor bed in the corner.

The room was such a one as his work made only too familiar to him—close, dark, bare of comforts, yet not without a certain lingering air of neatness and self-respect. The linen of the bed was clean, and the woman that lay there had marks of something refined and decent in her worn face. She was burning with fever; evidently, hard work and trouble had driven her to the breaking point.

"Well, my good woman, what can I do for you?" said Mr. St. John.

The woman roused from a feverish sleep and looked at him.

"Oh, sir, please send *her* here. She said she would come any time I needed her, and I want her now."

"Who is she? Who do you mean?"

"Please, sir, she means my teacher," said the child, with a bright, wise look in her thin little face. "It's Miss Angie. Mother wants her to come and talk to father; father's getting bad again."

"He isn't a bad man," put in the woman, "except they get him to drink; it's the liquor. God knows there never was a kinder man than John used to be."

"Where is he? I will try to see him," said Mr. St. John.

"Oh, don't; it won't do any good. He hates ministers; he wouldn't hear you; but Miss Angie he will hear; he promised her he wouldn't drink any more, but Ben Jones and Jim Price have been at him and got him off on a spree. O dear!"

At this, moment a feeble wail was heard from the basket cradle in the corner, and the little girl jumped from the bed, and in an important, motherly way, began to soothe an indignant baby, who put up his stomach and roared loudly after the manner of his kind, astonished and angry at not finding the instant solace and attention which his place in creation demanded.

Mr. St. John looked on in a kind of silent helplessness, while the little skinny creature lifted a child who seemed almost as large as herself and proceeded to soothe and assuage his ill humor by many inexplicable arts, till she finally quenched his cries in a sucking-bottle, and peace was restored.

"The only person in the world that can do John any good," resumed the woman, when she could be heard, "is Miss Angie. John would turn any *man*, specially any minister, out of the house, that said a word about his ways; but he likes to have Miss Angie come here. She has been here Saturday afternoons and read stories to the children, and taught them little songs, and John always listens, and she almost got him to promise he would give up drinking; she has such pretty ways of talking, a man can't get mad with her. What I want is, can't you tell her John's gone, and ask her to come to me? He'll be gone two days or more, and when he comes back he'll be sorry—he always is then; and then if Miss Angie will talk to him; you see she's so pretty, and dresses so pretty. John says she is the brightest, prettiest lady he ever saw, and it softer pleases him that she takes notice of us. John always puts his best foot foremost when she is round. John's used to being with gentlefolk," she said, with a sigh; "he knows a lady when he sees her."

"Well, my good woman," said Mr. St. John, "I shall see Miss Angie this evening, and you may be sure that I shall tell her all about this. Meanwhile, how are you off? Do you need money now?"

"I am pretty well off, sir. *He* took all my last week's money when he went, but Poll has gone to my wash-place to-day, and I told her to ask for pay. I hope they'll send it."

"If they don't," said Mr. St. John, "here is something to keep things going," and he slipped a bill into the woman's hand.

"Thank you, sir. When I get up, if you'll please give me some washing, I'll make it square. I've been held good at getting up linen."

Poor woman! She had her little pride of independence, and her little accomplishment—she could wash and iron! There she felt strong! Mr. St. John allowed her the refuge, and let her consider the money as an advance, not a charity.

He turned away, and went down the cracked and broken stairs with the thought struggling in an undefined manner in his breast, how much there was of pastoral work which transcended the power of man, and required the finer intervention of woman. With all, there came a glow of shy pleasure that there was a subject of intercommunication opened between him and Angie, something definite to talk about; and to a diffident man a definite subject is a mine of gold.

CHAPTER XVII.

THE Henderson's first "Evening" was a social success. The little parlors were radiant with the blaze
of the wood-fire, which gleamed and flashed and made
faces at itself in the tall, old-fashioned brass andirons,
and gave picturesque tints to the room.

Eva's tea-table was spread in one corner, dainty with
its white drapery, and with her pretty wedding-present
of china upon it—not china like Miss Dorcas Vanderheyden's, of the real old Chinese fabric, but china fresh
from the modern improvements of Paris, and so adorned
with violets and grasses and field flowers that it made a
December tea-table look like a meadow where one could
pick bouquets. Every separate tea-cup and saucer was
an artist's study, and a topic for conversation.

The arrangement of the rooms had been a day's
work of careful consideration between Eva and Angelique. There was probably not a perch or eyrie access-
ible by chairs, tables, or ottomans, where these little
persons had not been mounted, at divers times of the
day, trying the effect of various floral decorations. The
amount of fatigue that can be gone through in the mere
matter of preparing one little set of rooms for an evening
reception, is something that *men* know nothing about;
only the sisterhood could testify to that frantic "fanati-
cism of the beautiful" which seizes them when an evening company is in contemplation, and their house is to
put, so to speak, its best foot forward. Many an aching
back and many a drooping form could testify how the

woman spends herself in advance, in this sort of altar dressing for home worship.

But, as a consequence, the little rooms were bowers of beauty. The pictures were overshadowed with nodding wreaths of pressed ferns and bright bitter-sweet berries, with glossy holly leaves; the statuettes had backgrounds of ivy which threw out their whiteness. Harry's little workroom adjoining the parlor had become a green alcove, where engravings and books were spread out under the shade of a German student-lamp. Everywhere that a vase of flowers could make a pretty show, there was a vase of flowers, though it was December, and the ground frozen like lead. For the next door neighbor, sweet Ruth Baxter, had clipped and snipped every rosebud, and mignonette blossom, and even a splendid calla lily, with no end of scarlet geranium, and sent them in to Eva; and Miss Dorcas had cut away about half of an ancient and well-kept rose-geranium, which was the apple of her eye, to help out her little neighbor. So they reveled in flowers, without cutting those which grew on Eva's own bushes, which were all turned to the light and arranged in appropriate situations, blossoming their best. The little dining-room also was thrown open, and dressed, and adorned with flowers, pressed ferns, berries, and autumn leaves; with a distant perspective of light in it, that there might be a place of withdrawal and quiet chats over books and pictures. In every spot were disposed objects to start conversation. Books of autographs, portfolios of sketches, photographs of distinguished people, stereoscopic views, with stereoscope to explain them,—all sorts of intervening means and appliances by which people, not otherwise acquainted, should find something to talk about in common.

Eva was admirably seconded by her friends, from long experience versed in the art of entertaining. Mrs.

Van Arsdel, gentle, affable, society-loving, and with a quick tact at reading the feelings of others, was a host in herself. She at once took possession of Miss Dorcas Vanderheyden, who came in a very short dress of rich India satin, and very yellow and mussy but undeniably precious old lace, and walked the rooms with a high-shouldered independence of manner most refreshing in this day of long trains and modern inconveniences.

"Sensible old girl," was Jim Fellows's comment in Alice's ear as Miss Dorcas marched in; for which, of course, he got a reproof, and was ordered to remember and keep himself under.

As to Mrs. Betsey, with her white hair, and lace cap with lilac ribbons, and black dress, with a flush of almost girlish timidity in her pink cheeks, she won an instant way to the heart of Angelique, who took her arm and drew her to a cosy arm-chair before a table of engravings, and began an animated conversation on a book of etchings of the "Old Houses of New York." These were subjects on which Mrs. Betsey could talk, and talk entertainingly. They carried her back to the days of her youth; bringing back scenes, persons, and places long forgotten, her knowledge of which was full of entertainment. Angelique wonderingly saw her transfigured before her eyes. It seemed as if an after-glow from the long set sun of youthful beauty flashed back in the old, worn face, as her memory went back to the days of youth and hope. It is a great thing to the old and faded to feel themselves charming once more, even for an hour; and Mrs. Betsey looked into the blooming face and wide open, admiring, hazel eyes of Angelique, and felt that she was giving pleasure, that this charming young person was really delighted to hear her talk. It was one of those "cups of cold water" that Angelique was always giving to neglected and out-of-the-way people, without ever thinking that she did so, or why she did it, just because she was a sweet, kind-hearted, loving little girl.

When Mr. St. John, with an apprehensive spirit, adventured his way into the room, he felt safe and at ease in a moment. All was light, and bright, and easy— nobody turned to look at him, and it seemed the easiest thing in the world to thread his way through busy chatting groups to where Eva made a place for him by her side at the tea-table, passed him his cup of tea, and introduced him to Dr. Campbell, who sat on her other side, cutting the leaves of a magazine.

"You see," said Eva, laughing, "I make our Doctor useful on the Fourier principle. He is dying to get at those magazine articles, so I let him cut the leaves and take a peep along here and there, but I forbid reading— in our presence, men have got to give over absorbing, and begin radiating. Doesn't St. Paul say, Mr. St. John, that if women are to learn anything they are to ask their husbands at home? and doesn't that imply that their husbands at home are to talk to *them*, and not sit reading newspapers?"

"I confess I never thought of that inference from the passage," said Mr. St. John, smiling.

"But the modern woman," said Dr. Campbell, "scorns to ask her husband at home. She holds that her husband should ask her."

"Oh, well, I am not the modern woman. I go for the old boundaries and the old privileges of my sex; and besides, *I* am a good church woman and prefer to ask my husband. But I insist, as a necessary consequence, that he must *hear* me and answer me, as he cannot do if he is reading newspapers or magazines. Isn't that case fairly argued, Mr. St. John?"

"I don't see but it is."

"Well, then, the spirit of it applies to the whole of your cultured and instructive sex. Men, in the presence of women, ought always to be prepared to give them information, to answer questions, and make themselves generally entertaining and useful."

"You see, Mr. St. John," said Dr. Campbell, "that Mrs. Henderson has a dangerous facility for generalizing. Set her to interpreting and there's no saying where her inferences mightn't run."

"I'd almost release Mr. St. John from my rules, to allow him to look over this article of yours, though, Dr. Campbell," said Eva. "Harry has read it to me, and I said, along in different parts of it, if ministers only knew these things, how much good they might do!"

"What is the article?"

"It is simply something I wrote on 'Abnormal Influences upon the Will;' it covers a pretty wide ground as to the question of human responsibility and the recovery of criminals, and all that."

Mr. St. John remembered at this moment the case of the poor woman whom he had visited that afternoon, and the periodical fatality which was making her family life a shipwreck, and he turned to Dr. Campbell a face so full of eager inquiry and dawning thought that Eva felt that the propitious moment was come to leave them together, and instantly she moved from her seat between them, to welcome a new comer who was entering the room.

"I've got them together," she whispered to Harry a few minutes after, as she saw that the two were turned towards each other, apparently intensely absorbed in conversation.

The two might have formed a not unapt personification of flesh and spirit. Dr. Campcell, a broad-shouldered, deep-breathed, long-limbed man, with the proudly set head and quivering nostrils of a high-blooded horse— an image of superb physical vitality: St. John, so delicately and sparely built, with his Greek forehead and clear blue eye, the delicate vibration of his cleanly cut lips, and the cameo purity of every outline of his profile. Yet was he not without a certain air of vigor, the outshining of spiritual forces. One could fancy Campbell as the Berserker who could run, race, wrestle, dig, and wield the forces of nature, and St. John as the poet and orator who could rise to higher regions and carry souls upward with him. It takes both kinds to make up a world.

And now glided into the company the vision of two women in soft, dove-colored silks, with white crape kerchiefs crossed upon their breasts, and pressed crape caps bordering their faces like a transparent aureole. There was the neighbor, Ruth Baxter, round, rosy, young, blooming, but dressed in the straitest garb of her sect. With her back turned, you might expect to see an aged woman stricken in years, so prim and antique was the fashion of her garments; but when her face was turned, there was the rose of youth blooming amid the cool snows of cap and kerchief. The smooth pressed hair rippled and crinkled in many a wave, as if it would curl if it dared, and the round blue eyes danced with a scarce suppressed light of cheer that might have become mirthfulness, if set free; but yet the quaint primness of her attire set off her womanly charms beyond all arts of the toilet.

Her companion was a matronly person, who might be fifty or thereabouts. She had that calm, commanding serenity that comes to woman only from the habitual exaltation of the spiritual nature. Sibyl Selwyn was known in many lands as one of the most zealous and best accepted preachers of her sect. Her life had been an inspiration of pity and mercy; and she had been in far countries of the earth, where there was sin to be reproved or sorrow to be consoled, a witness to testify and a medium through whom guilt and despair might learn something of the Divine Pity.

She bore about with her a power of personal presence very remarkable. Her features were cast in large and noble mould; her clear cut, wide-open gray eyes had a penetrating yet kind expression, that seemed adapted both to search and to cheer, and went far to justify the opinion of her sect, which attributed to Sibyl in an eminent degree the apostolic gift of the discerning of spirits. Somehow, with her presence there seemed to come an atmosphere of peace and serenity, such as one might fancy clinging about even the raiment of one just stepped from a higher sphere. Yet, so gliding and so dove-like was the movement by which the two had come in—so perfectly, cheerfully, and easily had they entered into the sympathies of the occasion, that their entrance made no more break or disturbance in the social circle than the stealing in of a ray of light through a church window.

Eva had risen and gone to them at once, had seated them at the opposite side of the little tea-table and poured their tea, chatting the while and looking into their serene faces with a sincere cordiality which was reflected back from them in smiles of confidence.

Sibyl admired the pictures, flowers, and grasses on her tea-cup with the naïve interest of a child; for one often remarks, in intercourse with her sect, how the æsthetic sense, unfrittered and unworn by the petting of self-indulgence, is prompt to appreciate beauty.

Eva felt a sort of awed pleasure in Sibyl's admiration of her pretty things, as if an angel guide were stooping to play with her. She felt in her presence like one of earth's unweaned babies.

St. John, in one of the pauses of the conversation, looked up and saw this striking head and face opposite to him; a head reminding him of some of these saintly portraitures of holy women in which Overbeck delights. We have described him as peculiarly impressible under actual social influences. It was only the week before that an application had been made to him for one Sibyl Selwyn to hold a meeting in his little chapel, and sternly refused. His idea of a female preacher had been largely blended with the mediæval masculine contempt of woman and his horror of modern woman public teachers and lecturers. When this serene vision rose like an exhalation before him, he did not at first recall the applicant for his chapel, but he looked at her admiringly in a sort of dazed wonder, and inquired of Dr. Campbell in a low voice, "Who is that?"

"Oh," said Dr. Campbell. "don't you know? that's the Quaker preacher, Sibyl Selwyn; the woman who has faced and put down the devil in places where *you* couldn't and I *wouldn't* go."

St. John felt the blood flush in his cheeks, and a dim idea took possession of him that, if some had entertained angels unawares, others unawares had rejected them.

"Yes," said Dr. Campbell, "that woman has been alone, at midnight, through places where you and I could not go without danger of our heads; and she has said words to bar-tenders and brothel-keepers that would cost us our lives. But she walks out of it all, as calm as you see her to-night. I know that kind of woman—I was brought up among them. They are an interesting physiological study; the over-cerebration of the spiritual faculties among them occasions some very peculiar facts and phenomena. I should like to show you a record I have kept. It gives them at times an almost miraculous ascendancy over others. I fancy," he said carelessly, "that your legends of the saints could furnish a good many facts of the same sort."

At this moment, Eva came up in her authoritative way as mistress of ceremonies, took Mr. St. John by the arm, and, walking across with him, seated him by Sibyl Selwyn, introduced them to each other, and left them. St. John was embarrassed, but Sibyl received him with the perfect composure in which she sat enthroned.

"Arthur St. John," she said, "I am glad to meet thee. I am interested in thy work among the poor of this quarter, and have sought the Lord for thee in it."

"I am sure I thank you," said St. John, thus suddenly reduced to primitive elements and spoken to on the simple plane of his unvarnished humanity. It is seldom, after we come to mature years and have gone out into the world, that any one addresses us simply by our name without prefix or addition of ceremony. It is the province only of rarest intimacy or nearest relationship, and it was long since St. John had been with friend or relation who could thus address him. It took him back to childhood and his mother's knee. He was struggling with a vague sense of embarrassment, when he remembered the curt and almost rude manner in which he had repelled her overture to speak in his chapel, and the contempt he had felt for her at the time. In the presence of the clear, saintly face, it seemed as if he had been unconsciously guilty of violating a shrine. He longed to apologize, but he did not know how to begin.

"I feel," he said, "that I am inexperienced and that the work is very great. You," he added, "have had longer knowledge of it than I; perhaps I might learn something of you."

"Thou wilt be led," said Sibyl, with the same assured calmness, "be not afraid."

"I am sorry—I was sorry," said St. John, hesitating,

"to refuse the help you offered in speaking in my chapel, but it is contrary to the rules of the church."

"Be not troubled. Thee follows thy light. Thee can do no otherways. Thee is but young yet," she said, with a motherly smile.

"I did not know you personally then," he said. "I should like to talk more with you, some time. I should esteem it a favor to have you tell me some of your experiences."

"Some time, if we can sit together in stillness, I might have something given me for thee; this is not the time," said Sibyl, with quiet graciousness.

A light laugh seemed to cut into the gravity of the conversation.

Both turned. Angelique was the center of a gay group to whom she was telling a droll story. Angie had a gift for this sort of thing; and Miss Dorcas and Mrs. Betsey, Mrs. Van Arsdel and Mr. Van Arsdel were gathered around her as, with half-pantomime, half-mimicry, she was giving a street scene in one of her Sunday-school visitations. St. John laughed too; he could not help it. In a moment, however, he seemed to recollect himself, and sighed and said:

"It seems sometimes strange to me that we can allow ourselves to laugh in a world like this. She is only a child or she couldn't."

Sibyl looked tenderly at Angelique. "It is her gift," she said. "She is one of the children of the bride-chamber, who cannot mourn because the bridegroom is with them. It would be better for thee, Arthur St. John, to be more a child. Where the spirit of the Lord is, there is liberty."

St. John was impressed by the calm decision of this woman's manner, and the atmosphere of peace and assurance around her. The half-mystical character of her words fell in with his devout tendencies, and that strange, indefinable *something* that invests some persons with influence seemed to be with her, and he murmured to himself the words from Comus—

> " She fables not, and I do feel her words
> Set off by some superior power."

Mr. St. John had not for a moment during that whole evening lost the consciousness that Angelique was in the room. Through that double sense by which two trains of thought can be going on at the same time, he was sensible of her presence and of what she was doing, through all his talks with other people. He had given one glance, when he came into the room, to the place where she was sitting and entertaining Mrs. Betsey, and without any apparent watchfulness he was yet conscious of every movement she made from time to time. He knew when she dropped her handkerchief, he knew when she rose to get down another book, and when she came to the table and poured for Mrs. Betsey another cup of tea. A subtle exhilaration was in the air. He knew not why everything seemed so bright and cheerful; it is as when a violet or an orange blossom, hid in a distant part of a room, fills the air with a vague deliciousness.

He dwelt dreamily on Sibyl's half mystical words, and felt as if an interpreting angel had sanctioned the charm that he found in this bright, laughing child. He liked to call her a child to himself, it was a pleasant little nook into which he could retreat from a too severe scrutiny of his feelings towards her; for, quite unknown to himself, St. John's heart was fast slipping off into the good old way of Eden.

But we leave him for a peep at other parties. It is amusing to think how many people in one evening company are weaving and winding threads upon their own private, separate spools. Jim Fellows, in the dining-room, was saying to Alice:

"I'm going to bring Hal Stephens and Ben Hubert to you this evening; and by George, Alice, I want you to look after them a little, as *you can.* They are raw news-paper boys, tumbled into New York; and nobody cares a hang for them. Nobody does care a hang for any stranger body, you know. They haven't a decent place to visit, nor a woman to say a word to them; and yet I tell you they're good fellows. Everybody curses news-paper reporters and that sort of fellow. Nobody has a good word for them. It's small salary, and many kicks and cuffs they get at first; and yet that's the only way to get on the papers, and make a man of yourself at last; and so, as I've got up above the low rounds, I want to help the boys that are down there, and I'll tell you, Alice, it'll do 'em lots of good to know you."

And so Alice was gracious to the new-comers and made them welcome, and showed them pictures, and drew them out to talk, and made them feel that they were entertaining her.

Some women have this power of divining what a man can say, and giving him courage to say it. Alice was one of these; people wondered when they left her how they had been made to talk so well. It was the best and truest part of every one's nature that she gave courage and voice to. This power of young girls to ennoble young men is unhappily one of which too often they are unconscious. Too often the woman, instead of being a teacher in the higher life, is only a flatterer of the weak-nesses and lower propensities of the men whose admira-tion she seeks.

St. John felt frightened and embarrassed with his message to Angie. He had dwelt on it, all his way to the house, as an auspicious key to a conversation which he anticipated with pleasure; yet the evening rolled by, and though he walked round and round, and nearer and nearer, and conversed with this and that one, he did not come to the point of speaking to Angie. Sometimes she was talking to somebody else and he waited; sometimes she was not with anybody else, and then he waited lest his joining her should be remarked. He did not stop to ask himself why on earth it should be remarked any more than if he had spoken to Alice or Eva, or anybody else, but he felt as if it would be.

At last, however, after making several circles about the table where she sat with Mrs. Betsey, he sat down by them, and delivered his message with a formal precision, as if he had been giving her a summons. Angie was all sympathy and sweetness, and readily said she would go and see the poor woman the very next day, and then an awkward pause ensued. She was a little afraid of him as a preternaturally good man, and began to wonder whether she had been laughing too loud, or otherwise misbehaving, in the gaity of her heart, that evening.

So, after a rather dry pause, Mr. St. John uttered some commonplaces about the books of engravings before them, and then, suddenly seeming to recollect something he had forgotten, crossed the room to speak to Dr. Campbell.

"Dear me, child, and so that is your rector," said Mrs. Betsey. "Isn't he a little stiff?"

"I believe he is not much used to society," said Angie; "but he is a *very* good man."

The evening entertainment had rather a curious finale. A spirit of sociability had descended upon the company, and it was one of those rare tides that come sometimes where everybody is having a good time, and nobody looks at one's watch; and so, ten o'clock was long past, and eleven had struck, and yet there was no movement for dissolving the session.

Across the way, old Dinah had watched the bright windows with longing eyes, until finally the spirit of the occasion was too strong for her, and, bidding Jack lie down and be a good dog, she left her own precincts and ran across to the kitchen of the festal scene, to pick up some crumbs for her share.

Jack looked at her in winking obedience as she closed the kitchen door, being mindful in his own dog's head of a small slip of a pantry window which had served his roving purposes before now. The moment Dinah issued from the outer door, Jack bounced from the pantry window and went padding at a discreet distance from her heels. Sitting down on the front door-mat of the festive mansion, he occupied himself with his own reflections till the door opening for a late comer gave him an opportunity to slip in quietly.

Jack used his entrance ticket with discretion, watched, waited, reconnoitered, till finally, seeing an unemployed ottoman next Mrs. Betsey, he suddenly appeared in the midst, sprang up on the ottoman with easy grace, sat up on his hind paws, and waved his front ones affably to the public.

The general tumult that ensued, the horror of Miss Dorcas, the scolding she tried to give Jack, the storm of applause and petting which greeted him in all quarters, confirming him, as Miss Dorcas remarked, in his evil ways,—all these may better be imagined than described.

"A quarter after eleven, sister!"

"Can it be possible?" said Mrs. Betsey. "No wonder Jack came to bring us home."

Jack seconded the remark with a very staccato bark and a brisk movement towards the door, where, with much laughing, many hand shakings, ardent protestations that they had had a delightful evening, and promises to come again next week, the company dispersed.

CHAPTER XVIII

RAKING UP THE FIRE.

THE cream of an evening company is the latter end of it, after the more ceremonious have slipped away and only "we and our folks" remain to croon and rake up the fire.

Mr. and Mrs. Van Arsdel, Angelique, and Marie went home in the omnibus. Alice staid to spend the night with Eva, and help put up the portfolios, and put back the plants, and turn the bower back into a work-room, and set up the vases of flowers in a cool place where they could keep till morning; because, you know —you who are versed in these things—that flowers in December need to be made the most of, in order to go as far as possible.

Bolton yet lingered in his arm-chair, in his favorite corner, gazing placidly at the coals of the fire. Dr. Campbell was solacing himself, after the unsatisfied long-ings of the evening, with seeing how his own article looked in print, and Jim Fellows was helping miscella-neously in setting back flower-pots, re-arranging books, and putting chairs and tables, that had been arranged festively, back into humdrum household places. Mean-while, the kind of talk was going on that usually follows a social venture—a sort of review of the whole scene and of all the actors.

"Well, Doctor, what do you think of our rector?" said Eva, tapping his magazine briskly.

He lowered his magazine and squared himself round gravely.

"That fellow hasn't enough of the abdominal to carry his brain power," he said. "Splendid head—a little too high in the upper stories and not quite heavy enough in the basement. But if he had a good broad, square chest, and a good digestive and blood-making apparatus, he'd go. The fellow wants blood; he needs mutton and beef, and plenty of it. That's what he needs. What's called common sense is largely a matter of good diet and digestion."

"Oh, Doctor, you materialistic creature!" said Eva, "to think of talking of a clergyman as if he were a horse—to be managed by changing his feed!"

"Certainly, a man must be a good animal before he can be a good man."

"Well," said Alice, "all I know is, that Mr. St. John is perfectly, disinterestedly, heart and soul and body, devoted to doing good among men; and if that is not noble and grand and godlike, I don't know what is."

"Well," said Dr. Campbell, "I have a profound respect for all those fellows that are trying to mop out the Atlantic Ocean; and he mops cheerfully and with good courage."

"It's perfectly hateful of you, Doctor, to talk so," said Eva.

"Well, you know I don't go in for interfering with nature—having noble, splendid fellows waste and wear themselves down, to keep miserable scalawags and ill-begotten vermin from dying out as they ought to. Nature is doing her best to kill off the poor specimens of the race, begotten of vice and drunkenness; and what you call Christian charity is only interference."

"But you do it, Doctor; you know you do. Nobody does more of that very sort of thing than you do, now. Don't you visit, and give medicine and nursing, and all that, to just such people?"

I

"I may be a fool for doing it, for all that," said the Doctor. "I don't pretend to stick to my principles any better than most people do. We are all fools, more or less; but I don't believe in Christian charity: it's all wrong—this doctrine that the brave, strong good specimens of the race are to torment and tire and worry their lives out to save the scum and dregs. Here's a man who, by economy, honesty, justice, temperance and hard work, has grown rich, and has houses, and lands, and gardens, and pictures, and what not, and is having a good time as he ought to have, and right by him is another who, by dishonesty, and idleness, and drinking, has come to rags and poverty and sickness. Shall the temperate ·and just man deny himself enjoyment, and spend his time, and risk his health, and pour out his money, to take care of the wife and children of this scalawag? There's the question in a nutshell? and *I* say, no! If scalawags find that their duties will be performed for them when they neglect them, that's all they want. What should St. John live like a hermit for? deny himself food, rest and sleep? spend a fortune that might make him and some nice wife happy and comfortable, on drunkards' wives and children? No sense in it."

"That's just where Christianity stands above and opposite to nature," said Bolton, from his corner. "Nature says, destroy. She is blindly striving to destroy the maimed and imperfect. Christianity says, save. Its God is the Good Shepherd, who cares more for the one lost sheep than for the ninety and nine that went not astray."

"Yes," said Eva; "He who was worth more than all of us put together, came down from heaven to labor and suffer and die for sinners."

"That's supernaturalism," said Dr. Campbell. "I don't know about that."

"That's what we learn at church," said Eva, "and what we believe; and it's a pity you don't, Doctor."

"Oh, well," said Dr. Campbell, lighting his cigar, previous to going out, "I won't quarrel with you. You might believe worse things. St. John is a good fellow, and, if he wants a doctor any time, I told him to call me. Good night."

"Did you ever see such a creature?" said Eva.

"He talks wild, but acts right," said Alice.

"You had him there about visiting poor folks," said Jim. "Why, Campbell is a perfect fool about people in distress—would give a fellow watch and chain, and boots and shoes, and then scold anybody else that wanted to go and do likewise."

"Well, I say such discussions are fatiguing," said Alice. "I don't like people to talk all round the points of the compass so."

"Well, to change the subject, I vote our evening a success," said Jim. "Didn't we all behave beautifully!"

"We certainly did," said Eva.

"Isn't Miss Dorcas a beauty!" said Jim.

"Come, now, Jim; no slants," said Alice.

"I didn't mean any. Honest now, I like the old girl. She's sensible. She gets such clothes as she thinks right and proper, and marches straight ahead in them, instead of draggling and draggletailing after fashion; an it's a pity there weren't more like her."

"Dress is a vile, tyrannical Moloch," said Eva. "We are all too much enslaved to it."

"I know we are," said Alice. "I think it's *the* question of our day, what sensible women of small means are to do about dress; it takes so much time, so much strength, so much money. Now, if these organizing, convention-holding women would only organize a dress reform, they would do something worth while."

"The thing is," said Eva, "that in spite of yourself you have to conform to fashion somewhat."

"Unless you do as your Quaker friends do," said Bolton.

"By George," said Jim Fellows, "those two were the best dressed women in the room. That little Ruth was seductive."

"Take care; we shall be jealous," said Eva.

"Well," said Bolton, rising, "I must walk up to the printing-office and carry that corrected proof to Daniels."

"I'll walk part of the way with you," said Harry. "I want a bit of fresh air before I sleep."

WICKEDNESS, OR MISERY?

*"Bolton laid his hand on her shoulder, and, looking down on her,
said: 'Poor child, have you no mother?'"*—p. 197.

CHAPTER XIX.

A LOST SHEEP.

THE two sallied out and walked arm in arm up the street. It was a keen, bright, starlight night, with everything on earth frozen stiff and hard, and the stars above sparkling and glinting like white flames in the intense clear blue. Just at the turn of the second street, a woman who had been crouching in a doorway rose, and, coming up towards the two, attempted to take Harry's arm.

With an instinctive movement of annoyance and disgust, he shook her off indignantly.

Bolton, however, stopped and turned, and faced the woman. The light of a street lamp showed a face, dark, wild, despairing, in which the history of sin and punishment were too plainly written. It was a young face, and one that might once have been beautiful; but of all that nothing remained but the brightness of a pair of wonderfully expressive eyes. Bolton advanced a step towards her and laid his hand on her shoulder, and, looking down on her, said:

"Poor child, have you no mother?"

"Mother! Oh!"

The words were almost shrieked, and then the woman threw herself at the foot of the lamp-post and sobbed convulsively.

"Harry," said Bolton, "I will take her to the St. Barnabas; they will take her in for the night."

Then, taking the arm of the woman, he said in a voice of calm authority, "Come with me."

. He raised her and offered her his arm. "Child, there is hope for you," he said. "Never despair. I will take you where you will find friends."

A walk of a short distance brought them to the door of the refuge, where he saw her received, and then turning he retraced his steps to Harry.

"One more unfortunate," he said, briefly, and then immediately took up the discussion of a point in the proof-sheet just where he had left it. Harry was so excited by the incident that he could hardly keep up the discussion which Bolton was conducting.

"I wonder," he said, after an interval, "who that woman is, and what is her history."

"The old story, likely," said Bolton.

"What is curious," said Harry, "is that Eva described such a looking woman as hanging about our house the other evening. It was the evening when she was going over to the Vanderheyden house to persuade the old ladies to come to us this evening. She seemed then to have been hanging about our house, and Eva spoke in particular of her eyes—just such singular, wild, dark eyes as this woman has."

"It may be a mere coincidence," said Bolton. "She may have had some errand on your street. Whatever the case be, she is safe for the present. They will do the best they can for her. She's only one more grain in the heap!"

Shortly after, Harry took leave of Bolton and returned to his own house. He found all still, Eva waiting for him by the dying coals and smoking ashes of the fire. Alice had retired to her apartment.

"We've had an adventure," he said.

"What! to-night?"

Harry here recounted the scene and Bolton's course, and immediately Eva broke out: "There, Harry, it must be that very woman that I saw the night I was going into the Vanderheyden's; she seems to be hanging round this neighborhood. What can she be? Tell me, Harry, had she very brilliant dark eyes, and a sort of dreadfully haggard, hopeless look?"

"Exactly. Then I was provoked at her assurance in laying her hand on my arm; but when I saw her face I was so struck by its misery that I pitied her. You ought to have seen Bolton; he seemed so calm and command-ing, and his face, as he looked down on her, had a won-derful expression; and his voice,—you know that heavy, deep tone of his,—when he spoke of her mother it per-fectly overcame her. She seemed almost convulsed, but he assumed a kind of authority and led her away to the St. Barnabas. Luckily he knew all about that, for he had talked with St. John about it."

"Yes, indeed, I heard them talking about it this very evening; so it is quite a providence. I do wonder who she is or what she is. Would it do for me to go to-mor-row and inquire?"

"I don't know, my dear, as you could do anything. They will do all that is possible there, and I would not advise you to interfere merely from curiosity. You can do nothing."

"Strange!" said Eva, still looking in the fire while she was taking the hairpins out of her hair and loosening her neck ribbon, "strange, the difference in the lot of women. That girl has been handsome! People have loved her. She might have been in a home, happy like me, with a good husband—now there she is in the cold streets. It makes me very unhappy to think such things must be. You know how Bolton spoke of God, the Good Shepherd—how he cared more for one lost one than for all that went not astray. That is so beautiful— I do hope she will be saved."

"Let us hope so, darling."

"It seems selfish for me to wrap my comforts about me, and turn away my thoughts, and congratulate myself on my good luck—don't it?"

"But, darling, if you can't do anything, I don't know why you should dwell on it. But I'll promise you Bolton shall call and inquire of the Sisters, and if there is anything we can do, he will let us know. But now it's late, and you are tired and need rest."

CHAPTER XX

CONGRATULATE us, dear mother; we have had a success! Our first evening was all one could hope! Everybody came that we wanted, and, what is quite as good in such cases, everybody staid away that we didn't want. You know how it is; when you intend to produce real acquaintance, that shall ripen into intimacy, it is necessary that there should be no non-conductors to break the circle. There are people that shed around them coldness and constraint, as if they were made of ice, and it is a mercy when such people don't come to your parties. As it is, I have had the happiness to see our godly rector on most conversable terms with our heretic doctor, and each thinking better of the other. Oh! and, what was a greater triumph yet, I managed to introduce a Quaker preacheress to Mr. St. John, and had the satisfaction to see that he was completely charmed by her, as well he may be. The way it came about, you must know, is this:—

Little Ruth Baxter, our next door neighbor, has received this Sibyl Selwyn at her house, and is going with her soon on one of her preaching expeditions. I find it is a custom of their sect for the preachers to associate with themselves one or more lay sisters, who travel with them, and for a certain time devote themselves to works of charity and mercy under their superintendence. They visit prisons and penitentiaries; they go to houses of vice and misery, where one would think a woman would scarcely dare to go; they reprove sin, yet carry

always messages of hope and mercy.   Little Ruth is now
preparing to go with Sibyl on such a mission, and I am
much interested in the stories she tells me of the
strange unworldly experiences of this woman.   It is true
that these missions are temporary; they seem to be only
like what we could suppose the visits of angels might
be—something to arouse and to stimulate, but not to
exert a continuous influence.   What feeling they excite,
what good purposes and resolutions spring up under
their influence, they refer to the organized charities of
Christian churches of whatever name.   If Sibyl's peni-
tents are Romanists, she carries them to the Romish
Sisters; and so with Methodist, Baptist, or Ritualist,
wherever they can find shelter and care.   She seems to
regard her mission as like that of the brave Sisters of
Charity who go upon the field of battle amid belching
cannon and bursting shells, to bring away the wounded.
She leaves them in this or that hospital, and is off again
for more.

This she has been doing many years, as the spirit
within leads her, both in England and in this country.
I wish you could see her—I know how you would love
her.   As for me, I look up to her with a kind of awe;
yet she has such a pretty, simple-hearted innocence
about her.   I felt a little afraid of her at first, and
thought all my pins and rings and little bows and
fixtures would seem so many sins in her sight; but I
found she could admire a bracelet or a gem as much as
I did, and seemed to enjoy all my pretty things for me.
She says so prettily, "If thee acts up to thy light, Eva,
thee can do no more."   I only wish that I were as sure
as she is that I do.   It is quite sweet of her, and puts me
at ease in her presence.   They are going to be gone all
this week on some mission.   I don't know yet exactly
where, but I can't help feeling as if I wished some angel

woman like Sibyl would take me off with her, and let me do a little something in this great and never finished work of helping and healing. I have always had a longing to do a little at it, and perhaps, with some one to inspire and guide me, even I might do some good.

This reminds me of a strange incident. The other night, as I was crossing the street, I saw a weird-looking young woman, very haggard and miserable, who seemed to be in a kind of uncertain way, hanging about our house. There was something about her face and eyes that affected me quite painfully, but I thought nothing of it at the time. But, the evening after our reception, as Harry and Bolton were walking about a square beyond our house, this creature came suddenly upon them and took Harry's arm. He threw her off with a sudden impulse, and then Bolton, like a good man, as he always is, and with that sort of quiet self-possession he always has, spoke to her and asked where her *mother* was. That word was enough, and the poor thing began sobbing and crying, and then he took her and led her away to the St. Barnabas, a refuge for homeless people which is kept by some of our church Sisters, and there he left her; and Harry says he will tell Mr. St. John about it, so that he may find out what can be done for her, if anything.

When I think of meeting any such case personally, I feel how utterly weak and inexperienced I am, and how utterly unfit to guide or help, though I wish with my whole heart I could do something to help all poor desolate people. I feel a sort of self-reproach for being so very happy as I am while any are miserable. To take another subject,—I have been lately more and more intimate with Bolton. You know I sent you Caroline's letter about him. Well, really it seemed to me such a pity that two who are entirely devoted to each other

should be living without the least comfort of inter-
communion, that I could not help just trying the least
little bit to bring them together.   Harry rather warned
me not to do it.   These men are so prudent; their
counsels seem rather cold to our hearts—is it not so,
mother?   Harry advised me not to name the subject to
Bolton, and said *he* would not dare do it for the world.
Well, that's just because he's a man; he does not know
how differently men receive the approaches of a woman.
In fact, I soon found that there was no subject on which
Bolton was so all alive and eager to hear.   When I
had once mentioned Caroline, he kept recurring to the
subject, evidently longing to hear more from her; and
so, one way and another, in firelight talks and moonlight walks, and times and places when words slip out
before one thinks, the whole of what is to be known of
Caroline's feelings went into his mind, and all that might
be known of his to her passed into mine.   I, in short,
became a medium.   And do you think I was going to
let her fret her heart out in ignorance of anything I
could tell her?   Not if I know myself; in fact, I have
been writing volumes to Caroline, for I am determined
that no people made for each other shall go wandering
up and down this labyrinth of life, missing their way at
every turn, for want of what could be told them by some
friendly good fairy who has the clue.

Say now, mother, am I imprudent?   If I am, I can't
help it; the thing is done.   Bolton has broken the
silence and written to Caroline; and once letter-writing
is begun, you see, the rest follows.   Does it not?

Now the thing is done, Harry is rather glad of it, as
he usually is with the results of my conduct when I go
against his advice and the thing turns out all right; and,
what's of Harry better than that, when I get into a scrape
by going against his counsels, he never says, " I told you

so," but helps me out, and comforts me in the loveliest manner. Mother, dear, he does you credit, for you had the making of him! He never would have been the husband he is, if you had not been the mother you are.

You say you are interested in my old ladies across the way.

Yes, I really flatter myself that our coming into this neighborhood is quite a godsend to them. I don't know any that seemed to enjoy the evening more than they two. It was so long since they had been in any society, and their society power had grown cramped, stiff by disuse; but the light and brightness of our fireside, and the general friendly cheerfulness, seemed to wake them up. My sisters are admirable assistants. They are society girls in the best sense, and my dear little mamma is never so much herself as when she is devoting herself to entertaining others. Miss Dorcas told me, this morning, that she was thankful on her sister's account to have this prospect of a weekly diversion opened to her; for that she had so many sorrows and suffered so much, it was all she could do at times to keep her from sinking in utter despondency. What her troubles could have been Miss Dorcas did not say; but I know that her marriage was unhappy, and that she has lost all her children. But, at any rate, this acknowledgement from her that we have been a comfort and help to them gratifies me. It shows me that we were right in thinking that we need not run beyond our own neighborhood to find society full of interest and do our little part in the kindly work of humanity. Oh, don't let me forget to tell you that that lovely, ridiculous Jack of theirs, that they make such a pet of, insisted on coming to the party to look after them; waylaid the door, and got in, and presented himself in a striking attitude on an ottoman in the midst of the company, to Miss Dorcas's profound horror and our great amusement. Jack has now become the "dog of the regiment," and we think of issuing a season ticket in his behalf: for everybody pets him; he helps to make fun and conversation.

After all, my dear mother, I must say a grateful word in praise of my Mary. I pass for a first-rate house-keeper, and receive constant compliments for my lovely house, its charming arrangements, the ease with which I receive and entertain company, the smoothness and completeness with which everything goes on; and all the while, in my own conscience, I feel that almost all the credit is due to Mary. The taste in combination and arrangement is mine, to be sure—and I flatter myself on having some nice domestic theories; but after all, Mary's knowledge, and Mary's strength, and Mary's neatness and order, are the foundation on which all the structure is built. Of what use would be taste and beauty and refinement, if I had to do my own washing, or cook my own meals, or submit to the inroads of a tribe of untaught barbarians, such as come from the intelligence offices? How soon would they break my pretty teacups, and overwhelm my lovely *bijouterie* with a second Goth and Vandal irruption! So, with you, dear mother, you see I do justice to Mary, strong and kind, whom nobody thinks of and nobody praises, and yet who enables me to do all that I do. I believe she truly loves me with all the warmth of an Irish heart, and I love her in return; and I give her this credit with you, to absolve my own conscience for taking so much more than is due to myself in the world. But what a long letter I am writing! Writing to you is talking, and you know what a chatter-box I am; but you won't be tired of hearing all this from us. Your loving EVA.

ST. JOHN was seated in his study, with a book of meditations before him on which he was endeavoring to fix his mind. In the hot, dusty, vulgar atmosphere of modern life, it was his daily effort to bring around himself the shady coolness, the calm conventual stillness, that breathes through such writers as St. Francis de Sales and Thomas à Kempis, men with a genius for devotion, who have left to mankind records of the mile-stones and road-marks by which they traveled towards the highest things. Nor should the most stringent Protestant fail to honor that rich and grand treasury of the experience of devout spirits of which the Romish Church has been the custodian. The hymns and prayers and pious meditations which come to us through this channel are particularly worthy of a cherishing remembrance in this dusty, materialistic age. To St. John they had a double charm, by reason of their contrast with the sterility of the religious forms of his early life. While enough of the Puritan and Protestant remained in him to prevent his falling at once into the full embrace of Romanism, he still regarded the old fabric with a softened, poetic tenderness; he "took pleasure in her stones and favored the dust thereof."

Nor is it to be denied that in the history of the Romish Church are records of heroism and self-devotion which might justly inspire with ardor the son of a line of Puritans. Who can go beyond St. Francis Xavier in the signs of an apostle? Who labored with more utter

self-surrender than Father Claver for the poor negro
slaves of South America? And how magnificent are those
standing Orders of Charity, composed of men and women
of that communion, that have formed from age to age
a life-guard of humanity, devoted to healing the sick,
sheltering and educating the orphans, comforting the
dying!

A course of eager reading in this direction might
make it quite credible even that a Puritan on the rebound
should wish to come as near such a church as is possible
without sacrifice of conscience and reason.

In the modern Anglican wing of the English Church
St. John thought he had found the blessed medium.
There he believed were the signs of the devotion, the
heroism and self-sacrifice of the primitive Catholic
Church, without the hindrances and incrustations of
superstition.   That little record, "Ten Years in St.
George's Mission," was to him the seal of their calling.
There he read of men of property devoting their entire
wealth, their whole time and strength, to the work of
regenerating the neglected poor of London. He read
of a district that at first could be entered only under the
protection of the police, where these moral heroes began
their work of love amid the hootings and howlings of
the mob and threats of personal violence,—the scoff and
scorn of those they came to save; and how by the might
of Christian love and patience these savage hearts were
subdued, these blasphemies turned to prayers; and how
in this dark district arose churches, schools, homes for
the destitute, reformatories for the lost. No wonder St.
John, reading of such a history, felt, "This is the church
for me." Perhaps a wider observation might have shown
him that such labors and successes are not peculiar to
the ritualist, that to wear the cross outwardly is not
essential to bearing the cross inwardly, and that without

signs and the symbolism of devout forms, the spirit of love, patience and self-denial can and does accomplish the same results.

St. John had not often met Bolton before that evening at the Henderson's. There, for the first time, he had had a quiet, uninterrupted conversation with him; and, from the first, there had been felt between them that constitutional sympathy that often unites widely varying natures, like the accord of two different strings of an instrument.

Bolton was less of an idealist than St. John, with a wider practical experience and a heavier mental caliber. He was in no danger of sentimentalism, and yet there was about him a deep and powerful undertone of feeling that inclined him in the same direction with Mr. St. John. There are men, and very strong men, whose natures gravitate towards Romanism with a force only partially modified by intellectual convictions: they would be glad to believe it if they could.

Bolton was an instance of a man of high moral and intellectual organization, of sensitive conscience and intense sensibility, who, with the highest ideal of manhood and of the purposes to which life should be devoted, had come to look upon himself as an utter failure. An infirmity of the brain and the flesh had crept upon him in the unguarded period of youth, had struck its poison through his system, and weakened the power of the will, till all the earlier part of his life had been a series of the most mortifying failures. He had fallen from situation after situation, where he had done work for a season : and, each time, the agony of his self-reproach and despair had been doubled by the reproaches and expostulations of many of his own family friends, who poured upon bare nerves the nitric acid of reproach. He had seen the hair of his mother slowly and surely whitening in the sickening anxieties and disappointments which he had brought. Loving her with almost a lover's fondness, desiring above all things to be her staff and stay, he had felt himself to be to her only an anxiety and a disappointment.

When, at last, he had gained a foothold and a place in the press, he was still haunted with the fear of recurring failure. He who has two or three times felt his sanity give way, and himself become incapable of rational control, never thereafter holds himself secure. And so it was with this overpowering impulse to which Bolton had been subjected; he did not know at what time it might sweep over him again.

Of late, his intimacy had been sought by Eva, and he had yielded to the charm of her society. It was impossible for a nature at once so sympathetic and so transparent as hers to mingle intimately with another without learning and betraying much. The woman's tact at once divined that his love for Caroline had only grown with time, and the scarce suppressed eagerness with which he listened to any tidings from her led on from step to step in mutual confidence, till there was nothing more to be told, and Bolton felt that the only woman he had ever loved, loved him in return with a tenacity and intensity which would be controlling forces in her life.

It was with a bitter pleasure nearly akin to pain that this conviction entered his soul. To a delicate moral organization, the increase of responsibility, with distrust of ability to meet it, is a species of torture. He feared himself destined once more to wreck the life and ruin the hopes of one dearer than his own soul, who was devoting herself to him with a woman's uncalculating fidelity.

This agony of self-distrust, this conscious weakness in his most earnest resolutions and most fervent struggles, led Bolton to wish with all his heart that the beau-

tiful illusion of an all-powerful church in which still
resided the visible presence of Almighty God might be a
reality. His whole soul sometimes cried out for such a
visible Helper—for a church with power to bind and
loose, with sacraments which should supplement human
weakness by supernatural grace, with a priesthood competent to forgive sin and to guide the penitent. It was
simply and only because his clear, well-trained intelligence could see no evidence of what he longed to believe, that the absolute faith was wanting.

He was not the only one in this perplexed and hopeless struggle with life and self and the world who has
cried out for a visible temple, such as had the ancient
Jew; for a visible High-Priest, who should consult the
oracle for him and bring him back some sure message
from a living God.

When he looked back on the seasons of his failures,
he remembered that it was with vows and tears and
prayers of agony in his mouth that he had been swept
away by the burning temptation; that he had been
wrenched, cold and despairing, from the very horns of
the altar. Sometimes he looked with envy at those
refuges which the Romish Church provides for those
who are too weak to fight the battle of life alone, and
thought, with a sense of rest and relief, of entering some
of those religious retreats where a man surrenders his
whole being to the direction of another, and ends the
strife by laying down personal free agency at the feet
of absolute authority. Nothing but an unconvinced intellect—an inability to believe—stood in the way of this
entire self-surrender. This morning, he had sought Mr.
St. John's study, to direct his attention to the case of the
young woman whom he had rescued from the streets, the
night before.

Bolton's own personal experience of human weakness

and the tyranny of passion had made him intensely pitiful.   He looked on the vicious and the abandoned as a
man shipwrecked and swimming for his life looks on the
drowning who are floating in the waves around him;
and where a hand was wanting, he was prompt to stretch
it out.

There was something in that young, haggard face,
those sad, appealing eyes, that had interested him more
powerfully than usual, and he related the case with much
feeling to Mr. St. John, who readily promised to call and
ascertain if possible some further particulars about her.

"You did the very best possible thing for her," said
he, "when you put her into the care of the Church. The
Church alone is competent to deal with such cases."

Bolton ruminated within himself on the wild, dis-
eased impulses, the morbid cravings and disorders, the
complete wreck of body and soul that comes of such a
life as the woman had led, and then admired the serene
repose with which St. John pronounced that indefinite
power, the CHURCH, as competent to cast out the seven
devils of the Magdalen.

"I shall be very glad to hear good news of her," he
said; "and if the Church is strong enough to save such
as she, I shall be glad to know that too."

"You speak in a skeptical tone," said St. John.

"Pardon me: I know something of the difficulties,
physical and moral, which lie in the way," said Bolton.

"To them that believe, nothing shall be impossible,"
said St. John, his face kindling with ardor.

"And by the Church do you mean all persons who
have the spirit of Jesus Christ, or simply that portion of
them who worship in the form that you do?"

"Come, now," said St. John, "the very form of your
question invites to a long historic argument; and I am
sure you did not mean to draw that on your head."

"Some other time, though," said Bolton, "if you will undertake to convince me of the existence in this world of such a power as you believe in, you will find me certainly not unwilling to believe. But, this morning, I have but a brief time to spend. Farewell, for the present."

And with a hearty hand-shake the two parted.

CHAPTER XXII

BOLTON TO CAROLINE.

I HAD not thought to obtrude myself needlessly on you ever again. Oppressed with the remembrance that I have been a blight on a life that might otherwise have been happy, I thought my only expiation was silence. But it had not then occurred to me that possibly you could feel and be pained by that silence. But of late I have been very intimate with Mrs. Henderson, whose mind is like those crystalline lakes we read of—a pebble upon the bottom is evident. She loves you so warmly and feels for you so sympathetically that, almost unconsciously, when you pour your feelings into her heart, they are revealed to me through the transparent medium of her nature. I confess that I am still so selfish as to feel a pleasure in the thought that you cannot forget me. I cannot forget you. I never have forgotten you, I believe, for a waking conscious hour since that time when your father shut the door of his house between you and me. I have demonstrated in my own experience that there may be a double consciousness all the while going on, in which the presence of one person should seem to pervade every scene of life. You have been with me, even in those mad fatal seasons when I have been swept from reason and conscience and hope —it has added bitterness to my humiliation in my weak hours; but it has been motive and courage to rise up again and again and renew the fight—the fight that must last as long as life lasts; for, Caroline, this is so. In

some constitutions, with some hereditary predispositions,
the indiscretions and ignorances of youth leave a
fatal irremediable injury. Though the sin be in the
first place one of inexperience and ignorance, it is one
that nature never forgives. The evil once done can
never be undone; no prayers, no entreaties, no resolutions, can change the consequences of violated law.
The brain and nerve force, once vitiated by poisonous
stimulants, become thereafter subtle tempters and trai-
tors, forever lying in wait to deceive and urging to ruin;
and he who is saved, is saved so as by fire. Since it is
your unhappy fate to care so much for me, I owe to you
the utmost frankness. I must tell you plainly that I am
an unsafe man. I am like a ship with powder on board
and a smouldering fire in the hold. I must warn my
friends off, lest at any moment I carry ruin to them,
and they be drawn down in my vortex. We can be
friends, dear friends; but let me beg you, think as little
of me as you can. Be a friend in a certain degree, after
the manner of the world, rationally, and with a wise
regard to your own best interests—you who are worth
five hundred times what I am—you who have beauty,
talent, energy—who have a career opening before you,
and a most noble and true friend in Miss Ida; do not
let your sympathies for a very worthless individual lead
you to defraud yourself of all that you should gain in
the opportunities now open to you. Command my services for you in the literary line whenever they may be
of the slightest use. Remember that nothing in the
world makes me so happy as an opportunity to serve
you. Treat me as you would a loyal serf, whose only
thought is to live and die for you; as the princess of
the middle ages treated the knight of low degree, who
devoted himself to her service. There is nothing *you*
could ask me to do for you that would not be to me a

pleasure; and all the more so, if it involved any labor
or difficulty. In return, be assured, that merely by being
the woman you are, merely by the love which you have
given and still give to one so unworthy, you are a constant strength to me, an encouragement never to faint
in a struggle which must last as long as this life lasts.
For although we must not forget that life, in the *best*
sense of the word, lasts forever, yet this first mortal
phase of it is, thank God, but short. There is another
and a higher life for those whose life has been a failure
here. Those who die fighting—even though they fall,
many times trodden under the hoof of the enemy—will
find themselves there made more than conquerors
through One who hath loved them.

In this age, when so many are giving up religion,
hearts like yours and mine, Caroline, that know the real
strain and anguish of this present life, are the ones to
appreciate the absolute necessity of faith in the great
hereafter. Without this, how cruel is life! How bitter,
how even unjust, the weakness and inexperience with
which human beings are pushed forth amid the grind-
ing and clashing of natural laws—laws of whose operation they are ignorant and yet whose penalties are inexorable! If there be not a Guiding Father, a redeeming
future, how dark is the prospect of this life! and who
can wonder that the ancients, many of the best of them,
considered suicide as one of the reserved rights of human nature? Without religious faith, I certainly should.
I am making this letter too long; the pleasure of speaking to you tempts me still to prolong it, but I forbear.

Ever yours, devotedly, BOLTON.

CAROLINE TO BOLTON.

My Dear Friend: How can I thank you for the confidence you have shown me in your letter? You were

not mistaken in thinking that this long silence has been cruel to me. It is more cruel to a woman than it can possibly be to a man, because if to him silence be a pain, he yet is conscious all the time that he has the power to break it; he has the right to speak at any time, but a woman must die silent. Every fiber of her being says this. She cannot speak, she must suffer as the dumb animals suffer.

I have, I confess, at times, been bitterly impatient of this long reserve, knowing, as I did, that you had not ceased to feel what you once felt. I saw, in our brief interviews in New York, that you loved me still. A woman is never blind to that fact, with whatever care it is sought to be hidden. I saw that you felt all you once professed, and yet were determined to conceal it, and treat with me on the calm basis of ordinary friendship, and sometimes I was indignant: forgive me the injustice.

You see that such a course is of no use, as a means of making one forget. To know one's self passionately beloved by another who never avows it, is something dangerous to the imagination. It gives rise to a thousand restless conjectures, and is fatal to peace. We can reconcile ourselves in time to any *certainty;* it is only when we are called upon to accommodate ourselves to possibilities, uncertain as vaporous clouds, that we weary ourselves in fruitless efforts.

Your letter avows what I knew before; what you often told me in our happy days: and I now say in return that I, like you, have *never forgotten*; that your image and presence have been to me as mine to you, ever a part of my consciousness through all these years of separation. And now you ask me to change all this into a cool and prudent friendship, after the manner of the world; that is to say, to take *all* from you, to accept

K

the entire devotion of your heart and life, but be careful to risk nothing in return, to keep at a safe distance from your possible troubles, lest I be involved.

Do you think me capable of this? Is it like me? and what would you think and say to a friend who should make the same proposition to you? Put it to yourself: what would you think of yourself, if you could be so coldly wary and prudent with regard to a friend who was giving to you the whole devotion of heart and life?

No, dear friend, this is all idle talk. Away with it! I feel that I am capable of as entire devotion to you as I know you are to me; never doubt it. The sad fatality which clouds your life makes this feeling only the more intense; as we feel for those who are a part of our own hearts, when in suffering and danger. In one respect, my medical studies are an advantage to me. They have placed me at a stand-point where my judgment on these questions and subjects is different from those of ordinary women. An understanding of the laws of physical being, of the conditions of brain and nerve forces, may possibly at some future day bring a remedy for such sufferings as yours. I look for this among the possible triumphs of science,—it adds interest to the studies and lectures I am pursuing. I shall not be to you what many women are to the men whom they love, an added weight to fall upon you if you fall, to crush you under the burden of my disappointments and anxieties and distresses. Knowing that your heart is resolute and your nature noble, a failure, supposing such a possibility, would be to me only like a fever or a paralysis,—a subject for new care and watchfulness and devotion, not one for tears or reproaches or exhortations.

There are lesions of the will that are no more to be considered subject to moral condemnation than a strain of the spinal column or a sudden fall, from paralysis. It is a misfortune; and to real true affection, a misfortune only renders the sufferer more dear and redoubles devotion.

Your letter gives me courage to live—courage to pursue the course set before me here. I will make the most of myself that I can for your sake, since all I am or can be is yours. Already I hope that I am of use to you in opening the doors of confidence. Believe me, dear, nothing is so bad for the health of the mind or the body as to have a constant source of anxiety and apprehension that cannot be spoken of to anybody. The mind thus shut within itself becomes a cave of morbid horrors. I believe these unshared fears, these broodings, and dreads unspoken, often fulfill their own prediction by the unhealthy states of mind that they bring.

The chambers of the soul ought to be daily opened and aired; the sunshine of a friend's presence ought to shine through them, to dispel sickly damps and the malaria of fears and horrors. If I could be with you and see you daily, my presence should cheer you, my faith in you should strengthen your faith in yourself.

For my part, I can see how the very sensitiveness of your moral temperament which makes you so dread a failure, exposes you to fail. I think the near friends of persons who have your danger often hinder instead of helping them by the manifestation of their fears and anxieties. They think there is no way but to "pile up the agony," to intensify the sense of danger and responsibility, when the fact is, the subject of it is feeling now all the strain that human nerves can feel without cracking.

We all know that we can walk with a cool head across a narrow plank only one foot from the ground. But put the plank across a chasm a thousand feet in depth, and the head swims. We have the same capacity

in both cases; but, in the latter, the awfulness of the
risk induces a nervous anxiety that amounts to a paralysis of the will.

Don't, therefore, let this dread grow on you by the
horror of lonely brooding. Treat it as you would the
liability to any other disease, openly, rationally and hope-
fully; and keep yourself in the daily light and warmth
of sympathetic intercourse with friends who understand
you and can help you. There are Eva and Harry—
noble, true friends, indebted to you for many favors,
and devoted to you with a loyal faithfulness. Let their
faith and mine in you strengthen your belief in yourself.
And don't, above all things, take any load of responsibility about *my* happiness, and talk about being the
blight and shadow on my life. I trust I am learning that
we were sent into this world, not to clamor for happiness, but to do our part in a life-work. What matter is
it whether I am happy or not, if I do my part? I know
all the risks and all the dangers that come from being
identified, heart and soul, with the life of another as I
am with yours. I know the risks, and am ready to face
them. I am ready to live for you and die for you, and
count it all joy to the last.

I was much touched by what you said of those who
have died defeated yet fighting. Yes, it is my belief
that many a poor soul who has again and again failed
in the conflict has yet put forth more effort, practiced
more self-denial, than hundreds of average Christians;
and He who knows what the trial is, will judge them
tenderly—that is to say, justly.

But for you there must be a future, even in this life.
I am assured of it, and you must believe it: you must
believe with my faith, and hope in my hope. Come
what will, I am, heart and soul and forever,

Yours,   CAROLINE.

CHAPTER XXIII

THE SISTERS OF ST. BARNABAS.

WHO was St. Barnabas? We are told in the book of the Acts of the Apostles that he was a man whose name signified a "son of consolation." It must at once occur that such a saint is very much needed in this weary world of ours, and most worthy to be the patron of an "order."

To comfort human sorrow, to heal and help the desolate and afflicted, irrespective either of their moral worth or of any personal reward, is certainly a noble and praiseworthy object.

Nor can any reasonable objection be made to the custom of good women combining for this purpose into a class or order, to be known by the name of such a primitive saint, and wearing a peculiar livery to mark their service, and having rites and ceremonials such as to them seem helpful for this end. Surely the work is hard enough, and weary enough, to entitle the doers thereof to do it in their own way, as they feel they best can, and to have any sort of innocent helps in the way of signs and symbols that may seem to them desirable.

Yet the Sisters of St. Barnabas had been exposed to a sort of modern form of persecution from certain vigorous-minded Protestants, as tending to Romanism. A clamor had been raised about them for wearing large crosses, for bowing before altars, and, in short, for a hundred little points of Ritualism; and it was held that a proper zeal for Protestantism required their ejection

from a children's refuge, where, with much patience and
Christian mildness, they were taking care of sick babies
and teaching neglected street children.   Mrs. Maria
Wouvermans, with a committee of ladies equally zealous
for the order of the church and excited about the
dangers of Popery, had visited the refuge and pursued
the inquisition even to the private sleeping apartments of
the Sisters, unearthing every symptom of principle or
practice that savored of approach to the customs of the
Scarlet Woman; and, as the result of relentless inquisition and much vigorous catechising, she and her associates made such reports as induced the Committee of
Supervision to withdraw the charity from the Sisters of
St. Barnabas, and place it in other hands.   The Sisters,
thus ejected, had sought work in other quarters of the
great field of human suffering and sorrow.   A portion of
them had been enabled by the charity of friends to rent
a house to be devoted to the purposes of nursing destitute sick children, with dormitories also where homeless
women could find temporary shelter.

The house was not a bit more conventual or mediæval than the most common-place of New York houses.
It is true, one of the parlors had been converted into a
chapel, dressed out and arranged according to the
preferences of these good women.   It had an altar, with
a gilded cross flanked by candles, which there is no
denying were sometimes lighted in the day-time.   The
altar was duly dressed with white, red, green, violet or
black, according as the traditional fasts or feasts of the
Church came round.   There is no doubt that this simple
chapel, with its flowers, and candles, and cross, and its
little ceremonial, was an immense comfort and help to
these good women in the work that they were doing.
But the most rigid Protestant, who might be stumbled by
this little attempt at a chapel, would have been melted

into accord when he went into the long bright room full
of little cribs and cradles, where child invalids of different ages and in different stages of convalesence were
made happy amid flowers, and toys, and playthings, by
the ministration of the good women who wore the white
caps and the large crosses. It might occur to a thoughtful mind, that devotion to a work so sweetly unselfish
might well entitle them to wear any kind of dress and
pursue any kind of method, unchallenged by criticism.

In a neat white bed of one of the small dormitories
in the upper part of this house, was lying in a delirious
fever the young woman whom Bolton had carried there
on the night of our story. The long black hair had
become loosened by the restless tossing of her head
from side to side; her brow was bent in a heavy frown,
made more intense by the blackness of her eyebrows;
her large, dark eyes were wandering wildly to and fro
over every object in the room, and occasionally fixing
themselves with a strange look of inquiry on the Sister
who, in white cap and black robe, sat by her bedside,
changing the wet cloths on her burning head, and moist-
ening her parched lips from time to time with a spoonful
of water.

"I can't think who you are," she muttered, as the
Sister with a gentle movement put a fresh, cool cloth on
her forehead.

"Never mind, poor child," said the sweet voice in
reply; "try to be quiet."

"Quiet! *me* be quiet!—that's pretty well! Me!" and
she burst into weak, hysteric laughter.

"Hush, hush!" said the Sister, making soothing motions with her hands.

"The wandering eyes closed a few moments in a
feverish drowse. In a moment more, she started with a
wild look.

"Mother! mother! where are you? I can't find you. I've looked and looked till I'm so tired, and I can't find you. Mother, come to me,—I'm sick!"—and the girl rose and threw out her arms wildly.

The Sister passed her arm round her tenderly and spoke with a gentle authority, making her lie down again. Then, in a sweet low voice, she began singing a hymn :

"Jesus, lover of my soul,
 Let me to thy bosom fly,
While the billows near me roll,
 While the tempest still is high."

As she sung, the dark sad eyes fixed themselves upon her with a vague, troubled questioning. The Sister went on :

"Hide me, O my Saviour, hide,
 Till the storm of life is past,
Safe into the haven guide,
 Oh, receive my soul at last."

It was just day-dawn, and the patient had waked from a temporary stupor produced by a narcotic which had been given a few hours before to compose her.

The purple-and-rose color of dawn was just touching faintly everything in the room. Another Sister entered softly, to take the place of the one who had watched for the last four hours.

"How is she?" she said.

"Quite out of her head, poor thing. Her fever is very high."

"We must have the doctor," said the other. "She looks like a very sick girl."

"That she certainly is. She slept, under the opiate, but kept starting, and frowning, and muttering in her sleep; and this morning she waked quite wild."

"She must have got dreadfully chilled, walking so late in the street—so poorly clad, too!"

With this brief conversation, the second sister assumed her place by the bedside, and the first went to get some rest in her own room.

As day grew brighter, the singing of the matins in the chapel came floating up in snatches; and the sick girl listened to it with the same dazed and confused air of inquiry with which she looked on all around.

"Who is singing," she said to herself. "It's pretty, and good. But how came I here? I was so cold, so cold—out there!—and now it's so hot. Oh, my head! my head!"

A few hours later, Mr. St. John called at the Refuge to inquire after the new inmate.

Mr. St. John was one of the patrons of the Sisters. He had contributed liberally to the expenses of the present establishment, and stood at all times ready to assist with influence and advice.

The Refuge was, in fact, by the use of its dormitories, a sort of receiving station for homeless and desolate people, where they might find temporary shelter, where their wants might be inquired into, and help found for them according to their need.

After the interview with Bolton had made him acquainted with the state of the case, Mr. St. John went immediately to the Refuge. He was received in the parlor by a sweet-faced, motherly woman, with her white cap and black robe, and with a large black cross depending from her girdle. There was about her an air of innocent sanctity and seclusion from the out-door bustle of modern life that was refreshing.

She readily gave him an account of the new inmate, whose sad condition had excited the sympathy of all the Sisters.

She had come to them, she said, in a state of most woeful agitation and distress, having walked the streets on a freezing night till a late hour, in very insufficient clothing. Immediately on being received, she began to have violent chills, followed by burning fever, and had been all night tossing restlessly and talking wildly.

This morning, they had sent for the doctor, who pronounced her in a brain fever, and in a condition of great danger. She was still out of her mind, and could give no rational account of herself.

"It is piteous to hear her call upon her mother," said the Sister. "Poor child! perhaps her mother is distressing herself about her."

Mr. St. John promised to secure the assistance and sympathy of some benevolent women to aid the Sisters in their charge, and took his leave, promising to call daily.

CHAPTER XXIV

EVA TO HARRY'S MOTHER

MY DEAR MOTHER: When I wrote you last we were quite prosperous, having just come through with our first evening as a great success; and everybody since has been saying most agreeable things to us about it. Last Thursday, we had our second, and it was even pleasanter than the last, because people had got acquainted, so that they really wanted to see each other again. There was a most charming atmosphere of ease and sociability. Bolton and Mr. St. John are getting quite intimate. Mr. St. John, too, develops quite a fine social talent, and has come out wonderfully. The side of a man that one sees in the church and the pulpit is after all only one side, as we have discovered. I find that he has quite a gift in conversation, when you fairly get him at it. Then, his voice for singing comes into play, and he and Angie and Dr. Campbell and Alice make up a quartette quite magnificent for non-professionals. Angie has a fine soprano, and Alice takes the contralto, and the Doctor, with his great broad shoulders and deep chest, makes a splendid bass. Mr. St. John's tenor is really very beautiful. It is one of those penetrating, sympathetic voices that indicate both feeling and refinement, and they are all of them surprised and delighted to find how well they go together. Thursday evening they went on from thing to thing, and found that they could sing this and that and the other, till the evening took a good deal the form of a musical. But never mind, it brought them acquainted with each other and made them look forward to the next reunion as something agreeable. Ever since, the doctor goes round humming tunes, and says he wants St. John to try the tenor of this and that, and really has quite lost sight of his being anything else but a musical brother. So here is the common ground I wanted to find between them.

The doctor has told Mr. St. John to call on him whenever he can make him useful in his visits among the poor. Our doctor loves to *talk* as if he were a hard-hearted, unbelieving pirate, who didn't care a straw for his fellow-creatures, while he loses no opportunity to do anybody or anything a kindness.

You know I told you in my last letter about a girl that Harry and Bolton found in the street, the night of our first reception, and that they took her to the St. Barnabas Refuge. The poor creature has been lying there ever since, sick of a brain fever, caught by cold and exposure, and Dr. Campbell has given his services daily. If she had been the richest lady in the land, he could not have shown more anxiety and devotion to her than he has, calling twice and sometimes three times a day, and one night watching nearly all night. She is still too low and weak to give any account of herself; all we know of her is that she is one of those lost sheep, to seek whom the Good Shepherd would leave the ninety nine who went not astray. I have been once or twice to sit by her, and relieve the good Sisters who have so much else to do; and Angelique and Alice have also taken their turns. It seems very little for us to do, when these good women spend all their time and all their strength for those who have no more claim on them than they have on us.

It is a week since I began this letter, and something quite surprising to me has just developed.

I told you we had been to help nurse the poor girl at

the Sisters', and the last week she has been rapidly mending. Well, yesterday, as I didn't feel very well, and my Mary is an excellent nurse, I took her there to sit with the patient in my place, when a most strange scene ensued. The moment Mary looked on her, she recognized her own daughter, who had left her some years ago with a bad man. Mary had never spoken to me of this daughter, and I only knew, in a sort of general way, that she had left her mother under some painful circumstances. The recognition was dreadfully agitating to Mary and to the poor girl; indeed, for some time it was feared that the shock would produce a relapse. The Sisters say that the poor thing has been constantly calling for her mother in her distress.

It really seemed, for the time, as if Mary were going to be wholly unnerved. She has a great deal of that respectable pride of family character which belongs to the better class of the Irish, and it has been a bitter humiliation to her to have to acknowledge her daughter's shame to me; but I felt that it would relieve her to tell the whole story to some one, and I drew it all out of her. This poor Maggie had the misfortune to be very handsome. She was so pretty as a little girl, her mother tells me, as to attract constant attention; and I rather infer that the father and mother both made a pet and plaything of her, and were unboundedly indulgent. The girl grew up handsome, and thoughtless, and self-confident, and so fell an easy prey to a villain who got her to leave her home, on a promise of marriage which he never kept. She lived with him a while in one place and another, and he became tired of her and contrived to place her in a house of evil, where she was entrapped and enslaved for a long time. Having by some means found out where her mother was living, she escaped from her employers, and hung round the house irresolutely for some time, wishing but fearing to present herself, and when she spoke to Harry in the street, the night after our party, she was going in a wild, desperate way to ask something about her mother—knowing that he was the man with whom she was living.

Such seems to be her story; but I suppose, what with misery and cold, and the coming on of the fever, the poor thing hardly had her senses, or knew what she was about—the fever must have been then upon her.

So you see, dear mother, I was wishing in my last that I could go off with Sibyl Selwyn on her mission to the lost sheep, and now here is one brought to my very door. Is not this sent to me as my work? as if the good Lord had said, "No, child, your feet are not strong enough to go over the stones and briars, looking for the lost sheep; you are not able to take them out of the jaws of the wolf; but here is a poor wounded lamb that I leave at your door—that is your part of the great work." So I understand it, and I have already told Mary that as soon as Maggie is able to sit up, we will take her home with us, and let her stay with us till she is strong and well, and then we will try and put her back into good respectable ways, and keep her from falling again.

I think persons in our class of life cannot be too considerate of the disadvantages of poor working women in the matter of bringing up children.

A very beautiful girl in that walk of life is exposed to solicitation and temptation that never come near to people in our stations. We are guarded on all hands by our very position. I can see in this poor child the wreck of what must have been very striking beauty. Her hair is lovely, her eyes are wonderfully fine, and her hands, emaciated as she is, are finely formed and delicate. Well, being beautiful, she was just like any other young girl—her head was turned by flattery. She was silly and foolish, and had not the protections and barriers that are around us, and she fell. Well, then, we that have been more fortunate must help her up. Is it not so?

So, dear Mother, my mission work is coming to me. I need not go out for it. I shall write more of this in a day or two.

Ever yours,   EVA.

CHAPTER XXV

AUNT MARIA ENDEAVORS TO SET MATTERS RIGHT.

M RS. MARIA WOUVERMANS was one of those forces in creation to whom quiet is impossible. Watchfulness, enterprise and motion were the laws of her existence, as incessantly operating as any other laws of nature.

When we last saw her, she was in high ill-humor with her sister, Mrs. Van Arsdel, with Alice and Eva, and the whole family. She revenged herself upon them, as such good creatures know how to do, by heaping coals of fire on their heads in the form of ostentatiously untiring and uncalled-for labors for them all. The places she explored to get their laces mended and their quillings done up and their dresses made, the pilgrimages she performed in omnibuses, the staircases she climbed, the men and women whom she browbeat and circumvented in bargains—all to the advantage of the Van Arsdel purse— were they not recounted and told over in a way to appall the conscience of poor, easy Mrs. Van Arsdel, whom they summarily convicted of being an inefficient little know-nothing, and of her girls, who thus stood arraigned for the blackest ingratitude in not appreciating Aunt Maria?

"I'll tell you what it is, Alice," said Eva, when Aunt Maria's labors had come to the usual climax of such smart people, and laid her up with a sick-headache, "we girls have just got to make up with Aunt Maria, or she'll tear down all New York. I always notice that when she's out with us she goes tearing about in this way, using herself up for us—doing things no mortal wants her to do, and yet that it seems black ingratitude not to thank her for. Now, Alice, you are the one, this time, and you must just go and sit with her and make up, as I did."

"But, Eva, *I* know the trouble you fell into, letting her and mother entangle you with Wat Sydney, and I'm not going to have it happen again. I will not be compromised in any way or shape with a man whom I never mean to marry."

"Oh, well, I think by this time Aunt Maria understands this, only she wants you to come back and be loving to her, and say you're sorry you can't, etc. After all, Aunt Maria is devoted to us and is miserable when we are out with her."

"Well, I hate to have friends that one must be always bearing with and deferring to."

"Well, Alice, you remember Mr. St. John's sermons on the trials of the first Christians—when he made us all feel that it would have been a blessed chance to go to the stake for our religion?"

"Yes; it was magnificent. I felt a great exaltation."

"Well, I'll tell you what I thought. It may be as heroic, and more difficult, to put down our own temper and make the first concession to an unreasonable old aunt who really loves us than to be martyrs for Christ. Nobody wants us to be martyrs now-a-days; but I think these things that make no show and have no glory are a harder cross to take up."

"Well, Eva, I'll do as you say," said Alice, after a few moments of silence, "for really you speak the truth. I don't know anything harder than to go and make concessions to a person who has acted as ridiculously as Aunt

Maria has, and who will take all your concessions and
never own a word on her side."

"Well, dear, what I think in these cases is, that I am
not perfect. There are always enough things where I
didn't do quite right for me to confess; and as to her
confessing, that's not *my* affair. What *I* have to do is to
cut loose from my own sins; they are mine, and hers
are hers."

"True," said Alice; "and the fact is, I did speak
improperly to Aunt Maria. She is older than I am. I
ought not to have said the things I did. I'm hot tempered, and always say more than I mean."

"Well, Ally, do as I did—confess everything you can
think of and then say, as I did, that you must still be
firm upon one point; and, depend upon it, Aunt Maria
will be glad to be friends again."

This conversation had led to an amelioration which
caused Aunt Maria to appear at Eva's second reunion in
her best point lace and with her most affable company
manners, whereby she quite won the heart of simple
Mrs. Betsey Benthusen, and was received with patroniz-
ing civility by Miss Dorcas. That good lady surveyed
Mrs. Wouvermans with an amicable scrutiny as a specimen of a really creditable production of modern New
York life. She took occasion to remark to her sister
that the Wouvermans were an old family of unquestioned
position, and that really Mrs. Wouvermans had acquired
quite the family air.

Miss Dorcas was one of those people who sit habitually on thrones of judgment and see the children of this
world pass before them, with but one idea, to determine
what she should think of them. What they were likely
to think of her, was no part of her concern. Her scruti-
nies and judgments were extremely quiet, tempered with
great moderation and Christian charity, and were so sel-

dom spoken to anybody else that they did no one any harm.

She was a spectator at the grand theater of life; it interested and amused her to watch the acting, but she kept her opinions, for the most part, to herself. The re-unions at Eva's were becoming most interesting to her as widening her sphere of observation. In fact, her intercourse with her sister could hardly be called society, it was so habitually that of a nurse with a patient. She said to her, of the many things which were in her mind, only those which she thought she could bear. She was always planning to employ Mrs. Betsey's mind with varied occupations to prevent her sinking into morbid gloom, and to say only such things of everybody and everything to her as would tranquilize and strengthen her. To Miss Dorcas, the little white-haired lady was still the beautiful child of past days—the indiscreet, flighty, pretty pet, to be watched, nursed, governed, re-strained and cared for. As for conversation, in the sense of an unrestricted speaking out of thoughts as they arose, it was long since Miss Dorcas had held it with any human being. The straight, tall old clock in the corner was not more lonely, more self-contained and ret-icent.

The next day after the re-union, Aunt Maria came at the appointed hour, with all due pomp and circumstance, to make her call upon the two sisters, and was received in kid gloves in the best parlor, properly darkened, so that the faces of the parties could scarcely be seen ; and then the three remarked upon the weather, the state of the atmosphere to-day and its probable state to-morrow. Mrs. Wouvermans was properly complimented upon her niece's delightful re-unions; whereat she drew herself up with suitable modesty, as one who had been the source and originator of it all—claiming property in charming

Mrs. Henderson as the girl of her bringing up, the work of her hands, the specimen of her powers, marshalled and equipped by her for the field of life; and in her delightful soirées, as in some sort a result of her management. It may be a consolation to those who are ever called to wrestle with good angels like Aunt Maria, that if they only hold on and overcome them, and hold their own independent way, the angels, so far from being angry, will immediately assume the whole merit of the result. On the whole, Aunt Maria, hearing on all sides flattering things of Mrs. Henderson's lovely house and charming evenings, was pluming herself visibly in this manner.

Now, as Eva, in one of those bursts of confidence in which she could not help pouring herself out to those who looked kindly on her, had talked over with Miss Dorcas all Aunt Maria's objections to her soirées, and her stringent advice against them, the good lady was quietly amused at this assumption of merit.

"My! how odd, Dorcas!" said Mrs. Betsey to her sister, after Mrs. Wouvermans had serenely courtesied herself out. "Isn't this the 'Aunt Maria' that dear Mrs. Henderson was telling you about, that made all those objections to her little receptions?"

"Oh, yes," said Miss Dorcas.

"But how strange; she really talks now as if she had started them."

"People usually adopt a good thing, if they find they can't hinder it," said Miss Dorcas.

"I think it is just the oddest thing in the world; in fact, I don't think it's really honest," said Mrs. Betsey.

"It's the way people always do," said Miss Dorcas; "nothing succeeds like success. Mrs. Wouvermans opposed the plan because she thought it wouldn't go. Now that she finds it goes, she is so delighted she thinks she must have started it herself."

In fact, Aunt Maria was in an uncommonly loving and genial frame about this time. Her fits of petulance generally had the good effect of a clearing-up thunder-shower—one was sure of clear skies for some time afterwards.

The only difficulty about these charming periods of general reconciliation was that when the good lady once more felt herself free of the family, and on easy terms all around with everybody, she immediately commenced in some new direction that process of managing other people's affairs which was an inevitable result of her nature. Therefore she came, one afternoon not long after, into her sister's dressing-room with an air of pre-occupation and mystery, which Mrs. Van Arsdel had learned to dread as a sign that Maria had something new upon her mind.

Shutting the doors carefully, with an air of great precaution and importance, she said: "Nellie, I've been wanting to talk to you; something will have to be done about Eva: it will never do to let matters go on as they are going."

Mrs. Van Arsdel's heart began to sink within her; she supposed that she was to be required in some way to meddle or interfere with her daughter. Now, if anything was to be done of an unpleasant nature, Mrs. Van Arsdel had always far rather that Maria would do it herself. But the most perplexing of her applications were when she began stirring up her ease-loving, indulgent self to fulfill any such purposes on her children. So she said, in a faltering voice, "What *is* the matter now, Maria?"

"Well, *what* should you think?" said Mrs. Wouvermans, emphasizing the words. "You know that good-for-nothing daughter of Mary's that lived with me, years ago?"

"That handsome girl? To be sure."

"Handsome! the baggage! I've no patience when I think of her, with her airs and graces; dressing so that she really was mistaken for one of the family! And such impertinence! I made her walk Spanish very quick——"

"Well?"

"Well, who do you suppose this sick girl is that Angelique and Alice have been helping take care of in the new hospital, or whatever you call it, that those Popish women have started up there?"

Now Mrs. Van Arsdel knew very well what Aunt Maria was coming to, but she only said, faintly,

"Well?"

"Its just that girl and no other, and a more impudent tramp and huzzy doesn't live."

"It really is very shocking," said Mrs. Van Arsdel.

"Shocking! well I should think it was, but that isn't all. Eva actually has taken this creature to her house, and is going to let her stay there."

"Oh, indeed?" said Mrs. Van Arsdel, faintly.

Now Mrs. Van Arsdel had listened sympathetically to Eva when, in glowing and tender words, she had avowed her intention of giving this help to a poor, bewildered mother, and this chance of recovery to an erring child, but in the sharp, nipping atmosphere of Aunt Maria's hard, dry, selfish common sense, the thing looked so utterly indefensible that she only breathed this faint inquiry.

"Yes," said Aunt Maria, "and it's all that Mary's art. She has been getting old and isn't what she was, and she means to get both her children saddled upon Eva, who is ignorant and innocent as a baby. Eva and her husband are no more fit to manage than two babes in the woods, and this set of people will make them no end of trouble. The girl is a perfect witch, and it will never do in the world. You ought to talk to her and tell her about the danger."

"But, Maria, I am not at all sure that it may not be Eva's duty to help Mary take care of her daughter."

"Well, if it was a daughter that had behaved herself decently; but this creature is a tramp—a street-walker! It is not respectable to have her in the house a minute."

"But where can she go?"

"That's none of our look out. I suppose there are asylums, or refuges, or something or other, for such creatures."

"But if the Sisters could take her in and take care of her, I'm sure Eva might keep her awhile; at least till she gets strong enough to find some place."

"Oh, those Sisters! Don't tell me! I've no opinion of them. Wasn't I on the committee, and didn't I find crucifixes, and rosaries, and prie-dieus, and the Lord knows what of Popish trinkets in their rooms? They are regular Jesuits, those women. It's just like 'em to take in tramps and nurse 'em.

"You know, Nellie, I warned you I never believed in this Mr. St. John and his goings on up there, and I foresee just what trouble Eva is going to be got into by having that sort of creature put in upon her. Maggie was the most conceited, impertinent, saucy hussy I ever saw. She had the best of all chances in my house, if she'd been of a mind to behave herself, for I give good wages, pay punctually, and mine is about as good a house for a young woman to be trained in as there is. Nobody can say that Maggie didn't have a fair chance with me!"

"But really, Maria, I'm afraid that unless Mary can take care of her daughter at Eva's she'll leave her altogether and go to housekeeping, and Eva never would know how to get along without Mary."

"Oh, nonsense! I'll engage to find Eva a good, stout girl—or two of them, for that matter, since she thinks she could afford two—that will do better than Mary, who is getting older every year and less capable. I make it a principle to cut off girls that have sick friends and all such entanglements and responsibilities, right away; it unfits them for my service."

"Yes, but, Maria, you must consider that Eva isn't like you. Eva really is fond of Mary, and had rather have her there than a younger and stronger woman. Mary has been an old servant in the family. Eva has grown up with her. She loves Eva like a child."

"Oh, pshaw!" said Aunt Maria. "Now, of all things, don't be sentimental about servants. It's a little too absurd. We are to attend to our own interests!"

"But you see, sister," said Mrs. Van Arsdel, "Eva *is* just what you call sentimental, and it wouldn't do the least good for *me* to talk to her. She's a married woman, and she and her husband have a right to manage their affairs in their own way. Now, to tell the truth, Eva told me about this affair, and on the whole "—here Mrs. Van Arsdel's voice trembled weakly—"on the whole, I didn't think it would do any good, you know, to oppose her; and really, Maria, I was sorry for poor Mary. You don't know, you never had a daughter, but I couldn't help thinking that if I were a poor woman, and a daughter of mine had gone astray, I should be so glad to have a chance given her to do better; and so I really couldn't find it in my heart to oppose Eva."

"Well, you'll see what'll come of it," said Aunt Maria, who had stood, a model of hard, sharp, uncompromising common sense, looking her sister down during this weak apology for the higher wisdom. For now, as in the days of old, the wisdom of the cross is foolishness

to the wise and prudent of the world; and the heavenly
arithmetic, which counts the one lost sheep more than
the ninety and nine that went not astray, is still the
arithmetic, not of earth, but of heaven. There are many
who believe in the Trinity, and the Incarnation, and all
the articles of the Athanasian and Nicene Creeds, to
whom this wisdom of the Master is counted as folly:
"For the natural man understandeth not the things of
the kingdom of God; they are foolishness unto him:
neither can he know them."

Now Aunt Maria was in an eminent degree a specimen of the feminine sort of " natural man."

That a young and happy wife, with a peaceful, prosperous home, should put a particle of her own happiness
to risk, or herself to inconvenience, for the sake of a poor
servant woman and a sinful child, was, in her view, folly
amounting almost to fatuity; and she inly congratulated
herself with the thought that her sister and Eva would
yet see themselves in trouble by their fine fancies and
sentimental benevolence.

"Well, sister," she said, rising and drawing her cashmere shawl in graceful folds round her handsome shoulders, "I thought I should come to you first, as you
really are the most proper person to talk to Eva; but if
you should neglect your duty, there is no reason why I
should neglect mine.

"I hear of a very nice, capable girl that has lived
five years with the Willises, who has had permission to
advertise from the house, and I am going to have an interview with her, and engage her provisionally, so that, if
Eva has a mind to listen to reason, there may be a way
for her to supply Mary's place at once. I've made up
my mind that, on the whole, it's best Mary should go,"
she added reflectively, as if she were the mistress of Eva's
house and person.

L

"I'm sorry to have you take so much trouble, Maria; I'm sure it won't do any good."

"Did you ever know me to shrink from any trouble or care or responsibility by which I could serve you and your children, Nellie? I may not be appreciated—I don't expect it—but I shall not swerve from my duty to you; at any rate, it's my duty to leave no stone unturned, and so I shall start out at once for the Willises. They are going to Europe for a year or two, and want to find good places for their servants."

And so Mrs. Van Arsdel, being a little frightened at the suggestions of Aunt Maria, began to think with herself that perhaps she had been too yielding, and made herself very uncomfortable in reflecting on positive evils that might come on Eva.

She watched her sister's stately, positive, determined figure as she went down the stairs with the decision of a general, gave a weak sigh, wished that she had not come, and, on the whole, concluded to resume her story where she had left off at Aunt Maria's entrance.

SHE STOOD OUTSIDE THE GATE.

THE trial of human life would be a much simpler and easier thing to meet, if the lines of right and wrong were always perfectly definite. We are happy so far to believe in our kind as to think that there are vast multitudes who, if they only knew exactly what was right and proper to be done, would do it at all hazards.

But *what is right* for me, in these particular circumstances?—in that question, as it constantly rises, lies the great stress of the trial of life.

We have, for our guidance, a Book of most high and unworldly maxims and directions, and the life of a Leader so exalted above all the ordinary conceptions and maxims of this world that a genuine effort to be a Christian, after the pattern and directions of Christ, at once brings us face to face with daily practical inquiries of the most perplexing nature.

Our friend, Mrs. Maria Wouvermans, was the very type and impersonation of this world's wisdom of the ordinary level. The great object of life being to insure ease, comfort, and freedom from annoyance to one's self and one's family, her views of duty were all conveniently arranged along this line. In her view, it was the first duty of every good housekeeper to look ahead and avoid every occasion whence might arise a possible inconvenience or embarrassment. It was nobody's duty, in her opinion, to have any trouble, if it could be avoided, or to risk having any. There were, of course, duties to the poor, which she settled for by a regular annual subscription to some well-recommended board of charity in her

most respectable church. That done, she regarded herself as clear for action, and bound to shake off in detail
any troublesome or embarrassing person that threatened
to be a burden to her, or to those of her family that she
felt responsible for.

On the other hand, Eva was possessed by an earnest
desire to make her religious profession mean something
adequate to those startling and constantly recurring
phrases in the Bible and the church service which spoke
of the Christian as a being of a higher order, led by another Spirit, and living a higher life than that of the
world in general. Nothing is more trying to an ingenu-
ous mind than the conviction of anything like a sham
and a pretense in its daily life.

Mr. St. John had lately been preaching a series of
sermons on the history and customs of the primitive
church, in hearing which the conviction often forced
itself on her mind that it was the unworldly life of the
first Christians which gave victorious power to the faith.
She was intimately associated with people who seemed
to her to live practically on the same plan. Here was
Sibyl Selwyn, whose whole life was an exalted mission
of religious devotion; there was her neighbor Ruth Baxter, associated as a lay sister with the work of her more
gifted friend. Here were the Sisters of St. Barnabas,
lovely, cultivated women who had renounced all selfish
ends and occupations in life, to give themselves to the
work of comforting the sorrowful and saving the lost.
Such people, she thought, fully answered to the terms in
which Christians were spoken of in the Bible. But
could she, if she lived only to brighten one little spot of
her own, if she shut out of its charmed circle all sight
or feeling of the suffering and sorrow of the world around
her, and made her own home a little paradise of ease and
forgetfulness, could she be living a Christian life?

When, therefore, she heard from the poor mother under her roof the tale of her secretly-kept shames, sorrows, and struggles for the daughter whose fate had filled her with misery, she accepted with a large-hearted inconsiderateness a mission of love towards the wanderer.

She carried it to her husband; and, like two kind-hearted, generous-minded young people, they resolved at once to make their home sacred by bringing into it this work of charity.

Now, this work would be far easier in most cases, if the sinner sought to be saved would step forthwith right across the line, and behave henceforth like a saint. But unhappily that is not to be expected. Certain it was, that Maggie, with her great, black eyes and her wavy black hair, was no saint. A petted, indulged child, with a strong, ungovernable nature, she had been whirled hither and thither in the tides of passion, and now felt less repentance for sin than indignation at her own wrongs. It might have been held a hopeful symptom that Maggie had, at least, so much real truthfulness in her as not to profess what she did not feel.

It was a fact that the constant hymns and prayers and services of the pious Sisters wearied her. They were too high for her. The calm, refined spirituality of these exalted natures was too far above her, and she joined their services at best with a patient acquiescence, feeling the while how sinful she must be to be so bored by them.

But for Eva she had a sort of wondering, passionate admiration. When she fluttered into her sick room, with all her usual little graceful array of ribbons and fanciful ornament, Maggie's dull eye would brighten, and she looked after her with delighted wonder. When she spoke to her tenderly, smoothed her pillow, put cologne on her laced handkerchief and laid it on her brow, poor Maggie felt awed and flattered by the attention, far more, it is to be feared, than if somebody more resembling the traditional angel had done it. This lively, sprightly little lady, so graceful, so pretty in all her motions and in all her belongings, seemed to poor worldly Maggie much more nearly what she would like an angel to be, in any world where she would have to live with them.

The Sisters, with their black robes, their white caps, and their solemn prayers, seemed to her so awfully good that their presence chilled her. She felt more subdued, but more sinful and more hopeless with them than ever.

In short, poor Maggie was yet a creature of this world, and of sense, and the spiritual world to her was only one dark, confused blurr, rather more appalling than attractive. A life like that of the Sisters, given to prayer and meditation and good works, was too high a rest for a soul growing so near the ground and with so few tendrils to climb by. Maggie could conceive of nothing more dreary. To her, it seemed like being always thinking of her sins; and that topic was no more agreeable a subject of meditation to Maggie than it is to any of us. Many people seem to feel that the only way of return for those who have wandered from the paths of virtue is the most immediate and utter self-abasement. There must be no effort at self-justification, no excusing one's self, no plea for abatement of condemnation. But let us Christians who have never fallen, in the grosser sense, ask ourselves if, with regard to our own particular sins and failings, we hold the same strict line of reckoning. Do we come down upon ourselves for our ill temper, for our selfishness, for our pride, and other respectable sins, as we ask the poor girl to do who has been led astray from virtue?

Let us look back and remember how the Master once coupled an immaculate Pharisee and a fallen woman in one sentence as two debtors, both owing a sum to a creditor, and both having nothing to pay,—both freely forgiven by infinite clemency. It is a summing up of the case that is too often forgotten.

Eva's natural tact and delicacy stood her in stead in her dealings with Maggie, and made *her* touch upon the wounds of the latter more endurable than any other. Without reproof for the past, she expressed hope for the future.

"You shall come and stay with your mother at my house, Maggie," she said, cheerfully, "and we will make you useful. The fact is, your mother needs you; she is not so strong as she was, and you could save her a great many steps."

Now, Maggie still had skillful hands and a good many available worldly capacities. The very love of finery and of fine living which had once helped to entrap her, now came in play for her salvation. Something definite to do, is, in some crises, a far better medicine for a sick soul than any amount of meditation and prayer. One step fairly taken in a right direction, goes farther than any amount of agonized back-looking.

In a few days, Maggie made for herself in Eva's family a place in which she could feel herself to be of service. She took charge of Eva's wardrobe, and was zealous and efficient in ripping, altering and adapting articles for the adornment of her pretty mistress; and Eva never failed to praise and encourage her for every right thing she did, and never by word or look reminded her of the past.

Eva did not preach to Maggie; but sometimes, sitting at her piano while she sat sewing in an adjoining room, she played and sung some of those little melodies which

Sunday-schools have scattered as a sort of popular ballad literature. Words of piety, allied to a catching tune, are like seeds with wings—they float out in the air and drop in odd corners of the heart, to spring up in good purposes.

One of these little ballads reminded Eva of the night she first saw Maggie lingering in the street by her house:

> " I stood outside the gate,
>   A poor wayfaring child ;
> Within my heart there beat
>   A tempest fierce and wild.
> A fear oppressed my soul
>   That I might be too late ;
> And, oh, I trembled sore
>   And prayed—outside the gate,
>
> " ' Mercy,' I loudly cried,
>   ' Oh, give me rest from sin !'
> ' I will,' a voice replied,
>   And Mercy let me in.
> She bound my bleeding wounds
>   And carried all my sin ;
> She eased my burdened soul,
>   Then Jesus took me in.
>
> " In Mercy's guise I knew
>   The Saviour long abused,
> Who oft had sought my heart,
>   And oft had been refused.
> Oh, what a blest return
>   For ignorance and sin !
> I stood outside the gate
>   And Jesus let me in."

After a few days, Eva heard Maggie humming this tune over her work. "There," she said to herself, "the good angels are near her! *I* don't know what to say to her, but they do."

In fact, Eva had that delicacy and self-distrust in

regard to any direct and personal appeal to Maggie which is the natural attendant of personal refinement. She was little versed in any ordinary religious phraseology, such as very well-meaning persons often so freely deal in. Her own religious experiences, fervent and sincere though they were, never came out in any accredited set of phrases; nor had she any store of cut-and-dried pious talk laid by, to be used for inferiors whom she was called to admonish. But she had stores of kind artifices to keep Maggie usefully employed, to give her a sense that she was trusted in the family, to encourage hope that there was a better future before her.

Maggie's mother, fond and loving as she was, seconded these tactics of her mistress but indifferently. Mary had the stern pride of chastity which distinguishes the women of the old country, and which keeps most of the Irish girls who are thrown unprotected on our shores superior to temptation.

Mary keenly felt that Maggie had disgraced her, and as health returned and she no longer trembled for her life, she seemed called upon to keep her daughter's sin ever before her. Her past bad conduct and the lenity of her young mistress, her treating her so much better than she had any reason to expect, were topics on which Mary took every occasion to enlarge in private, leading to passionate altercations between herself and her daughter, in which the child broke over all bounds of goodness and showed the very worst aspects of her nature. Nothing can be more miserable, more pitiable, than these stormy passages between wayward children and honest, good-hearted mothers, who love them to the death, and yet do not know how to handle them, sensitive and sore with moral wounds. Many a time poor Mary went to sleep with a wet pillow, while Maggie, sullen and hard-hearted, lay with her great black eyes wide

open, obdurate and silent, yet in her secret heart longing to make it right with her mother. Often, after such
a passage she would revolve the line of the hymn—

> "I stood outside the gate."

It seemed to her that that gate was her mother's heart,
and that she stood outside of it; and yet all the while
the poor mother would have died for her. Eva could
not at first account for the sullen and gloomy moods
which came upon Maggie, when she would go about the
house with lowering brows, and all her bright, cheerful
ways and devices could bring no smile upon her face.

"What is the matter with Maggie?" she would say to
Mary.

"Oh, nothing, ma'am, only she's bad; she's got to
be brought under, and brought down,—that's what she
has."

"Mary, I think you had better not talk to Maggie
about her past faults. She knows she has been wrong,
and the best way is to let her get quietly into the right
way. We mustn't keep throwing up the past to her.
When we do wrong, we don't like to have people keep
putting *us* in mind of it."

"You're jest an angel, Miss Eva, and it isn't many
ladies that would do as you do. You're too good to her
entirely. She ought to be made sensible of it."

"Well, Mary, the best way to make her sensible and
bring her to repentance is to treat her kindly and never
bring up the past. Don't you see it does no good, Mary?
It only makes her sullen, and gloomy, and unhappy, so
that I can't get anything out of her. Now please, Mary,
just keep quiet, and let *me* manage Maggie."

And then Mary would promise, and Eva would
smooth matters over, and affairs would go on for a day
or two harmoniously. But there was another authority

in Mary's family, as in almost every Irish household,—a man who felt called to have a say and give a sentence.

Mary had an elder brother, Mike McArtney, who had established himself in a grocery business a little out of the city, and who felt himself to stand in position of head of the family to Mary and her children.

The absolute and entire reverence and deference with which Irish women look up to the men of their kindred is something in direct contrast to the demeanor of American women. The male sex, if repulsed in other directions, certainly are fully justified and glorified by the submissive daughters of Erin. Mike was the elder brother, under whose care Mary came to this country. He was the adviser and director of all her affairs. He found her places; he guided her in every emergency. Mike, of course, had felt and bitterly resented the dishonor brought on their family by Maggie's fall. In his view, there was danger that the path of repentance was being made altogether too easy for her, and he had resolved on the first leisure Sunday evening to come to the house and execute a thorough work of judgment on Maggie, setting her sin in order before her, and, in general, bearing down on her in such a way as to bring her to the dust and make her feel it the greatest possible mercy and favor that any of her relations should speak to her.

So, after Eva had hushed the mother and tranquilized the girl, and there had been two or three days of serenity, came Sunday evening and Uncle Mike.

The result was, as might have been expected, a loud and noisy altercation. Maggie was perfectly infuriated, and talked like one possessed of a demon; using, alas! language with which her sinful life had made her only too familiar, and which went far to justify the rebukes which were heaped upon her.

In his anger at such contumacious conduct, Uncle Mike took full advantage of the situation, and told Maggie that she was a disgrace to her mother and her relations—a disgrace to any honest house—and that he wondered that decent gentle-folks would have her under their roof.

In short, in one hour, two of Maggie's best friends—the mother that loved her as her life and the uncle that had been as a father to her—contrived utterly to sweep away and destroy all those delicate cords and filaments which the hands of good angels had been fastening to her heart, to draw her heavenward.

When a young tree is put in new ground, its roots put forth fibres delicate as hairs, but in which is all the vitality of a new phase of existence. To tear up those roots and wrench off those fibres is too often the destructive work of well-intending friends; it is done too often by those who would, if need be, give their very heart's blood for the welfare they imperil. Such is life as we find it.

CHAPTER XXVII

ROUGH HANDLING OF SORE NERVES.

THE same Sunday evening that Mary and her brother Mike had devoted to the disciplinary processes with Maggie, had been spent by Eva and her husband at her father's house.

Mrs. Van Arsdel, to say the truth, had been somewhat shaken and disturbed by Aunt Maria's suggestions; and she took early occasion to draw Eva aside, and make many doubtful inquiries and utter many admonitory cautions with regard to the part she had taken for Maggie.

"Of course, dear, it's very kind in you," said Mrs. Van Arsdel; "but your aunt thinks it isn't quite prudent; and, come to think it over, Eva, I'm afraid it may get you into trouble. Everything is going on so well in your house, I don't want you to have anything disagreeable, you know."

"Well, after all, mother, how can I be a Christian, or anything like a Christian, if I am never willing to take any trouble? If you heard the preaching we do every Sunday, you would feel so."

"I don't doubt that Mr. St. John is a good preacher," said Mrs. Van Arsdel; "but then I never could go so far, you know; and your aunt is almost crazy now because the girls go up there and don't sit in our pew in church. She was here yesterday, and talked very strongly about your taking Maggie. She really made me quite uncomfortable."

"Well, I should like to know what concern it is of

Aunt Maria's!" said Eva. "It's a matter in which Harry and I must follow our own judgment and conscience; Harry thinks we are doing right, and I suspect Harry knows what is best to do as well as Aunt Maria."

"Well, certainly, Eva, I must say it's an unusual sort of thing to do. I know your motives are all right and lovely, and I stood up for you with your aunt. I didn't give in to her a bit; and yet, all the while, I couldn't help thinking that maybe she was right and that maybe your good-heartedness would get you into difficulty."

"Well, suppose it does; what then? Am I never to have any trouble for the sake of helping anybody? I am not one of the very good women with missions, like Sibyl Selwyn, and can't do good that way; and I'm not enterprising and courageous, like sister Ida, to make new professions for women: but here is a case of a poor woman right under my own roof who is perplexed and suffering, and if I can help her carry her load, ought I not to do it, even if it makes me a good deal of trouble?"

"Well, yes, I don't know but you ought," said Mrs. Van Arsdel, who was always convinced by the last speaker.

"You see," continued Eva, " the priest and the Levite who passed by on the other side when a man lay wounded were just of Aunt Maria's mind. They didn't want trouble, and if they undertook to do anything for him they would have a good deal; so they left him. And if I turn my back on Mary and Maggie I shall be doing pretty much the same thing."

"Well, if you only are sure of succeeding. But girls that have fallen into bad ways are such dangerous creatures; perhaps you can't do her any good, and will only get yourself into trouble."

"Well, if I fail, why then I shall fail. But I think

it's better to try and fail in doing our part for others than never to try at all."

"Well, I suppose you are right, Eva; and after all I'm sorry for poor Mary. She had a hard time with her marriage all round; and I suppose it's no wonder Maggie went astray. Mary couldn't control her; and handsome girls in that walk of life are so tempted. How does she get on?"

"Oh, nicely, for the most part. She seems to have a sort of adoration for me. I can say or do anything with her, and she really is very handy and skillful with her needle; she has ripped up and made over an old dress for me so you'd be quite astonished to see it, and seems really pleased and interested to have something to do. If only her mother will let her alone, and not keep nagging her, and bringing up old offenses. Mary is so eager to make her do right that she isn't judicious, she doesn't realize how sensitive and sore people are that know they have been wrong. Maggie is a proud girl."

"Oh, well, she's no business to be proud," said Mrs. Van Arsdel. "I'm sure she ought to be humbled in the very dust; that's the least one should expect."

"And so ought we all," said Eva, "but we are not, and she isn't. She makes excuses for herself, and feels as if she had been abused and hardly treated, just as most of us do when we go wrong, and I tell Mary not to talk to her about the past, but just quietly let her do better in future; but it's very hard to get her to feel that Maggie ought not to be willing to be lectured and preached to from morning till night."

"Your Aunt Maria, no doubt, will come up and free her mind to you about this affair," said Mrs. Van Arsdel. "She has a scheme in her head of getting another girl for you in Mary's place. The Willises are going abroad for three years and have given their servants leave to

advertise from the house; and your aunt left me Saturday, saying she was going up there to ascertain all about
them and get you the refusal of one of them, provided
you wished to get rid of Mary."

"Get rid of Mary! I think I see myself turning
upon my good·Mary that loves me as she does her life,
and scheming to get her out of my house because she's
in trouble. No, indeed; Mary has been true and faithful to me, and I will be a true and faithful friend to her.
What could I do with one of the Willises' servants, with
their airs and their graces? Would they come to a little
house like mine, and take all departments in turn, and do
for me as if they were doing for themselves, as Mary
does?"

"Just so," said Mrs. Van Arsdel. "That's just what
I told Maria. I told her that you never would consent.
But you know how it is with her when she gets an idea
in her head, there's no turning her. You might as well
talk to a steam engine. She walked off down stairs
straight as a ramrod, and took the omnibus for the
Willises, in spite of all I could say; and, sure as the
world, she'll be up to talk with you about it. She insisted
that it was *my* duty to interfere; and I told her you
had a right to manage your matters in your own way.
Then she said if I didn't do my duty by you, *she*
should."

"Well, you have done your duty, Mamma dear," said
Eva, kissing her mother. "I'll bear witness to that, and
it isn't your fault if I am not warned. But you, dear
little mother, have sense to let your children sail their
own boat their own way, without interfering."

"Well, I think your ways generally turn out the best
ways, Eva," said her mother. "And I think Aunt Maria
herself comes into them finally. She is proud as a peacock of your receptions, and takes every occasion to tell

people what charming, delightful evenings you have; and she praises your house and your housekeeping and you to everybody, so you may put up with a little bother now and then."

"Oh, I'll manage Aunt Maria, never you fear," said Eva, as she rose confidently and took her husband from a discussion with Mr. Van Arsdel.

"Come, Harry, it's nine o'clock, and we have a long walk yet to get home."

It was brisk, clear winter moonlight in the streets as Harry and Eva took their way homeward—she the while relieving her mind by reciting her mother's conversation.

"Don't it seem strange," she said, "how the minute one actually tries to do some real Christian work everything goes against one?"

"Yes," said Harry; "the world isn't made for the unfortunate or unsuccessful. In general, the instinct of society is the same among men as among animals—anything sickly or maimed is to be fought off and got rid of. If there is a sick bird, all the rest fly at it and peck it to death. So in the world, when man or woman doesn't keep step with respectable people, the first idea is to get them out of the way. We can't exactly kill them, but we can wash our hands of them. Saving souls is no part of the world's work—it interferes with its steady business; it takes unworldly people to do that."

"And when one begins," said Eva, "shrewd, sensible folks, like Aunt Maria, blame us; and little, tender-hearted folks, like mamma, think it's almost a pity we should try, and that we had better leave it to somebody else; and then the very people we are trying to do for are really troublesome and hard to manage—like poor Maggie. She is truly a very hard person to get along with, and her mother is injudicious, and makes it harder;

but yet, it really does seem to be our work to help take care of her. Now, isn't it?"

" Well, then, darling, you may comfort your heart with one thought: when you are doing for pure Christian motives a thing that makes you a great deal of trouble, and gets you no applause, you are trying to live just that unworldly life that the first .Christians did. They were called a peculiar people, and whoever acts in the same spirit now-a-days will be called the same. I think it is the very highest wisdom to do as you are doing; but it isn't the wisdom of this world. It's the kind of thing that Mr. St. John is sacrificing his whole life to; it is what Sibyl Selwyn is doing all the time, and your little neighbor Ruth is helping in. We can at least try to do a little. We are inexperienced, it may be that we shall not succeed, it may be that the girl is past saving; but it's worth while to try, and try our very best."

Harry was saying this just as he put his latch-key into the door of his house.

It was suddenly opened from within, and Maggie stood before them with her bonnet and shawl on, ready to pass out. There was a hard, sharp, desperate expression in her face as she pressed forward to pass them.

" Maggie, child," said Eva, laying hold of her arm, " where are you going?"

" Away—anywhere—I don't care where," said Maggie, fiercely, trying to pull away.

" But you mustn't," said Eva, laying hold of her.

" Maggie," said Harry, stepping up to her and speaking in that calm, steady voice which controls passionate people, "go into the house immediately with Mrs. Henderson; she will talk with you."

Maggie turned, and sullenly followed Eva into a little sewing room adjoining the parlor, where she had often sat at work.

"Now, Maggie," said Eva, "take off your bonnet, for I'm not going to have you go into the streets at this hour of the night, and sit down quietly here and tell me all about it. What has happened? What is the matter? You don't want to distress your mother and break her heart?"

"She hates me," said Maggie. "She says I've disgraced her and I disgrace you, and that it's a disgrace to have me here. She and Uncle Mike both said so, and I said I'd go off, then."

"But where could you go?" said Eva.

"Oh, I know places enough! They're bad, to be sure. I wanted to do better, so I came away; but I can go back again."

"No, Maggie, you must never go back. You must do as I tell you. Have I not been a friend to you?"

"Oh, yes, yes, *you* have; but they say I disgrace you."

"Maggie, I don't think so. *I* never said so. There is no need that you should disgrace anybody. I hope you'll live to be a credit to your mother—a credit to us all. You are young yet; you have a good many years to live; and if you'll only go on and do the very best you can from this time, you can be a comfort to your mother and be a good woman. It's never too late to begin, Maggie, and I'll help you now."

Maggie sat still and gazed gloomily before her.

"Come, now, I'll sing you some little hymns," said Eva, going to her piano and touching a few chords. "You've got your mind all disturbed, and I'll sing to you till you are more quiet."

Eva had a sweet voice, and a light, dreamy sort of touch on the piano, and she played and sung with feeling.

There were truths in religion, higher, holier, deeper

than she felt capable of uttering, which breathed themselves in these hymns; and something within her gave
voice and pathos to them.

The influence of music over the disturbed nerves and
bewildered moral sense of those who have gone astray
from virtue, is something very remarkable. All modern
missions more or less recognize that it has a power which
goes beyond anything that spoken words can utter, and
touches springs of deeper feeling.

Eva sat playing a long time, going from one thing to
another; and then, rising, she found Maggie crying softly
by herself.

"Come, now, Maggie," she said, "you are going to be
a good girl, I know. Go up and go to bed now, and
don't forget your prayers. That's a good girl."

Maggie yielded passively, and went to her room.

Then Eva had another hour's talk, to persuade Mary
that she must not be too exacting with Maggie, and that
she must for the future avoid all such encounters with
her. Mary was, on the whole, glad to promise anything;
for she had been thoroughly alarmed at the altercation
into which their attempt at admonition had grown, and
was ready to admit to Eva that Mike had been too hard
on her. At all events, the family honor had been suffi-
ciently vindicated, and, if Maggie would only behave herself, she was ready to promise that Mike should not be
allowed to interfere in future. And so, at last, Eva
succeeded in inducing Mary to go to her daughter's
room with a reconciling word before she went to bed,
and had the comfort of seeing the naughty girl crying in
her mother's arms, and the mother petting and fondling
her as a mother should.

Alas! it is only in the good old Book that the father
sees the prodigal a great way off, and runs and falls on
his neck and kisses him, before he has confessed his sin

or done any work of repentance. So far does God's heavenly love outrun even the love of fathers and mothers.

"Well, I believe I've got things straightened out at last," said Eva, as she came back to Harry; "and now, if Mary will only let me manage Maggie, I think I can make all go smooth."

CHAPTER XXVIII

REASON AND UNREASON.

THE next morning being Monday, Dr. Campbell dropped in to breakfast. Since he and Eva had met so often in Maggie's sick room, and he had discussed the direction of her physical well-being, he had rapidly grown in intimacy with the Hendersons, and the little house had come to be regarded by him as a sort of home. Consequently, when Eva sailed into her dining-room, she found him quietly arranging a handful of cut flowers which he had brought in for the center of her breakfast table.

"Good morning, Mrs. Henderson," he said, composedly. "I stepped into Allen's green-house on my way up, to bring in a few flowers. With the mercury at zero, flowers are worth something."

"How perfectly lovely of you, Doctor," said she. "You are too good."

"I don't say, however, that I had not my eye on a cup of your coffee," he replied. "You know I have no faith in disinterested benevolence."

"Well, sit down then, old fellow," said Harry, clapping him on the shoulder. "You're welcome, flowers or no flowers."

"How are you all getting on?" he said, seating himself.

"Charmingly, of course," said Eva, from behind the coffee-pot, "and as the song says, 'the better for seeing you.'"

"And how's my patient—Maggie?"

"Oh, she's doing well, if only people will let her alone; but her mother, and uncle, and relations will keep irritating her with reproaches. You see, I had got her in beautiful training, and she was sewing for me and making herself very useful, when, Sunday evening, when I was gone out, her uncle came to see her, and talked and bore down upon her so as to completely upset all I had done. I came home and found her just going out of the house, perfectly desperate."

"And ready to go to the devil straight off, I suppose?" said the Doctor. "His doors are always open."

"You see," said Harry, "things seem to be so arranged in this world that if man, woman or child does wrong or gets out of the way, all society is armed to the teeth to prevent their ever doing right again. Their own flesh and blood pitch into them with reproaches and expostulations, and everybody else looks on them with suspicion, and nobody wants them and nobody dares trust them."

"Just so," said Dr. Campbell, "the world is an army —it can't stop for anything. 'Wounded to the rear,' is the word, and the army must go on and leave the sick and wounded to die or be taken by the enemy. For my part, I never thought Napoleon was so much out of the way when he recommended poisoning the sick and wounded that could not be moved. I think I should prefer to be comfortably and decently poisoned myself in such a case. The world isn't ripe yet for the doctrine; but I think all people who get broken down, and don't keep step physically and morally, had better be killed at once. Then we could get on comfortably, and in a few generations should have a nice population."

"Come, now, Doctor; I'm not going to have that sort of talk," said Eva. "In short, you've got to keep on as you have been doing—working for the wounded in the

rear. And now tell me if I could do a better thing for
Maggie than keep her here in our house, under my own
eye and influence, till she gets quite strong and well,
and help her to live down the past?"

"Well, that's a sensible putting of the thing," said
Dr. Campbell, "if you will be foolish enough to take the
trouble; but I forewarn you that girls that have been
through her experiences are troublesome to manage.
Their nerves are all in a jangle; they are sore everywhere, and the very good that is in them is turned
wrong side outward; and, as you say, the world will be
against you, in a general way. Relations, as far as ever I
have observed, are rather harder on sinners than anybody
else—especially on a woman that goes astray; and next to
them sensible, worldly-wise, respectable people—people
who live to get rid of trouble, and feel that 'bother'
is the sum and substance of evil. Now, taking up a girl
like Maggie, you must count on that. Her relations
will hinder all they can; and the more respectable they
are, the harder they will bear down upon her. Your
relations will think you a sentimental little fool, and do
all they can to hinder you. The rank and file of comfortable, religious, church-going people will call you imprudent, and only fanatics, like Mr. St. John and Sibyl
Selwyn, will understand you or stand by you; and, to
crown all, the girl herself is as unreliable as the wind.
The evil done to a woman in this kind of life is the de-
rangement of her whole nervous system, so that she is
swept by floods of morbid influences, and liable to wild,
passionate gusts of feeling. The cessation from this free
Bohemian life, with its strong excitements, leaves them
in unnatural states of craving for stimulus; and when you
have done all you can for them,—in a moment, off they
go. That's the reason why most prudent people prefer
to wash their hands of them, and stop before they begin."

"It's all very well to talk so, Doctor, if the case related to a stranger; but here is my poor, good Mary, who has been in our family ever since I was a little girl, and has always loved me and been devoted to me—shall I now give her the cold shoulder and not help her in this crisis of her life, because I am afraid of trouble? Isn't it worth trouble, and a great deal of trouble, and a great deal of patience, to save this daughter of hers from ruin? I think it is."

"I think you and your husband will do it," said the Doctor, "because you are just what you are; and I shall help you, because I'm what I am; but, nevertheless, I set the reasonable side before you. I think this Maggie is a fine creature. There are, in a confused way, the beginnings of a great deal that is right, and even noble, in her; but nobody ought to begin with her without taking account of risks."

"Well," said Eva, "you know I am a Christian, and I look in the New Testament for my principles, and there I find it plainly set down that the Lord values one sinner that is brought to repentance more than ninety and nine just persons that need no repentance; and that he would leave the ninety and nine sheep, and go into the wilderness to look up one lost lamb."

"That is the Christian religion, undoubtedly," said Dr. Campbell; "but there is exactly where the Christian religion parts company with worldly prudence. The world and all its institutions are organized and arranged for the strong, the wise, the prudent, and the successful. The weak, the sick, the sinners, and all that sort of thing, are to have as much care as they can without interfering with the healthy and strong. Now, in the good old times of English law, they used to hang summarily anybody that made trouble in society in any way—the woman who stole a loaf of bread, and the man who stole

M

a horse, and the vagrant who picked a pocket; then there was no discussion and no bother about reformation, such as is coming down upon our consciences now-a-days. Good old times those were, when there wasn't any of this gush over the fallen and lost; the slate was wiped clean of all the puzzling sums at the yearly assizes and the account started clear. Now-a-days, there is such a bother about taking care of criminals that an honest man has no decent chance of comfort."

"Well, Doctor," said Eva, "if the essence of Christianity is restoration and salvation, I don't see but your profession is essentially a Christian one. You seek and save the lost. It is your business by your toil and labor to help people who have sinned against the laws of nature, to get them back again to health; isn't it so?"

"Well, yes, it is," said the doctor, "though I find everything going against me in this direction, as much as you do."

"But you find mercy in nature," said Harry. "In the language of the Psalms: 'There is forgiveness with her that she may be feared.' The first thing, after one of her laws has been broken, comes in her effort to restore and save; it may be blind and awkward, but still it points toward life and not death, and you doctors are her ministers and priests. You bear the *physical* gospel; and we Christians take the same process to the spiritual realm that lies just above yours, and that has to work through yours. Our business in both realms seems to be, by our own labor, self-denial and suffering, to save those who have sinned against the laws of their being."

"Well," said the doctor; "even so, I go in for saving in my line by an instinct apart from my reason, an instinct as blind as nature's when she sets out to heal a broken bone in the right arm of a scalawag, who never used his arm for anything but thrashing his wife and

children, and making himself a general nuisance; yet I
have been amazed sometimes to see how kindly and
patiently old Mother Nature will work for such a man.
Well, I am something like her. I have the blind instinct
of healing in my profession, and I confess to sitting up
all night, watching to keep the breath of life in sick
babies that I know ought to be dead, and had better be
dead, inasmuch as there's no chance for them to be even
decent and respectable, if they live; but I *can't* let 'em
die, any more than nature can, without a struggle. The
fact is, reason is one thing and the human heart
another; and, as St. Paul says, 'these two are contrary
one to the other, so that ye cannot do the thing ye
would.' You and your husband, Mrs. Henderson, have
got a good deal of this troublesome human heart in you,
so that you cannot act reasonably, any more than I can."

"That's it, Doctor," said Eva, with a bright, sudden movement towards him and laying her hand on his
arm, "let's not act reasonably—let's act by something
higher. I know there is something higher—something
we dare to do and feel able to do in our best moments.
You are a Christian in heart, Doctor, if not in faith."

"Me? I'm the most terrible heretic in all the con-
tinent."

"But when you sit up all night with a sick baby
from mere love of saving, you are a Christian ; for,
doesn't Christ say, 'inasmuch as ye did it unto the least
of these, ye did it unto me'? Christians are those who
have Christ's spirit, as I think, and sacrifice themselves
to save others."

"May the angels be of your opinion when I try the
gate hereafter," said the Doctor. "But now, seriously,
about this Maggie. I apprehend that you will have
trouble from the fact that, having been kept on stimulants in a rambling, loose, disorderly life, she will not be

able long to accommodate herself to any regular habits.
I don't know how much of a craving for drink there may
be in her case, but it is a usual complication of such
cases. Such people may go for weeks without yielding,
and then the furor comes upon them, and away they go.
Perhaps she may not be one of those worst cases; but,
in any event, the sudden cessation of all the tumultuous
excitement she has been accustomed to, may lead to a
running down of the nervous system that will make her
act unreasonably. Her mother, and people of her class,
may be relied on for doing the very worst thing that the
case admits of, with the very best intentions. And now
if these complications get you into any trouble, rely
upon me so far as I can do anything to help. Don't
hesitate to command me at any hour and to any extent,
because I mean to see the thing through with you.
When spring comes on, if you get her through the winter, we must try and find her a place in some decent,
quiet farmer's family in the country, where she may feed
chickens and ducks, and make butter, and live a natural,
healthful, out-door life; and, in my opinion, that will
be the best and safest way for her."

"Come, Doctor," said Harry, "will you walk up town
with me? It's time I was off."

"Now, Harry, please remember; don't forget to match
that worsted," said Eva. "Oh! and that tea must be
changed. You just call in and tell Haskins that."

"Anything else?" said Harry, buttoning on his overcoat.

"No; only be sure you come back early, for mamma
says Aunt Maria is coming down here upon me, and I
shall want you to strengthen me. The Doctor appreciates Aunt Maria."

"Certainly I do," said the Doctor; "a devoted relation who carries you all in her heart hourly, and there-

fore has an undoubted right to make you as uncomfortable as she pleases. That's the beauty of relations. If you have them you are bothered *with* them, and if you haven't you are bothered for want of 'em. So it goes. Now I would give all the world if I had a good aunt or grandmother to haul me over the coals, and fight me, out of pure love—a fellow feels lonesome when he knows nobody would care if he went to the devil."

"Oh, as to that," said Eva, "come here whenever you're lonesome, and we'll fight and abuse you to your heart's content; and you sha'n't go to that improper person without our making a fuss about it. We'll abuse you as if you were one of the family."

"Good," said the Doctor, as he stepped towards the front window; "but here, to be sure, is your aunt, bright and early."

CHAPTER XXIX

AUNT MARIA FREES HER MIND.

THE door opened, to let out the two gentlemen, just as Mrs. Wouvermans was coming up the steps, fresh and crisp as one out betimes on the labors of a good conscience.

The dear woman had visited the Willises, at the remote end of the city, had had diplomatic conversations with both mistress and maid in that establishment, and had now arrived as minister plenipotentiary to set all matters right in Eva's establishment. She had looked all through the subject, made up her mind precisely what Eva ought to do, revolved it in her own mind as she sat apparently attending to a rather drowsy sermon at her church, and was now come, as full of sparkling vigor and brisk purposes as a well-corked bottle of champagne.

Eva met her at the door with the dutiful affection which she had schooled herself to feel towards one whose intentions were always so good, but with a secret reserve of firm resistance as to the lines of her own proper personality.

"I have a great deal to do, to-day," said the lady, "and so I came out early to see you before you should be gone out or anything, because I had something very particular I wanted to say to you."

Eva took her aunt's things and committed them to the care of Maggie, who opened the parlor-door at this moment.

Aunt Maria turned towards the girl in a grand superior way and fixed a searching glance on her.

"Maggie," she said, "is this you? I'm astonished to see *you* here."

The words were not much, but the intonation and manner were meant to have all the effect of an awful and severe act of judgment on a detected culprit—to express Mrs. Wouvermans' opinion that Maggie's presence in any decent house was an impertinence and a disgrace.

Maggie's pale face turned a shade paler, and her black eyes flashed fire, but she said nothing; she went out and closed the door with violence.

"Did you see that?" said Aunt Maria, turning to Eva.

"I saw it, Aunty, and I must say I think it was more your fault than Maggie's. People in our position ought not to provoke girls, if we do not want to excite temper and have rudeness."

"Well, Eva, I've come up here to have a plain talk with you about this girl, for I think you don't know what you're doing in taking her into your house. I've talked with Mrs. Willis, and with your Aunt Atkins, and with dear Mrs. Elmore about it, and there is but just one opinion—they are all united in the idea that you ought not to take such a girl into your family. You never can do anything with them; they are utterly good for nothing, and they make no end of trouble. I went and talked to your mother, but she is just like a bit of tow string, you can't trust her any way, and she is afraid to come and tell you what she really thinks, but in her heart she feels just as the rest of us do."

"Well, now, upon my word, Aunt Maria, I can't see what right you and Mrs. Willis and Aunt Atkins and Mrs. Elmore have to sit as a jury on my family affairs and send me advice as to my arrangements, and I'm not in the least obliged to you for talking about my affairs to them. I think I told you, some time ago, that Harry and I intend to manage our family according to our own

judgment; and, while we respect you, and are desirous
of showing that respect in every proper way, we cannot
allow you any right to intermeddle in our family matters.
I am guided by my husband's judgment (and you yourself admit that, for a wife, there is no other proper appeal)
and Harry and I act as one. We are entirely united in
all our family plans."

"Oh, well, I suppose there is no harm in my taking
an interest in your family matters, since you are my god-
child, and I brought you up, and have always cared as
much about you as any mother could do—in fact, I think
I have felt more like a mother to you than Nellie has."

"Well, Aunty," said Eva, "of course, I feel how kind
and good you have always been, and I'm sure I thank
you with all my heart; but still, after all, we must be
firm in saying that you cánnot govern our family."

"Who is wanting to govern your family?—what
ridiculous talk that is! Just as if I had ever tried;
but you may, of course, allow your old aunt, that
has had experience that you haven't had, to propose
arrangements and tell you of things to your advantage,
can't you?"

"Oh, of course, Aunty."

"Well, I went up to the Willises, because they are
going to Europe, to be gone for three years, and I
thought I could secure their Ann for you. Ann is a
treasure. She has been ten years with the Willises, and
Mrs. Willis says she don't know of a fault that she has."

"Very well, but, Aunty, I don't want Ann, if she were
an angel; I have my Mary, and I prefer her to anybody
that could be named."

"But, Eva, Mary is getting old, and she is encumbered with this witch of a daughter, whom she is putting
upon your shoulders and making you carry; and I
perceive that you'll be ridden to death—it's a perfect

Old Man of the Sea on your backs. Now, get rid of
Mary, and you'll get rid of the whole trouble. It isn't
worth while, just because you've got attached to Mary,
to sacrifice your interests for her sake. Just let her go."

"Well, now, Aunty, the short of the matter is, that I
will do nothing of the kind. I won't let Mary go, and I
don't want any other arrangement than just what I have.
I am perfectly satisfied."

"Well, you'll see that your keeping that girl in your
house will bring you all into disgrace yet," said Aunt
Maria, rising hastily. "But it's no use talking. I
spent a good half-day attending to this matter, and
making arrangements that would have given you the
very best of servants; but if you choose to take in
tramps, you must take the consequences. I can't help
it;" and Aunt Maria rose vengefully and felt for her
bonnet.

Eva opened the door of the little sewing-room, where
Maggie had laid it, and saw her vanishing out of the
opposite door.

"I hope she did not hear you, Aunty," she said, in-
voluntarily.

"I don't care if she did," was the reply, as the injured lady resumed her bonnet and departed from the
house, figuratively shaking the dust from her feet.

Eva went out also to attend to some of her morning
business, and, on her return, was met by Mary with an
anxious face. Maggie had gone out and taken all her
things with her, and was nowhere to be found. After
some search, Eva found a paper pinned to the cushion
of her toilet-table, on which was written:

"*Dear Mrs. Henderson:* You have tried hard to save me ; but
it's no use. I am only a trouble to mother, and I disgrace you. So
I am going, and don't try to find me. May God bless you and
mother.   MAGGIE."

CHAPTER XXX

A DINNER ON WASHING DAY.

THE world cannot wait for anybody. No matter whose heart breaks or whose limbs ache, the world must move on. Life always has its next thing to be done, which comes up imperatively, no matter what happens to you or me.

So when it appeared that Maggie was absolutely gone—gone without leaving trace or clue where to look for her, Mary, though distressed and broken-hearted, had small time for lamentations.

For just as Maggie's note had been found, read, and explained to Mary, and in the midst of grief and wonderment, a note was handed in to Eva by an office-boy, running thus:

"*Dear Little Wife :* I have caught Selby, and we can have him at dinner to-night; and as I know there's nothing like you for emergencies, I secured him, and took the liberty of calling in on Alice and Angie, and telling them to come. I shall ask St. John, and Jim, and Bolton, and Campbell—you know, the more the merrier, and, when you are about it, it's no more trouble to have six or seven than one; and now you have Maggie, one may as well spread a little. Your own HARRY."

"Was ever such a man!" said Eva; "poor Mary! I'm sorry all this is to come upon you just as you have so much trouble, but just hear now! Mr. Henderson has invited an English gentleman to dinner, and a whole parcel of folks with him. Well, most of them are *our* folks, Mary—Miss Angie, and Miss Alice, and Mr. Fellows, and Mr. Bolton, and Mr. St. John—of course we must have him."

"Oh, well, we must just do the best we can," said Mary, entering into the situation at once; "but really, the turkey that's been sent in isn't enough for so many. If you'd be so good as to step down to Simon's, ma'am, and order a pair of chickens, I could make a chicken pie, and then there's most of that cold boiled ham left, and trimmed up with parsley it would do to set on table —you'll ask him to send parsley—and the celery's not enough, we shall want two or three more bunches. I'm sorry Mr. Henderson couldn't have put it off, later in the week, till the washing was out of the way," she concluded, meekly, "but we must do the best we can."

Now, Christian fortitude has many more showy and sublime forms, but none more real than that of a poor working-woman suddenly called upon to change all her plans of operations on washing day, and more especially if the greatest and most perplexing of life's troubles meets her at the same moment. Mary's patience and self-sacrifice showed that the crucifix and rosary and prayer-book in her chamber were something more than ornamental appendages—they were the outward signs of a faith that was real.

"My dear, good Mary," said Eva, "it's just sweet of you to take things so patiently, when I know you're feeling so bad; but the way it came about is this: this gentleman is from England, and he is one that Harry wants very much to show attention to, and he only stays a short time, and so we have to take him when we can get him. You know Mr. Henderson generally is so considerate."

"Oh, I know," said Mary, "folks can't always have things just as they want."

"And then, you know, Mary, he thought we should

have Maggie here to help us. He couldn't know, you
see——"

Mary's countenance fell, and Eva's heart smote her,
as if she were hard and unsympathetic in forcing her
own business upon her in her trouble, and she hastened
to add :

"We sha'n't give Maggie up I will tell Mr. Henderson about her when he comes home, and he will know
just what to do. You may be sure, Mary, he will stand
by you, and leave no stone unturned to help you. We'll
find her yet."

"It's my fault partly, I'm afraid; if I'd only done
better by her," said Mary; "and Mike, he was hard on
her; she never would bear curbing in, Maggie would n't.
But we must just do the best we can," she added, wiping
her eyes with her apron. "What would you have for
dessert, ma'am ?"

"What would you make easiest, Mary ?"

"Well there's jelly, blanc-mange or floating island,
though we didn't take milk enough for that; but I guess
I can borrow some of Dinah over the way. Miss Dorcas
would be willing, I'm sure."

"Well, Mary, arrange it just as you please. I'll go
down and order more celery and the chickens, and I
know you'll bring it all right; you always do. Meanwhile, I'll go to a fruit store, and get some handsome
fruit to set off the table."

And so Eva went out, and Mary, left alone with her
troubles, went on picking celery, and preparing to make
jelly and blanc mange, with bitterness in her soul. People must eat, no matter whose hearts break, or who go
to destruction; but, on the whole, this incessant drive of
the actual in life is not a bad thing for sorrow.

If Mary had been a rich woman, with nothing to do
but to go to bed with a smelling-bottle, with full leisure

to pet and coddle her griefs, she could not have made half as good headway against them as she did by help of her chicken pie, and jelly, and celery and what not, that day.

Eva had, to be sure, given her the only comfort in her power, in the assurance that when her husband came home she would tell him about it, and they would see if anything could be done to find Maggie and bring her back. Poor Mary was full of self-reproach for what it was too late to help, and with concern for the trouble which she felt her young mistress had been subjected to. Added to this was the wounded pride of respectability, even more strong in her class than in higher ones, because with them a good name is more nearly an only treasure. To be come of honest, decent folk is with them equivalent to what in a higher class would be called coming of gentle blood. Then Mary's brother Mike, in his soreness at Maggie's disgrace, had not failed to blame the mother's way of bringing her up, after the manner of the world generally when children turn out badly.

"She might have expected this. She ought to have known it would come. She hadn't held her in tight enough; had given her her head too much; his wife always told him they were making a fool of the girl."

This was a sharp arrow in Mary's breast; because Mike's wife, Bridget, was one on whom Mary had looked down, as in no way an equal match for her brother, and her consequent want of cordiality in receiving her had rankled in Bridget's mind, so that she was forward to take advantage of Mary's humiliation.

It is not merely professed enemies, but decent family connections, we are sorry to say, who in time of trouble sometimes say "aha! so would we have it." All whose advice has not been taken, all who have felt themselves

outshone or slighted, are prompt with the style of consolation exemplified by Job's friends, and eager above
all things to prove to those in trouble that they have
nobody but themselves to thank for it.

So, no inconsiderable part of Mary's bitter herbs this
day, was the prick and sting of all the possible things
which might be said of her and Maggie by Bridget and
Mike, and the rest of the family circle by courtesy included in the term "her best friends." Eva, tender-
hearted and pitiful, could not help feeling a sympathetic
cloud coming over her as she watched poor Mary's woe-
struck and dejected air. She felt quite sure that Maggie had listened, and overheard Aunt Maria's philippic
in the parlor, and that thus the final impulse had been
given to send her back to her miserable courses; and
somehow Eva could not help a vague feeling of blame
from attaching to herself, for not having made sure that
those violent and cruel denunciations should not be
overheard.

"I ought to have looked and made sure, when I
found what Aunt Maria was at," she said to herself. "If
I had kept Maggie up stairs, this would not have happened." But then, an English literary man, that Harry
thought a good deal of, was to dine there that night,
and Eva felt all a housekeeper's enthusiasm and pride, to
have everything charming. You know how it is, sisters.
Each time that you have a social enterprise in hand you
put your entire soul into it for the time being, and have
a complete little set of hopes and fears, joys, sorrows and
plans, born with the day and dying with the morrow.

Just as she was busy arranging her flowers, the door-
bell rang, and Jim Fellows came in with a basket of fruit.

"Good morning," he said; "Harry told me you were
going to have a little blow-out to-night, and I thought
I'd bring in a contribution."

"Oh! thanks, Jim; they are exactly the thing I was going out to look for. How lovely of you!"

"Well, they've come to you without looking, then," said Jim. "Any commands for me? Can't I help you in any way?"

"No, Jim, unless—well, you know my good Mary is the great wheel of this establishment, and if she breaks down we all go too—for I should n't know what to do a single day without her."

"Well, what has happened to this great wheel?" said Jim. "Has it a cold in its head, or what?"

"Come, Jim, don't make fun of my metaphors; the fact is, that Mary's daughter, Maggie, has run off again and left her."

"Just what she might have expected," said Jim.

"No; Maggie was doing very well, and I really thought I should make something of her. She thought everything of me, and I could get along with her perfectly well, and I found her very ingenious and capable; but her relations all took up against her, and her uncle came in last night and talked to her till she was in a perfect fury."

"Of course," said Jim, "that's the world's way; a fellow can't repent and turn quietly, he must have his sins well rubbed into him, and his nose held to the grindstone. I should know that Maggie would flare up under that style of operation; those great black eyes of hers are not for nothing, I can tell you."

"Well, you see it was last night, while I was up at papa's, that her uncle came, and they had a stormy time, I fancy; and when Harry and I came home we found Maggie just flying out of the door in desperation, and I brought her back, and quieted her down, and brought her to reason, and her mother too, and made it all smooth and right. But, this morning, came in Aunt Maria—"

Jim gave a significant whistle.

"Yes, you may well whistle. You see, Maggie once lived with Aunt Maria, and she's dead set against her, and came to make me turn her out of my house, if she could. You ought to have seen the look of withering scorn and denunciation she gave Maggie when she opened the door!—and she talked about her so loud to me, and said so much to induce me to turn away both her and Mary, and take another set of girls, that I don't wonder Maggie went off; and now poor Mary is quite broken-hearted. It makes me feel sad to see her go about her work so forlorn and patient, wiping her eyes every once in a while, and yet doing everything for me, like the good soul she always is."

"By George!" said Jim; "I wish I could help her. Well, I'll put somebody on Maggie's track and we'll find her out. I know all the detectives and the police— trust us newspaper fellows for that—and Maggie is a pretty marked article, and I think I may come on the track of her; there are not many things that Jim can't find out, when he sets himself to work. Meanwhile, have you any errands for me to run, or any message to send to your folks? I may as well take it, while I'm about it."

"Well, yes, Jim; if you'd be kind enough, as you go by papa's, to ask Angie to come down and help me. She is always so brisk and handy, and keeps one in such good spirits, too."

"Oh, yes, Angie is always up and dressed, whoever wants her, and is good for any emergency. The little woman has Christmas tree on her brain just now—for our Sunday-school; only the other night, she was showing me the hoods and tippets she had been knitting for it, like a second Dorcas—"

"Yes," said Eva, "we must all have a consultation

about that Christmas tree. I wanted to see Mr. St. John about it.'

"Do you think there were any Christmas trees in the first centuries," said Jim, "or any churchly precedent for them?—else I don't see how St. John is going to allow such a worldly affair in his chapel."

"Oh, pshaw! Mr. St. John is sensible. He listened with great interest to Angie, the other night, while she was telling about one that she helped get up last year in Dr. Cushing's Sunday-school room, and he seemed quite delighted with the idea; and Angie and Alice and I are on a committee to get a list of children and look up presents, and that was one thing I wanted to talk about to-night."

"Well, get St. John and Angie to talking tree together, and she'll edify him. St. John is O. K. about all the particulars of how they managed in the catacombs, without doubt, and he gets ahead of us all preaching about the primitive Christians, but come to a Christmas tree for New York street boys and girls, in the 19th century, I'll bet on Angie to go ahead of him. He'll have to learn of her—and you see he won't find it hard to take, either. Jim knows a thing or two." And Jim cocked his head on one side, like a saucy sparrow, and looked provokingly knowing.

"Now, Jim, what do you mean?"

"Oh, nothing. Alice says I mustn't think anything or say anything, on pain of her high displeasure. But, you just watch the shepherd and Angie to-night."

"Jim, you provoking creature, you mustn't talk so."

"Bless your heart, who is talking so? Am I saying anything? Of course I'm not saying anything. Alice won't let me. I always have to shut my eyes and look the other way when Angie and St. John are around, for

fear I should say something and make a remark. Jim
says nothing, but he thinks all the more."

Now, we'll venture to say that there isn't a happy
young wife in the first months of wifehood that isn't pre-
disposed to hope for all her friends a happy marriage, as
about the summit of human bliss; and so Eva was not
shocked like Alice by the suggestion that her rector
might become a candidate for the sacrament of matri-
mony. On the contrary, it occurred to her at once that
the pretty, practical, lively, efficient little Angie might be
a true angel, not merely of church and Sunday-school,
but of a rector's house. He was ideal and theoretic, and
she practical and common-sense; yet she was pretty
enough, and picturesque, and fanciful enough for an ideal
man to make a poem of, and weave webs around, and
write sonnets to; and as all these considerations flashed
at once upon Eva's mind, she went on settling a spray
of geranium with rose-buds, a pleased dreamy smile on
her face. After a moment's pause, she said:

"Jim, if you see a bird considering whether to build
a nest in the tree by your window, and want him there,
the way is to keep pretty still about it and not go to the
window, and watch, and call people, saying, 'Oh, see here,
there's a bird going to build!' Don't you see the sense
of my parable?"

"Well, why do you talk to me? Haven't I kept away
from the window, and walked round on tip-toe like a cat,
and only given the quietest look out of the corner of my
eye?"

"Well, it seems you couldn't help calling my attention
and Alice's. Don't extend the circle of observers, Jim."

"See if I do. You'll find me discretion itself. I
shall be so quiet that even a humming bird's nerves
couldn't be disturbed. Well, good by, for the present."

"Oh, but, Jim, don't forget to do what you can about

Maggie. It really seems selfish in me to be absorbed in my own affairs, and not doing anything to help Mary, poor thing, when she's so good to me."

"Well, I don't see but you are doing all you can. I'll see about it right away and report to you," said Jim; "so, *au revoir.*"

Angie came in about lunch time; the two sisters, once at their tea and toast, discussed the forthcoming evening's preparations and the Christmas Sunday-school operations: and Eva, with the light of Jim's suggestions in her mind, began to observe certain signs of increasing intimacy between Angie and Mr. St. John.

"O Eva, I want to tell you: I went to see those poor Prices, Saturday afternoon; and there was John, just back from one of those dreadful sprees that he will have every two or three weeks. You never saw a creature so humble and so sorry, and so good, and so anxious to make up with his wife and me, and everybody all round, as he was. He was sitting there, nursing his wife and tending his baby, just as handy as a woman,—for she, poor thing, has had a turn of fever, in part, I think, brought on by worry and anxiety; but she seemed so delighted and happy to have him back!—and I couldn't help thinking what a shame it is that there should be any such thing as rum, and that there should be people who make it their business and get their living by tempting people to drink it. If I were a Queen, I'd shut up all the drinking-shops right off!"

"I fancy, if we women could have our way, we should do it pretty generally."

"Well, I don't know about that," said Angie. "One of the worst shops in John's neighborhood is kept by a woman."

"Well, it seems so hopeless—this weakness of these men," said Eva.

"Oh, well, never despair," said Angie. "I found him in such a good mood that I could say anything I wanted to, and I found that he was feeling terribly because he had lost his situation in Sanders' store on account of his drinking habits. He had been a porter and errand boy there, and he is so obliging and quick that he is a great favorite; but they got tired of his being so unreliable, and had sent him word that they didn't want him any more. Well, you see, here was an opportunity. I said to him: 'John, I know Mr. Sanders, and if you'll sign a solemn pledge never to touch another drop of liquor, or go into a place where it is sold, I will try and get him to take you back again.' So I got a sheet of paper and wrote a pledge, strong and solemn, in a good round hand, and he put his name to it; and just then Mr. St. John came in and I showed it to him, and he spoke beautifully to him, and prayed with him, and I really do hope, now, that John will stand."

"So, Mr. St. John visits them?"

"Oh, to be sure; ever since I had those children in my class, he has been very attentive there. I often hear of his calling; and when he was walking home with me afterwards, he told me about that article of Dr. Campbell's and advised me to read it. He said it had given him some new ideas. He called this family my little parish, and said I could do more than he could. Just think of our rector saying that."

Eva did think of it, but forbore to comment aloud. "Jim was right," she said to herself.

CHAPTER XXXI

THE dinner party, like many impromptu social ventures, was a success. Mr. Selby proved one of that delightful class of English travelers who travel in America to see and enter into its peculiar and individual life, and not to show up its points of difference from old-world social standards. He seemed to take the sense of a little family dinner, got up on short notice, in which the stereotyped doctrine of courses was steadfastly ignored ; where there was no soup or fish, and only a good substantial course of meat and vegetables, with a slight dessert of fruit and confectionery ; where there was no black servant, with white gloves, to change the plates, but only respectable, motherly Mary, who had tidied herself and taken the office of waiter, in addition to her services as cook.

A real high-class English gentleman, when he fairly finds himself out from under that leaden pale of conventionalities which weighs down elasticity like London fog and smoke, sometimes exhibits all the hilarity of a boy out of school on a long vacation, and makes himself frisky and gamesome to a degree that would astonish the solemn divinities of insular decorum. Witness the stories of the private fun and frolic of Thackeray and Dickens, on whom the intoxicating sense of social freedom wrought results sometimes surprising to staid Americans; as when Thackeray rode with his heels out of the carriage window through immaculate and gaping Boston and Dickens perpetrated his celebrated walking wager.

Mr. Selby was a rising literary man in the London writing world, who had made his own way up in the world, and known hard times and hard commons, though now in a lucrative position. It would have been quite possible, by spending a suitable sum and deranging the whole house, to set him down to a second-rate imitation of a dull, conventional London dinner, with waiters in white chokers, and protracted and circuitous courses; and in that case Mr. Selby would have frozen into a stiff, well preserved Briton, with immaculate tie and gloves, and a guarded and diplomatic reserve of demeanor. Eva would have been nervously thinking of the various unusual arrangements of the dinner table, and a general stiffness and embarrassment would have resulted. People who entertain strangers from abroad often re-enact the mistake of the two Englishmen who traveled all night in a diligence, laboriously talking broken French to each other, till at dawn they found out by a chance slip of the tongue that they were both English. So, at heart, every true man, especially in a foreign land, is wanting what every true household can give him—sincere homely feeling, the sense of domesticity, the comfort of being off parade and among friends; and Mr. Selby saw in the first ten minutes that this was what he had found in the Hendersons' house.

In the hour before dinner, Eva had shown him her ivies and her ferns and her manner of training them, and found an appreciate observer and listener. Mr. Selby was curious about American interiors and the detail of domestic life among people of moderate fortune. He was interested in the modes of warming and lighting, and arranging furniture, etc.; and soon Eva and he were all over the house, while she eloquently explained to him the working of the furnace, the position of the water pipes, and the various comforts and con-

CONFIDENCES.

*"In due course followed an introduction to 'my wife,' whose photo-
graph Mr. Selby wore dutifully in his coat-pocket over the exact
region of the heart."*—p. 287.

veniences which they had introduced into their little territories.

"I've got a little box of my own at Kentish town," Mr. Selby said, in a return burst of confidence, "and I shall tell my wife about some of your contrivances; the fact is," he added, "we literary people need to learn all these ways of being comfortable at small expense. The problem of our age is, that of perfecting small establishments for people of moderate means; and I must say, I think it has been carried further in your country than with us."

"In due course followed an introduction to "my wife," whose photograph Mr. Selby wore dutifully in his coat-pocket, over the exact region of the heart; and then came "my son," four years old, with all his playthings round him; and, in short, before an hour, Eva and he were old acquaintances, ready to tell each other family secrets.

Alice and Angelique were delightful girls to reinforce and carry out the home charm of the circle. They had eminently what belongs to the best class of American girls,—that noble frankness of manner, that fearless giving forth of their inner nature, which comes from the atmosphere of free democratic society. Like most high-bred American girls, they had traveled, and had opportunities of observing European society, which added breadth to their range of conversation without taking anything from their frank simplicity. Foreign travel produces two opposite kinds of social effect, according to character. Persons who are narrow in their education, sensitive and self-distrustful, are embarrassed by a foreign experience: they lose their confidence in their home life, in their own country and its social habitudes, and get nothing adequate in return; their efforts at hospitality are repressed by a sort of mental comparison of themselves with foreign models; they shrink from entertaining strangers, through an indefinite fear that they shall come short of what would be expected somewhere else.   But persons of more breadth of thought and more genuine courage see at once that there is a characteristic American home life, and that what a foreigner seeks in a foreign country is the *peculiarity* of that country, and not an attempt to reproduce that which has become stupid and tedious to him by constant repetition at home.

Angelique and Alice talked readily and freely; Alice with the calm, sustained good sense and dignity which was characteristic of her, and Angelique in those sunny jets and flashes of impulsive gaiety which rise like a fountain at the moment.   Given the presence of three female personages like Eva, Alice, and Angelique, and it would not be among the possibilities for a given set of the other sex to be dull or heavy.   Then, most of the gentlemen were more or less *habitués* of the house, and somewhat accorded with each other, like instruments that have been played in unison; and it is not, therefore to be wondered at that Mr. Selby made the mental comment that, taken at home, these Americans are delightful, and that cultivated American women are particularly so from their engaging frankness of manner.

There would be a great deal more obedience to the apostolic injunction, "Be not forgetful to entertain strangers," if it once could be clearly got into the heads of well-intending people *what* it is that strangers want. What do *you* want, when away from home, in a strange city?   Is it not the warmth of the home fireside, and the sight of people that you know care for you?   Is it not the blessed privilege of speaking and acting yourself out unconstrainedly among those who you know understand you?   And had you not rather dine with an old friend on simple cold mutton, offered with a warm heart, than go to a splendid ceremonious dinner party among people who don't care a rush for you?

Well, then, set it down in your book that other people are like you; and that the art of entertaining is the art of really caring for people. If you have a warm heart, congenial tastes, and a real interest in your stranger, don't fear to invite him, though you have no best dinner set, and your existing plates are sadly chipped at the edges, and even though there be a handle broken off from the side of your vegetable dish. Set it down in your belief that you can give something better than a dinner, however good,—you can give a part of yourself. You can give love, good will, and sympathy, of which there has, perhaps, been quite as much over cracked plates and restricted table furniture as over Sèvres china and silver.

It soon appeared that Mr. Selby, like other sensible Englishmen, had a genuine interest in getting below the surface life of our American world, and coming to the real "hard-pan" on which our social fabric is founded. He was full of intelligent curiosity as to the particulars of American journalism, its management, its possibilities, its remunerations compared with those of England; and here was where Bolton's experience, and Jim Fellows's many-sided practical observations, came out strongly.

Alice was delighted with the evident impression that Jim made on a man whose good opinion appeared to be worth having; for that young lady, insensibly perhaps to herself, held a sort of right of property in Jim, such as the princesses of the middle ages had in the knights that wore their colors, and Jim, undoubtedly, was inspired by the idea that bright eyes looked on, to do his *devoir* manfully in the conversation. So they went over all the chances and prospects of income and living for literary men and journalists in the two countries; the facilities

N

for marriage, and the establishment of families, including salaries, rents, prices of goods, etc.   In the course of the conversation, Mr. Selby made many frank statements of his own personal experience and observation, which were responded to with equal frankness on the part of Harry and Eva and others, till it finally seemed as if the whole company were as likely to become *au courant* of each other's affairs as a party of brothers and sisters.   Eva, sitting at the head, like a skillful steerswoman, turned the helm of conversation adroitly, now this way and now that, to draw out the forces of all her guests, and bring each into play.   She introduced the humanitarian questions of the day; and the subject branched at once upon what was doing by the Christian world: the high church, the ritualists, the broad church, and the dissenters all rose upon the carpet, and St. John was wide awake and earnest in his inquiries.   In fact, an eager talking spirit descended upon them, and it was getting dark when Eva made the move to go to the parlor, where a bright fire and coffee awaited them.

"I always hate to drop very dark shades over my windows in the evening," said Eva, as she went in and began letting down the lace curtains; "I like to have the firelight of a pleasant room stream out into the dark, and look cheerful and hospitable outside; for that reason I don't like inside shutters.   Do you know, Mr. Selby, how your English arrangements used to impress me? They were all meant to be very delightful to those *in*-side, but freezingly repulsive to those without.   Your beautiful grounds that one longs to look at, are guarded by high stone-walls with broken bottles on the top, to keep one from even hoping to get over.   Now, I think beautiful grounds are a public charity, and a public education; and a man shouldn't build a high wall round them, so that even the sight of his trees, and the odor of his flowers, should be denied to his poor neighbors."

"It all comes of our national love of privacy," said Mr. Selby; "it isn't stinginess, I beg you to believe, Mrs. Henderson, but *shyness*,—you find our hearts all right when you get in."

"That we do; but, I beg pardon, Mr. Selby, oughtn't shyness to be put down in the list of besetting sins, and fought against; isn't it the enemy of brotherly kindness and charity?"

"Certainly, Mrs. Henderson, you practice so delightfully, one cannot find fault with your preaching," said Mr. Selby; "but, after all, is it a sin to want to keep one's private life to himself, and unexposed to the comments of vulgar, uncongenial natures? It seems to me, if you will pardon the suggestion, that there is too little of this sense of privacy in America. Your public men, for instance, are required to live in glass cases, so that they may be constantly inspected behind and before. Your press interviewers beset them on every hand, take down their chance observations, record everything they say and do, and how they look and feel at every moment of their lives. I confess that I would rather be comfortably burned at the stake at once than to be one of your public men in America; and all this comes of your *not* being shy and reserved. It's a state of things impossible in the kind of country that has high walls with glass bottles around its private grounds."

"He has us there, Eva," said Harry; "our vulgar, jolly, democratic level of equality over here produces just these insufferable results; there's no doubt about it."

"Well," said Jim, "I have one word to say about newspaper reporters. Poor boys! everybody is down on them, nobody has a bit of charity for them; and yet, bless you, it isn't their fault if they're impertinent and prying. That is what they are engaged for and paid for, and kicked out if they're not up to. Why, look you, here are four or five big dailies running the general gossip-mill for these great United States, and if any one of them gets a bit of news before another, it's a victory —a "beat." Well, if the boys are not sharp, if other papers get things that they don't or can't, off they must go; and the boys have mothers and sisters to support— and want to get wives some day—and the reporting business is the first round of the ladder; if they get pitched off, it's all over with them."

"Precisely," said Mr. Selby; "it is, if you will pardon my saying it, it is your great American public that wants these papers and takes them, and takes the most of those that have the most gossip in them, that are to blame. *They* make the reporters what they are, and keep them what they are, by the demand they keep up for their wares; and so, I say, if Mrs. Henderson will pardon me, that, as yet, I am unable to put down our national shyness in the catalogue of sins to be fought against. I confess I would rather, if I should ever happen to have any literary fame, I would rather shut my shutters, evenings, and have high walls with glass bottles on top around my grounds, and *not* have every vulgar, impertinent fellow in the community commenting on my private affairs. Now, in England, we have all arrangements to keep our families to ourselves, and to such intimates as we may approve."

"Oh, yes, I knew it to my cost when I was in England," said Eva. "You might be in a great hotel with all the historic characters of your day, and see no more of them than if you were in America. They came in close family carriages, they passed to close family rooms, they traveled in railroad compartments specially secured to themselves, and you knew no more about them than if you had stayed at home."

"Well," said Mr. Selby, "you describe what I think are very nice, creditable, comfortable ways of managing."

"With not even a newspaper reporter to tell the people what they were talking about, and what gowns their wives and daughters wore," said Bolton, dryly. "I confess, of the two extremes, the English would most accord with my natural man."

"So it is with all of us," said St. John; "the question is, though, whether this strict caste system which links people in certain lines and ruts of social life, doesn't make it impossible to have that knowledge of one another as human beings which Christianity requires. It struck me in England that the high clergy had very little practical comprehension of the feelings of the lower classes, and their wives and daughters less. They were prepared to dispense charity to them from above, but not to study them on the plane of equal intercourse. They never mingle, any more than oil and water; and that, I think, is why so much charity in England is thrown away—the different classes do not understand each other, and never can."

"Yes," said Harry; "with all the disadvantages and disagreeable results of our democratic jumble in society, our common cars where all ride side by side, our hotel parlors where all sit together, and our *tables d' hote* where all dine together, we do know each other better, and there is less chance of class misunderstandings and jealousies, than in England."

"For my part, I sympathize with Mr. Selby, according to the flesh," said Mr. St. John. "The sheltered kind of life one leads in English good society is what I prefer; but, if our Christianity is good for anything, we cannot choose what we prefer."

" I have often thought," said Eva, "that the pressure of vulgar notoriety, the rush of the crowd around our Saviour, was evidently the same kind of trial to him that it must be to every refined and sensitive nature; and yet how constant and how close was his affiliation with the lowest and poorest in his day. He *lived* with them, he gave them just what we shrink from giving—his personal presence—himself."

Eva spoke with a heightened color and with a burst of self-forgetful enthusiasm. There was a little pause afterwards, as if a strain of music had suddenly broken into the conversation, and Mr. Selby, after a moment's pause, said :

" Mrs. Henderson, I give way to *that* suggestion. Sometimes, for a moment, I get a glimpse that Christianity is something higher and purer than any conventional church shows forth, and I feel that we nominal Christians are not living on that plane, and that if we only could live thus, it would settle the doubts of modern skeptics faster than any Bampton Lectures."

" Well," said Eva, "it does seem as if that which is best for society on the whole is always gained by a sacrifice of what is agreeable. Think of the picturesque scenery, and peasantry, and churches, and ceremonials in Italy, and what a perfect scattering and shattering of all such illusions would be made by a practical, common-sense system of republican government, that would make the people thrifty, prosperous, and happy! The good is not always the beautiful."

" Yes," said Bolton to Mr. Selby, "and you Liberals in England are assuredly doing your best to bring on the very state of society which produces the faults that annoy you here. The reign of the great average masses never can be so agreeable to taste as that of the cultured few."

But we will not longer follow a conversation which was kept up till a late hour around the blazing hearth. The visit was one of those happy ones in which a man enters a house a stranger and leaves it a friend. When all were gone, Harry and Eva sat talking it over by the decaying brands.

"Harry, you venturesome creature, how dared you send such a company in upon me on washing day?"

"Because, my dear, I knew you were the one woman in a thousand that could face an emergency and never lose either temper or presence of mind; and you see I was right."

"But it isn't me that you should praise, Harry; it's my poor, good Mary. Just think how patiently she turned out of her way and changed all her plans, and worked and contrived for me, when her poor old heart was breaking! I must run up now and say how much I thank her for making everything go off so well."

Eva tapped softly at the door of Mary's room. There was no answer. She opened it softly. Mary was kneeling with clasped hands before her crucifix, and praying softly and earnestly; so intent that she did not hear Eva coming in. Eva waited a moment, and then kneeled down beside her and softly put her arm around her.

"Oh, dear, Miss Eva!" said Mary, "my heart's just breaking."

"I know it, I know it, my poor Mary."

"It's so cold and dark out-doors, and where is she?" said Mary, with a shudder. "Oh, I wish I'd been kinder to her, and not scolded her."

"Oh, dear Mary, don't reproach yourself; you did it for the best. We will pray for her, and the dear Father will hear us, I know he will. The Good Shepherd will go after her and find her."

CHAPTER XXXII.

A MISTRESS WITHOUT A MAID.

[Eva to Harry's Mother.]

VALLEY OF HUMILIATION.

DEAR MOTHER : I have kept you well informed of all our prosperities in undertaking and doing : how everything we have set our hand to has turned out beautifully; how "our evenings" have been a triumphant success; and how *we and our neighbors* are all coming into the spirit of love and unity, getting acquainted, mingling and melting into each other's sympathy and knowledge. I have had the most delightful run of compliments about my house, as so bright, so cheerful, so social and cosy, and about my skill in managing to always have every thing so nice, and in entertaining with so little parade and trouble, that I really began to plume myself on something very uncommon in the way of what Aunt Prissy Diamond calls "faculty." Well, you know, next in course after the Palace Beautiful comes the Valley of Humiliation—whence my letter is dated—where I am at this present writing. Honest old John Bunyan says that, although people do not descend into this place with a very good grace, but with many a sore bruise and tumble, yet the air thereof is mild and refreshing, and many sweet flowers grow here that are not found in more exalted regions.

I have not found the flowers yet, and feel only the soreness and bruises of the descent. To drop the metaphor: I have been now three days conducting my establishment without Mary, and with no other assistant than her daughter, the little ten-year-old midget I told you about. You remember about poor Maggie, and what we were trying to do for her, and how she fled from our house? Well, Jim Fellows set the detectives upon her track, and the last that was heard of her, she had gone up to Poughkeepsie; and, as Mary has relations somewhere in that neighborhood, she thought, perhaps, if she went immediately, she should find her among them. The dear, faithful soul felt dreadfully about leaving me, knowing that, as to all practical matters, I am a poor "sheep in the wilderness;" and if I had made any opposition, or argued against it, I suppose that I might have kept her from going, but I did not. I did all I could to hurry her off, and talked heroically about how I would try to get along without her, and little Midge swelled with importance, and seemed to long for the opportunity to display her latent powers; and so Mary departed suddenly one morning, and left me in possession of the field.

The situation was the graver that we had a gentleman invited to dinner, and Mary had not time even to stuff the turkey, as she had to hurry off to the cars. "What will you do, Miss Eva?" she said, ruefully; and I said cheerily: "Oh, never fear, Mary; I never found a situation yet that I was not adequate to," and I saw her out of the door, and then turned to my kitchen and my turkey. My soul was fired with energy. I would prove to Harry what a wonderful and unexplored field of domestic science lay in my little person. Everything should be so perfect that the absence of Mary should not even be suspected!

So I came airily upon the stage of action, and took an observation of the field. This turkey should be stuffed, of course; turkeys always were stuffed; but

what with? How very shadowy and indefinite my
knowledge grew, as I contemplated those yawning rifts
and caverns which were to be filled up with something
savory—I didn't precisely know what! But the cook-
book came to my relief. I read and studied the
directions, and proceeded to explore for the articles.
"Midge, where does your mother keep the sweet herbs?"
Midge was prompt and alert in her researches and
brought them to light, and I proceeded gravely to measure and mix, while Midge, delighted at the opportunity
of exploring forbidden territory, began a miscellaneous
system of rummaging and upsetting in Mary's orderly
closets. "Here's the mustard, ma'am, and here's the
French mustard, and here's the vanilla, and the cloves is
here, and the nutmeg-grater, ma'am, and the nutmegs is
here;" and so on, till I was half crazy.

"Midge, put all those things back and shut the cupboard door, and stop talking," said I, decisively. And
Midge obeyed.

"Now," said I, "I wonder where Mary keeps her
needles; this must be sewed up."

Midge was on hand again, and pulled forth needles,
and thread, and twine, and after some pulling and pinch-
ing of my fingers, and some unsuccessful struggles with
the stiff wings that wouldn't lie down, and the stiff legs
that would kick out, my turkey was fairly bound and
captive, and handsomely awaiting his destiny.

"Now, Midge," said I, triumphant; "open the oven
door!"

"Oh! please, ma'am, it's only ten o'clock. You
don't want to roast him all day."

Sure enough; I had not thought of that. Our dinner hour was five o'clock; and, for the first time in my
life, the idea of time as connected with a roast turkey
rose in my head.

"Midge, when *does* your mother put the turkey in?"

"Oh! not till some time in the afternoon," said Midge, wisely.

"How long does it take a turkey to roast?" said I.

"Oh! a good while," said Midge, confidently, "'cordin' as how large they is."

I turned to my cook-book, and saw that so much time must be given to so many pounds; but I had not the remotest idea how many pounds there were in the turkey. So I set Midge to cleaning the silver, and ran across the way, to get light of Miss Dorcas.

How thankful I was for the neighborly running-in terms on which I stood with my old ladies; it stood me in good stead in this time of need. I ran in at the back door and found Miss Dorcas in her kitchen, presiding over some special Eleusinean mysteries in the way of preserves. The good soul had on a morning-cap calculated to strike terror into an inexperienced beholder, but her face beamed with benignity, and she entered into the situation at once.

"Cookery books are not worth a fly in such cases," she remarked, sententiously. "You must use your judgment."

"But what if you haven't got any judgment to use?" said I. "I haven't a bit."

"Well, then, dear child, you must use Dinah's, as I do. Dinah can tell to a T, how long a turkey takes to roast, by looking at it. Here, Dinah, run over, and 'talk turkey' to Mrs. Henderson."

Dinah went back with me, boiling over with giggle. She laughed so immoderately over my turkey that I began to fear I had made some disgraceful blunder; but I was relieved by a facetious poke in the side which she gave me, declaring:

"Lord's sakes alive, Mis' Henderson, you's dun it

like a bawn cook, you has. Land sake! but it just *kills*
me to see ladies work," she added, going into another
chuckle of delight.   "Waall, now, Mis' Henderson, dat
'are turkey 'll want a mighty sight of doin'.   Tell ye
what—I'll come over and put him in for you, 'bout three
o'clock," she concluded, giving me a matronizing pat on
the back.

"Besides," said little Midge, wisely, "there's all the
chambers and the parlors to do."

Sure enough! I had forgotten that beds do not make
themselves, nor chambers arrange themselves, as always
had seemed to me before.   But I went at the work, with
little Midge for handmaid, guiding her zeal and directing
and superintending her somewhat erratic movements,
till bedrooms, parlors, house, were all in wonted order.
In the course of this experience, it occurred to me a
number of times how much activity, and thought, and
care and labor of some one went to make the foundation
on which the habitual ease, quiet and composure of my
daily life was built; and I mentally voted Mary a place
among the saints.

Punctually to appointment, Dinah came over and
lifted my big turkey into the oven, and I shut the door
on him, and thought my dinner was fairly under way.

But the kitchen stove, which always seemed to me
the most matter-of-fact, simple, self-evident verity in
nature, suddenly became an inscrutable labyrinth of
mystery in my eyes.   After putting in my turkey, I went
on inspecting my china-closet, and laying out napkins,
and peering into preserve-jars, till half an hour had
passed, when I thought of taking a peep at him.   There
he lay, scarcely warmed through, with a sort of chilly
whiteness upon him.

"Midge," I cried, "why don't this fire burn? This
turkey isn't cooking."

"Oh, dear me, mum! you've forgot the drafts is shut," said Midge, just as if I had ever thought of drafts, or supposed there was any craft or mystery about them.

Midge, however, proceeded to open certain mysterious slides, whereat the stove gave a purr of satisfaction, which soon broadened into a roar.

"That will do splendidly," said I; "and now, Midge, go and get the potatoes and turnips, peel them, and have them ready."

The stove roared away merrily, and I went on with my china-closet arrangements, laying out a dessert, till suddenly I smelled a smell of burning. I went into the kitchen, and found the stove raging like a great red dragon, and the top glowing hot, and, opening the oven door, a puff of burning fume flew in my face.

"Oh, Midge, Midge," I cried, "what *is* the matter? The turkey is all burning up!" and Midge came running from the cellar.

"Why, mother shuts them slides *part* up, when the fire gets agoing too fast," said Midge—"so;" and Midge manipulated the mysterious slides, and the roaring monster grew calm.

But my turkey needed to be turned, and I essayed to turn him—a thing which seems the simplest thing in life, till one tries it and becomes convinced of the utter depravity of matter. The wretched contrary bird of evil! how he slipped and slid, and went every way but the right way! How I wrestled with him, getting hot and combative, outwardly and inwardly! How I burned my hand on the oven door, till finally over he flounced, spattering hot gravy all over my hand and the front breadth of my dress. I had a view then that I never had had before of the amount of Christian patience needed by a cook. I really got into quite a vengeful state of feeling with the monster, and shut the oven door with a malignant bang, as Hensel and Gretel did when they burned the old witch in the fairy story.

But now came the improvising of my dessert! I had projected an elegant arrangement of boiled custard, with sponge-cake at the bottom, and feathery snow of egg-froth on top—a showy composition, which, when displayed in a high cut-glass dish, strikingly ornaments the table.

I felt entirely equal to boiled custard. I had seen Mary make it dozens of times. I knew just how many eggs went to the quart of milk, and that it must be stirred gently all the time, in a kettle of boiling water, till the golden moment of projection arrived. So I stirred and stirred, with a hot face and smarting hands; for the burned places burned so much worse in the heat as to send a doubt through my mind whether I ever should have grace enough to be a martyr at the stake, for any faith or cause whatever.

But I bore all for the sake of my custard; when, oh! from some cruel, mysterious, unexplained cause, just at the last moment, the golden creamy preparation suddenly separated into curd and whey, leaving my soul desolate within me!

What had I done? What had I omitted? I was sure every rite and form of the incantation had been performed just as I had seen Mary do it hundreds of times; yet hers proved a rich, smooth, golden cream, and mine unsightly curd and watery whey!

The mysteriousness of natural laws was never so borne in upon me. There is a kink in every one of them, meant to puzzle us. In my distress, I ran across to the back door again and consulted Dinah.

" What can be the matter, Dinah? My custard won't come, when I've mixed everything exactly right, according to the rules; and it's all turned to curd and whey!"

"Land sake, missis, it's jest cause it will do so sometimes—dat are's de reason," said Dinah, with the certainty of a philosopher. "Soft custard is jest de aggravatinest thing! you don't never know when it's goin' to be contrary and flare up agin you."

"Well, Dinah," said Miss Dorcas, "you try your luck with some of our fresh morning's milk—you always have luck—and carry it over to Mrs. Henderson."

The dear old angel! No morning cap, however fearful, could disguise her. I fell upon her neck and kissed her, then and there, she was so good! She is the best old soul, mother, and I feel proud of having discovered her worth. I told her how I did hope some time she would let me do something for her, and we had quite a time, pledging our friendship to each other in the kitchen.

Well, Dinah brought over the custard, thick and smooth, and I arranged it in my high cut-glass dish and covered it with foamy billows of whites of egg tipped off with sparkles of jelly, so that Dinah declared that it looked as well "as dem perfectioners could do it;" and she staid to take my turkey out for me at the dinner hour; and I, remembering my past struggle and burned fingers, was only too glad to humbly accept her services.

Dinah is not a beauty, by any of the laws of art, but she did look beautiful to me, when I left her getting up the turkey, and retired to wash my hot cheeks and burning hands and make my toilette; for I was to appear serene and smiling in a voluminous robe, and with unsullied ribbons, like the queen of the interior, whose morning had been passed in luxurious ease and ignorant of care.

To say the truth, dear mother, I was so tired and worn out with the little I had done that I would much rather have lain down for a nap than to have enacted the

part of charming hostess.   Talk about women meeting
men with a smile, when they come in from the cares of
business!   I reflected that, if this sort of thing went on
much longer, Harry would have to meet me with a smile,
and a good many smiles, to keep up my spirits at this end
of the lever.   However, it was but for once; I sum-
moned my energies and was on time, nicely dressed, serene and fresh as if nothing had happened, and we went
through our dinner without a break down, for little
Midge was a well-trained waiter and did heroically.

Only, when I came to pour the coffee after dinner, I
was astonished at its unusual appearance.   Our clear,
limpid, golden coffee had always been one of our strong
points, and one on which I had often received special
compliments.   People had said, "How do you contrive
to always have such coffee?" and I had accepted with a
graceful humility, declaring, as is proper in such cases,
that I was not aware of any particular merit in it, etc.

The fact is, I never had thought about coffee at all.
I had seen, as I supposed, how Mary made it, and never
doubted that mine would be like hers; so that when a
black, thick, cloudy liquid poured out of my coffee pot,
I was, I confess, appalled.

Harry, like a good fellow, took no notice, and covered
my defect by beginning an animated conversation on the
merits of the last book our gentleman had published.
The good man forgot all about his coffee in his delight
at the obliging things Harry was saying, and took off the
muddy draught with a cheerful zeal, as if it was so much
nectar.

But, on our way to the parlor, Harry contrived to
whisper,

"What has got into Mary about her coffee to-day?"

"O Harry," I replied, "Mary's gone.   I had to get
the dinner all alone."

"You did! You wonderful little puss!" said the good boy. "Never mind the coffee! Better luck next time."

And, after we were alone that night, Harry praised and admired me, and I got out the cookery book to see how I ought to have made my coffee.

The directions, however, were not near as much to the point as the light I got from Dinah, who came across on a gossiping expedition to our kitchen that evening, and to whom I propounded the inquiry, "Why wasn't my coffee clear and nice like Mary's?"

"Land sakes, Mis' Henderson, ye did n't put in no fish-skin, nor nothing to clar it."

"No. I never heard of such a thing."

"Some uses fish-skin, and some takes an egg," continued Dinah. "When eggs is cheap, I takes an egg. Don't nobody have no clarer coffee 'n mine."

I made Dinah illustrate her theme by one practical experiment, after the manner of chemical lecturers, and then I was mistress of the situation. Coffee was a vanquished realm, a subjugated province, the power whereof was vested henceforth, not in Mary, but myself.

Since then, we have been anxiously looking for Mary every day; for Thursday is coming round, and how are we to have "our evening" without her? Alice and Angie are both staying with me now to help me, and on the whole we have pretty good times, though there isn't any surplus of practical knowledge among us. We have all rather plumed ourselves on being sensible domestic girls. We can all make lovely sponge cake, and Angie excels in chocolate caramels, and Alice had a great success in currant jelly. But the thousand little practical points that meet one in getting the simplest meal, nobody knows till he tries. For instance, we fried our sausages in butter, the first morning, to the great scandal of little

Midge, who instructed us gravely that they were made to fry themselves.

Since "our boys" have found out that we are sole mistresses of the kitchen, they often drop in to lighten our labors and to profess their own culinary accomplishments. Jim Fellows declares that nobody can equal him in coffee, and that he can cook a steak with tomato sauce in a manner unequaled; and Bolton professes a peculiar skill in an omelette; so we agreed yesterday to let them try their hand, and we had a great frolic over the getting up of a composition dinner. Each of us took a particular thing to be responsible for; and so we got up a pic-nic performance, which we ate with great jollity. Dr. Campbell came in with a glass coffee-making machine by which coffee was to be made on table for the amusement of the guests as well as for the gratification of appetite; and he undertook, for his part, to engineer it. Altogether we had a capital time, and more fun than if we had got the dinner under the usual auspices; and, to crown all, I got a letter from Mary that she is coming back to-morrow,—so all's well that ends well. Meanwhile, dear mother, though I have burned my hands and greased the front breadth of my new winter dress, yet I have gained something quite worth having by the experience of the last few days.

I think I shall have more patience with the faults and short-comings of the servants after this; and if the custard is a failure, or the meat is burned, or the coffee doesn't come perfectly clear, I shall remember that she is a sister woman of like passions with myself, and perhaps trying to do her very best when she fails, just as I was when I failed. I am quite sure that I shall be a better mistress for having served an apprenticeship as a maid.

So good by, dear mother.

Your loving　　　　　Eva.

CHAPTER XXXIII

A FOUR-FOOTED PRODIGAL.

THERE was dismay and confusion in the old Vanderheyden house, this evening. Mrs. Betsey sat abstracted at her tea, as one refusing to be comforted. The chair on which Jack generally sat alert and cheerful at meal times was a vacant chair, and poor soft-hearted Mrs. Betsey's eyes filled with tears every time she looked that way. Jack had run away that forenoon and had not been seen about house or premises since.

"Come now, Betsey," said Miss Dorcas, "eat your toast; you really are silly."

"I can't help it, Dorcas; it's getting dark and he doesn't come. Jack never did stay out so long before; something must have happened to him."

"Oh, you go 'way, Miss Betsey!" broke in Dinah, with the irreverent freedom which she generally asserted to herself in the family counsels, "never you fear but what Jack 'll be back soon enough—too soon for most folks; *he* knows which side *his* bread 's buttered, dat dog does. Bad penny allers sure to come home 'fore you want it."

"And there's no sort of reason, Betsey, why you shouldn't exercise self-control and eat your supper," pursued Miss Dorcas, authoritatively. "A well-regulated mind "—

"You needn't talk to me about a well-regulated mind, Dorcas," responded Mrs. Betsey, in an exacerbated tone. "I haven't got a well-regulated mind and never had, and never shall have; and reading Mrs. Chapone and Dr.

Watts on the Mind, and all the rest of them, never did
me any good. I'm one of that sort that when I'm anxious I *am* anxious; so it don't do any good to talk *that*
way to me."

"Well, you know, Betsey, if you'll only be reasonable,
that Jack always has come home."

"And good reason," chuckled Dinah. "Don't he
know when he's well off? you jest bet he does. I know
jest where he is; he's jest off a gallivantin' and a pran-
cin' and a dancin' now 'long o' dem low dogs in Flower
Street, and he'll come back bimeby smellin' 'nuff to
knock ye down, and I shall jest hev the washin' on him,
that's what I shall; and if I don't give him sech a soap-
in' and scrubbin' as he never hed, I tell you! So you jest
eat your toast, Mis' Betsey, and take no thought for de
morrer, Scriptur' says."

This cheerful picture, presented in Dinah's overpow-
eringly self-confident way, had some effect on Mrs. Betsey, who wiped her eyes and finished her slice of toast
without further remonstrance.

"Dinah, if you're sure he's down on Flower Street,
you might go and look him up, after tea," she added,
after long reflection.

"Oh, well, when my dishes is done up, ef Jack ain't
come round, why, I'll take a look arter him," quoth
Dinah. "I don't hanker arter no dog in a gineral way,
but since you've got sot on Jack, why, have him you
must. Dogs is nothin' but a plague; for my part I's glad
there won't be no dogs in heaven."

"What do you know about that?" said Mrs. Betsey,
with spirit.

"Know?" said Dinah. "Hain't I heard my Bible
read in Rev'lations all 'bout de golden city, and how it
says, 'Widout are dogs'? Don't no dogs walk de golden
streets, now I tell you; got Bible on dat ar. Jack 'll hev

to take his time in dis world, for he won't get in dere a promenadin'."

"Well then, Dinah, we must make the most we can of him here," pursued Miss Dorcas, "and so, after you've done your dishes, I wish you'd go out and look him up. You know you can find him, if you only set your mind to it."

"To think of it!" said Mrs. Betsey. "I had just taken such pains with him; washed him up in nice warm water, with scented soap, and combed him with a fine-tooth comb till there was n't a flea on him, and tied a handsome pink ribbon round his neck, because I was going to take him over to Mrs. Henderson's to call, this afternoon; and just as I got him all perfectly arranged out he slipped, and that's the last of him."

"I'll warrant!" said Dinah, "and won't he trail dat ar pink ribbon through all sorts o' nastiness, and come home smellin' wus 'n a sink-drain! Dogs hes total depravity, and hes it *hard;* it's no use tryin' to make Christians on 'em. But I'll look Jack up, never you fear. I'll bring him home, see if I don't," and Dinah went out with an air of decision that carried courage to Mrs. Betsey's heart.

"Come, now," said Miss Dorcas, "we'll wash up the china, and then, you know, it's Thursday—we'll dress and go across to Mrs. Henderson's and have a pleasant evening; and by the time we come back Jack 'll be here, I dare say. Never mind looking out the window after him now," she added, seeing Mrs. Betsey peering wistfully through the blinds up and down the street.

"People talk as if it were silly to love dogs," said Mrs. Betsey, in an injured tone. "I don't see why it is. It may be better to have a baby, but if you haven't got a baby, and have got a dog, I don't see why you shouldn't love that; and Jack was real loving, too," she added, "and such company for me; he seemed like a reasonable creature; and you were fond of him, Dorcas, you just *know* you were."

"Of course, I'm very fond of Jack," said Miss Dorcas, cheerfully; "but I'm not going to make myself miserable about him. I know, of course, he'll come back in good time. But here's Dinah, bringing the water. Come now, let's do up the china—here's your towel—and then you shall put on that new cap Mrs. Henderson arranged for you, and go over and let her see you in it. It was so very thoughtful in dear Mrs. Henderson to do that cap for you; and she said the color was very becoming."

"She is a dear, sweet little woman," said Mrs. Betsey; "and that sister of hers, Miss Angelique, looks like her, and is so lovely. She talked with me ever so long, the last time we were there. She isn't like some young girls, she can see something to like in an old woman."

Poor good Miss Dorcas had, for the most part, a very exalted superiority to any toilet vanities; but, if the truth were to be told, she was moved to an unusual degree of indulgence towards Mrs. Betsey by the suppressed fear that something grave might have befallen the pet of the household. In a sort of vague picture, there rose up before her the old days, when it was not a dog, but a little child, that filled the place in that desolate heart. When there had been a patter of little steps in those stiff and silent rooms; and questions of little shoes, and little sashes, and little embroidered robes, had filled the mother's heart. And then there had been in the house the racket and willful noise of a school-boy, with his tops, and his skates, and his books and tasks; and then there had been the gay young man, with his smoking-caps and cigars, and his rattling talk, and his coaxing, teasing ways; and then, alas! had come bad courses, and irregular hours, and watchings, and fears for one who refused to be guided; night-watchings for one who came late, and brought sorrow in his coming; till, finally, came a darker hour, and a coffin, and a funeral, and a grave, and long weariness and broken-heartedness,—a sickness of the heart that had lasted for years, that had blanched the hair, and unstrung the nerves, and made the once pretty, sprightly little woman a wreck. All these pictures rose up silently before Miss Dorcas's inner eye as she busied herself in wiping the china, and there was a touch of pathos about her unaccustomed efforts to awaken her sister's slumbering sensibility to finery, and to produce a diversion in favor of the new cap.

The love of a pet animal is something for which people somehow seem called upon to apologize to our own species, as if it were a sort of *mésalliance* of the affections to bestow them on anything below the human race; and yet the Book of books, which reflects most faithfully and tenderly the nature of man, represents the very height of cruelty by the killing of a poor man's pet lamb. It says the rich man had flocks and herds, but the poor man had nothing save one little ewe lamb, which he had brought and nourished up, which grew up together with him and his children, which ate of his bread, and drank of his cup, and lay in his bosom, and was to him as a daughter.

And how often on the unintelligent head of some poor loving animal are shed the tears of some heart-sorrow; and their dumb company, their unspoken affection, solace some broken heart which hides itself to die alone.

Dogs are the special comforters of neglected and forgotten people; and to hurt a poor man's dog, has always seemed to us a crime akin to sacrilege.

We are not at all sure, either, of the boasted superiority of our human species. A dog who lives up to the laws of his being is, in our view, a nobler creature than a man who sinks below his: he is certainly a much more profitable member of the community.   We suggest, moreover, that a much more judicious use could be made of the city dog-pound in thinning out human brutes than in smothering poor, honest curs who always lived up to their light and did just as well as they knew how.

To say the honest truth about poor Jack, his faults were only those incident to his having been originally created a dog—a circumstance for which he was in no way responsible.   He was as warm-hearted, loving, demonstrative a creature as ever wagged a tail, and he was anxious to please his mistress to the best of his light and knowledge.   But he had that rooted and insuperable objection to soap and water, and that preference for dirt and liberty, which is witnessed also in young animals of the human species, and Mrs. Betsey's exquisite neatness was a sore cross and burden to him. · Then his destiny having made him of the nature of the flesh-eaters, as the canine race are generally, and Miss Dorcas having some strict dietetic theories intended to keep him in genteel figure, Jack's allowance of meat and bones was far below his cravings: and so he was led to explore neighboring alleys, and to investigate swill-pails; to bring home and bury bones in the Vanderheyden garden-plot, which formed thus a sort of refrigerator for the preservation of his marketing.   Then Jack had his own proclivities for society.   An old lady in a cap, however caressing and affectionate, could not supply all the social wants of a dog's nature; and even the mixed and low company of Flower Street was a great relief to him from the very slelect associations and good behavior to which he was restricted the greater part of his time.   In short, Jack, like the rest of us, had his times when he was fairly tired out of being good, and acting the part of a cultivated drawing-room dog; and then he reverted with a bound to his freer doggish associates. Such an impulse is not confined to four-footed children of nature. Rachel, when mistress of all the brilliancy and luxury of the choicest *salon* in Paris, had fits of longing to return to the wild freedom of a street girl's life, and said that she felt within herself a "*besoin de s'encanailler.*" This expresses just what Jack felt when he went trailing his rose-colored bows into the society of Flower Street, little thinking, as he lolled his long pink ribbon of a tongue jauntily out of his mouth, and enjoyed the sensation he excited among the dogs of the vicinity, of the tears and anxieties his frolic was creating at home. But, in due time, the china was washed, and Mrs. Betsey entered with some interest into preparations for the evening.

Miss Dorcas and Mrs. Betsey were the earliest at the Henderson fireside, and they found Alice, Angelique and Eva busy arranging the tea-table in the corner.

"Oh, don't you think, Miss Dorcas, Mary hasn't come back yet, and we girls are managing all alone," said Angelique; "you can't think what fun it is!"

"Why didn't you tell me, Mrs. Henderson?" said Miss Dorcas. "I would have sent Dinah over to make your coffee."

"Oh, dear me, Miss Dorcas, Dinah gave me private lessons day before yesterday," said Eva, "and from henceforth I am personally adequate to any amount of coffee, I grow so self-confident. But I tried my hand in making those little biscuit Mary gets up, and they were a failure. Mary makes them with sour milk and soda, and I tried to do mine just like hers. I can't tell why, but they came out of the oven a brilliant grass-green— quite a preternatural color."

"Showing that they were the work of a green hand," said Angelique.

o

"It was an evident reflection on me," said Eva. "At any rate, I sent to the bakery for my biscuit to-night, for I would not advertise my greenness in public."

"But we are going to introduce a novelty this evening," said Angelique; "to wit: boiled chestnuts; anybody can cook chestnuts."

"Yes," said Eva; "Harry's mother has just sent us a lovely bag of chestnuts, and we are going to present them as a sensation. I think it will start all sorts of poetic and pastoral reminiscences of lovely fall days, and boys and girls going chestnutting and having good times; it will make themes for talk."

"By the by," said Angelique, "where's Jack, Mrs. Benthusen?"

"Oh! my dear, you touch a sore spot. We are in distress about Jack. He ran away this morning, and we haven't seen him all day."

"How terrible!" said Eva. "This is a neighborhood matter. Jack is the dog of the regiment. We must all put our wits together to have him looked up. Here comes Jim; let's tell him," continued she, as Jim Fellows walked up.

"What's up, now?"

"Why, our dog is missing," said Eva. "The pride of our hearts, the ornament of our neighborhood, is gone."

"Do you think anybody has stolen him?" said Alice.

"I shouldn't wonder," said Mrs. Betsey; "Jack is a dog of a very pure breed, and very valuable. A boy might get quite a sum for him."

"I'll advertise him in our paper," said Jim.

"Thank you, Mr. Fellows," said Mrs. Betsey, with tears in her eyes.

"I don't doubt he'll get back to you, even if he has

been stolen," said Harry. "I have known wonderful instances of the contrivance, and ingenuity, and perseverance of these creatures in getting back home."

"Well," said Jim, "I know a regiment of our press boys and reporters, who go all up and down the highways and byways, alleys and lanes of New York, looking into cracks and corners, and I'll furnish them with a description of Jack, and tell them *I* want him; and I'll be bound we'll have him forthcoming. There's some use in newspaper boys, now and then."

And Jim sat down by Mrs. Betsey, and entered into the topic of Jack's characteristics, ways, manners and habits, with an interest which went to the deepest heart of the good little old lady, and excited in her bosom the brightest hopes.

The evening passed off pleasantly. By this time, the habitual comers felt enough at home to have the sort of easy enjoyment that a return to one's own fireside always brings.

Alice, Jim, Eva, Angelique, and Mr. St. John discussed the forthcoming Christmas-tree for the Sunday-school, and made lists of purchases to be made of things to be distributed among them.

" Let's give them things that are really useful," said St. John.

"For my part," said Eva, "in giving to such poor children, whose mothers have no time to entertain them, and no money to buy pretty things, I feel more disposed to get bright, attractive playthings—dolls with fine, fancy dresses, and so on; it gives a touch of poetry to the poor child's life."

"Well, I've dressed four dolls," said Angie; "and I offer my services to dress a dozen more. My innate love of finery is turned to good account here."

" I incline more to useful things," said Alice.

"Well," said Eva, "suppose we do both, give each child one useful thing and one for fancy?"

"Well," said Alice, "the shopping for all this list of eighty children will be no small item. Jim, we shall have to call in your services."

"I'm your man," said Jim. "I know stores where the fellows would run their feet off to get a good word from us of the press. I shall turn my influence in to the service of the church."

"Well," said Alice, "we shall take you with us, when we go on our shopping tour."

"I know a German firm where you can get the real German candles, and glass balls, and all the shiners and tinklers to glorify your tree, and a little angel to stick on the top. A tip-top notice from me in the paper will make them shell out for us like thunder."

Mr. St. John opened his large, thoughtful, blue eyes on Jim with an air of innocent wonder. He knew as little of children and their ways as most men, and was as helpless about all the details of their affairs as he was desirous of a good result.

"I leave it all in your hands," he said, meekly; "only, wherever I can be of service, command me."

It was probably from pure accident that Mr. St. John as he spoke looked at Angie, and that Angie blushed a little, and that Jim Fellows twinkled a wicked glance across at Alice. Such accidents are all the while happening, just as flowers are all the while springing up by the wayside. Wherever man and woman walk hand in hand, the earth is sown thick with them.

It was a later hour than usual when Miss Dorcas and Mrs. Betsey came back to their home.

"Is Jack come home?" was the first question.

No, Jack had not come.

CHAPTER XXXIV.

GOING TO THE BAD.

IT was the week before Christmas, and all New York was stirring and rustling with a note of preparation. Every shop and store was being garnished and furbished to look its best. Christmas-trees for sale lay at the doors of groceries; wreaths of ground-pine, and sprigs and branches of holly, were on sale, and selling briskly. Garlands and anchors and crosses of green began to adorn the windows of houses, and were a merchantable article in the stores. The toy-shops were flaming and flaunting with a delirious variety of attractions, and mammas and papas with puzzled faces were crowding and jostling each other, and turning anxiously from side to side in the suffocating throng that crowded to the counters, while the shopmen were too flustered to answer questions, and so busy that it seemed a miracle when anybody got any attention. The country-folk were pouring into New York to do Christmas shopping, and every imaginable kind of shop had in its window some label or advertisement or suggestion of something that might answer for a Christmas gift. Even the grim, heavy hardware trade blossomed out into festal suggestions. Tempting rows of knives and scissors glittered in the windows; little chests of tools for little masters, with cards and labels to call the attention of papa to the usefulness of the present. The confectioners' windows were a glittering mass of sugar frostwork of every fanciful device, gay boxes of bonbons, marvelous fabrications of chocolate, and sugar rainbows in candy of every possible device; and bewildered crowds of well-dressed purchasers came and saw and bought faster than the two hands of the shopmen could tie up and present the parcels. The grocery stores hung out every possible suggestion of festal cheer. Long strings of turkeys and chickens, green bunches of celery, red masses of cranberries, boxes of raisins and drums of figs, artistically arranged, and garnished with Christmas greens, addressed themselves eloquently to the appetite, and suggested that the season of festivity was·at hand.

The weather was stinging cold—cold enough to nip one's toes and fingers, as one pressed round, doing Christmas shopping, and to give cheeks and nose alike a tinge of red. But nobody seemed to mind the cold. "Cold as Christmas" has become a cheery proverb; and for prosperous, well-living people, with cellars full of coal, with bright fires and roaring furnaces and well-tended ranges, a cold Christmas is merely one of the luxuries. Cold is the condiment of the season; the stinging, smarting sensation is an appetizing reminder of how warm and prosperous and comfortable are all within doors.

But did any one ever walk the streets of New York, the week before Christmas, and try to imagine himself moving in all this crowd of gaiety, outcast, forsaken and penniless? How dismal a thing is a crowd in which you look in vain for one face that you know! how depressing the sense that all this hilarity and abundance and plenty is not for you! Shakespeare has said, "How miserable it is to look into happiness through another man's eyes—to see that which you might enjoy and may not, to move in a world of gaiety and prosperity where there is nothing for you!"

Such were Maggie's thoughts, the day she went out

from the kindly roof that had sheltered her, and cast
herself once more upon the world. Poor hot-hearted,
imprudent child, why did she run from her only friends?
Well, to answer that question, we must think a little. It
is a sad truth, that when people have taken a certain
number of steps in wrong-doing, even the good that is in
them seems to turn against them and become their
enemy. It was in fact a residuum of honor and generosity, united with wounded pride, that drove Maggie
into the street, that morning. She had overheard the
conversation between Aunt Maria and Eva; and certain
parts of it brought back to her mind the severe reproaches which had fallen upon her from her Uncle
Mike. He had told her she was a disgrace to any honest
house, and she had overheard Aunt Maria telling the
same thing to Eva,—that the having and keeping such
as she in her home was a disreputable, disgraceful thing,
and one that would expose her to very unpleasant comments and observations. Then she listened to Aunt
Maria's argument, to show Eva that she had better send
her mother away and take another woman in her place,
because she was encumbered with such a daughter.

"Well," she said to herself, "I'll go then. I'm in
everybody's way, and I get everybody into trouble that's
good to me. I'll just take myself off. So there!" and
Maggie put on her things and plunged into the street
and walked very fast in a tumult of feeling.

She had a few dollars in her purse that her mother
had given her to buy winter clothing; enough, she
thought vaguely, to get her a few days' lodging somewhere, and she would find something honest to do.

Maggie knew there were places where she would be
welcomed with an evil welcome, where she would have
praise and flattery instead of chiding and rebuke; but
she did not intend to go to them just yet.

The gentle words that Eva had spoken to her, the hope and confidence she had expressed that she might yet retrieve her future, were a secret cord that held her back from going to the utterly bad.

The idea that somebody thought well of her, that somebody believed in her, and that a lady pretty, graceful, and admired in the world, seemed really to care to have her do well, was a redeeming thought. She would go and get some place, and do something for herself, and when she had shown that she could do something, she would once more make herself known to her friends. Maggie had a good gift at millinery, and, at certain odd times, had worked in a little shop on Sixteenth Street, where the mistress had thought well of her, and made her advantageous offers. Thither she went first, and asked to see Miss Pinhurst. The moment, however, that she found herself in that lady's presence, she was sorry she had come. Evidently, her story had preceded her. Miss Pinhurst had heard all the particulars of her ill conduct, and was ready to the best of her ability to act the part of the flaming sword that turned every way to keep the fallen Eve out of paradise.

"I am astonished, Maggie, that you should even think of such a thing as getting a place *here*, after all's come and gone that you know of; I am astonished that you could for one moment think of it. None but young ladies of good character can be received into our workrooms. If I should let such as you come in, my respectable girls would feel insulted. I don't know but they would leave in a body. I think *I* should leave, under the same circumstances. No, I wish you well, Maggie, and hope that you may be brought to repentance; but, as to the shop, it isn't to be thought of."

Now, Miss Pinhurst was not a hard-hearted woman; not, in any sense, a cruel woman; she was only on that

picket duty by which the respectable and well-behaved
part of society keeps off the ill-behaving. Society has
its instincts of self-protection and self-preservation, and
seems to order the separation of the sheep and the goats,
even before the time of final judgment. For, as a general thing, it would not be safe and proper to admit
fallen women back into the ranks of those unfallen,
without some certificate of purgation. Somebody must
be responsible for them, that they will not return again
to bad ways, and draw with them the innocent and inexperienced. Miss Pinhurst was right in requiring an
unblemished record of moral character among her shop-
girls. It was her mission to run a shop and run it well;
it was not her call to conduct a Magdalen Asylum:
hence, though we pity poor Maggie, coming out into the
cold with the bitter tears of rejection freezing her cheek,
we can hardly blame Miss Pinhurst. She had on her
hands already all that she could manage.

Besides, how could she know that Maggie was really
repentant? Such creatures were so artful; and, for
aught she knew, she might be coming for nothing else
than to lure away some of her girls, and get them into
mischief. She spoke the honest truth, when she said she
wished well to Maggie. She did wish her well. She
would have been sincerely glad to know that she had
gotten into better ways, but she did not feel that it was
her business to undertake her case. She had neither
time nor skill for the delicate and difficult business of
reformation. Her helpers must come to her ready-made,
in good order, and able to keep step and time: she
could not be expected to make them over.

"How hard they all make it to do right!" thought
Maggie. But she was too proud to plead or entreat.
"They all act as if I had the plague, and should give it
to them; and yet I don't want to be bad. I'd a great

deal rather be good if they'd let me, but I don't see any way. Nobody will have me, or let me stay," and Maggie felt a sobbing pity for herself. Why should she be treated as if she were the very off-scouring of the earth, when the man who had led her into all this sin and sorrow was moving in the best society, caressed, admired, flattered, married to a good, pious, lovely woman, and carrying all the honors of life?

Why was it such a sin for *her*, and no sin for him? Why could he repent and be forgiven, and why must she never be forgiven? There wasn't any justice in it, Maggie hotly said to herself—and there wasn't; and then, as she walked those cold streets, pictures without words were rising in her mind, of days when everybody flattered and praised her, and he most of all. There is no possession which brings such gratifying homage as personal beauty; for it is homage more exclusively belonging to the individual self than any other. The tribute rendered to wealth, or talent, or genius, is far less personal. A child or woman gifted with beauty has a constant talisman that turns all things to gold—though, alas! the gold too often turns out like fairy gifts; it is gold only in seeming, and becomes dirt and slate-stone on their hands.

Beauty is a dazzling and dizzying gift. It dazzles first its possessor and inclines him to foolish action; and it dazzles outsiders, and makes them say and do foolish things.

From the time that Maggie was a little chit, running in the street, people had stopped her, to admire her hair and eyes, and talk all kinds of nonsense to her, for the purpose of making her sparkle and flush and dimple, just as one plays with a stick in the sparkling of a brook. Her father, an idle, willful, careless creature, made a show plaything of her, and spent his earnings for her gratification and adornment. The mother was only too proud and fond; and it was no wonder that when Maggie grew up to girlhood her head was a giddy one, that she was self-willed, self-confident, obstinate. Maggie loved ease and luxury. Who doesn't? If she had been born on Fifth Avenue, of one of the magnates of New York, it would have been all right, of course, for her to love ribbons and laces and flowers and fine clothes, to be imperious and self-willed, and to set her pretty foot on the neck of the world. Many a young American princess, gifted with youth and beauty and with an indulgent papa and mamma, is no wiser than Maggie was; but nobody thinks the worse of her. People laugh at her little saucy airs and graces, and predict that she will come all right by and by. But then, for her, beauty means an advantageous marriage, a home of luxury and a continuance through life of the petting and indulgence which every one loves, whether wisely or not.

But Maggie was the daughter of a poor working-woman—an Irishwoman at that—and what marriage leading to wealth and luxury was in store for her?

To tell the truth, at seventeen, when her father died and her mother was left penniless, Maggie was as unfit to encounter the world as you, Miss Mary, or you, Miss Alice, and she was a girl of precisely the same flesh and blood as yourself. Maggie cordially hated everything hard, unpleasant or disagreeable, just as you do. She was as unused to crosses and self-denials as you are. She longed for fine things and pretty things, for fine sight-seeing and lively times, just as you do, and felt just as you do that it was hard fate to be deprived of them. But, when worse came to worst, she went to work with Mrs. Maria Wouvermans. Maggie was parlor-girl and waitress, and a good one too. She was ingenious, neat-handed, quick and bright; and her beauty drew favorable

attention.   But Mrs. Wouvermans never commended,
but only found fault.   If Maggie carefully dusted every
one of the five hundred knick-knacks of the drawing-
room five hundred times, there was nothing said ; but if,
on the five hundred and first time, a moulding or a crev-
ice was found with dust in it, Mrs. Wouvermans would
summon Maggie to her presence with the air of a judge,
point out the criminal fact, and inveigh, in terms of general severity, against her carelessness, as if carelessness
were the rule rather than the exception.

Mrs. Wouvermans took special umbrage at Maggie's
dress—her hat, her feathers, her flowers—not because
they were ugly, but because they were pretty, a great
deal too pretty and dressy for her station.   Mrs. Wouvermans's ideal of a maid was a trim creature, content
with two gowns of coarse stuff and a bonnet devoid of
adornment ; a creature who, having eyes, saw not anything in the way of ornament or luxury ; whose whole
soul was absorbed in work, for work's sake ; content with
mean lodgings, mean furniture, poor food, and scanty
clothing ; and devoting her whole powers of body and
soul to securing to others elegancies, comforts and luxuries to which she never aspired.   This self-denied sister
of charity, who stood as the ideal servant, Mrs. Wouvermans's maid did not in the least resemble.   Quite another thing was the gay, dressy young lady who, on Sunday mornings, stepped forth from the back gate of her
house with so much the air of a Murray Hill demoiselle
that people sometimes said to Mrs. Wouvermans, " Who
is that pretty young lady that you have staying with
you ?"—a question that never failed to arouse a smothered sense of indignation in that lady's mind, and added
bitterness to her reproofs and sarcasms, when she found
a picture-frame undusted, or pounced opportunely on a
cobweb in some neglected corner.

Maggie felt certain that Mrs. Wouvermans was on the watch to find fault with her—that she wanted to condemn her, for she had gone to service with the best of resolutions. Her mother was poor and she meant to help her; she meant to be a good girl, and, in her own mind, she thought she was a very good girl to do so much work, and remember so many different things in so many different places, and forget so few things.

Maggie praised herself to herself, just as you do, my young lady, when you have an energetic turn in household matters, and arrange and beautify, and dust, and adorn mamma's parlors, and then call on mamma and papa and all the family to witness and applaud your notability. At sixteen or seventeen, household virtue is much helped in its development by praise. Praise is sunshine; it warms, it inspires, it promotes growth : blame and rebuke are rain and hail; they beat down and bedraggle, even though they may at times be necessary. There was a time in Maggie's life when a kind, judicious, thoughtful, Christian woman might have kept her from falling, might have won her confidence, become her guide and teacher, and piloted her through the dangerous shoals and quicksands which beset a bright, attractive, handsome young girl, left to make her own way alone and unprotected.

But it was not given to Aunt Maria to see this opportunity ; and, under her system of management, it was not long before Maggie's temper grew fractious, and she used to such purpose the democratic liberty of free speech, which is the birthright of American servants, that Mrs. Wouvermans never forgave her.

Maggie told her, in fact, that she was a hard-hearted, mean, selfish woman, who wanted to get all she could out of her servants, and to give the least she could in return; and this came a little too near the truth ever to

be forgotten or forgiven.   Maggie was summarily warned
out of the house, and went home to her mother, who
took her part with all her heart and soul, and declared
that Maggie shouldn't live out any longer—she should
be nobody's servant.

This, to be sure, was silly enough in Mary, since service is the law of society, and we are all more or less
servants to somebody ; but uneducated people never
philosophize or generalize, and so cannot help themselves to wise conclusions.

All Mary knew was that Maggie had been scolded
and chafed by Mrs. Wouvermans ; her handsome darling
had been abused, and she should get into some higher
place in the world ; and so she put her as workwoman
into the fashionable store of S. S. & Co.

There Maggie was seen and coveted by the man who
made her his prey.   Maggie was seventeen, pretty, silly,
hating work and trouble, longing for pleasure, leisure,
ease and luxury; and he promised them all.   He told
her that she was too pretty to work, that if she would
trust herself to him she need have no more care; and
Maggie looked forward to a rich marriage and a home
of her own.   To do her justice, she loved the man that
promised this with all the warmth of her Irish heart.
To her, he was the splendid prince in the fairy tale,
come to take her from poverty and set her among
princes; and she felt she could not do too much for him.
She would be such a good wife, she would be so devoted,
she would improve herself and learn so that she might
never discredit him.

Alas! in just such an enchanted garden of love, and
hope, and joy, how often has the ground caved in and
let the victim down into dungeons of despair that never
open !

Maggie thinks all this over as she pursues her cheer-

GOING TO THE BAD.

" The sweet-faced woman calls the attention of her husband. He
frowns, whips up the horse, and is gone. . . Bitterness possesses
Maggie's soul. . . Why not go to the bad ?"—p. 327.

less, aimless way through the cold cutting wind, and looks into face after face that has no pity for her. Scarcely knowing why she did it, she took a car and rode up to the Park, got out, and wandered drearily up and down among the leafless paths from which all trace of summer greenness had passed.

Suddenly, a carriage whirred past her. She looked up. There he sat, driving, and by his side so sweet a lady, and between them a flaxen-haired little beauty, clasping a doll in her chubby arms!

The sweet-faced woman looks pitifully at the haggard, weary face, and says something to call the attention of her husband. An angry flush rises to his face. He frowns, and whips up the horse, and is gone. A sort of rage and bitterness possess Maggie's soul. What is the use of trying to do better? Nobody pities her. Nobody helps her. The world is all against her. Why not go to the bad?

CHAPTER XXXV

A SOUL IN PERIL.

IT will be seen by the way in which we left poor Maggie that she stood in just one of those critical steep places of life where a soul is in pain and peril; where the turning of a hair's breadth may decide between death and life. And it is something, not only to the individual, but to the whole community, what a woman may become in one of these crises of life.

Maggie had a rich, warm, impulsive nature, full of passion and energy; she had personal beauty and the power that comes from it; she had in her all that might have made the devoted wife and mother, fitted to give strong sons and daughters to our republic, and to bring them up to strengthen our country. But, deceived, betrayed, led astray by the very impulses which should have ended in home and marriage, with even her best friends condemning her, her own heart condemning her, the whole face of the world set against her, her feet stood in slippery places.

There is another life open to the woman whom the world judges and rejects and condemns; a life short, bad, desperate; a life of revenge, of hate, of deceit; a life in which woman, outraged and betrayed by man, turns bitterly upon him, to become the tempter, the betrayer, the ruiner of man,—to visit misery and woe on the society that condemns her.

Many a young man has been led to gambling, and drinking, and destruction; many a wife's happiness has been destroyed; many a mother has wept on a sleepless pillow over a son worse than dead,—only because some woman, who at a certain time in her life might have been saved to honor and good living, has been left to be a vessel of wrath fitted to destruction. For we have seen in Maggie's history that there were points all along, where the girl might have been turned into another and a better way.

If Mrs. Maria Wouvermans, instead of railing at her love of feathers and flowers, watching for her halting, and seeking occasion against her, had only had grace to do for her what lies in the power of every Christian mistress; if she had won her confidence, given her motherly care and sympathy, and trained her up under the protection of household influences, it might have been otherwise. Or, supposing that Maggie were too self-willed, too elate with the flatteries that come to young beauty, to be saved from a fall, yet, after that fall, when she rose, ashamed and humbled, there was still a chance of retrieval.

Perhaps there is never a time when man or woman has a better chance, with suitable help, of building a good character than just after a humiliating fall which has taught the sinner his own weakness, and given him a sad experience of the bitterness of sin.

Nobody wants to be sold under sin, and go the whole length in iniquity; and when one has gone just far enough in wrong living to perceive in advance all its pains and penalties, there is often an agonized effort to get back to respectability, like the clutching of the drowning man for the shore. The waters of death are cold and bitter, and nobody wants to be drowned.

But it is just at this point that the drowning hand is wrenched off; society fears that the poor wet wretch will upset its respectable boat; it pushes him off, and rows over the last rising bubbles.

And this is not in the main because men and women

are hard-hearted or cruel, but because they are busy,
every one of them, with their own works and ways, hurried, driven, with no time, strength, or heart-leisure for
more than they are doing. What is one poor soul struggling in the water, swimming up stream, to the great
pushing, busy, bustling world?

Nothing in the review of life appears to us so pitiful
as the absolute nothingness of the individual in the great
mass of human existence. To each living, breathing,
suffering atom, the consciousness of what it desires and
suffers is so intense, and to every one else so faint. It is
faint even to the nearest and dearest, compared to what
it is to one's self. "The heart knoweth its own bitterness, and a stranger intermeddleth not therewith."

Suppose you were suddenly struck down to-day by
death in any of its dreadful forms, how much were this
to you, how little to the world! how little even to the
friendly world, who think well of you and wish you
kindly! The paper that tells the tale scarcely drops from
their hand; a few shocked moments of pity or lamentation, perhaps, and then returns the discussion of what
shall be for dinner, and whether the next dress shall be
cut with flounces or folds: the gay waves of life dance
and glitter over the last bubble which marks where you
sank.

So we have seen poor Maggie, with despair and bitterness in her heart, wandering, on a miserable cold day,
through the Christmas rejoicings of New York, on the
very verge of going back to courses that end in unutterable degradation and misery; and yet, how little it was
anybody's business to seek or to save her.

"So," said Mrs. Wouvermans, in a tone of exultation,
when she heard of Maggie's flight, "I *hope*, I'm sure,
Eva's had enough of her fine ways of managing! Miss
Maggie's off, just as I knew she'd be. That girl is a

baggage! And now, of course, nothing must do but Mary must be off to look for her, and then Eva is left with all her house on her hands. I should think this would show her that my advice wasn't so altogether to be scorned."

Now, it is not to be presumed that Mrs. Wouvermans really was so cruel as to exult in the destruction of Maggie, and the perplexity and distress of her mother, or in Eva's domestic discomfort; yet there was something very like this in the tone of her remarks.

Whence is the feeling of satisfaction which we have when things that we always said we knew, turn out just as we predicted? Had we really rather our neighbor would be proved a thief and a liar than to be proved in a mistake ourselves? Would we be willing to have somebody topple headlong into destruction for the sake of being able to say, "I told you so"?

Mrs. Wouvermans did not ask herself these pointed questions, and so she stirred her faultless coffee without stirring up a doubt of her own Christianity—for, like you and me, Mrs. Wouvermans held herself to be an ordinarily good Christian.

Gentle, easy Mrs. Van Arsdel heard this news with acquiescence. "Well, girls, so that Maggie's run off and settled the question; and, on the whole, I'm not sorry, for that ends Eva's responsibility for her; and, after all, I think your aunt was half right about that matter. One doesn't want to have too much to do with such people."

"But, mamma," said Alice, "it seems such a dreadful thing that so young a girl, not older than I am, should be utterly lost."

"Yes, but you can't help it, and such things are happening all the time, and it isn't worth while making ourselves unhappy about it. I'm sure Eva acted like a little saint about it, and the girl can have no one to blame but herself."

"I know," said Alice; "Eva told me about it. It was Aunt Maria, with her usual vigor and activity, who precipitated the catastrophe. Eva had just got the girl into good ways, and all was going smoothly, when Aunt Maria came in and broke everything up. I must say, I think Aunt Maria is a nuisance."

"Oh, Alice, how can you talk so, when you know that your aunt is thinking of nothing so much as how to serve and advance you girls?"

"She is thinking of how to carry her own will and pleasure; and we girls are like so many ninepins that she wants to set up or knock down to suit her game. Now she has gone and invited those Stephenson girls to spend the holidays with her."

"Well, you know it's entirely on your account, Alice, —you girls. The Stephensons are a very desirable family to cultivate."

"Yes; it's all a sort of artifice, so that they may have to invite us to visit them next summer at Newport. Now, I never was particularly interested in those girls. They always seemed to me insipid sort of people; and to feel obliged to be very attentive to them and cultivate their intimacy, with any such view, is a sort of maneuvering that is very repulsive to me; it doesn't seem honest."

"But now your aunt has got them, and we must be attentive to them," pleaded Mrs. Van Arsdel.

"Oh, of course. What I am complaining of is that my aunt can't let us alone; that she is always scheming for us, planning ahead for us, getting people that we must be attentive to, and all that; and then, because she's our aunt and devoted to our interests, our conscience is all the while troubling us because we don't like her better.

The truth is, Aunt Maria is a constant annoyance to me, and I reproach myself for not being grateful to her. Now, Angelique and I are on a committee for buying the presents for the Christmas-tree of our mission-school, and we shall have to go and get the tree up; and it's no small work to dress a Christmas-tree—in fact, we shall just have our hands full, without the Stephensons. We are going up to Eva's this very morning, to talk this matter over and make out our lists of things ; and, for my part, I find the Stephensons altogether *de trop.*"

Meanwhile, in Eva's little dominion, peace and prosperity had returned with the return of cook to the kitchen cabinet. A few days' withdrawal of that important portion of the household teaches the mistress many things, and, among others, none more definitely than the real dignity and importance of that sphere which is generally regarded as least and lowest.

Mary had come back disheartened from a fruitless quest. Maggie had indeed been at Poughkeepsie, and had spent a day and a night with a widowed sister of Mary's, and then, following a restless impulse, had gone back to New York—none knew whither; and Mary was going on with her duties with that quiet, acquiescent sadness with which people of her class bear sorrow which they have no leisure to indulge. The girl had for two or three years been lost to her; but the brief interval of restoration seemed to have made the pang of losing her again still more dreadful. Then, the anticipated mortification of having to tell Mike of it, and the thought of what Mike and Mike's wife's would say, were a stinging poison. Though Maggie's flight was really due in a great measure to Mike's own ungracious reception of her and his harsh upbraidings, intensified by what she had overheard from Mrs. Wouvermans, yet Mary was quite sure that Mike would receive it as a confirmation of his own sagacity in the opinion he had pronounced.

The hardness and apathy with which even near relations will consign their kith and kin to utter ruin is one of the sad phenomena of life. Mary knew that Mike would say to her, "Didn't I tell you so? The girl's gone to the bad; let her go! She's made her bed; let her lie in it."

It was only from her gentle, sympathetic mistress that Mary met with a word of comfort. Eva talked with her, and encouraged her to pour out all her troubles and opened the door of her own heart to her sorrows. Eva cheered and comforted her all she could, though she had small hopes, herself.

She had told Mr. Fellows, she said, and Mr. Fellows knew all about New York—knew everybody and everything—and if Maggie were there he would be sure to hear of her; "and if she is anywhere in New York I will go to her," said Eva, "and persuade her to come back and be a good girl. And don't you tell your brother anything about it. Why need he know? I dare say we shall get Maggie back, and all going right, before he knows anything about it."

Eva had just been talking to this effect to Mary in the kitchen, and she came back into her parlor, to find there poor, fluttering, worried little Mrs. Betsey Benthusen, who had come in to bewail her prodigal son, of whom, for now three days and nights, no tidings had been heard.

"I came in to ask you, dear Mrs. Henderson, if anything has been heard from the advertising of Jack? I declare, I haven't been able to sleep since he went, I am so worried. I dare say you must think it silly of me," she said, wiping her eyes, "but I *am* just so silly. I really had got so fond of him—I feel so lonesome without him."

"Silly, dear friend!" said Eva in her usual warm, impulsive way, "no, indeed; I think it's perfectly natural that you should feel as you do. I think, for my part, these poor dumb pets were given us to love; and if we do love them, we can't help feeling anxious about them when they are gone."

"You see," said Mrs. Betsey, "if I only knew—but I don't—if I knew just where he was, or if he was well treated; but then, Jack is a dog that has been used to kindness, and it would come hard to him to have to suffer hunger and thirst, and be kicked about and abused. I lay and thought about things that might happen to him, last night, till I fairly cried"—and the tears stood in the misty blue eyes of the faded little old gentlewoman, in attestation of the possibility. "I got so wrought up," she continued, "that I actually prayed to my Heavenly Father to take care of my poor Jack. Do you think that was profane, Mrs. Henderson?—I just could not help it."

"No, dear Mrs. Betsey, I don't think it was profane; I think it was just the most sensible thing you could do. You know our Saviour says that not a sparrow falls to the ground without our Father, and I'm sure Jack is a good deal larger than a sparrow."

"Well, I didn't tell Dorcas," said Mrs. Betsey, "because she thinks I'm foolish, and I suppose I am. I'm a broken-up old woman now, and I never had as much strength of mind as Dorcas, anyway. Dorcas has a *very* strong mind," said little Mrs. Betsy in a tone of awe; "she has tried all she could to strengthen mine, but she can't do much with me."

Just at this instant, Eva, looking through the window down street, saw Jim Fellows approaching, with Jack's head appearing above his shoulder in that easy, jaunty attitude with which the restored lamb is represented in a modern engraving of the Good Shepherd.

There he sat, to be sure, with a free and easy air of bright, doggish vivacity; perched aloft with his pink tongue hanging gracefully out of his mouth, and his great, bright eyes and little black tip of a nose gleaming out from the silvery thicket of his hair, looking anything but penitent for all the dismays and sorrows of which he had been the cause.

"Oh, Mrs. Betsey, do come here," cried Eva; "here is Jack, to be sure!"

"You don't say so! Why, so he is; that *dear*, good Mr. Fellows! how can I ever thank him enough!"

And, as Jim mounted the steps, Eva hastened to open the door in anticipation of the door-bell.

"Any dogs to-day, ma'am?" said Jim in the tone of a pedlar.

"Oh, Mrs. Henderson!" said Mrs. Betsey. But what further she said was lost in Jack's vociferous barking. He had recognized Mrs. Betsey and struggled down out of Jim's arms, and was leaping and capering and barking, overwhelming his mistress with obstreperous caresses, in which there was not the slightest recognition of any occasion for humility or penitence. Jack was forgiving Mrs. Betsey with all his might and main for all the trouble he had caused, and expressing his perfect satisfaction and delight at finding himself at home again.

"Well," said Jim, in answer to the numerous questions showered upon him, "the fact is that Dixon and I were looking up something to write about in a not very elegant or reputable quarter of New York, and suddenly, as we were passing one of the dance houses, that girl Maggie darted out with Jack in her arms, and calling after me by name, she said: 'This poor dog belongs to the people opposite Mrs. Henderson's. He has been stolen away, and won't you take him back?' I said I would, and then I said, 'Seems to me, Maggie, you'd better come back, too, to your mother, who is worrying dreadfully about you.' But she turned quickly and said, 'The less said about me the better,' and ran in."

"Oh, how dreadful that anybody should be so depraved at her age," said little Mrs. Betsey, complacently caressing Jack. "Mrs. Henderson, you have had a fortunate escape of her; you must be glad to get her out of your house. Well, I must hurry home with him and get him washed up, for he's in *such* a state! And do look at this ribbon! Would you know it ever had been a ribbon? it's thick with grease and dirt, and I dare say he's covered with fleas. O Jack, Jack, what trouble you have made me!"

And the little woman complacently took up her criminal, who went off on her shoulder with his usual waggish air of impudent assurance.

"See what luck it is to be a dog," said Jim. "Nobody would have half the patience with a ragamuffin boy, now!"

"But, seriously, Jim, what can be done about poor Maggie? I've promised her mother to get her back, if she could be discovered."

"Well, really she is in one of the worst drinking saloons of that quarter, kept by Mother Mogg, who is, to put the matter explicitly, a sort of she devil. It isn't a place where it would do for me or any of the boys to go. We are not calculated for missionary work in just that kind of field."

"Well, who *can* go? What can be done? I've promised Mary to save her. I'll go myself, if you'll show me the way."

"You, Mrs. Henderson? You don't know what you

P

are talking about. You never could go there. It isn't to be thought of."

"But somebody must go, Jim; we can't leave her there."

"Well, now I think of it," said Jim, "there is a Methodist minister who has undertaken to set up a mission in just that part of the city. They bought a place that used to be kept for a rat-pit, and had it cleaned up, and they have opened a mission house, and have prayer-meetings and such things there. I'll look that thing up; perhaps he can find Maggie for you. Though I must say you are taking a great deal of trouble about this girl."

"Well, Jim, she has a mother, and her mother loves her as yours does you."

"By George, now, that's enough," said Jim. "You don't need to say another word. I'll go right about it, this very day, and hunt up this Mr. What's-his-name, and find all about this mission. I've been meaning to write that thing up this month or so."

CHAPTER XXXVI

LOVE IN CHRISTMAS GREENS.

THE little chapel in one of the out-of-the-way streets of New York presented a scene of Christmas activity and cheerfulness approaching to gaiety. The whole place was fragrant with the spicy smell of spruce and hemlock. Baskets of green ruffles of ground-pine were foaming over their sides with abundant contributions from the forest; and bright bunches of vermilion bittersweet, and the crimson-studded branches of the black alder, added color to the picture. Of real traditional holly, which in America is a rarity, there was a scant supply, reserved for more honorable decorations.

Mr. St. John had been busy in his vestry with paper, colors, and gilding, illuminating some cards with Scriptural mottoes. He had just brought forth his last effort and placed it in a favorable light for inspection. It is the ill-fortune of every successful young clergyman to stir the sympathies and enkindle the venerative faculties of certain excitable women, old and young, who follow his footsteps and regard his works and ways with a sort of adoring rapture that sometimes exposes him to ridicule if he accepts it, and which yet it seems churlish to decline. It is not generally his fault, nor exactly the fault of the women, often amiably sincere and unconscious; but it is a fact that this kind of besetment is more or less the lot of every clergyman, and he cannot help it. It is to be accepted as we accept any of the shadows which are necessary in the picture of life, and got along with by the kind of common sense with which we dispose of any of its infelicities.

Mr. St. John did little to excite demonstrations of this kind; but the very severity with which he held himself in reserve seemed rather to increase a kind of sacred prestige which hung around him, making of him a sort of churchly Grand Llama. When, therefore, he brought out his illuminated card, on which were inscribed in Anglo Saxon characters,

> " The Word was made flesh
> And dwelt among us,"

there was a loud acclaim of " How lovely! how sweet!" with groans of intense admiration from Miss Augusta Gusher and Miss Sophronia Vapors, which was echoed in "ohs!" and "ahs!" from an impressible group of girls on the right and left.

Angelique stood quietly gazing on it, with a wreath of ground-pine dangling from her hand, but she said nothing.

Mr. St. John at last said, "And what do *you* think, Miss Van Arsdel?"

"I think the colors are pretty," Angie said, hesitating, "but "—

"But what?" said Mr. St. John, quickly.

"Well, I don't know what it means—I don't understand it."

Mr. St. John immediately read the inscription in concert with Miss Gusher, who was a very mediæval young lady and quite up to reading Gothic, or Anglo Saxon, or Latin, or any Churchly tongue.

"Oh!" was all the answer Angie made; and then, seeing something more was expected, she added again, "I think the effect of the lettering very pretty," and turned away, and busied herself with a cross of ground-pine that she was making in a retired corner.

The chorus were loud and continuous in their ac-

SKIRMISHING.

"I like your work," he said, "better than you do mine." "I didn't say that I didn't like yours," said Angie, coloring.—p. 341.

claims, and Miss Gusher talked learnedly of lovely inscriptions in Greek and Latin, offering to illuminate some of them for the occasion. Mr. St. John thanked her and withdrew to his sanctum, less satisfied than before.

About half an hour after, Angie, who was still quietly busy upon her cross in her quiet corner, under the shade of a large hemlock tree which had been erected there, was surprised to find Mr. St. John standing, silently observing her work.

"I like your work," he said, "better than you did mine."

"I didn't say that I didn't like yours," said Angie, coloring, and with that sort of bright, quick movement that gave her the air of a bird just going to fly.

"No, you did not *say*, but you left approbation unsaid, which amounts to the same thing. You have some objection, I see, and I really wish you would tell me frankly what it is."

"O Mr. St. John, don't say that! Of course I never thought of objecting; it would be presumptuous in me. I really don't understand these matters at all, not at all. I just don't know anything about Gothic letters and all that, and so the card doesn't say anything to me. And I must confess, I thought "—

Here Angie, like a properly behaved young daughter of the Church, began to perceive that her very next sentence might lead her into something like a criticism upon her rector; and she paused on the brink of a gulf so horrible, "with pious awe that feared to have offended."

Mr. St. John felt a very novel and singular pleasure in the progress of this interview. It interested him to be differed with, and he said, with a slight intonation of dictation:

"I must insist on your telling me what you thought, Miss Angie."

"Oh, nothing, only this—that if *I*, who have had more education than our Sunday-school scholars, can't read a card like that, why, *they* could not. I'm quite sure that an inscription in plain modern letters that I could read would have more effect upon my mind, and I am quite sure it would on them."

"I thank you sincerely for your frankness, Miss Angie; your suggestion is a valuable one."

"I think," said Angie, "that mediæval inscriptions, and Greek and Latin mottoes, are interesting to educated, cultivated people. The very fact of their being in another language gives a sort of piquancy to them. The idea gets a new coloring from a new language; but to people who absolutely don't understand a word, they say nothing, and of course they do no good; so, at least, it seems to me."

"You are quite right, Miss Angie, and I shall immediately put my inscription into the English of to-day. The fact is, Miss Angie," added St. John after a silent pause, "I feel more and more what a misfortune it has been to me that I never had a sister. There are so many things where a woman's mind sees so much more clearly than a man's. I never had any intimate female friend." Here Mr. St. John began assiduously tying up little bunches of the ground-pine in the form which Angie needed for her cross, and laying them for her.

Now, if Angie had been a sophisticated young lady, familiar with the tactics of flirtation, she might have had precisely the proper thing at hand to answer this remark; as it was, she kept on tying her bunches assiduously and feeling a little embarrassed.

It was a pity he should not have a sister, she thought. Poor man, it must be lonesome for him; and Angie's

face at this moment must have expressed some com-
miseration or some emotion that emboldened the young
man to say, in a lower tone, as he laid down a bunch of
green by her:

"If you, Miss Angie, would look on me as you do on
your brothers, and tell me sincerely your opinion of me,
it might be a great help to me."

Now Mr. St. John was certainly as innocent and
translucently ignorant of life as Adam at the first hour
of his creation, not to know that the tone in which he
was speaking and the impulse from which he spoke, at
that moment, was in fact that of man's deepest, most
absorbing feeling towards woman. He had made his
scheme of life; and, as a set purpose, had left *love* out
of it, as something too terrestrial and mundane to consist with the sacred vocation of a priest. But, from the
time he first came within the sphere of Angelique, a
strange, delicious atmosphere, vague and dreamy, yet
delightful, had encircled him, and so perplexed and diz-
zied his brain as to cause all sorts of strange vibrations.
At first, there was a sort of repulsion—a vague alarm, a
suspicion and repulsion singularly blended with an
attraction. He strove to disapprove of her; he resolved
not to think of her; he resolutely turned his head away
from looking at her in her place in Sunday-school and
church, because he felt that his thoughts were alarmingly
drawn in that direction.

Then came his invitation into society, of which the
hidden charm, unacknowledged to himself, was that he
should meet Angelique; and that mingling in society had
produced, inevitably, modifying effects, which made him
quite a different being from what he was in his recluse
life passed between the study and the altar.

It is not in man, certainly not in a man so finely
fibered and strung as St. John, to associate intimately

with his fellows without feeling their forces upon himself, and finding many things in himself of which he had
not dreamed.

But if there be in the circle some one female presence
which all the while is sending out an indefinite though
powerful enchantment, the developing force is still more
marked.

St. John had never suspected himself of the ability
to be so agreeable as he found himself in the constant
reunions which, for one cause or another, were taking
place in the little Henderson house. He developed a
talent for conversation, a vein of gentle humor, a turn
for versification, with a cast of thought rising into the
sphere of poetry, and then, with Dr. Campbell and Alice
and Angie, he formed no mean quartette in singing.

In all these ways he had been coming nearer and
nearer to Angie, without taking the alarm. He remembered appositely what Montalembert in his history of the
monks of the Middle Ages says of the female friendships
which always exerted such a modifying power in the lives
of celebrated saints; how St. Jerome had his Eudochia,
and St. Somebody-else had a sister, and so on. And as
he saw more and more of Angelique's character, and felt
her practical efficiency in church work, he thought it
would be very lovely to have such a friend all to himself.
Now, friendship on the part of a young man of twenty-
five for a young saint with hazel eyes and golden hair,
with white, twinkling hands and a sweet voice, and an
assemblage of varying glances, dimples and blushes, is
certainly a most interesting and delightful relation; and
Mr. St. John built it up and adorned it with all sorts of
charming allegories and figures and images, making a
sort of semi-celestial affair of it.

It is true, he had given up St. Jerome's love, and
concluded that it was not necessary that his "heart's

elect" should be worn and weary and wasted, or resemble a dying altar-fire; he had learned to admire Angie's blooming color and elastic step, and even to take an appreciative delight in the prettinesses of her toilette; and, one evening, when she dropped a knot of peach-blow ribbons from her bosom, the young divine had most unscrupulously appropriated the same, and, taking it home, gloated over it as a holy relic, and yet he never suspected that he was in love—oh, no! And, at this moment, when his voice was vibrating with that strange revealing power that voices sometimes have in moments of emotion, when the very tone is more than the words, he, poor fellow, was ignorant that his voice had said to Angie, "I love you with all my heart and soul."

But there is no girl so uninstructed and so inexperienced as not to be able to interpret a tone like this at once, and Angie at this moment felt a sort of bewildering astonishment at the revelation. All seemed to go round and round in dizzy mazes—the greens, the red berries—she seemed to herself to be walking in a dream, and Mr. St. John with her.

She looked up and their eyes met, and at that moment the veil fell from between them. His great, deep, blue eyes had in them an expression that could not be mistaken.

"Oh, Mr. St. John!" she said.

"Call me *Arthur*," he said, entreatingly.

"Arthur!" she said, still as in a dream.

"And may I call you Angelique, my good angel, my guide? Say so!" he added, in a rapid, earnest whisper, "say so, dear, dearest Angie!"

"Yes, Arthur," she said, still wondering.

"And, oh, *love* me," he added, in a whisper; "a little, ever so little! You cannot think how precious it will be to me!"

"Mr. St. John!" called the voice of Miss Gusher.

He started in a guilty way, and came out from behind the thick shadows of the evergreen which had concealed this little *tête-à-tête*. He was all of a sudden transformed to Mr. St. John, the rector—distant, cold, reserved, and the least bit in the world dictatorial. In his secret heart, Mr. St. John did not like Miss Gusher. It was a thing for which he condemned himself, for she was a most zealous and efficient daughter of the Church. She had worked and presented a most elegant set of altar-cloths, and had made known to him her readiness to join a sisterhood whenever he was ready to ordain one. And she always admired him, always agreed with him, and never criticised him, which perverse little Angie sometimes did; and yet ungrateful Mr. St. John was wicked enough at this moment to wish Miss Gusher at the bottom of the Red Sea, or in any other Scriptural situation whence there would be no probability of her getting at him for a season.

"I wanted you to decide on this decoration for the font," she said. "Now, there is this green wreath and this red cross of bitter-sweet. To be sure, there is no tradition about bitter-sweet; but the very name is symbolical, and I thought that I would fill the font with calla lilies. Would lilies at Christmas be strictly Churchly? That is my only doubt. I have always seen them appropriated to Easter. What should you say, Mr. St. John?"

"Oh, have them by all means, if you can," said Mr. St. John. "Christmas is one of the Church's highest festivals, and I admit anything that will make it beautiful."

Mr. St. John said this with a radiancy of delight which Miss Gusher ascribed entirely to his approbation of her zeal; but the heavens and the earth had assumed a new aspect to him since that little talk in the corner. For when Angie lifted her eyes, not only had she read the unutterable in his, but he also had looked far down into the depths of her soul, and seen something he did not quite dare to put into words, but in the light of which his whole life now seemed transfigured.

It was a new and amazing experience to Mr. St. John, and he felt strangely happy, yet particularly anxious that Miss Gusher and Miss Vapors, and all the other tribe of his devoted disciples, should not by any means suspect what had fallen out; and therefore it was that he assumed such a cheerful zeal in the matter of the font and decorations.

Meanwhile, Angie sat in her quiet corner, like a good little church mouse, working steadily and busily on her cross. Just as she had put in the last bunch of bittersweet, Mr. St. John was again at her elbow.

"Angie," he said, "you are going to give me that cross. I want it for my study, to remember this morning by."

"But I made it for the front of the organ."

"Never mind. I can put another there; but this is to be *mine*," he said, with a voice of appropriation. "I want it because you were making it when you promised what you did. You must keep to that promise, Angie."

"Oh, yes, I shall."

"And I want one thing more," he said, lifting Angie's little glove, where it had fallen among the refuse pieces.

"What!—my glove? Is not that silly?"

"No, indeed."

"But my hands will be cold."

"Oh, you have your muff. See here: I want it," he said, "because it seems so much like you, and you don't know how lonesome I feel sometimes."

Poor man ! Angie thought, and she let him have the glove. "Oh," she said, apprehensively, "please don't stay here now. I hear Miss Gusher calling for you."

"She is always so busy," said he, in a tone of discontent.

"She is so good," said Angie, "and does so much."

"Oh, yes, good enough," he said, in a discontented tone, retreating backward into the shadow of the hemlock, and so finding his way round into the body of the church.

But there is no darkness or shadow of death where a handsome, engaging young rector can hide himself so that the truth about him will not get into the bill of some bird of the air.

The sparrows of the sanctuary are many, and they are particularly wide awake and watchful.

Miss Gusher had been witness of this last little bit of interview; and, being a woman of mature experience, versed in the ways of the world, had seen, as she said, through the whole matter.

"Mr. St. John is just like all the rest of them, my dear," she said to Miss Vapors, "he will flirt, if a girl will only let him. I saw him just now with that Angie Van Arsdel. Those Van Arsdel girls are famous for drawing in any man they happen to associate with."

"You don't say so," said Miss Vapors; "what did you see?"

"Oh, my dear, I sha'n't tell; of course, I don't approve of such things, and it lowers Mr. St. John in my esteem,—so I'd rather not speak of it. I did hope he was above such things."

"But do tell me, did he *say* anything?" said Miss Vapors, ready to burst in ignorance.

"Oh, no. I only saw some appearances and expressions—a certain manner between them that told all.

Sophronia Vapors, you mark my words: there is something going on between Angie Van Arsdel and Mr. St. John. I don't see, for my part, what it is in those Van Arsdel girls that the men see; but, sure as one of them is around, there is a flirtation got up."

" Why, they're not so very beautiful," said Miss Vapors.

" Oh, dear, no. I never thought them even pretty; but then, you see, there's no accounting for those things."

And so, while Mr. St. John and Angie were each wondering secretly over the amazing world of mutual understanding that had grown up between them, the rumor was spreading and growing in all the band of Christian workers.

CHAPTER XXXVII.

ACCORDING to the view of the conventional world, the brief, sudden little passage between Mr. St. John and Angelique among the Christmas-greens was to all intents and purposes equivalent to an engagement; and yet, St. John had not actually at that time any thought of marriage.

"Then," says Mrs. Mater-familias, ruffling her plumage, in high moral style, "he is a man of no principle—and acts abominably." You are wrong, dear madam; Mr. St. John is a man of high principle, a man guided by conscience, and who would honestly sooner die than do a wrong thing.

"Well, what does he mean then, talking in this sort of way to Angie, if he has no intentions? He ought to know better."

Undoubtedly, he ought to know better, but he does not. He knows at present neither his own heart nor that of womankind, and is ignorant of the real force and meaning of what he has been saying and looking, and of the obligations which they impose on him as a man of honor. Having been, all his life, only a *recluse* and student, having planned his voyage of life in a study, where rocks and waves and breakers and shoals are but so many points on paper, it is not surprising that he finds himself somewhat ignorant in actual navigation, where rocks and shoals are quite another affair. It is one thing to lay down one's scheme and law of life in a study, among supposititious men and women, and another to carry it out in life among real ones, each one of whom acts upon us with the developing force of sun-shine on the seed-germ.

In fact, no man knows what there is in himself till he has tried himself under the influence of other men; and if this is true of man over man, how much more of that subtle developing and revealing power of woman over man. St. John, during the first part of his life, had been possessed by that sort of distant fear of womankind which a person of acute sensibility has of that which is bright, keen, dazzling, and beyond his powers of man-agement, and which, therefore, seems to him possessed of indefinite powers for mischief. It was something with which he felt unable to cope. He had, too, the common prejudice against fashionable girls and women as of course wanting in earnestness; and he entered upon his churchly career with a sort of hard determina-tion to have no trifling, and to stand in no relation to this suspicious light guerrilla force of the church but that of a severe drill-sergeant.

To his astonishment, the child whom he had under-taken to drill had more than once perforce, and from the very power of her womanly nature, proved herself competent to guide him in many things which belonged to the very essence of his profession—church work. Angie had been able to enter places whence he had been excluded; able to enter by those very attractions of life and gaiety and prettiness which had first led him to set her down as unfit for serious work.

He saw with his own eyes that a bright little spirit, with twinkling ornaments, and golden hair, and a sweet voice, could go into the den of John Price in his surliest mood, could sing, and get his children to singing, till he was as persuadable in her hands as a bit of wax; that she could scold and lecture him at her pleasure, and get him to making all kinds of promises;.in fact that he, St. John himself, owed his *entrée* into the house, and his recognition there as a clergyman, to Angie's good offices and persistent entreaties.

Instead of being leader, he was himself being led. This divine child was becoming to him a mystery of wisdom; and, so far from feeling himself competent to be her instructor, he came to occupy, as regards many of the details of his work, a most catechetical attitude towards her, and was ready to accept almost anything she told him.

St. John was, from first to last, an idealist. It was ideality that inclined him from the barren and sterile chillness of New England dogmatism to the picturesque forms and ceremonies of a warmer ritual. His conception of a church was a fair ideal; such as a poet might worship, such as this world has never seen in reality, and probably never will. His conception of a life work—of the priestly office, with all that pertains to it—belonged to that realm of poetry that is above the matter-of-fact truths of experience, and is sometimes in painful conflict with them. What wonder, then, if love, the eternal poem, the great ideal of ideals, came over him without precise limits and exact definitions—that when the divine cloud overshadowed him he "wist not what he said."

St. John certainly never belonged to that class of clergymen who, on being assured of a settlement and a salary, resolve, in a general way, to marry, and look up a wife and a cooking-stove at the same time; who take lists of eligible women, and have the conditional refusal of a house in their pockets, when they go to make proposals.

In fact, he had had some sort of semi-poetical ideas of a diviner life of priestly self-devotion and self-consecration, in which woman can have no part. He had been fascinated by certain strains of writing in some of the devout Anglicans whose works furnished most of the studies of his library; so that far from setting it down in a general way that he must some time marry, he had, up to this time, shaped his ideal of life in a contrary direction. He had taken no vows; he had as yet taken no steps towards the practical working out of any scheme; but there floated vaguely through his head the idea of a celibate guild—a brotherhood who should revive, in dusty modern New York, some of the devout conventual fervors of the middle ages. A society of brothers, living in a round of daily devotions and holy ministration, had been one of the distant dreams of his future cloud-land.

And now, for a month or two, he had been like a charmed bird, fluttering in nearer and nearer circles about this dazzling, perplexing, repellent attraction.

For weeks, unconsciously to himself, he had had but one method of marking and measuring his days: there were the days when he expected to see *her*, and the days when he did not; and wonderful days were interposed between, when he saw her unexpectedly—as, somehow, happened quite often.

We believe it is a fact not yet brought clearly under scientific investigation as to its causes, but a fact, nevertheless, that young people who have fallen into the trick of thinking about each other when separated are singularly apt to meet each other in their daily walks and ways. Victor Hugo has written the *Idyl of the Rue Plumette;* there are also Idyls of the modern city of New York. At certain periods in the progress of the poem, one such chance glimpse, or moment of meeting, at a street corner or on a door-step, is the event of the day.

St. John was sure of Angie at her class on Sunday

mornings, and at service afterwards. He was sure of her on Thursday evenings, at Eva's reception; and then, besides, somehow, when she was around looking up her class on Saturday afternoons, it was so natural that he should catch a glimpse of her now and then, coming out of that house, or going into that door; and then, in the short days of winter, the darkness often falls so rapidly that it often struck him as absolutely necessary that he should see her safely home: and, in all these moments of association, he felt a pleasure so strange and new and divine that it seemed to him as if his whole life until he knew her had been flowerless and joyless. He pitied himself, when he thought that he had never known his mother and had never had a sister. That must be why he had known so little of what it was so lovely and beautiful to know.

Love, to an idealist, comes not first from earth, but heaven. It comes as an exaltation of all the higher and nobler faculties, and is its own justification in the fuller nobleness, the translucent purity, the larger generosity, and warmer piety, it brings. The trees do not examine themselves in spring-time, when every bud is thrilling with a new sense of life—they *live*.

Never had St. John's life-work looked to him so attractive, so possible, so full of impulse; and he worshiped the star that had risen on his darkness, without as yet a thought of the future. As yet, he thought of her only as a vision, an inspiration, an image of almost childlike innocence and purity, which he represented to himself under all the poetic forms of saintly legend.

She was the St. Agnes, the child Christian, the sacred lamb of Christ's fold. She was the holy Dorothea, who wore in her bosom the roses of heaven, and had fruits and flowers of Paradise to give to mortals; and when he left her, after ever so brief an interview, he fancied that one leaf from the tree of life had fluttered to his bosom. He illuminated the text, "Blessed are the pure in heart," in white lilies, and hung it over his *prie dieu* in memorial of her, and sometimes caught himself singing:

> " I can but know thee as my star,
> My angel and my dream."

As yet, the thought had not yet arisen in him of appropriating his angel guide. It was enough to love her with the reverential, adoring love he gave to all that was holiest and purest within him, to enshrine her as his ideal of womanhood.

He undervalued himself in relation to her. He seemed to himself coarse and clumsy, in the light of her intuitions, as he knew himself utterly unskilled and untrained in the conventional modes and usages of the society in which he had begun to meet her, and where he saw her moving with such deft ability, and touching every spring with such easy skill.

Still he felt a craving to be something to her. Why might she not be a *sister* to him, to him who had never known a sister? It was a happy thought, one that struck him as perfectly new and original, though it was—had he only known it—a well-worn, mossy old mile-stone that had been passed by generations on the pleasant journey to Eden. He had not, however, had the least intention of saying a word of this kind to Angie when he came to the chapel that morning. But he had been piqued by her quiet, resolute little way of dissent from the flood of admiration which his illumination had excited. He had been a little dissatisfied with the persistent adulation of his flock, and, like Zeuxis, felt a disposition to go after the blush of the maiden who fled. It was not the first time that Angie had held her own opinion against him, and turned away with that air of quiet resolution

which showed that she had a reserved force in herself
that he longed to fathom. Then, in the little passage
that followed, came one of those sudden overflows that
Longfellow tells of :

> " There are moments in life when the heart is so full of emotion
> That if by chance it be shaken, or into its depths like a pebble
> Drops some careless word, it overflows, and its secret,
> Spilt on the ground like water, can never be gathered together."

St. John's secret looked out of his eager eyes; and,
in fact, he was asking for Angie's whole heart, while his
words said only, " love me as a brother." A man, unfortunately, cannot look into his own eyes, and does not
always know what they say. But a woman may look
into them; and Angie, though little in person and childlike in figure, had in her the concentrated, condensed
essence of womanhood—all its rapid foresight; its keen
flashes of intuition; its ready self-command, and something of that maternal care-taking instinct with which
Eve is ever on the alert to prevent a blunder or mistake on the part of the less perceiving Adam.

She felt the tones of his voice. She knew that he
was saying more than he was himself aware of, and that
there were prying eyes about; and she knew, too, with a
flash of presentiment, what would be the world's judgment of so innocent a brotherly and sisterly alliance as
had been proposed and sealed by the sacrifice of her glove.

She laughed a little to herself, fancying her brother
Tom's wanting her glove, or addressing her in the reverential manner and with the beseeching tones that she
had just heard. Certainly she would be a sister to him,
she thought, and, the next time she met him at Eva's
alone, she would use her liberty to reprove him for his imprudence in speaking to her in that way when so many
were looking on. The little empress knew her ground;
and that it was hers now to dictate and his to obey.

CHAPTER XXXVIII

"WE MUST BE CAUTIOUS."

EVA was at the chapel that morning and overheard, of the conversation between Miss Gusher and Miss Vapors, just enough to pique her curiosity and rouse her alarm. Of all things, she dreaded any such report getting into the whirlwind of gossip that always eddies round a church door where there is an interesting, unmarried rector, and she resolved to caution Angie on the very first opportunity; and so, when her share of wreaths and crosses was finished, and the afternoon sun began to come level through the stained windows, she crossed over to Angie's side, to take her home with her to dinner.

"I've something to tell you," she said, "and you must come home and stay with me to-night." And so Angie came.

"Do you know," said Eva, as soon as the sisters found themselves alone in her chamber, where they were laying off their things and preparing for dinner, "do you know that Miss Gusher?"

"I—no, very slightly," said Angie, shaking out her shawl to fold it. "She's a very cultivated woman, I believe."

"Well, I heard her saying some disagreeable things about you and Mr. St. John this morning," said Eva.

The blood flushed in Angie's cheek, and she turned quickly to the glass and began arranging her hair.

"What did she say?" she inquired.

"Something about the Van Arsdel girls always getting up flirtations."

"Nonsense! how hateful! I'm sure it's no fault of mine that Mr. St. John came and spoke to me."

"Then he did come?"

"Oh, yes; I was perfectly astonished. I was sitting all alone in that dark corner where the great hemlock tree was, and the first I knew he was there. You see, I criticised his illuminated card—that one in the strange, queer letters—I said I couldn't understand it; but Miss Gusher, Miss Vapors, and all the girls were oh-ing and ah-ing about it, and I felt quite snubbed and put down. I supposed it must be my stupidity, and so I just went off to my tree and sat down to work quietly in the dark corner, and left Miss Gusher expatiating on mottoes and illuminations. I knew she was very accomplished and clever and all that, and that I didn't know anything about such things."

"Well, then," said Eva, "he followed you?"

"Yes, he came suddenly in from the vestry behind the tree, and I thought, or hoped, he stood so that nobody noticed us, and he insisted on my telling him why I didn't like his illumination. I said I did like it, that I thought it was beautifully done, but that I did not think it would be of any use to those poor children and folks to have inscriptions that they didn't understand; and he said I was quite right, and that he should alter it and put it in plain English; and then he said, what a help it was to have a woman's judgment on things, what a misfortune it was that he had never had a sister or any friend of that kind, and then he asked me to be a sister to him, and tell him frankly always just what I thought of him, and I said I would. And then "—

"What then?"

"Oh, Eva, I can't tell you; but he spoke so earnestly and quick, and asked me if I couldn't love him just a little; he asked me to call him Arthur, and then, if you believe me, he would have me give him my glove, and so I let him take it, because I was afraid some of those girls would see us talking together. I felt almost frightened that he should speak so, and I wanted him to go away."

"Well, Angie dear, what do you think of all this?"

"I know he cares for me very much," said Angie, quickly, "more than he says."

"And you, Angie?"

"I think he's good and noble and true, and I love him."

"As a sister, of course," said Eva, laughing.

"Never mind how—I love him," said Angie; "and I shall use my sisterly privilege to caution him to be very distant and dignified to me in future, when those prying eyes are around."

"Well now, darling," said Eva, with all the conscious dignity of early matronage, "we shall have to manage this matter very prudently—for those girls have had their suspicions aroused, and you know how such things will fly through the air. The fact is, there is nothing so perplexing as just this state of things; when you know as well as you know anything that a man is in love with you, and yet you are not engaged to him. I know all about the trouble of that, I'm sure; and it seems to me, what with Mamma, Aunt Maria, and all the rest of them, it was a perfect marvel how Harry and I ever came together. Now, there's that Miss Gusher, she'll be on the watch all the time, like a cat at a mouse-hole; and she's going to be there when we get the Christmas-tree ready and tie on the things, and you must manage to keep as far off from him as possible. I shall be there, and I shall have my eyes in my head, I promise you. We must try to lull their suspicions to sleep."

"Dear me," said Angie, "how disagreeable!"

"I'm sorry for you, darling, but I've kept it off as long as I could; I've seen for a long time how things are going."

"You have? Oh, Eva!"

"Yes; and I have had all I could do to keep Jim Fellows from talking, and teasing you, as he has been perfectly longing to do for a month past."

"You don't say that Jim has noticed anything?"

"Yes, Jim noticed his looking at you, the very first thing after he came to Sunday-school."

"Well, now, at first I noticed that he looked at me often, but I thought it was because he saw something he disapproved of—and it used to embarrass me. Then I thought he seemed to avoid me, and I wondered why. And I wondered, too, why he always would take occasion to look at me. I noticed, when your evenings first began, that he never came near me, and never spoke to me, and yet his eyes were following me wherever I went. The first evening you had, he walked round and round me nearly the whole evening, and never spoke a word; then suddenly he came and sat down by me, when I was sitting by Mrs. Betsey, and gave me a message from the Prices; but he spoke in such a stiff, embarrassed way, and then there was an awful pause, and suddenly he got up and went away again; and poor little Mrs. Betsey said, ' Bless me, how stiff and ungracious he is '; and I said that I believed he wasn't much used to society— but, after a while, this wore away, and he became very social, and we grew better and better acquainted all the time. Although I was a little contradictious, and used to controvert some of his notions, I fancy it was rather a novelty to him to find somebody that didn't always give up to him, for, I must say, some of the women that go to our chapel do make fools of themselves about him. It really provokes me past all bearing. If any body *could* set me against a man, it would be those silly, admiring women who have their hands and eyes always raised in adoration, whatever he does. It annoys him, I can see, for it is very much against his taste, and he likes me because, he says, I always will tell him the truth."

*　　*　　*　　*　　*　　*　　*　　*　　*

Meanwhile St. John had gone back to his study, walking as on a cloud. The sunshine streaming into a western window touched the white lilies over his *prie dieu* till they seemed alive. He took down the illumination and looked at it. He had a great mind to give this to her as a Christmas present. Why not? Was she not to be his own sister? And his thoughts strolled along through pleasant possibilities and all the privileges of a brother. Certainly, he longed to see her now, and talk them over with her; and suddenly it occurred to him that there were a few points in relation to the arrangement of the tree about which it would be absolutely necessary to get the opinion of Mrs. Henderson. Whether this direction of the path of duty had any relation to the fact that he had last seen her going away from the vestry arm in arm with Angie, we will not assume to say; but the solemn fact was that, that evening, just as it came time to drop the lace curtains over the Henderson windows, when the blazing wood fire was winking and blinking roguishly at the brass audirons, the door-bell rang, and in he walked.

Angelique had her lap full of dolls, and was sitting like Iris in the rainbow, in a confused *mélange* of silks, and gauzes, and tissues, and spangles. Three dressed dolls were propped up in various attitudes around her, and she was holding the fourth, while she fitted a sky-blue mantilla which she was going to trim with silver braid. Where Angie got all her budget of fineries was a stand-

Q

ing mystery in the household, only that she had an infinitely persuasive tongue, and talked supplies out of admiring clerks and milliners' apprentices. It was a pretty picture to see her there in the warm, glowing room, tossing and turning her filmy treasures, and cocking her little head on one side and the other with an air of profound reflection.

Harry was gone out. Eva was knitting a comforter in her corner, and everything was as still and as cosy as heart could desire, when St. John made his way into the parlor and got himself warmly ensconced in his favorite niche. What more could mortal man desire? He talked gravely with Eva, and watched Angie. He thought of a lean, haggard picture of a St. Mary of Egypt, praying forlornly in the desert, that had hitherto stood in his study, and the idea somehow came over him that modern New York saints had taken a much more agreeable turn than those of old. Was it not better to be dressing dolls for poor children than to be rolling up one's eyes and praying alone out in a desert? In his own mind he resolved to take down that picture forthwith. He had, in his overcoat in the hall, his illuminated lilies, wrapped snugly in tissue paper and tied with a blue ribbon; and, all the while he was discoursing with Eva, he was ruminating how he could see Angie alone a minute, just long enough to place it in her hands. Surely, somebody ought to make her a Christmas present, she who was thinking of every one but herself.

Eva was one of the class of diviners, and not at all the person to sit as Madame de Trop in an exigency of this sort, and so she had a sudden call to consult with Mary in the kitchen.

"Now for it," thought St. John, as he rose and drew nearer. Angie looked up with a demure consciousness.

He began fingering her gauzes and her scissors unconsciously.

"Now, now! I don't allow that," she said, playfully, as she took them altogether from his hand.

"I have something for you," he said suddenly.

"Something for me!" with a bright, amused look. "Where is it?"

St. John fumbled a moment in the entry and brought in his parcel. Angie watched him untying it with a kittenish gravity. He laid it down before her. "From your brother, Angie," he said.

"Oh, how lovely! how beautiful! O Mr. St. John, did you do this for me?"

"It was of you I was thinking; you, my inspiration in all that is holy and good; you who strengthen and help me in all that is pure and heavenly."

"Oh, don't say that!"

"It's true, Angie, my Angie, my angel. I knew nothing worthily till I knew you."

Angie looked up at him; her eyes, clear and bright as a bird's, looked into his; their hands clasped together, and then, it was the most natural thing in the world, he kissed her.

"But, Arthur," said Angie, "you must be careful not to arouse disagreeable reports and gossip. What is so sacred between us must not be talked of. Don't look at me, or speak to me, when others are present. You don't know how very easy it is to make people talk."

Mr. St. John promised all manner of prudence, and walked home delighted. And thus these two Babes in the Wood clasped hands with each other, to wander up and down the great forest of life, as simply and sincerely as if they had been Hensel and Grettel in the fairy story. They loved each other, wholly trusted each other without a question, and were walking in dream-land. There was no question of marriage settlements, or rent and taxes; only a joyous delight that they two in this wilderness world had found each other.

We pity him who does not know that there is nothing purer, nothing nearer heaven than a young man's first-enkindled veneration and adoration of womanhood in the person of her who is to be his life's ideal. It is the morning dew before the sun arises.

CHAPTER XXXIX

SAYS SHE TO HER NEIGHBOR—WHAT?

"MY dear," said Mrs. Dr. Gracey to her spouse, "I have a great piece of news for you about Arthur —they say that he is engaged to one of the Van Arsdel girls."

"Good," said the Doctor, pushing up his spectacles. "It's the most sensible thing I have heard of him this long while. I always knew that boy would come right if he were only let alone. How did you hear?"

"Miss Gusher told Mary Jane. She charged her not to tell; but, oh, it's all over town! There can be no doubt about it."

"Why hasn't he been here, then, like a dutiful nephew, to tell us, I should like to know?" said Dr. Gracey.

"Well, I believe they say it isn't announced yet; but there's no sort of doubt of it. There's no doubt, at any rate, that there's been a very decided intimacy, and that if they are not engaged, they ought to be; and as I know Arthur is a good fellow, I know it must be all right. Those Ritualistic young ladies are terribly shocked. Miss Gusher says that her idol is broken; that she never again shall reverence a clergyman."

"Very likely. A Mrs. St. John will be a great interruption in the way of holy confidences and confessionals, and all their trumpery; but it's the one thing needful for Arthur. A good, sensible woman for a wife will make him a capital worker. The best adviser in church work is a good wife; and the best school of the church is a Christian family. That's my doctrine, Mrs. G."

Mrs. G. blushed at the implied compliment, while the Doctor went on:

"Now, I never felt the least fear of how Arthur was coming out, and I take great credit to myself for not opposing him. I knew a young man must do a certain amount of fussing and fizzling before he settles down strong and clear; and fighting and opposing a crotchety fellow does no good. I think I have kept hold on Arthur by never rousing his combativeness and being sparing of good advice; and you see he is turning right already. A wife will put an end to all the semi-monkish trumpery that has got itself mixed up with his real self-denying labor. A woman is capital for sweeping down cobwebs in Church or State. Well, I shall call on Arthur and congratulate him forthwith."

Dr. Gracey was Arthur's maternal uncle, and he had always kept an eye upon him from boyhood, as the only son of a favorite sister.

The Doctor, himself rector of a large and thriving church, was a fair representative of that exact mixture of conservatism and progress which characterizes the great, steady middle class of the American Episcopacy. He was tolerant and fatherly both to the Ritualists, who overdo on one side, and the Low Church, who underdo on the other. He believed largely in good nature, good sense, and the expectant treatment, as best for diseases both in the churchly and medical practice.

So, when he had succeeded in converting his favorite nephew to Episcopacy, and found him in danger of using it only as a half-way house to Rome, he took good heed neither to snub him, nor to sneer at him, but to give him sympathy in all the good work he did, and, as far as possible, to shield him from that species of persecution which is sure to endear a man's errors to him, by investing them with a kind of pathos.

" The world isn't in danger from the multitudes rushing into extremes of self-sacrifice," the Doctor said, when
his wife feared that Arthur was becoming an ascetic.
" Keep him at work; work will bring sense and steadi-
ness. Give him his head, and he'll pull in harness all
right by and by. A colt that don't kick out of the
traces a little, at first, can't have much blood in
him."

It will be seen by the subject-matter of this conversation that the good seed which had been sown in the
heart of Miss Gusher had sprung up and borne fruit—
thirty, sixty and a hundred fold, as is the wont of the
gourds of gossip,—more rapid by half in their growth
than the gourd of Jonah, and not half as consolatory.

In fact, the gossip plant is like the grain of mustard
seed, which, though it be the least of all seeds, becom-
eth a great tree, and the fowls of the air lodge in its
branches and chatter mightily there at all seasons.

Miss Gusher, and Miss Vapors, and Miss Rapture,
and old Mrs. Eyelet, and the Misses Glibbett, so well
employed their time, about the season of Christmas, that
there was not a female person in the limits of their
acquaintance that had not had the whole story of all
that had been seen, surmised, or imagined, related as a
profound secret. Notes were collected and compared.
Mrs. Eyelet remembered that she had twice seen Mr.
St. John attending Angie to her door about nightfall.
Miss Sykes, visiting one afternoon in the same district,
deposed and said that she had met them coming out of a
door together. She was quite sure that they must have
met by appointment. Then, oh, the depths of possibility
that the gossips saw in that Henderson house! Always
there, every Thursday evening! On intimate terms with
the family.

" Depend upon it, my dear," said Mrs. Eyelet, " Mrs.

Henderson has been doing all she could to catch him. They say he's at her house almost constantly."

Aunt Maria's plumage rustled with maternal solicitude. "I don't know but it is as good a thing as we could expect for Angie," said she to Mrs. Van Arsdel. "He's a young man of good family and independent property. I don't like his ritualistic notions, to be sure; but one can't have everything. And, at any rate, he can't become a Roman Catholic if he gets married— that's one comfort."

"'There he goes!" said little Mrs. Betsey, as she sat looking through the blinds, with the forgiven Jack on her knee. "He's at the door now. Dorcas, I *do* believe there's something in it."

"Something in what?" said Miss Dorcas, "and who *are* you talking about, Betsey?"

"Why, Mr. St. John and Angie. He's standing at the door, this very minute. It must be true. I'm glad of it; only he isn't half good enough for her."

"Well, it don't follow that there is an engagement because Mr. St. John is at the door," said Miss Dorcas.

"But all the things Mrs. Eyelet said, Dorcas!"

"Mrs. Eyelet is a gossip," said Miss Dorcas, shortly.

"But, Dorcas, I really thought his manner to her last Thursday was particular. Oh, I'm sure there's something in it! They say he's such a good young man, and independently rich. I wonder if they'll take a house up in this neighborhood? It would be so nice to have Angie within calling distance! A great favorite of mine is Angie."

CHAPTER XL

MEANWHILE Dr. Gracey found his way to Arthur's study.

"So, Arthur," he said, " that pretty Miss Van Arsdel's engaged."

The blank expression and sudden change of color in St. John's face was something quite worthy of observation.

"Miss Van Arsdel engaged!" he repeated with a gasp, feeling as if the ground were going down under him.

" Yes, that pretty fairy, Miss Angelique, you know."

" How did you hear—who told you ?"

" How did I hear? Why, it's all over town. Arthur, you bad boy, why haven't *you* told *me* ?"

" Me ?"

" Yes, you ; you are the happy individual. I came to congratulate you."

St. John looked terribly confused.

" Well, we are not really exactly engaged."

" But you are going to be, I understand. So far so good. I like the family—good stock—nothing could be better ; but, Arthur, let me tell you, you'd better have it announced and above board forthwith. You are not my sister's son, nor the man I took you for, if you could take advantage of the confidence inspired by your position to carry on a flirtation."

The blood flushed into St. John's cheeks.

" I'm not flirting, uncle ; that vulgar word is no name

for my friendship with Miss Van Arsdel. It is as sacred
as the altar. I reverence her; I love her with all my
heart. I would lay down my life for her."

"Good! but nobody wants you to lay down your life.
That is quite foreign to the purpose. What is wanting
is, that you step out like a man and define your position
with regard to Miss Van Arsdel before the world; otherwise all the gossips will make free with her name and
yours. Depend upon it, Arthur, a man has done too
much or too little when a young lady's name is in every
one's mouth in connection with his, without a definite
engagement."

"It is all my fault, uncle. I hadn't the remotest
idea. It's all my fault—all. I had no thought of what
the world would say; no idea that we were remarked—
but, believe me, our intimacy has been, from first to last,
entirely of my seeking. It has grown on us gradually,
till I find she is more to me than any one ever has been
or can be. Whether I am as much to her, I cannot tell.
My demands have been humble. We are not engaged,
but it shall not be my fault if another day passes and we
are not."

"Right, my boy. I knew you. You were no nephew
of mine if you didn't feel, when your eyes were open,
the honor of the thing. God made you a gentleman
before he made you a priest, and there's but one way for
a gentleman in a case like this. If there's anything I
despise, it's a priest who uses his priestly influence,
under this fine name and that, to steal from a woman love
that does n't belong to him, and that he never can return,
and never ought to   If a man thinks he can do more
good as a single man and a missionary, well; I honor
him, but let him make the sacrifice honestly. Don't
let him want pretty girls for intimate friends or guardian
angels, or Christian sisters, or any such trumpery. It's

dishonest and disloyal; it is unfair to the woman and selfish in the man."

"Well, uncle, I trust you say all this because you don't think it of me; as I know my heart before God, I say I have not been doing so mean and cowardly a thing There was a time when I thought I never should marry. Those were my days of ignorance. I did not know how much a true woman might teach me, and how much I needed such a guide, even in my church work."

"In short, my boy, you found out that the Lord was right when he said, 'It is not good for man to be alone.' We pay the Lord the compliment once in a while to believe he knows best. Depend on it, Arthur, that Christian families are the Lord's church, and better than any guild of monks and nuns whatsoever."

All which was listened to by Mr. St. John with a radiant countenance. It is all down-hill when you are showing a man that it is his duty to do what he wants to do. Six months before, St. John would have fought every proposition of this speech, and brought up the whole of the Middle Ages to back him. Now, he was as tractable as heart could wish.

"After all, Uncle," he said, at last, "what if she will not have me? And what if I am not the man to make her happy?"

"Oh, if you ask prettily, I fancy she won't say nay; and then you *must* make her happy. There are no two ways about that, my boy."

"I'm not half good enough for her," said St. John.

"Like enough. We are none of us good enough for these women; but, luckily, that isn't apt to be their opinion."

St. John started out from the conference with an alert step. In two days more, rumor was met with open confirmation. St. John had had the decisive interview with

Angie, had seen and talked with her father and mother, and been invited to a family dinner; and Angie wore on her finger an engagement-ring. There was no more to be said now. Mr. St. John was an idol who had stepped down from his pedestal into the ranks of common men. He was no longer a mysterious power—an angel of the churches, but a *man* of the nineteenth century. Nevertheless, it is an undoubted fact that, for all the purposes of this mortal life, a good man is better than an angel.

But not so thought the ecstasia of his chapel. A holy father, in a long black gown, with a cord round his waist, and with a skull and hour-glass in his cell, is somehow thought to be nearer to heaven than a family man with a market-basket on his arm ; but we question whether the angels themselves think so. There may be as holy and unselfish a spirit in the way a market-basket is filled as in a week of fasting; and the oil of gladness may make the heavenward wheels run more smoothly than the spirit of heaviness. The first bright day, St. John took Angie a drive in the park, a proceeding so evidently of the earth, earthy, that Miss Gusher hid her face, after the manner of the seraphim, as he passed; but he and Angie were too happy and too busy in their new world to care who looked or who didn't, and St. John rather triumphantly remembered the free assertion of the great apostle, " Have we not power to lead about a sister or a wife?" and felt sure that he should have been proud and happy to show Angie to St. Paul himself.

Alice was at first slightly disappointed, but the compensation of receiving so very desirable a brother-in-law reconciled her to the loss of her poetic and distant ideal.

As to little Mrs. Betsey, she fell upon Angie's neck in rapture; and her joy was heightened in the convincing proof that she was now able to heap upon the unbelieving head of Dorcas that she had been in the right all along.

When dear little Mrs. Betsey was excited, her words and thoughts came so thick that they were like a flock of martins, all trying to get out of a martin-box together, —chattering, twittering, stumbling over each other, and coming out at heads and points in a wonderful order. When the news had been officially sealed to her, she begged the right to carry it to Dorcas, and ran home and burst in upon her with shining eyes and two little pink spots in her cheeks.

"There, Dorcas, they are engaged. Now, *didn't* I say so, Dorcas? I knew it. I told you so, that Thursday evening. Oh, you can't fool me; and that day I saw him standing on the doorstep! I was just as certain! I saw it just as plain! What a shame for people to talk about him as they do, and say he's going to Rome. I wonder what they think now? The sweetest girl in New York, certainly. Oh! and that ring he bought! Just as if he could be a Roman Catholic! It's big as a pea, and sparkles beautiful, and's got the 'Lord is thy keeper' in Hebrew on the inside. I want to see Mrs. Wouvermans and ask her what she thinks now. Oh, and he took her to ride in such a stylish carriage, white lynx lap-robe, and all! I don't care if he does burn candles in his chapel. What does that prove? It don't prove anything. I like to see people have some logic about things, for my part, don't you, Dorcas? *Don't* you?"

"Mercy! yes, Betsey," said Miss Dorcas, delighted to see her sister so excitedly happy, "though I don't exactly see my way clear through yours; but no matter."

"I'm going to crochet a toilet cushion for a wedding present, Dorcas, like that one in the red room, you know. I wonder when it will come off? How lucky I have that sweet cap that Mrs. Henderson made. Wasn't it good of her to make it? I hope they'll invite us. Don't you think they will? I suppose it will be in his chapel, with candles and all sorts of new ways. Well, I don't care, so long as folks are good people, what their ways are; do *you*, Dorcas? I must run up and count the stitches on that cushion this minute!" And Mrs. Betsey upset her basket of worsteds in her zeal, and Jack flew round and round, barking sympathetically. In fact, he was so excited by the general breeze that he chewed up two balls of worsted before recovering his composure. Such was the effect of the news at the old Vanderheyden house.

CHAPTER XLI

LETTER FROM EVA TO HARRY'S MOTHER.

MY DEAR MOTHER: I sit down to write to you with a heart full of the strangest feelings and expeririences. I feel as if I had been out in some other world and been brought back again; and now I hardly know myself or where I am. You know I wrote you all about Maggie, and her leaving us, and poor Mary's trouble about her, and how she had been since seen in a very bad neighborhood: I promised Mary faithfully that I would go after her; and so, after all our Christmas labors were over, Harry and I went on a midnight excursion with Mr. James, the Methodist minister, who has started the mission there.

It seemed to me very strange that a minister could have access to all those places where he proposed to take us, and see all that was going on without insult or danger but he told me that he was in the constant habit of passing through the dance-houses, and talking with the people who kept them, and that he had never met with any rudeness or incivility.

He told us that in the very center of this worst district of New York, among drinking saloons and dance-houses, a few Christian people had bought a house in which they had established a mission family, with a room which they use for a chapel; and they hold weekly prayer-meetings, and seek to draw in the wretched people there.

On this evening, he said, they were about to give a midnight supper at the Home to any poor houseless wanderer whom they could find in those wretched streets, or who hung about the drinking-saloons.

"Our only hope in this mission," he said, "is to make these wretched people feel that we really are their friends and seek their good; and, in order to do this, we must do something for them that they can understand. They can all understand a good supper, when they are lying about cold and hungry and homeless, on a stinging cold night like this; and we don't begin to talk to them till we have warmed and fed them. It surprises them to have us take all this trouble to do them good; it awakens their curiosity; they wonder what we do it for, and then, when we tell them it is because we are Christians, and love them, and want to save them, they believe us. After that, they are willing to come to our meetings, and attend to what we say."

Now, this seemed to me good philosophy, but I could not help saying: "Dear Mr. James, how could you have the courage to begin a mission in such a dreadful place; and how can you have any hope of saving such people?" And he answered: With God, all things are possible. That was what Christ came for—to seek and save the *lost*. The Good Shepherd," he said, "leaves the ninety and nine safe sheep in the fold, and goes after one that is lost *until he finds it.*" I asked him who supported the Home, and he said it was supported by God, in answer to prayer; that they made no public solicitation; had nobody pledged to help them; but that contributions were constantly coming in from one Christian person or another, as they needed them; that the superintendent and matron of the Home had no stated salary, and devoted themselves to the work in the same faith that the food and raiment needed would be found for them; and so far it had not failed.

All this seemed very strange to me. It seemed a

sort of literal rendering of some of the things in the Bible that we pass over as having no very definite meaning. Mr. James seemed so quiet, so assured, so calm and unexcited, that one could n't help believing him.

It seemed a great way that we rode, in parts of the city that I never saw before, in streets whose names were unknown to me, till finally we alighted before a plain house in a street full of drinking-saloons. As we drove up, we heard the sound of hymn-singing, and looked into a long room set with benches which seemed full of people. We stopped a moment to listen to the words of an old Methhodist hymn;

> "Come, ye weary, heavy-laden,
> Lost and ruined by the fall,
> If you tarry till you're better,
> You will never come at all.
>   Not the righteous—
>   Sinners, Jesus came to call.

> "Come, ye thirsty, come and welcome,
> God's free bounty glorify.
> True belief and true repentance,
> Every grace that brings us nigh,
>   Without money,
>   Come to Jesus Christ and buy."

It was the last hymn, and they were about breaking up as we went into the house. This building, Mr. James told us, used to be a rat-pit, where the lowest, vilest, and most brutal kinds of sport were going on. It used to be, he said, foul and filthy, physically as well as morally; but scrubbing and paint and whitewash had transformed it into a comfortable home. There was a neat sitting-room, carpeted and comfortably furnished, a dining-room, a pantry stocked with serviceable china, a work-room with two or three sewing-machines, and a kitchen, from which at this moment came a most appe-

tizing smell of the soup which was preparing for the
midnight supper. Above, were dormitories, in which
were lodging about twenty girls, who had fled to this
refuge to learn a new life. They had known the depth
of sin and the bitterness of punishment, had been
spurned, disgraced and outcast. Some of them had been
at Blackwell's Island—on the street—in the very gutter
—and now, here they were, as I saw some of them, decently and modestly dressed, and busy preparing for the
supper. When I looked at them setting the tables, or
busy about their cooking, they seemed so cheerful and
respectable, I could scarcely believe that they had been
so degraded. A portion of them only were detailed for
the night service; the others had come up from the
chapel and were going to bed in the dormitories, and we
heard them singing a hymn before retiring. It was very
affecting to me—the sound of that hymn, and the thought
of so peaceful a home in the midst of this dreadful
neighborhood. Mr. James introduced us to the man
and his wife who take charge of the family. They are
converts—the fruits of these labors. He was once a
singer, and connected with a drinking-saloon, but was
now giving his whole time and strength to this work, in
which he had all the more success because he had so
thorough an experience and knowledge of the people to
be reached. We were invited to sit down to a supper
in the dining-room, for Mr. James said we should be out
so late before returning home that we should need something to sustain us. So we took some of the soup which
was preparing for the midnight supper, and very nice and
refreshing we found it. After this, we went out with
Mr. James and the superintendent, to go through the
saloons and dance-houses and drinking places, and to
distribute tickets of invitation to the supper. What we
saw seems now to me like a dream. I had heard that

such things were, but never before did I see them. We went from one place to another, and always the same features—a dancing-room, with girls and women dressed and ornamented, sitting round waiting for partners; men of all sorts walking in and surveying and choosing from among them and dancing, and, afterwards or before, going with them to the bar to drink. Many of these girls looked young and comparatively fresh; their dresses were cut very low, so that I blushed for them through my veil. I clung tight to Harry's arm, and asked myself where I was, as I moved round among them. Nobody noticed us. Everybody seemed to have a right to be there, and see what they could.

I remember one large building of two or three stories, with larger halls below, all lighted up, with dancing and drinking going on, and throngs and throngs of men, old and young, pouring and crowding through it. These tawdrily bedizened, wretched girls and women seemed to me such a sorrow and disgrace to womanhood and to Christianity that my very heart sunk, as I walked among them. I felt as if I could have cried for their disgrace. Yet nobody said a word to us. All the keepers of the places seemed to know Mr. James and the superintendent. He spoke to them all kindly and politely, and they answered with the same civility. In one or two of the saloons, the superintendent asked leave to sing a song, which was granted, and he sung the hymn that begins:

> "I love to tell the story
>   Of unseen things above,
> Of Jesus and his glory,
>   Of Jesus and his love;
> I love to tell the story—
>   It did so much for me—
> And that is just the reason
>   I tell it unto thee."

At another place, he sung "Home, sweet home," and I thought I saw many faces that looked sad. Either our presence was an embarrassment, or for some other reason it seemed to me there was no real gaiety, and that the dancing and the keeping up of a show of hilarity were all heavy work.

There seems, however, to be a gradation in these dreadful places. Besides these which were furnished with some show and pretension, there were cellars where the same sort of thing was going on—dancing and drinking, and women set to be the tempters of men. We saw miserable creatures standing out on the sidewalk, to urge the passers-by to come into these cellars. It was pitiful, heart-breaking to see.

But the lowest, the most dreadful of all, was what they called the bucket shops. There the vilest of liquors are mixed in buckets and sold to wretched, crazed people who have fallen so low that they cannot get anything better. It is the lowest depth of the dreadful deep.

Oh, those bucket shops! Never shall I forget the poor, forlorn, forsaken-looking creatures, both men and women, that I saw there. They seemed crouching in from the cold—hanging about, or wandering uncertainly up and down. Mr. James spoke to many of them, as if he knew them, kindly and sorrowfully. "This is a hard way you are going," he said to one. "Ar'n't you most tired of it?" "Well," he said to another poor creature, "when you have gone as far as you can, and come to the end, and nobody will have you, and nobody do anything for you, then come to us, and we'll take you in."

During all this time, and in all these places, the Superintendent, who seemed to have a personal knowledge of many of those among whom he was moving, was busy distributing his tickets of invitation to the supper. He knew where the utterly lost and abandoned ones were most to be found, and to them he gave most regard.

But as yet, though I looked with anxious eyes, I had seen nothing of Maggie. I spoke to Mr. James at last, and he said, " We have not yet visited Mother Moggs's establishment, where she was said to be. We are going there now."

" Mother Moggs is a character in her way," he told us. " She has always treated me with perfect respect and politeness, because I have shown the same to her. She seems at first view like any other decent woman, but she is one that, if she were roused, would be as prompt with knife and pistol as any man in these streets." As he said this, we turned a corner, and entered a dancing-saloon, in its features much like many others we had seen. Mother Moggs stood at a sort of bar at the upper end, where liquors were displayed and sold. She seemed really so respectably dressed, and so quiet and pleasant-looking, that I could scarcely believe my eyes when I saw her.

Mr. James walked up with us to where she was standing, and spoke to her, as he does to every one, gently and respectfully, inquiring after her health, and then, in a lower tone, he said, " And how about the health of your soul?"

She colored, and forced a laugh, and answered with some smartness: "Which soul do you mean? I've got two—one on each foot."

He took no notice of the jest, but went on :

"And how about the souls of these girls? What will become of them?"

"I ain't hurting their souls," she said. "I don't force 'em to stay with me; they come of their own ac-

cord, and they can go when they please. I don't keep
'em. If any of my girls can better themselves anywhere
else, I don't stand in their way."

The air of virtuous assurance with which she spoke
would have given the impression that she was pursuing,
under difficult circumstances, some praiseworthy branch
of industry at which her girls were apprentices.

Just at this moment, I turned, and saw Maggie standing behind me. She was not with the other girls, but
standing a little back, toward the bar. Instantly I
crossed over, and, raising my veil, said, "Maggie, poor
child! come back to your mother."

Her face changed in a moment; she looked pale, as
if she were going to faint, and said only, "Oh! Mrs.
Henderson, you here?"

"Yes, I came to look for you, Maggie. Come right
away with us," I said. "O Maggie! come," and I burst
into tears.

She seemed dreadfully agitated, but said:

"Oh, I can't; it's too late!"

"No, it isn't. Mr. James," I said, "here she is. Her
mother has sent for her."

"And you, madam," said Mr. James to the woman,
" have just said you wouldn't stand in the way, if any of
your girls could better themselves."

The woman was fairly caught in her own trap. She
cast an evil look at us all, but said nothing, as we
turned to leave, I holding upon Maggie, determined not
to let her go.

We took her with us to the Home. She was crying
as if her heart would break. The girls who were getting
the supper looked at her with sympathy and gathered
round her. One of them interested me deeply. She
was very pale and thin, but had such a sweet expression
of peace and humility in her face! She came and sat

down by Maggie and said, "Don't be afraid; this is Christ's home, and he will save you as he has me. I was worse than you are—worse than you ever could be— and He has saved *me*. I am *so* happy here!"

And now the miserable wretches who had been invited to the supper came pouring in. Oh, such a sight! Such forlorn *wrecks* of men, in tattered and torn garments, with such haggard faces, such weary, despairing eyes! They looked dazed at the light and order and quiet they saw as they came in. Mr. James and the superintendent stood at the door, saying, "Come in, boys, come in; you're welcome heartily! Here you are, glad to see you," seating them on benches at the lower part of the room.

While the supper was being brought in, the table was set with an array of bowls of smoking hot soup and a large piece of nice white bread at each place. When all had been arranged, Mr. James saw to seating the whole band at the tables, asked a blessing, standing at the head, and then said, cheerily, " Now, boys, fall to; eat all you want; there is plenty more where this came from, and you shall have as much as you can carry."

The night was cold, and the soup was savory and hot, and the bread white and fine, and many of them ate with a famished appetite; the girls meanwhile stood watchful to replenish the bowls or hand more bread. All seemed to be done with such a spirit of bountiful, cheerful good-will as was quite inspiriting.

It was not till hunger was fully satisfied that Mr. James began to talk to them, and when he did, I wondered at his tact.

"This is quite the thing, now, isn't it, boys, of a cold night like this, when a fellow is hungry? See what it is to have friends.

"I suppose, boys, you get better suppers than these

from those fellows that you buy your drink of. They make suppers for you sometimes, I suppose?"

"No, indeed," growled some of the men. "Catch 'em doing it!"

"Why, I should think they ought to, when you spend all your money on them. You pay all your money to them, and make yourselves so poor that you haven't a crust, and then they won't even get you a supper?"

"No, that they won't," growled some. "They don't care if we starve."

"Boys," said Mr. James, "aren't you fools? Here these men get rich, and you get poor. You pay all your earnings to them. You can't have anything, and they have everything. They can have plate-glass windows, and they can keep their carriages, and their wives have their silk dresses and jewels, and you pay for it all; and then, when you've spent your last cent over their counters, they kick you into the street. Aren't you fools to be supporting such men? Your wives don't get any silk dresses, I'll bet. O boys, where are your wives?—where are your mothers?—where are your children?"

By this time they were looking pretty sober, and some of them had tears in their eyes.

"Oh, boys, boys! this is a bad way you've been in—a bad way. Haven't you gone long enough? Don't you want to give it up? Look here—now, boys, I'll read you a story." And then he read from his pocket Testament the Parable of the Prodigal Son. He read it beautifully: I thought I had never understood it before. When he had done, he said, "And now, boys, hadn't you better come back to your Father? Do you remember, some of you, how your mother used to teach you to say, 'Our Father, who art in heaven?' Come now, kneel down, every one of you, and let's try it once more."

They all knelt, and I never heard anything like that prayer. It was so loving, so earnest, so pitiful. He prayed for those poor men, as if he were praying for his own soul. They must have *felt* how he loved them. It almost broke my heart to hear him: it did seem for the time as if the wall were down that separates God's love from us, and that everybody must feel it, even these poor wretched creatures.

There were among them some young men, and some whose heads and features were good, and indicative of former refinement of feeling. I could not help thinking how many histories of sorrow, for just so many families, were written in those faces.

"Is it possible that you can save any of these?" I said to Mr. James, as they were going out.

"*We* cannot, but God can," he said. "With God, all things are possible. We have seen a great many saved that were as low as these; but it was only by the power of God converting their souls. That is at all times possible."

"But," said Harry, "the craving for drink gets to be a physical disease."

"Yet I have seen that craving all subdued and taken away by the power of the Holy Spirit. They become new creatures in Christ."

"That would be almost miraculous," said Harry.

"We must expect miracles, and we shall have them," replied he.

Meanwhile the girls had gathered around Maggie, and were talking with her, and when we spoke of going, she said:

"Dear Mrs. Henderson, let me stay here awhile; the girls here will help me, and I can do some good here, and by-and-by, perhaps, when I am stronger, I can come back to mother. It's better for me here now."

R

Mr. James and the matron both agreed that, for the present, this would be best.

There is a current of sympathy, an energy of Christian feeling, a sort of enthusiasm, about this house, that helps one to begin anew.

It was nearly morning before we found ourselves in our home again—but, for me, the night has not been spent in vain. Oh, mother, can it be that in a city full of churches and Christians such dreadful things as I saw are going on every night? Certainly, if all Christians felt about it as those do who have begun this Home, there would be a change. If every Christian would do a little, a great deal would be done; for there are many Christians. But now it seems as if a few were left to do all, while the many do nothing. But Harry and I are resolved henceforth to do our part in helping this work.

Mary is comforted about Maggie and unboundedly grateful to me for going.

I think she herself prefers her staying there awhile; she has felt so keenly what Aunt Maria said about her being a burden and disgrace to us.

We shall watch over her there, and help her forward in life as fast as she is strong enough to go. But I am making this letter too long, so good-by for the present.

Your loving   Eva.

CHAPTER XLII

"WELL, hurrah for Jim!" exclaimed our friend Jim Fellows, making tumultuous entrance into the Henderson house, with such a whirl and breeze of motion as to flutter the music on the piano, and the papers on Harry's writing-desk, while he skipped round the room, executing an extemporary *pas seul.*

"Jim, for goodness sake, what now?" said Harry, rising. "What's up?"

"I've got it! I've got it!—the first place on 'the Forum!' Think of the luck! I've been talking with Ivison and Sears about it, and the papers are all drawn. I'm made now, you'd better believe. It's firm land at last, and I tell you, if I have n't scratched for it!"

"Wish you joy, my boy, with all my heart," said Harry, shaking his hand. "It's the top of the ladder."

"And I, too, Jim," said Eva, offering her hand frankly. "Sit down and have a cup of tea with us."

"*You* don't care, I suppose, what happens to *me*," said Jim in an abused tone, turning to Alice, who had sat quietly in a shaded corner through this outburst.

"Bless me, Jim, I've been holding my breath, for I did n't know what you'd do next. I'm sure I wish you joy with all my heart. There's my hand on it," and Alice reached out her hand as frankly as Eva.

It was a hand as fair, soft and white as a man might wish to have settle like a dove of peace and rest in his own; and, as it went into his palm, Jim could not help giving it a warm, detaining grasp that had a certain significance, especially as his eyes rested upon her with a flash of expression before which hers fell.

Alice had come to Eva's to dine, and they were now just enjoying that pleasant after-dinner hour around the fireside, when they sat and played with their tea in pretty teacups, and chatted, and looked into the fire. It is the hour dear to memory, when the home fireside seems like a picture, when the gleams of light that fall on one's plants and pictures and books and statuettes, bring forth some new charm in each one, giving rise to the exulting feeling, " Nowhere in the world is there a place so pretty and so cosy as this."

Now, Alice had been meditating a return to her own home that night, trusting to Harry for escort; but, at the moment that Jim took her hand and she saw the expression of his eyes, she mentally altered her intentions and resolved to remain all night. She was sure if she rose to go Jim would, of course, be her escort. She was not going to walk home alone with him in his present mood, and trust herself to hear, and be obliged to answer, anything he might be led to say.

The fact is well known to observers of mental phenomena, that an engagement suddenly sprung upon a circle of intimate acquaintances is often productive of great searchings of heart, and that it is apt to have a result similar to the knocking down of one brick at the extreme of a line of them.

Alice had been startled and astonished by finding her rector descending from the semi-angelic sphere where she had, in her imagination, placed him, and coming into the ranks of mortal and marrying men. She had seen and handled the engagement ring which sparkled on Angie's finger, and it looked like any other ring that a gentleman of good taste might buy, and she had heard all the comments of the knowing ones thereon. Already there was activity in the direction of a prospective trousseau. Aunt Maria, with her usual alertness, was prizing stuffs and giving records of prices and of cheap and desirable shopping places, and racing from one end of the city to the other in self-imposed pilgrimages of research. There were discussions of houses for the future rectory. Everything was in a whirl of preparation. There was marriage in the very air: and the same style of reflection which occurs when there is a death, is apposite also to the betrothal—" Whose turn shall come next?" "*Hodie mihi—cras tibi.*"

Jim Fellows, the most excitable, sympathetic of all mortal Jims, may well be supposed to have felt something of the general impulse.

Now, Miss Alice was as fine a specimen of young-lady-hood at twenty-two as is ordinarily to be met with in New York or otherwhere. She was well read, well bred, high-minded and high-principled. She was a little inclined to the ultra-romantic in her views, and while living along contentedly, and with a moderate degree of good sense and comfort, with such people as were to be found on earth, was a little prone to indulge dreams of super-celestial people—imaginary heroes and heroines. In the way of friendship, she imagined she liked many of her gentlemen associates; but the man she was to marry was to be a hero—somebody before whom she and every one else should be irresistibly constrained to bow down and worship. She knew nobody of this species as yet.

Harry was all very well; a nice fellow—a bright, lively, wide-awake fellow—a faultless husband—a desirable brother-in-law; but still Harry was not a hero. He was a man subject to domestic discipline for at times littering the parlor table with too many pamphlets, for giving imprudent invitations to dinner on an ill-considered bill of fare, and for confounding solferino with pink when describing colors or matching worsteds. All these things brought him down into the sphere of the actual, and took off the halo. In review of all the married men of her acquaintance, she was constrained to acknowledge that the genus *hero* was rare. Nobody that she was acquainted with ever had married this kind of being; and, in fact, within her own mind his lineaments were cloudy and indistinct, like the magic looking-glass of Agrippa before the destined image shone out. She only knew of this or that mortal man of her acquaintance, that he was not in the least like this ideal of her dreams.

Meanwhile, Miss Alice was not at all insensible to the charm of having a friend of the other sex wholly and entirely devoted to her.

She thought she had with most exemplary frankness and directness indicated to Jim that they were to be friends and only friends; she had contended for her right to be just as intimate with him as he and she pleased, in the face of Aunt Maria and of all the ranks and orders of good gossips who make the regulation of other people's affairs a specialty; and she flattered herself that she had at last conquered this territory and secured for herself this independent right.

People had almost done telling her they had heard that she was engaged to Jim Fellows, and asking her when it was going to be announced. She plumed herself, in a quiet way, on the independence and spirit she had shown in the matter.

Now, Jim was one of those fellows who, in certain respects, remain a boy forever. The boy in him was certainly booked for as long a mortal journey as the man; and, at threescore years and ten, one ought not to expect to meet in him other than a white-headed, vivacious old boy. He was a driving, industrious, efficient creature. He was, in all respects, ideally fitted to success in the profession he had chosen; the very image and body of the New York press man—lively, versatile, acute, unsleeping, untiring, always wide-awake, up and dressed, and in full command of his faculties, at any hour of day or night, ready for any emergency, overflowing with inconsiderate fun and frolic, and, like the public he served, going for his joke at any price. Since his intimacy with Alice she had assumed to herself the right of looking over his ways and acting the part of an exterior conscience; and Jim had formed the habit of bringing to her his articles for criticism. And Alice flattered herself that she was not altogether selfish in accepting his devotion, but was saving him from many an unwise escapade, and exciting him to higher standards and nobler ways of looking at life.

Of all the Christian and becoming *rôles* in the great drama of life, there is none that so exactly suits young ladies of a certain degree of gravity and dignity as that of guardian angel.

Now, in respect to Jim, Alice certainly was fitted to sustain this *rôle*. She was well-poised, decided, sensible and serious in her conceptions of life, truthful and conscientious; and the dash of ideality which pervaded all her views gave to her, in the eyes of the modern New York boy, a sort of sacred prestige, like the halo around a saint.

No one sees life on a harder, colder, more utterly unscrupulous side than the *élève* of the New York press. He grinds in a mill of competition. He serves sharp and severe masters, who in turn are driven up by an exacting, irresponsible public, panting for excitement, grasping for the latest sensation. The man of the press sees behind the scenes in every illusion of life; the shapeless pulleys,

the dripping tallow candles that light up the show, all are
familiar to him.

To him come all the tribes who have axes to grind,
and want him to turn their grindstones.   Avarice, ambition, petty vanity, private piques, mean intrigues, sly
revenges, all unbosom themselves to him as to a father
confessor, and invoke his powerful aid.   To him it is
given to see the back door and back stairs of much that
the world venerates, and he finds there filthy sweepings
and foul *débris*. Even the church of every name and
sect has its back door, its unsightly sweepings.   He who
is in so many secrets, who expolres so many cabals, who
sees the wrong side of so many a fair piece of goods, with
all its knots, and jags, and thrums, what wonder if he
come to that worse form of scepticism—the doubt of all
truth, of all virtue, of all honor?   When he sees how
reputations can be made and unmade in the secret con-
claves of printing offices, how generous and holy enthusiasms are assumed as a cloak for low and selfish designs,
how the language which stirs man's deepest nature lies
around loose in the hands of skilled word-experts, to be
used in getting up cabals and carrying party intrigues,
it is scarcely to be wondered at if he come to regard life
as a mere game of skill, where the shrewdest player wins.
It is exactly here that a true, good woman is the moral
salvation of man.   Such a woman seems to a man more
than she can ever seem to her female acquaintances.
She is to him the proof of a better world, of a truer life,
of the reality of justice, purity, honor, and unselfishness.
He regards her, to be sure, as unpractical, and ignorant
of the world's ways, but with a holy ignorance which
belongs to a higher region.

Jim had dived into New York life at first with the
mere animal recklessness with which an expert swimmer
shows his skill in difficult navigation. Life was an

adventure, a game, a game at which he was determined nobody should cheat him, a race in which he was determined to come out ahead. Nobody should catch *him* napping; nobody should outwit him; he would be nobody's fool. His acquaintance with a certain class of girls was only a continuation of the bright, quick, adroit game of fencing which he played in the world. If a girl would flirt, so would Jim. He was *au courant* of all the positions and strategy of that sort of encounter; he had all the *persiflage* of flattery and compliment at his tongue's end, and enjoyed the rustle and flutter of ribbons, the tapping of fans, and the bustle and mystery of small secrets, the little "ohs and ahs," and feminine commotions that he could stir up in almost any bevy of nymphs in evening dresses. Speaking of female influence, there are some exceptions to be taken to the general theory that woman has an elevating power over man. It may be doubted whether there goes any of this divine impulse from giggling, flirting girls, whose highest aim is to secure the admiration and attention of men, and who, to get it, will flatter and fawn, profess to adore tobacco smoke, and even to have a warm side towards whiskey punch,—girls whose power over men is based on an indiscriminate deference to what men themselves feel to be their lower and less worthy nature.

The woman who really wins for herself a worthy influence with a man is she who recognizes in him the divine under all worldly disguises, and invariably and strongly takes part with his higher against his lower nature. This was the secret of Alice's power over Jim; and this was why she had become, in the secret and inner world of his life, almost a religious image. All his dawning aspirations to be somewhat better than a mere chaser of expedients, to be a man of lofty objects and

noble purposes, had come from her acquaintance with
him—an acquaintance begun on both sides in the spirit
of mere flirtation, and passing from that to esteem and
friendship.   But, in the case of a marriageable young
man of twenty-five, friendship is like some of those rare
cacti of the greenhouses which, in an unexpected hour,
burst out into blossoms of untold splendor.   An engagement just declared in their circle had breathed a warmer
atmosphere of suggestion around them, and upon that
had come a position in his profession which offered him
both consideration and money; and when Jim was
assured of this, his first thought was of Alice.

"Friendship is a humbug," was that young gentlemen's mental decision.   "It may do all very well with
some kinds of girls"—and Jim mentally reviewed some of
his lady acquaintances—"but with Alice Van Arsdel, it·
is all humbug for me to go on talking friendship.   I
can't, and *shan't*, and WON'T."   And in this mood it was
that he gave to Alice's hand that startling kind of
pressure, and something of this flashed from his eyes
into hers.   It was that something, like the gleam of a
steel blade, determined, resolute, assured, that discon-
certed and alarmed her.   It was like the sounding of a
horn, summoning a parley at the postern gate of a fortress, and the lady chatelaine not ready either to sur-
render or to defend.   So, in a moment, Alice resolved
not to walk the four or five squares between her present
position and home, *tête-à-tête* with Jim Fellows; and she
sat very composed and very still in her corner, and put
in demand all those quiet, repressive tactics by which
dignified young ladies keep back issues they are not
precisely ready to meet.

The general subject under discussion when Jim came
in, was a party to be given at Aunt Maria's the next
evening in honor of the Stephenses, when Angie and Mr.

St. John would make their first appearance together as a betrothed couple.

"Now, Jim," said Eva, "how lucky that you came in, for I was just going to send a note to you! Here's Harry has got to give a lecture to-morrow night and can't come in till towards the end of the evening. Alice is coming to dine and dress down here with me, and I want you to dine with us and be our escort to the party—that is, if you will put up with our dressing time and not get into such a state of perfect amazement as Harry always does when we are not ready at the moment."

"If you ever get a wife, Jim, you'll be made perfect in this science of waiting," said Harry. "The only way to have a woman ready in season for a party is to shut her up just after breakfast and keep her at it straight along through the day. Then you may have her before ten o'clock."

"You see," said Eva, "Harry's only idea, when he is going to a party, is to get home again early. We almost never go, and then he is in such a hurry to get there, so as to have it over with and be at home again."

"Well, I confess, for my part, I hate parties," said Harry. "They always get agoing just about my usual bed-time."

"Well, Harry, you know Aunt Maria wants an old-fashioned, early party, at eight o'clock at the latest; and when *she* says she wants a thing, she *means* it. She would never forgive us for being late."

"Dear me, Eva, do begin to dress over night then," said Harry. "You certainly never will get through to-morrow, if you don't."

"Harry, you sauce-box, I think you talk abominably about me. Just because I have so many more things to see to than he has! A woman's dress, of course, takes more time; there's a good deal more to do and every little thing has to be just right.

"Of course, I know that," said Harry. "Have n't I stood, and stood, and stood, while bows were tied, and picked out, and patted, and flatted, and then pulled out and tied over, and when we were half an hour behind time already ?"

"I fancy," said Alice, "that if the secrets of some young gentlemen's toilets were unveiled, we should see that we were not alone in tying bows and pulling them out. I've known Tom to labor over his neck-ties by the hour together; it took him quite as long to prink as any of us girls."

" But do n't you be alarmed, Jim," said Eva; "we intend to be on time."

"No, do n't," said Harry; " you can have my writing-table, and get up your editorials, while the conjuration is going on up-stairs."

"Just think," said Alice, "how Aunt Maria is coming out."

"Why; yes, it's a larger affair than usual," said Eva. "A hundred invitations! That must be on account of Angie."

"Oh, yes," said Alice, "Aunt Maria is pluming herself on Angie's engagement. Since she has discovered that Mr. St. John has an independent fortune, there is no end to her praises and felicitations. Oh, and she has altered her opinion entirely about his ritualism. The Bishop, she says, stands by him; and what the Bishop doesn't condemn, nobody has any right to; and then she sets forth what a good family he belongs to, and so well connected! I'd like to see anybody say anything against Mr. St. John's practices before Aunt Maria now!"

" I'm sure this party is quite an outlay for Aunt Maria," said Eva.

"Oh," said Alice, "she's making all her jellies, and blanc-manges, and ice creams in the house. You know how perfectly she always does things. I've been up helping her. She will have a splendid table. She was rather glorifying herself to me that she could get up so fine a show at so little expense."

"Well, she can," said Eva. "No one can get more for a given amount of money than Aunt Maria. I suppose that is one of the womanly virtues, and one can learn as much of it from her as anybody."

"Yes," said Alice, "if a stylish party is the thing to be demonstrated, Aunt Maria will get one up more successfully, more perfect in all points, and for less money; than any other woman in New York. She will have exactly the right people, and exactly the right things to give them. Her rooms will be lovely. She will be dressed herself to a T, and she will say just the right thing to everybody. All her nice silver and her pretty things will come out of their secret crypts and recesses to do honor to the occasion, and, for one night, all will be suavity and sociability personified; and then everything will go back into lavender, the silver to the safe, the chairs and lounges to their cover, the shades will come down, and her part of the world's debt of sociability will be done up for the year. Then she will add up the expense, and set it down in her account book, and that thing 'll be finished and checked off."

"A mode of proceeding which she was very anxious to engraft upon me," said Eva; "but I am a poor stock. My instincts are for what she would call an expensive, chronic state of hospitality, as we live down here."

"Well," said Jim, "when I get a house of my own, I'm going to do as you do."

"Jim has got sight of the domestic tea-kettle in the

future," said Harry. "That's the first effect of his promotion."

"Oh, don't be in a hurry about setting up a house of your own," said Eva. "I'm afraid we should miss you here, and you're an institution, Jim; we could n't get on without you."

"Oh, Jim ought not to give up to one what was meant for mankind," said Alice, hardily. "I think there would be a universal protest against his retiring to private life."

And Alice looked into the fire, apparently as sweetly unconscious of anything particular on Jim's part as if she had not read aright the flash of his eye and the pressure of his hand.

Jim seemed vexed and nervous, and talked extravaganzas all the evening, with more than even his usual fluency, and towards ten o'clock said to Alice:

"I am at your command at any time, when you are ready to return home."

"Thank you, Jim," said Alice, with that demure and easy composure with which young ladies avoid a crisis without seeming to see it. "I am going to stay here to-night, to discuss some important points of party costume with Eva; so mind you don't fail us to-morrow night. *Au revoir !*"

CHAPTER XLIII

A MIDNIGHT CAUCUS OVER THE COALS.

"NOW, do n't you girls sit up and talk all night," said Harry from the staircase, as he started bedward, after Jim Fellows had departed, and the house-door was locked for the night.

Now, Eva was one of that class of household birds whose eyes grow wider awake and brighter as the small hours of the night approach; and, just this night, she felt herself swelling with a world of that distinctively feminine talk which women keep for each other, when the lordly part of creation are out of sight and hearing. Harry, who worked hard in his office all day and came home tired at night, and who had the inevitable next day's work ever before him, was always an advocate for early and regular hours, and regarded these sisterly night-watches with suspicion.

"You know, now, Eva, that you oughtn't to sit up late. You're not strong," he preached from the staircase in warning tones, as he slowly ascended.

"Oh, no, dear; we won't be long. We've just got a few things to talk over."

"Well, you know you never know what time it is."

"Oh, never you mind, Harry; you'll be asleep in ten minutes. I want to talk with Ally."

"There, now, he's off," said Eva, gleefully shutting the door and drawing an easy chair to the remains of the fire, while she disposed the little unburned brands and ends so as to make a last blaze; then, leaning back, she began taking out hair-pins and shaking down curls and untying ribbons, as a sort of preface to a wholly free and easy conversation. " I think, Ally," she said, with an air of profound reflection, "if I were you, I should wear my white tarletan to-morrow night, with cherry-colored trimming, and cherry velvet in your hair. You see that altering the trimming changes the whole effect, so that it will look exactly like a new dress."

"I was thinking of doing something with the tarletan," said Alice, who had also taken out her hair-pins and let down her long dark masses of hair around her handsome oval face, while her great dark eyes were studying the coals abstractedly. It was quite evident by the deep intense gaze she fixed before her that it was not the tarletan or the trimmings that at that moment occupied her mind, but something deeper.

Eva saw and suspected, and went on designedly:

" How nice and lucky it was that Jim came in just as he did."

"Yes, it was lucky," repeated Alice, abstractedly, taking off her neck-scarf, and folding and smoothing it with an unnecessary amount of precision.

" Jim is such a nice fellow," said Eva. "I am thoroughly delighted that he has got that situation. It is really quite a position for him."

"Yes, Jim is doing very well," said Alice, with a certain uneasy motion.

" I really think," pursued Eva, " that your friendship has been everything to Jim. We all notice how much he has improved."

" It's only that we know him better," said Alice. " Jim always was a nice fellow; but it takes a very intimate acquaintance to get at the real earnest nature there is under all his nonsense. But after all, Eva, I'm a little afraid of trouble in that friendship."

"Trouble—how?" said Eva, with the most innocent

A MIDNIGHT CAUCUS.

"'There, now he's off,' said Eva, . . . then, leaning back, she
began taking out hair-pins and shaking down curls and untying
ribbons as a preface to a wholly free conversation."—p. 400.

air in the world, as if she did not feel perfectly sure of what was coming next.

"Well, I do think, and I always have said, that an intimate friendship between a lady and a gentleman is just the best thing for both parties."

"Well, is n't it?" said Eva.

"Well, yes. But the difficulty is, it won't stay. It will get to be something more than you want, and that makes a trouble. Now, did you notice Jim's manner to me to-night?"

"Well, I *thought* I saw something rather suspicious," said Eva, demurely; "but then you always have been so sure that there was nothing, and was to be nothing, in that quarter."

"Well, I never have meant there should be. I have been perfectly honorable and above-board with Jim; treated him just like a sister, and I thought there was the most perfect understanding between us."

"Well, you see, darling," said Eva, "I've sometimes thought whether it was quite fair to let any one be so very intimate with one, unless one were willing to take the consequences, in case his feelings should become deeply involved. Now, we should have thought it a bad thing for Mr. St. John to go on cultivating an intimate friendship with Angie, if he never meant to marry. It would be taking from her feelings and affections that might be given to some one who would make her happy for life; and I think some women, I don't mean you, of course, but some women I have seen and heard of, like to absorb all the feeling and devotion a man has without in the least intending to marry him. They keep him from being interested in any one else who might make him a happy home, and won't have him themselves."

"Eva, you are too hard," said Alice.

"Understand me, dear; I said I didn't mean you, for

I think your course has been perfectly honorable and honest so far; but I do think you have got to a place that needs care.   It's my positive belief that Jim not only loves you, Alice, but that he is *in* love with you in a way that will have the most serious effect on his life and character."

"Oh, dear me, that's just what I've been fearing," said Alice, "is n't it too bad?   I really do n't think it's my fault.   Do you know, Eva, I came here meaning to go home to-night, and I stayed only because I was afraid to walk home with Jim.   I was sure if I did there would be a crisis of some kind."

"For my part, Ally," said Eva, "I'm not so very sure that there has n't been some advance in your feelings, as well as in Jim's.   I don't see why you should set it down among the impossibles that you should marry Jim Fellows."

"Oh! well," said Alice, "I like—yes, I really love Jim very much; he is very agreeable to me, always.   I know nobody, on the whole, more so; but then, Eva, he's not at all the sort of man I have ever thought of as possible for me to marry.   Oh! not at all," and Alice gazed before her into the coals, as if she saw her hero through them.

"And what sort of a man is this phenix?"

"Oh! something grave, and deep, and high, and heroic."

Eva gave a light, little shrug to her shoulders, and rippled a laugh.   "And when you have got such a man, you will have to ask him to go to market for beef and cranberry sauce.   You will have to get him to match your worsted, and carry your parcels, and talk over with him about how to cure the chimney of smoking and make the kitchen range draw.   Don't you think a hero will be a rather cumbersome help in housekeeping?

Besides, your heroes like to sit on pedestals and have you worship them. Now, for my part, I'd rather have a good kind *man* that will worship me.

> "'A creature not too bright and good
> For human nature's daily food.'

A man like Harry, for instance. Harry isn't a hero; he's a good, true, noble-hearted boy, though, and I'd rather have him than the angel Gabriel, if I could choose now. I don't see what's to object to in Jim, if you like him and love him, as you say. He's handsome; he's lively and cheerful; he's kind-hearted and obliging; and he's certainly true and constant in his affections: and now he has a good position, and one where he can do a good work in the world, and your influence might help him in it."

"Why, Eva, you seem to be pleading for him like a lawyer," said Alice, apparently not at all displeased to hear that side of the question discussed.

"Well, really," said Eva, "I do think it would be a nice thing for us all if you could like Jim, for he's one of us; we all know him and like him, and he wouldn't take you away to the ends of the earth; you might settle right down here, and live near us, and all go on together cosily. Jim is just the fellow to make a bright, pleasant, hospitable home; and he's certain to be a devoted husband to whomever he marries."

"Jim ought to be married, certainly," said Alice, in a reflective tone. "Just the right kind of a marriage would be the making of him."

"Well, look over the girls you know, and see if there's any one that you would like to have Jim marry."

"I know," said Alice, with a quickened flush of color, "that there isn't a girl he cares a snap of his finger for."

"There's Jane Stuyvesant."

"Oh, nonsense! don't mention Jane Stuyvesant!"

"Well, she's rich, and brilliant, and very gracious to Jim."

"Well, I happen to know just how much that amounts to. Jim never would have a serious thought of Jane Stuyvesant—that I'm certain of. She's a perfectly frivolous girl, and he knows it."

"I've thought sometimes he was quite attentive to one of those Stephenson girls, at Aunt Maria's."

"What, Sophia Stephenson! You could n't have got more out of the way. Why, no! Why, she's nothing but a breathing wax doll; that's all there is to her. Jim never could care for her."

"Well, what was it about that Miss Du Hare?"

"Oh, nothing at all, except that she was a dashing, flirting young thing that took a fancy to Jim and invited him to her opera box, and of course Jim went. The fact is, Jim is good-looking and lively and gay, and will go a certain way with any nice girl. He likes to have a jolly, good time; but he has his own thoughts about them all, as I happen to know. There is n't one of these that he has a serious thought of."

"Well, then, darling, since nobody else will suit him, and it's for his soul's health and wealth to be married, I don't see but you ought to undertake him yourself."

Alice smiled thoughtfully, and twisted her sash into various bows, in an abstracted manner.

"You see," continued Eva, "that it would be altogether improper for you to enact the fable of the dog in the manger—neither take him yourself nor let any one else have him."

"Oh, as to that," said Alice, flushing up, "he has my free consent to take anybody else he wants to; only I know there is n't anybody he does want."

"Except—" said Eva.

"Well, except present company," said Alice. "I'll tell you, Eva, if anything could incline me more to such a decision, it's the way Aunt Maria has talked about Jim to me—setting him down as if he was the last and most improbable *parti* I could choose; and as if, of course, I never could even think of him. I don't see what right she has to think so, when there are girls a great deal richer and standing higher in fashionable society than I do that would have Jim in a minute, if they could get him. Jim is constantly beset with more invitations to parties and to go into society than he can at all meet, and I know there are plenty that would be glad enough to take him."

"Oh, but Aunt Maria has moderated a good deal as to Jim, lately," said Eva. "She told me herself, the other day, that he really was one of the most gentlemanly, agreeable young fellows she knew of, and said what a pity it was he hadn't a fortune."

"Oh, that witch of a creature!" said Alice, laughing. "He has been just amusing himself with getting round Aunt Maria."

"And I dare say," said Eva, "that, if she finds Jim has a really good position, she might at last come to a state of resignation. I will say that for Aunt Maria, that after fighting you for a while she comes round handsomely—when she is certain that fighting is in vain; but the most amusing thing is to see how she has come down about Mr. St. John's ritualism. Think of her actually going up there to church last Sunday, and not saying a word about the candles, or the chantings, or any of the abominations! She only remarked that she was sure she never heard a better Gospel sermon than Mr. St. John preached—which was true enough. Harry and I were so amused we could hardly keep our faces straight; but we said not a word to remind her of past denunciations."

"The danger of going to Rome is sensibly abated, it appears," said Alice.

"Oh, yes. I believe Aunt Maria must be cherishing distant visions of a time when she shall be aunt to Mr. St. John, and set him all straight."

"She'll have her match for once," said Alice, "if she has any such intentions."

"One thing is a comfort," said Eva. "Aunt Maria has her hands so full, getting up Angie's trousseau, and buying her sheets and towels and table-cloths, and tearing all about, up stairs and down, and through dark alleys, to get everything of the very best at the smallest expense, that her nervous energies are all used up, and there is less left to be expended on you and me. A wedding in the family is a godsend to us all."

The conversation here branched off into an animated discussion of some points in Angie's wedding-dress, and went on with an increasing interest till it was interrupted by a dolorous voice from the top of the entry staircase.

"Girls, have you the least idea what time it is?"

"Why, there's Harry, to be sure," said Eva. "Dear me, Alice, what time is it?"

"Half-past one! Mercy on us! is n't it a shame?"

"Coming, Harry, coming this minute," called Eva, as the two sisters began turning down the gas and raking up the fire; then, gathering together collars, hair-pins, ribbons, sashes and scarfs, they flew up the stairway, and parted with a suppressed titter of guilty consciousness.

"It was abominable of us," said Eva; "but I never looked at the clock."

CHAPTER XLIV

FLUCTUATIONS.

MIDNIGHT conversations of the sort we have chronicled between Alice and Eva, do not generally lead to the most quiet kind of sleep. Such conversations suggest a great deal, and settle nothing; and Alice, after retiring, lay a long time with her great eyes wide open, looking into the darkness of futurity, and wondering, as girls of twenty-two or thereabouts do wonder, what she should do next.

There is no help for it; the fact may as well be confessed at once, that no care and assiduity in fencing and fortifying the conditions of a friendship between an attractive young woman and a lively, energetic young man, will ensure their always remaining simply and purely those of companionship and good fellowship, and never becoming anything more.

In the case of St. John and Angie, the stalk of friendship had had but short growth before developing the flower of love; and now, in Alice's mind and conscience, it was becoming quite a serious and troublesome question whether a similar result were not impending over her.

The wise man of old said : " He that delicately bringeth up his servant from a child shall have him for his son at last." The proverb is significant, as showing the gradual growth of kindly relations into something more and more kindly, and more absorbing.

So, in the night-watches, Alice mentally reviewed all those looks, words and actions of Jim's which produced a conviction in her mind that he was passing beyond the

allotted boundaries, and approaching towards a point in
which there would inevitably be a crisis, calling for a
decision on her part which should make him either more
or less than he had been.　Her talk with Eva had only
set this possibility more distinctly before her.

Was she, then, willing to give him up entirely, and
to shut the door resolutely on all intimacy tending to
keep up and encourage feelings that could come to no
result?　When she proposed this to herself, she was surprised at her own unwillingness to let him go.　She
could scarcely fancy herself able to do without his ready
friendship, his bright, agreeable society—without the
sense of ownership and power which she felt in him.
Reviewing the matter strictly in the night-watches, she
was obliged to admit to herself that she could not afford
to part with Jim; that there was no woman she could
fancy—certainly none in the circle of her acquaintance—
whom she could be sincerely glad to have him married
to; and when she fancied him absorbed in any one else,
there was a dreary sense of loss which surprised her.
Was it possible, she asked herself, that he had become
necessary to her happiness—he whom she never thought
of otherwise than as a pleasant friend, a brother, for
whose success and good fortune she had interested herself?

Well then, was she ready for an engagement?　Was
the great ultimate revelation of woman's life—that dark
Eleusinian mystery of fate about which vague conjecture
loves to gather, and which the imagination invests with
all sorts of dim possibilities—suddenly to draw its curtains and disclose to her neither demi-god nor hero, but
only the well-known, every-day features of one with
whom she had been walking side by side for months
past—"only Jim and nothing more?"

Alice could not but acknowledge to herself that she

knew no man possible or probable that she liked better; and yet this shadowy, ideal rival—this cross between saint and hero, this Knight of the Holy Grail—was as embarrassing to her conclusions as the ghost in "Hamlet" It was only to be considered that the ideal hero had not put in an actual appearance. He was nowhere to be found or heard from; and here was this warm-hearted, helpful, companionable Jim, with faults as plenty as blackberries, but with dozens of agreeable qualities to every fault; and the time seemed to be rapidly coming when she must make up her mind either to take him or leave him, and she was not ready to do either! No wonder she lay awake, and studied the squares of the dim window and listened to the hours that struck, one after another, bringing her no nearer to fixed conclusions than before! A young lady who sees the time coming when she must make a decision, and who does n't want to take either alternative presented, is certainly to be pitied. Alice felt herself an abused and afflicted young woman. She murmured at destiny. Why would men fall in love? she queried. Why would n't they remain always devoted, admiring friends, and get no further? She was having such good times! and why must they end in a dilemma of this sort? How nice to have a gentleman friend, all devotion, all observance, all homage, without its involving any special consequences!

When she came to shape this feeling into words and look at it, she admitted that it savored of the worst kind of selfishness, and might lead to trifling with what is most precious and sacred. Alice was a conscientious, honorable girl, and felt all the force of this. She had justified herself all along by saying that her intimacy with Jim had so far been for his good; that he had often expressed to her his sense that she was leading him to a higher and better life, to more worthy and honorable

s

aims and purposes: but how if he should claim that
this very ministry had made her necessary to him, and
that, if she threw him off, it would be worse than if she
had never known him? Looking over the history of
the last few months, she could not deny to herself that,
as their acquaintance had grown more and more confidential, her manners possibly had expressed a degree of
kindness which might justly have inspired hopes. Was
she not bound to fulfill such hopes if she could?

These were most uncomfortable inquiries, and she
was glad of morning and a cheerful breakfast-table to
dispel them. Things never look so desperate by day-
light, and Alice managed a good breakfast with a toler-
able appetite. Then there was the tarlatan dress to be
made over and rearranged, and Eva's toilette to be put
into party order—quite enough to keep two young women
of active fancy and skillful fingers busy for one day. It
was a snowy, unpleasant day, and, as they lived on an
out-of-the-way street, they were secure from callers and
took their work into the parlor so soon as Harry had
gone for the day. The little room soon became a
brilliant maelstrom of gauzy stuffs and bright ribbons,
among which the two sat chatting, arranging, combining,
compounding; as of old, one might imagine a pair of
heathen goddesses in the clouds, getting up rainbows.
No matter how solemn and serious we of womankind
are in our deepest hearts, or how philosophically we
may look down on the vanity of dress, we must all
confess that a party is a party; and the sensible, economical woman who does not often go, and does not
make a point of having all the paraphernalia in constant
readiness, has to give all the more care and thought to
the exceptional occasion when she does. Even Scripture recognizes the impossibility of appearing at a feast
without the appropriate garment; and so Eva and Alice

cut and fitted and trimmed and tried experiments in head-dresses and arrangements of hair, and meanwhile Alice had the comfort of talking over and over to Eva all the varying shades of the subject that was on her mind.

What woman does not appreciate the blessing of a patient, sympathetic listener, who will hear with unabated interest the same story repeated over and over as it rises in one's thoughts? Eva listened complacently and with the warmest interest to the same things that Alice had said the night before, and went on repeating to her the same lessons of matronly wisdom with which she had then enriched her, neither of them betraying the slightest consciousness that the things they were saying were not just fresh from the mint—entirely new and hitherto unconsidered.

Jim's character was discussed, and with that fine, skillful faculty of analysis and synthesis which forms the distinctive interest of feminine conversation. In the course of these various efforts of character portrait-painting, it became quite evident to Eva that Alice was in just that state in which some people's admitted faults are more interesting and agreeable than the virtues of some others. When a woman gets thus far, her final decision is not a matter of doubt to any far-sighted reader of human nature.

Alice was by nature exact and conscientious as to all rules, forms, and observances. Her pronunciation, whether of English or French, was critically perfect; her hand-writing and composition were faultless to a comma. She was an enthusiastic and thorough maintainer of all the boundaries and forms of good society and of churchly devotion. Jim, without being in any sense really immoral or wicked, was a sort of privileged Arab, careering in and out through the boundaries of all departments,

shocking respectable old prejudices and fluttering reverential usages, talking slang and making light of dignita-
ries with a free and easy handling that was alarming.

But it is a fact that very correct people, who would
not violate in their own persons one of the *convenances*,
are often exceedingly amused and experience a peculiar
pleasure in seeing them tossed hither and thither by
somebody else. Nothing is so tiresome as perfect cor-
rectness, and we all know that everything that amuses
us and makes us laugh lies outside of it; and Alice, if
the truth were to be told, liked Jim all the better for the
very things in which he was most unlike herself. Well,
such being the state of the garrison on the one side,
what was the position of the attacking party?

Jim had gone home discontented at not having a
private interview with Alice, but more and more resolved, with every revolving hour since the accession of
good fortune which had given him a settled position,
that he would have a home of his own forthwith, and
that the queen of that home should be Alice Van Arsdel.
She must not, she could not, she would not say him
Nay; and if she did, he wouldn't take No for an answer. He would have her, if he had to serve for her as
long as Jacob did for Rachel. But when Jim remembered how many times he had persuaded Alice to his
own way, how many favors she had granted him, he was
certain that it was not in her to refuse. He had looked
with new interest at the advertisements of houses to
let, and the furniture stores for the last few days had
worn a new and suggestive aspect. He had commenced
transactions with regard to parlor furniture, and actually
bought a pair of antique brass andirons, which he was
sure would be just the thing for their fireside. Then
he had bought an engagement ring, which lay snugly ensconced in its satin case in a corner of his vest pocket,

and he was inly resolved that he would make to himself a chance to lodge it on the proper finger in the
next twenty-four hours. How he was to get an interview did not yet appear; but he trusted to Providence.
It is a fact on record, that before the twenty-four hours
were up the deed was done, and Jim and Alice were engaged; but it came about in a way far different from
any foreseen by any party, as we shall proceed to show.

CHAPTER XLV

THE VALLEY OF THE SHADOW.

IT wanted yet twenty minutes to eight o'clock, and Jim was sitting alone in the glow of the evening fireside. The warm, red light, flickering and shadowing, made the room seem like a mysterious grotto. Jim, in best party trim, sat gazing dreamily into the fire, turning the magic ring now and then in his vest pocket, and looking at his watch at intervals, while the mysterious rites of the toilet were going on upstairs.

Alice had never made a more elaborate or more careful toilet. Did she want to precipitate that which she said to herself she dreaded? Certainly she did not spare one possible attraction. She evidently saw no reason, under present circumstances, why she should not make herself look as well as she could.

As the result of the whole day's agitations and discussions, she had come to the conclusion that if Jim had anything to say she would listen to it advisedly, and take it into mature consideration. So she braided her long, dark hair, and crowned herself therewith, and then earrings and brooches came twinkling out here and there like stars, and bits of ribbon and velvet fluttered hither and thither, and fell into wonderfully apposite places, and the woman grew and brightened before the glass, as a picture under the hands of the artist.

It wanted yet a quarter of an hour of the time for the carriage, when there came a light fluff of gauzy garments, and the two party goddesses floated in in all misty splendor, and seemed to fill the whole room with the flutter of dresses.

Alice was radiant; her eyes were never more brilliant, and she was full of that subtle brightness which comes from the tremor of fully-awakened feeling. She was gayer than was her usual wont as she swept about the room and courteseyed with much solemnity to Jim, and turned herself round and round after the manner of a revolving figure in the shop windows.

Suddenly—and none of them knew how—there was a quick flash; the gauzy robe had swept into the fire, and, before any of them could speak, the dress was in flames. There was a scream, an utterance of agony from all parties at once, and Eva was just doing the most fatal thing possible in rushing desperately towards her sister, when Jim came between them, caught the woolen cloth from the table, and wrapped it around Alice; then, taking her in his arms, he laid her on the sofa, and crushed out the fire, beating it with his hands, and tearing the burning fragments away and casting them under foot. It all passed in one fearful, awe-struck moment, while Eva stood still, with the very shadow of death upon her, and saw Jim fighting back the fire, which in a moment or two was entirely extinguished. Alice had fainted, and Jim and Eva looked at each other as people do who have just seen death rising up between them.

"She is safe now," said Jim, as he stood there, pale as death and quivering from head to foot, while the floor around was strewed with the blackened remains of the gauzy material which he had torn away. "She is all right," he added; "the cloth has saved her throat and lungs."

It seemed now the most natural thing in the world that Jim should lay Alice's head upon his arm and administer restoratives; and, when she opened her eyes, that he should call her his darling, his life, his love. They had been in the awful valley of the shadow to-

gether—that valley where all that is false perishes and
drops off, and what is true becomes the only reality.
Alice felt that she loved Jim—that she belonged to him,
and she did not dispute his right to speak as he did,
and to care for her as one had a right to care for his own.

"Well," said Eva, drawing a long breath, when the
bell rang and the carriage was announced, "we cannot
go to the party, that is certain ; and, Jim, tell him to go
for Doctor Campbell. Mary, bring down a wrapper;
we'll slip it over your torn finery, Alice, for the present,"
said Eva, endeavoring to be practical and self-possessed,
though with a little hysterical sob every now and then
betraying the shock to her nerves. "Then there must
be a note sent to Aunt Maria, or what will she think ?"
pursued Eva, when Alice had been made comfortable on
the sofa, where Jim was devoting himself to her.

"Don't, pray, tell all about it," said Alice. "One
does n't want to become the talk of all New York."

"I'll tell her that you have met with an accident
that will detain you and me, but that you are not dangerous," said Eva, as she wrote her note and sent Mary
up with it.

It was not until tranquillity had somewhat settled
down on the party that Jim began to feel that his own
hands were blistered ; for, though a man under strong
excitement may handle fire for a while and not feel it,
yet nature keeps account and brings in her bill in due
season.

"Why, Jim, you brave fellow," said Alice, suddenly
raising herself, as she saw an expression of pain on his
face, "here I am thinking only of myself, and you are
suffering."

"Oh, nothing; nothing at all," said Jim; but Eva
and Alice, now thoroughly aroused, were shocked at the
state of his hands.

"The doctor will have you to attend to first," said Alice, " You have saved me by sacrificing yourself."

"Thank God for that!" said Jim, fervently.

Well, the upshot of the story is that Eva would not hear of Jim's leaving them that night. Doctor Campbell pronounced that the burns on his hands needed serious attention, and the prospect was that he would be obliged to rest from using them for a day or two.

But these two or three days of hospital care were not on the whole the worst of Jim's life, for Alice insisted on being his amanuensis, and writing his editorials for him, and, as she wrote with the engagement ring sparkling on her finger, Jim thought that he had never seen it appear to so great advantage. It was said that Jim's editorials, that week, had a peculiar vigor and pungency. We should not at all wonder, under the circumstances, if that were the case.

CHAPTER XLVI

AND so Jim Fellows and Alice Van Arsdel were engaged at last. The reader, who has cared to follow the workings of that young lady's mind has doubtless seen from the first that she was on the straight highway to such a result.

Intimate friendship—what the French call "*camaraderie*"—is, in fact, the healthiest and the best commencement of the love that is needed in married life; because it is more like what the staple of married life must at last come to. It gives opportunity for the knowledge of all those minor phases of character under which a married couple must at last see each other.

Alice and Jim had been side by side in many an every-day undress rehearsal. They had laughed and frolicked together like two children; they had known each other's secrets; they had had their little miffs and tiffs, and had gotten over them; but, through all, there had been a steady increase on Jim's part of that deeper feeling which makes a woman the ideal guide and governor and the external conscience of life. But his habit of jesting, and of talking along the line of his most serious feelings in language running between joke and earnest, had prevented the pathos and the power of what was really deepest in him from making itself felt. There wanted something to call forth the expression of the deep manly feeling that lay at the bottom of his heart. There wanted, on her part, something to change friendship to a warmer feeling. Those few dreadful moments, when they stood under the cloud of a sudden and frightful danger, did more to reveal to them how much they were to each other than years of ordinary acquaintance. It was as if they had crossed the river of death together, and saw each other in their higher natures. Do we not all remember how suffering and danger will bring out in well-known faces a deep and spiritual expression never there before? It was a marked change in the faces of our boys who went to the recent war. Looking in a photograph book, one sees first the smooth lines of a boyish face indicating nothing more than a boy's experience, but, as he turns the following pages, he sees the same face, after suffering and danger and death have called up the strength of the inner man, and imparted a higher and more spiritual expression to the countenance.

The sudden nearness into which they had come to the ever possible tragedy that underlies human life, had given a deep and solemn tenderness to their affection. It was a baptism into the love which is stronger than death. Alice felt her whole heart going out, without a fear or a doubt, in return for the true love that she felt was ready to die for her.

Those few first days that they spent mostly in each other's society, were full of the real, deep, enthusiastic tenderness of that understanding of each other which had suddenly arisen between them.

So, to her confidential female correspondent—the one who had always held her promise to be the first recipient of the news of her engagement—she wrote as follows:

"Yes, dear Belle, I have to tell you at last that I *am engaged*—engaged, with all my heart and soul, to Jim Fellows. I see your wonder, I hear you saying, 'You said it never was to be ; that there *never* would be anything in it.' Well, dear Belle, when I said that

I thought it; but it seems I didn't know myself or him. But Eva has told you of the dreadful danger I ran; the shock to my nerves, the horror, the fright, were something I never shall forget. By God's mercy he saved my life, and I saw and felt at that time how dear I was to him, and how much he was willing to suffer for me. The poor fellow is not yet fully recovered, and I cannot recall that sudden fright without being almost faint. I cared a good deal for him before, and knew he cared for me; but this dreadful shock revealed us to each other as we had never known each other before. I am perfectly settled now and have not a doubt. There is all the seriousness and *all the depth that is in me* in the promise I have at last given him.

"Jim is not rich, but he has just obtained a good position as one of the leading editors of the *Forum*, enough to make it prudent for him to think of having a home of his own; and I thank God for the reverses of fortune that have taught me how to be a helpful and sensible wife. We don't either of us care for show or fashion, but mean to have another fireside like Eva's. Exactly when this thing is to be, is not yet settled; but you shall have due notice to get your bridesmaid's dress ready."

So wrote Alice to her bridesmaid that was to be. Meanwhile, the declared engagement went its way, traveling through the circle, making everywhere its sensation.

We believe there is nothing so generally interesting to human nature as a newly-declared engagement. It is a thing that everybody has an opinion of; and the editorial comments, though they do not go into print, are fully as numerous and as positive as those following a new appointment at Washington.

Especially is this the case where the parties, being long under suspicion and accusation, have denied the impeachment, and vehemently protested that "there was, and there would be, nothing in it," and that "it was only friendship." When, after all the strength of such asseveration, the flag is finally struck, and the suspected parties walk forth openly, hand in hand, what a number of people immediately rise in their own opinion, saying with complacency: "There! what did I tell you? I knew it was so. People may talk as much as they please, they can't deceive me!"

Among the first to receive the intelligence was little Mrs. Betsey, who, having been over with Jack to make a morning call at the Henderson house, had her very cap lifted from her head with amazement at the wonderful news. So, panting with excitement, she rushed back across the way to astonish Miss Dorcas, and burst in upon her, with Jack barking like a storming party in the rear.

"Good gracious, Betsey, what's the matter now?" said Miss Dorcas. "What has happened?"

"Well, what should you think? You can't guess! Jack, be still! stop barking! Stop, sir!"—as Jack ran under a chair in a distant corner of the room, and fired away with contumacious energy.

"Yes, Dorcas, I have such a piece of news! I declare, that dog!—I'll *kill* him if he don't stop!" and Mrs. Betsey, on her knees, dragged Jack out of his hiding-place, and cuffed him into silence, and then went on with her news, which she determined to make the most of, and let out a bit at a time, as children eat gingerbread.

"Well, now, Betsey, since the scuffle is over between you and Jack, perhaps you will tell me what all this is about," said Miss Dorcas, with dignity.

"Well, Dorcas, it's another engagement; and who *do* you guess it is? You never will guess in the world, I know; now guess."

"I don't know," said Miss Dorcas, critically surveying Mrs. Betsey over her spectacles, "unless it is you and old Major Galbraith."

"Aren't you ashamed, Dorcas?" said the little old lady, two late pink roses coming in either cheek. "Major Galbraith!—old and deaf and with the rheumatism!"

"Well, you wanted me to guess, and I guessed the two most improbable people in the circle of our acquaintance." Now, Major Galbraith was an old admirer of Mrs. Betsey's youth, an ancient fossil remain of the distant period to which Miss Dorcas and Mrs. Betsey belonged.

He was an ancient bachelor, dwelling in an ancient house on Murray hill, and subsisting on the dry hay of former recollections. Once a year, on Christmas or New Year's, the old major caused himself to be brought carefully in a carriage to the door of the Vanderheyden house, creaked laboriously up the steps, pulled the rusty, jangling old bell, and was shown into the somber twilight of the front parlor, where he paid his respects to the ladies with the high-shouldered, elaborate stateliness and gallantry of a former period. The compliments which the major brought out on these occasions were of the most elaborate and well-considered kind, for he had an abundance of leisure to compose them, and very few ladies to let them off upon. They had, for the parties to whom they were addressed, all the value of those late roses and violets which one now and then finds in the garden, when the last black frosts have picked off the blooms of summer. The main difficulty of the interview always was the fact that the poor major was stone-deaf, and, in spite of both ladies screaming themselves hoarse, he carried away the most obviously erroneous impressions, to last him through the next year. Yet, in ages past, the major had been a man of high fashion, and he was, if one only could get at him, on many accounts better worth talking to than many modern beaux; but as age and time had locked him in a case and thrown away the key, the suggestion of tender relations between him and Mrs. Betsey was impossible enough to answer Miss Dorcas's purpose.

But Mrs. Betsey was bursting to begin on the contents of her news-bag, and so, out it came.

"Well now, Dorcas, if you won't go to being ridiculous, and talking about Major Galbraith, I'll tell you who it is. It's that dear, good Mr. Fellows that got Jack back again for us, and I'm sure I never feel as if I could do enough for him when I think of it, and besides that, he always is so polite and considerate, and talks with one so nicely and is so attentive, seems to think something of you, if you *are* an old woman, so that I'm glad with all my heart, for I think it's a splendid thing, and she's just the one for him, and do you know I've been thinking a great while that it was going to be? I have noticed signs, and have had my own thoughts, but I didn't let on. I despise people that are always prying and spying and expressing opinions before they know."

This lucid exposition might have proceeded at greater length, had not Miss Dorcas, whose curiosity was now fully roused, cut into the conversation with an air of judicial decision.

"Well now, after all, Betsey, *will* you have the goodness, since you began to tell the news, to tell it like a reasonable creature? Mr. Fellows is the happy man, you say. Now, *who*—is—the *woman?*"

"Oh, didn't I tell you? Why, what is the matter with me to-day? I thought I said Miss Alice Van Arsdel. Won't she make him a splendid wife? and I'm sure he'll make a good husband; he's so kind-hearted. Oh! you ought to have seen how kind he was to Jack that day he brought him back; and such a sight as Jack was, too—all dirt and grease! Why it took Dinah and me at least two hours to get him clean, and there are not many young gentlemen that would be so patient as he was. I never shall forget it of him."

" Patient as *who* was?" said Miss Dorcas. " I believe Jack was the last nominative case in that sentence ; do pray compose yourself, Betsey, and don't take entire leave of your senses."

"I mean Mr. Fellows was patient, of course, you know."

"Well, then, do take a little pains to say what you mean," said Miss Dorcas.

"Well, don't you think it a good thing—and were you expecting it?"

"So far as I know the parties, it's as good a thing as engagements in general," said Miss Dorcas. " They have my very best wishes."

"Well, did you ever think it would come about?"

"No; I never troubled my head with speculations on what plainly is none of my concern," said Miss Dorcas.

It was evident that Miss Dorcas was on the highest and most serene mountain-top of propriety this morning, and all her words and actions indicated that calm superiority to vulgar curiosity which, in her view, was befitting a trained lady. Perhaps a little pique that Betsey had secured such a promising bit of news in advance of herself, added to her virtuous frigidity of demeanor. We are all mortal, and the best of us are apt to undervalue what we did not ourselves originally produce. But if Miss Dorcas wished in a gentle manner to remind Mrs. Betsey that she was betraying too much of an inclination for gossip, she did not succeed. The clock of time had gone back on the dial of the little old lady, and she was as full of chatter and detail as a school-girl, and determined at any rate to make the most of her incidents, and to create a sensation in her sister's mind—for what is more provoking than to have people sit calm and unexcited when we have a stimulating bit of news to tell? It is an evident violation of Christian charity. Mrs. Betsey now drew forth her next card.

"Oh, and, Dorcas! you've no idea. They've been having the most dreadful time over there! Miss Alice has had the greatest escape! The most wonderful providence! It really makes my blood run cold to think of it. Don't you think, she was all dressed to go to Mrs. Wouvermans's party, and her dress caught on fire, and if it hadn't been for Mr. Fellows's presence of mind she might have been burned to death—really burned to death! Only think of it!"

"You don't say so!" said Miss Dorcas, who now showed excitement enough to fully satisfy Mrs. Betsey. "How very dreadful! Why, how was it?"

"Yes—she was passing in front of the fire, in a thin white tarlatan, made very full, with flounces, and it was just drawn in and flashed up like tinder. Mr. Fellows caught the cloth from the table, wrapped her in it and laid her on the sofa, and then tore and beat out the fire with his hands."

"Dear—me! dear—me!" said Miss Dorcas, "how dreadful! But he did just the right thing."

"Yes, indeed; you ought to have seen! Mrs. Henderson showed me what was left of the dress, and it was really awful to see! I could not help thinking, 'In the midst of life we are in death.' All trimmed up with scarlet velvet and bows, and just hanging in rags and tatters, where it had been burned and torn away! I never saw any thing so solemn in my life."

"A narrow escape, certainly," said Miss Dorcas. "And is she not injured at all?"

"Nothing to speak of, only a few slight burns; but poor Mr. Fellows has to have his hands bandaged and dressed every day; but of course he doesn't mind that

since he has saved her life.   But just think of it, Dorcas,
we shall have two weddings, and it'll make two more
visiting places.   I'm going to tell Dinah all about it,"
and the little woman fled to the kitchen, with Jack at
her heels, and was soon heard going over the whole
story again.

Dinah's effusion and sympathy, in fact, were the final
refuge of Mrs. Betsey on every occasion, whether of joy
or sorrow or perplexity—and between her vigorous
exclamations and loud responses, and Jack's running
commentary of unrestrained barking, there was as much
noise over the announcement as could be made by an
average town meeting.

Thus were the tidings received across the way.   In
the Van Arsdel family, Jim was already an established
favorite.   Mr. Van Arsdel always liked him as a bright,
agreeable evening visitor, and, now that he had acquired
a position that promised a fair support, there was no opposition on his part to overcome.   Mrs. Van Arsdel was
one of the motherly, complying sort of women, generally
desirous of doing what the next person to her wanted
her to do; and, though she was greatly confused by
remembering Alice's decided asseverations that "*it* never
was and never would be anything, and that Jim was not
at all the person she ever should think of marrying," yet,
since it was evident that she was now determined upon
the affair, Mrs. Van Arsdel looked at it on the bright
side.

"After all, my dear," she said to her spouse, "if I
must lose both my daughters, it's a mercy to have them
marry and settle down here in New York, where I can
have the comfort of them.   Jim will always be an attentive husband and a good family man.   I saw *that* when
he was helping us move; but I'm sure I don't know
what Maria will say now!"

"No matter what Maria says, my dear," said Mr. Van Arsdel. "It don't make one hair white or black. It's time you were emancipated from Maria."

But Aunt Maria, like many dreaded future evils, proved less formidable on this occasion than had been feared.

The very submissive and edifying manner in which Mr. Jim Fellows had received her strictures and cautions on a former occasion, and the profound respect he had shown for her opinion, had so far wrought upon her as to make her feel that it was really a pity that he was not a young man of established fortune. If he only had anything to live on, why, he might be a very desirable match; and so, when he had a good position and salary, he stood some inches higher in her esteem. Besides this, there was another balm which distilled resignation in the cup of acquiescence, and that was the grand chance it gave her to say, "I told you so." How dear and precious this privilege is to the very best of people, we need not insist. There are times when it would comfort them, if all their dearest friends were destroyed, to be able to say, "I told you so. It's just as I always predicted!" We all know how Jonah, though not a pirate or a cut-throat, yet wished himself dead because a great city was not destroyed, when he had taken the trouble to say it would be. Now, though Alice's engagement was not in any strict sense an evil, yet it was an event which Aunt Maria had always foreseen, foretold and insisted on.

So when, with heart-sinkings and infinite precautions, Mrs. Van Arsdel had communicated the news to her, she was rather relieved at the response given, with a toss of the head and a vigorous sniff:

"Oh, that's no news to me; it's just what I have foreseen all along—what I told you was coming on, and

you would n't believe it.   *Now* I hope all of you will see
that I was right."

"I think," said Mrs. Van Arsdel, "that it was Jim's
presence of mind in saving her life that decided Alice at
last.   She always liked him; but I don't think she really
loved him till then."

"Well, of course, it was a good thing that there was
somebody at hand who had sense to do the right thing,
when girls will be so careless; but it was n't that.   She
meant to have him all along; and I knew it," said Aunt
Maria.   "Well, Jim Fellows, after all, is n't the worst
match a girl could make, either, now that he has some
prospects of his own—but, at any rate, it has turned out
just as I said it would.   I knew she'd marry him, six
months ago, just as well as I know it now, unless you
and she listened to my advice then.   So now all we have
to do is to make the best of it.   You've got two weddings on your hands, now Nellie, instead of one, and I
shall do all I can to help you.   I was out all day yesterday looking at sheeting, and I think that at Shanks &
Maynard's is decidedly the firmest and the cheapest, and
I ordered three pieces sent home; and I carried back
the napkins to Taggart's, and then went rambling off up
by the Park to find that woman that does marking."

"I'm sure, Maria, I am ever so much obliged to
you," said Mrs. Van Arsdel.

"Well, I hope I'm good for something.   Though I 'm
not fit to be out; I 've such a dreadful cold in my head,
I can hardly see; and riding in these New York omnibuses always makes it worse."

" Dear Maria, why will you expose yourself in that
way ?"

" Well, somebody 's got to do it—and your judgment
is n't worth a fip, Nellie.   That sheeting that you were
thinking of taking was n't half so good, and cost six cents

a yard more. I could n't think of having things go that
way."

"But I 'm sure we do n't any of us want you to make
yourself sick."

"Oh, I sha'n't be sick. I may suffer; but I sha'n't
give up. I 'm not one of the kind. If you had the cold
in your head that I have, Nellie, you 'd be in bed, with
both girls nursing you; but that is n't my way. I keep
up, and attend to things. I want these things of Angie's
to be got up properly, as they ought to be, and there 's
nobody to do it but me."

And little Mrs. Van Arsdel, used, from long habit, to
be thus unceremoniously snubbed, dethroned, deposed,
and set down hard by her sister when in full career of
labor for her benefit, looked meekly into the fire, and
comforted herself with the reflection that it "was just
like Maria. She always talked so; but, after all, she was
a good soul, and saved her worlds of trouble, and made
excellent bargains for her."

CHAPTER XLVII

"IN THE FORGIVENESS OF SINS."

THIS article of faith forms a part of the profession of all Christendom, is solemnly recited every Sunday and many week-days in the services of all Christian churches that have a liturgy, whether Roman or Greek or Anglican or Lutheran, and may, therefore, bid fair to pass for a fundamental doctrine of Christianity.

Yet, if narrowly looked into, it is a proposition under which there are more heretics and unbelievers than all the other doctrines of religion put together.

Mrs. Maria Wouvermans, standing, like a mother in Israel, in the most eligible pew of Dr. Cushing's church, has just pronounced these words with all the rest of the Apostles' Creed, which she has recited devoutly twice a day every Sunday for forty years or more. She always recited her creed in a good, strong, clear voice, designed to rebuke the indolent or fastidious who only mumbled or whispered, and made a deep reverence in the proper place at the name of Jesus ; and somehow it seemed to feel as if she were witnessing a good confession, and were part and parcel with the protesting saints and martyrs that, in blue and red and gold, were shining down upon her through the painted windows. This solemn standing up in her best bonnet and reciting her Christian faith every Sunday, was a weekly testimony against infidelity and schism and lax doctrines of all kinds, and the good lady gave it with unfaltering regularity. Nothing would have shocked her more than to have it intimated to her that she did not believe the articles of her own faith ; and yet, if there was anything in the world that Mrs. Maria Wouvermans practically did n't believe in, and did n't mean to believe in, it was "*the forgiveness of sins.*"

As long as people did exactly right, she had fellow-ship and sympathy with them. When they did wrong, she wished to have nothing more to do with them. Nay, she seemed to consider it a part of public justice and good morals to clear her skirts from all contact with sinners. If she heard of penalties and troubles that befell evil doers, it was with a face of grim satisfaction. "It serves them right—just what they ought to expect. I don't pity them in the least," were familiar phrases with her. If anybody did her an injury, crossed her path, showed her disrespect or contumely, she seemed to feel as free and full a liberty of soul to hate them as if the Christian religion had never been heard of. And, in particular, for the sins of women, Aunt Maria had the true ingrain Saxon ferocity which Sharon Turner describes as characteristic of the original Saxon female in the earlier days of English history, when the unchaste woman was pursued and beaten, starved and frozen, from house to house, by the merciless justice of her sisters.

It is the same spirit that has come down through English law and literature, and shows itself in the old popular ballad of "Jane Shore," where, without a word of pity, it is recorded how Jane Shore, the king's mistress, after his death, first being made to do public penance in a white sheet, was thereafter turned out to be frozen and starved to death in the streets, and died miserably in a ditch, from that time called Shoreditch. A note tells us that there was one man who, moved by pity, at one time sheltered the poor creature and gave her food, for which he was thrown into prison, to the great increase of her sorrow and misery.

It was in a somewhat similar spirit that Mrs. Wouvermans regarded all sinning women. Her uniform ruling in such cases was that they were to be let alone by all decent people, and that if they fell into misery and want, it was only just what they deserved, and she was glad of it. What business had they to behave so? In her view, all efforts to introduce sympathy and mercy into prison discipline—all forbearance and pains-taking with the sinful and lost in all places in society—was just so much encouragement given to the criminal classes, and one of the lax humanitarian tendencies of the age. It is quite certain that had Mrs. Wouvermans been a guest in old times at a certain Pharisee's house, where the Master allowed a fallen woman to kiss His feet, she would have joined in saying: "If this man were a prophet he would have known what manner of woman this is that toucheth him, for she is a sinner." There was certainly a marked difference of spirit between her and that Jesus to whom she bowed so carefully whenever she repeated the creed.

On this particular Sunday, Eva had come to church with her aunt, and was going to dine with her, intent on a mission of Christian diplomacy.

Some weeks had now passed since she left Maggie in the mission retreat, and it was the belief of the matron there, and the attending clergyman, that a change had taken place in her, so radical and so deep that, if now some new and better course of life were opened to her, she might, under careful guidance, become a useful member of society. Whatever views modern skepticism may entertain in regard to what is commonly called the preaching of the gospel, no sensible person conversant with actual facts can help acknowledging that it does produce in some cases the phenomenon called *conversion*, and that conversion, when real, is a solution of all diffi-

culties in our days as it was in those of the first
apostles.

The first Christians were gathered from the dregs of
society, and the Master did not fear to say to the Phar-
isees, "The publicans and harlots go into the kingdom
of heaven before you;" and St. Paul addresses those
who he says had been thieves and drunkards and revilers
and extortioners, with the words, "Ye are washed; ye
are sanctified; ye are justified in the name of the Lord
Jesus and by the spirit of God."

It is on the power of the Divine spirit to effect such
changes, even in the most hopeless and forlorn subjects,
that Christians of every name depend for success; and
by this faith such places as the Home for the Fallen are
undertaken and kept up.

What people look for, and labor for, as is proved by
all experience, is more liable to happen than what they
do not expect and do not labor for. The experiment of
Mr. James was attended by many marked and sudden
instances of conversion and permanent change of character. Maggie had been entrapped and drawn in by
Mother Moggs in one of those paroxysms of bitter despair which burned in her bosom, when she saw, as she
thought, every respectable door of life closed upon her
and the way of virtue shut up beyond return. When she
thought how, while *she* was cast out as utterly beyond
hope, the man who had betrayed her and sinned with her
was respected, flattered, rich, caressed, and joined in
marriage to a pure and virtuous wife, a blind and keen
sense of injustice awoke every evil or revengeful passion
within her. "If they won't let me do good, I *can* do
mischief," she thought, and she was now ready to do all
she could to work misery and ruin for a world that
would give her no place to do better. Mother Moggs
saw Maggie's brightness and smartness, and the remains

T

of her beauty. She flattered and soothed her. To say the truth, Mother Moggs was by no means all devil. She had large remains of that motherly nature which is common to warm-blooded women of easy virtue. She took Maggie's part, was indignant at her wrongs, and offered her a shelter and a share in her business. Maggie was to tend her bar; and by her talents and her good looks and attractions Mother Moggs hoped to double her liquor sales. What if it did ruin the men? What if it was selling them ruin, madness, beggary—so much the better;—had they not ruined her?

If Maggie had been left to her own ways, she might have been the ruin of many. It was the Christ in the heart of a woman who had the Christian love and Christian courage to go after her and seek for her, that brought to her salvation. The invisible Christ must be made known through human eyes; he must speak through a voice of earthly love, and a human hand inspired by his spirit must be reached forth to save.

The sight of Eva's pure, sweet face in that den of wickedness, the tears of pity in her eyes, the imploring tones of her voice, had produced an electric revulsion in Maggie's excitable nature. She was not, then, forsaken: she was cared for, loved, followed even into the wilderness, by one so far above her in rank and station. It was an illustration of what Christian love was, which made it possible to believe in the love of Christ. The hymns, the prayers, that spoke of hope and salvation, had a vivid meaning in the light of this interpretation. The enthusiasm of gratitude that arose first towards Eva, overflowed and bore the soul higher towards a Heavenly Friend.

Maggie was now longing to come back and prove by her devotion ard obedience her true repentance, and Eva had decided to take her again. With two weddings impending in the family, she felt that Maggie's skill with the needle and her facility in matters pertaining to the female toilet might do good service, and might give her the sense of usefulness—the strength that comes from something really accomplished.

· Her former experience made her careful, however, of those sore and sensitive conditions which attend the return to virtue in those who have sinned, and which are often severest where there is the most moral vitality, and she was anxious to prevent any repetition on Aunt Maria's part of former unwise proceedings. All the other *habitués* of the house partook of her own feeling; Alice and Angie were warmly interested for the poor girl; and if Aunt Maria could be brought to tolerate the arrangement, the danger of a sudden domiciliary visit from her attended with inflammatory results might be averted.

So Eva was very sweet and very persuasive in her manner to-day, for Aunt Maria had been devoting herself so entirely to the family service during the few weeks past, that she felt in some sort under a debt of obligation to her. The hardest person in the world to manage is a sincere, willful, pig-headed, pertinacious friend who will insist on doing you all sorts of kindnesses in a way that plagues about as much as it helps you.

But Eva was the diplomatist of the family; the one with the precise mixture of the *suaviter in modo* with the *fortiter in re*. She had hitherto carried her points with the good lady in a way that gave her great advantage, for Aunt Maria was one of those happily self-complacent people who do not fail to arrogate to themselves the after the most strenuous efforts, to hinder, and Eva's credit of all the good things that they have not been able, housekeeping and social successes, so far, were quite a feather in her cap. So, after dinner, Eva began with:

"Well, you know, Aunt Maria, what with these two weddings coming on, there is to be a terrible pressure of work—both coming the week after Easter, you see. So," she added quickly, "I think it quite lucky that I have found Maggie and got her back again, for she is one of the quickest and best seamstresses that I know of." Aunt Maria's brow suddenly darkened. Every trace of good-humor vanished from her face as she said:

"Now do tell me, Eva, if you *are* going to be such a fool, when you were once fairly quit of that girl, to bring her back into your family."

"Yes, Aunt, I thought it my Christian duty to take care of her, and see that she did not go to utter ruin."

"I don't know what you mean," said Aunt Maria. "*I* should say she *had* gone there now. Do you think it your duty to turn your house into a Magdalen asylum?"

"No, I do not; but I do think it is our duty to try to help and save this *one* girl whom we know—who is truly repentant, and who wants to do well."

"Repentant!" said Aunt Maria in a scornful tone. "Don't tell me. I know their tricks, and you'll just be imposed on and get yourself into trouble. I know the world, and I know all about it." Eva now rose and played her last card. "Aunt Maria," she said, "You profess to be a Christian and to follow the Saviour who came to seek and save the lost, and I don't think you do right to treat with such scorn a poor girl that is trying to do better."

"It's pretty well of you, Miss, to lecture *me* in this style! Trying to do better!" said Aunt Maria, "then what did she go off for, when she was at your house and you were doing all you could for her? It was just that she wanted to go to the bad."

"She went off, Aunt Maria," said Eva, "because she

overheard all you said about her, the day you were at my house. She heard you advising me to send her mother away on her account, and saying that she was a disgrace to me. No wonder she ran off."

"Well, serves her right for listening! Listeners never hear any good of themselves," said Aunt Maria.

"Now, Aunty," said Eva, "nobody has more respect for your good qualities than I have, or more sense of what we all owe you for your kindness to us; but I must tell you fairly that, now I am married, you must not come to my house to dictate about or interfere with my family arrangements. You must understand that Harry and I manage these matters ourselves and will not allow any interference; and I tell you now that Maggie is to be at our house, and under my care, and I request that you will not come there to say or do anything which may hurt her mother's feelings or hers."

"Mighty fine," said Aunt Maria, rising in wrath, "when it has come to this, that servants are preferred before me!"

"It has not come to that, Aunt Maria. It has simply come to this: that I am to be sole mistress in my own family, and sole judge of what it is right and proper to do; and when I need your advice I shall ask it; but I don't want you to offer it unless I do."

Having made this concluding speech while she was putting on her bonnet and shawl, Eva now cheerfully wished her aunt good afternoon, and made the best of her way down-stairs.

"I don't see, Eva, how you could get up the courage to face your aunt down in that way," said Mrs. Van Arsdel, to whom Eva related the interview.

"Dear Mamma, it'll do her good. She will be as sweet as a rose after the first week of indignation. Aunt Maria is a sensible woman, after all, and resigns herself

to the inevitable.   She worries and hectors you, my
precious Mammy, because you will let her.   If you'd
show a brave face, she would n't do it; but it is n't in
you, you poor, lovely darling, and so she just preys upon
you ; but Harry and I are resolved to make her stand
and give the countersign when she comes to our camp."

And it is a fact that, a week after, Aunt Maria spent
a day with Eva in the balmiest state of grace, and made
no allusion whatever to the conversation above cited.
Nothing operates so healthfully on such moral constitutions as a good dose of certainty.

CHAPTER XLVIII

THE PEARL CROSS.

EVERY thoughtful person who exercises the least supervision over what goes on within, is conscious of living two distinct lives—the outward and the inward.

The external life is positive, visible, definable; easily made the subject of conversation. The inner life is shy, retiring, most difficult to be expressed in words, often inexplicable, even to the subject of it, yet no less a positive reality than the outward.

We have not succeeded in the picture of our Eva unless we have shown her to have one of those sensitive moral organizations, whose nature it is to reflect deeply, to feel intensely, and to aspire after a high moral ideal.

If we do not mistake the age we live in, the perplexities and anxieties of such natures form a very large item in our modern life.

It is said that the Christian religion is losing its hold on society. On the contrary, we believe there never was a time when faith in Christianity was so deep and all-pervading, and when it was working in so many minds as a disturbing force.

The main thing which is now perplexing modern society, is the effort which is making to reduce the teachings of the New Testament to actual practice in life and to regulate society by them. There is no skepticism as to the ends sought by Jesus in human life. Nobody doubts that love is the fulfilling of the law, and that to

do as we would be done by, applied universally, would
bring back the golden age, if ever such ages were.

But the problem that meets the Christian student,
and the practical person who means to live the Christian
life, is the problem of redemption and of self-sacrifice.

In a world where there is always ruin and misery,
where the inexperienced are ensnared and the blind
misled, and where fatal and inexorable penalties follow
every false step, there must be a band of redeemers,
seekers and savers of the lost.   There must be those
who sacrifice ease, luxury and leisure, to labor for the
restoration of the foolish and wicked who have sold
their birthright and lost their inheritance; and here is
just the problem that our age and day present to the
thoughtful person who, having professed, in whatever
church or creed, to be a Christian, wishes to make a
reality of that profession.

The night that Eva had spent in visiting the worst
parts of New York had been to her a new revelation of
that phase of paganism which exists in our modern city
life, within sound of hundreds of church bells of every
denomination.   She saw authorized as a regular trade,
and protected by law, the selling of that poisoned liquor
which brings on insanity worse than death; which en-
genders idiocy, and the certainty of vicious propensities
in the brain of the helpless unborn infant; which is the
source of all the poverty, and more than half the crime,
that fills alms-houses and prisons, and of untold miseries
and agonies to thousands of families.   She saw woman
degraded as the minister of sin and shame; the fallen
and guilty Eve, forever plucking and giving to Adam
the forbidden fruit whose mortal taste brings death into
the world; and her heart had been stirred by the sight
of those multitudes of poor ruined wrecks of human
beings, men and women, that she had seen crowding in

to that midnight supper, and by the earnest pleadings of faith and love that she had heard in the good man's prayers for them. She recalled his simple faith, his undaunted courage in thus maintaining this forlorn hope in so hopeless a region, and she could not rest satisfied with herself, doing nothing to help.

In talking with Mr. James on his prospects, he had said that he very much wished to enlarge this Home so as to put there some dormitories for the men who were willing to take the pledge to abandon drinking, where they could find shelter and care until some kind of work could be provided for them. He stated further that he wished to connect with the enterprise a farm in the country where work could be found for both men and women, of a kind which would be remunerative, and which might prove self-supporting.

Eva reflected with herself whether she had anything to give or to do for a purpose so sacred. Their income was already subject to a strict economy. The little elegancies and adornments of her house were those that are furnished by thought and care rather than by money. Even with the most rigorous self-scrutiny, Eva could not find fault with the home philosophy by which their family life had been made attractive and delightful, because she said and felt that her house had been a ministry to others. It had helped to make others stronger, more cheerful, happier.

But when she brought Maggie away from the Home, she longed to send back some helpful token to those earnest laborers.

On revising her possessions, she remembered that, once, in the days when she was a rich and rather self-indulgent daughter of luxury, she had spent the whole of one quarter's allowance in buying for herself a pearl cross. It cost her not even a sacrifice, for when with a kiss or two she confessed her extravagance to her father, he only pinched her cheek playfully, told her not to do so again, and gave a check for the amount. There it lies, at this moment, in Eva's hands; and as she turns it abstractedly round and round, and marks the play of light on the beautiful pearls, she thinks earnestly what that cross means, and wonders that she should ever have worn it as a mere bauble.

Does it not mean that man's most generous Friend, the highest, the purest, the sweetest nature that ever visited this earth, was agonized, tortured, forsaken, and left to bleed life away, unpitied and unrelieved, for love of us and of all sinning, suffering humanity? Suddenly the words came with overpowering force to her mind: "He died for all, that they which live should not henceforth live unto themselves."

Immediately she resolved that she would give this cross to the sacred work of saving the lost. She resolved to give it secretly—without the knowledge even of her husband. The bauble was something personal to herself that never would be missed or inquired for, and she felt about such an offering that reserve and sacredness which is proper to natures of great moral delicacy. With the feeling she had at this moment, it was as much an expression of personal loyalty and devotion to Jesus Christ as was the precious alabaster vase of Mary. It satisfied, moreover, a kind of tender, vague remorse that she had often felt; as if, in her wedded happiness and her quiet home, she were too blessed, and had more than her share of happiness in a world where there were such sufferings and sorrows.

She had always had a longing to do something towards the world's work, and, if nothing more, to be a humble helper of the brave and heroic spirits who press on in the front ranks of this fight for the good.

She did not wish to be thanked or praised, as if the giving up of such a toy for such a cause were a sacrifice worth naming; for, in the mood that she was in, it was no sacrifice—it was a relief to an over-charged feeling, an act of sacramental union between her soul and the Saviour who gave himself wholly for the lost. So she put the velvet case in its box, and left it at Mr. James's door, with the following little note:

" *My Dear Sir :* Ever since that most sad evening when I went with you in your work of mercy to those unhappy people, I have been thinking of what I saw, and wishing I could do something to help you. You say that you do not solicit aid except from the dear Father who is ever near to those that are trying to do such work as this; yet, as long as he is ever near to Christian hearts, he will inspire them with desires to help in a cause so wholly Christ-like. I send you this ornament, which was bought in days when I thought little of its sacred meaning. Sell it, and let the avails go towards enlarging your Home for those poor people who find no place for repentance in the world. I would rather you would tell nobody from whom it comes. It is something wholly my own ; it is a relief to offer it, to help a little in so good a work, and I certainly shall not forget to pray for your success.

" Yours, very truly,   E. H.

" P.S.—I am very happy to be able to say that poor M. seems indeed a changed creature. She is gentle, quiet, and humble ; and is making, in our family, many friends.

" I feel hopeful that there is a future for her, and that the dear Saviour has done for her what no human being could do."

We have seen the question raised lately in a religious paper, whether the sacrifice of personal ornaments for benevolent objects was not obligatory; and we have seen the right to retain these small personal luxuries defended with earnestness.

To us, it seems an unfortunate mode of putting a very sacred subject.

The Infinite Saviour, in whose hands all the good works of the world are moving, is *rich*. The treasures of the world are his. He is as able now as he was when on earth to bid us cast in our line and find a piece of silver in the mouth of the first fish. Our gifts are only valuable to him for what they express in us.

Had Mary not shed the precious balm upon his head, she would not have been reproved for the omission; yet the exaltation of love which so expressed itself was appreciated and honored by him.

It is written, too, that he looked upon and loved the young man who had not yet attained to the generous enthusiasm that is willing to sacrifice *all* for suffering humanity.

Religious offerings, to have value in his sight, must be like the gifts of lovers, not extorted by conscience, but by the divine necessity which finds relief in giving.

He can wait, as mothers do, till we outgrow our love of toys and come to feel the real sacredness and significance of life. The toy which is dear to childhood will be easily surrendered in the nobler years of maturity.

But Eva's was a nature so desirous of sympathy that whatever dwelt on her mind overflowed first or last into the minds of her friends; and, an evening or two after her visit to the mission home, she told the whole story at her fireside to Dr. Campbell, St. John, and Angie, Bolton, Jim, and Alice, who were all dining with her. Eva had two or three objects in this. In the first place, she wanted to touch the nerve of real Christian unity which she felt existed between the heart of St. John and that of every true Christian worker—that same Christian unity that associated the Puritan apostle Eliot with the Roman Catholic missionaries of Canada. She wished him to see in a Methodist minister the same faith, the same moral heroism which he had so warmly responded to in the ritualistic mission of St. George, and which was his moral ideal in his own work.

She wished to show Dr. Campbell the pure and simple faith in God and prayer by which so effective a work
of humanity had already been done for a class so hopeless.

"It's all very well," he said, "and I'm glad, if anybody can do it; but I don't believe prayer has anything
to do with it."

"Well, I do," said Bolton, energetically. "I would n't
think life worth having another minute, if I did n't think
there was a God who would stand by a man whose whole
life was devoted to work like this."

"Well," said Campbell, "it is n't, after all, an appeal
to God; it's an appeal to human nature. Nobody that
has a heart in him can see such a work doing and not
want to help it. Your minister takes one and another to
see his Home, and says nothing, and, by-and-by, the
money comes in."

"But in the beginning," said Eva, "he had no money,
and nothing to show to anybody. He was going to do
a work that nobody believed in, among people that
everybody thought so hopeless that it was money thrown
away to help him. To whom could he go but God? He
went and asked *Him* to help him, and began, and has
been helped day by day ever since; and *I* believe God
did help him. What is the use of believing in God at
all, if we don't believe that?"

"Well," said Jim, "I'm not much on theology, but
we newspaper fellows get a considerable stock of facts,
first and last; and I've looked through this sort of thing,
and I believe in it. A man don't go on doing a business
of six or seven or eight thousand a year on prayer,
unless prayer amounts to something; and I know, first
and last, the expenses of that concern can't be less than
that."

"Well," said Harry, "we have a lasting monument

in the great orphan house of Halle—a whole city square
of solid stone buildings. I have stood in the midst of
them, and they were all built by one man, without fortune of his own, who has left us his written record how,
day by day, as expenses thickened, he went to God and
asked for his supplies, and found them."

"But I maintain," said Dr. Campbell, "that his appeal was to human nature. People found out what he
was doing, their sympathies were moved, and they sent
him help. The very sight of such a work is an application."

"I don't think that theory accounts for the facts,"
said Bolton. "Admitting that there is a God who is
near every human heart in its most secret retirement,
who knows the most hidden moods, the most obscure
springs of action, how can you prove that this God did
not inspire the thoughts of sympathy and purposes of
help there recorded? For we have in this Franke's
journal, year after year, records of help coming in when
it was wanted, having been asked for of God, and obtained with as much regularity and certainty as if checks
had been drawn on a banker."

"Well," said Dr. Campbell, "do you suppose that, if
I should now start to build a hospital without money,
and pray every week for funds to settle with my work-
men, it would come?"

"No, Doctor, *you 're* not the kind of fellow that such
things happen to," said Jim, "nor am I."

"It supposes an exceptional nature," said Bolton,
"an utter renunciation of self, an entire devotion to an
unselfish work, and an unshaken faith in God. It is a
moral genius, as peculiar and as much a gift as the genius
of painting, poetry, or music."

"It is an inspiration to do the work of humanity,
and it presupposes faith," said Eva. "You know the

Bible says, 'He that cometh to God must *believe* that HE IS, and that he is a rewarder of those that diligently seek him.' "

The result of that fireside talk was not unfruitful. The next week was a harvest for the Home.

In blank envelopes, giving no names, came various sums. Fifty dollars, with the added note:

> " From a believer in human nature."

This was from Dr. Campbell.

A hundred dollars was found in another envelope, with the note:

> " To help up the fallen,
> From one who has been down."

This was from Bolton.

Mr. St. John sent fifty dollars, with the words:

> " From a fellow-worker."

And, finally, Jim Fellows sent fifty, with the words:

> " From one of the boys."

None of these consulted with the other; each contribution was a silent and secret offering. Who can prove that the " Father that seeth in secret " did not inspire them?

CHAPTER XLIX

THE UNPROTECTED FEMALE.

" THE Squantum and Patuxet Manufacturing Company have concluded not to make any dividends for the current year."

Such was the sum and substance that Miss Dorcas gathered from a very curt letter which she had just received from the Secretary of that concern, at the time of the semi-annual dividend.

The causes of this arrangement were said to be that the entire income of the concern (which it was cheerfully stated had never been so prosperous) was to be devoted to the erection of a new mill and the purchase of new machinery, which would in the future double the avails of the stock.

Now, as society is, and, for aught we see, as it must be, the masculine half of mankind have it all their own way; and the cleverest and shrewdest woman, in making investments, has simply the choice between what this or that *man* tells her. If she falls by chance into the hands of an honest man, with good sense, she may make an investment that will be secure to pay all the expenses of her mortal pilgrimage, down to the banks of Jordan; but if, as quite often happens, she falls into the hands of careless or visionary advisers, she may suddenly find herself in the character of "the unprotected female" at some half-way station of life, with her ticket lost and not a cent to purchase her further passage.

Now, this was precisely the predicament that this letter announced to Miss Dorcas. For the fact was that, although she and her sister owned the house they lived in, yet every available cent of income that supplied their establishment came from the dividends of these same Squantum and Patuxet mills.

It is a fact, too, that women, however strong may be their own sense and ability, do, as a general fact, rely on the judgment of the *men* of the family, and consider their rulings in business matters final.

Miss Dorcas had all this propensity intensified by the old-world family feeling. Her elder brother, Dick Vanderheyden, was one of those handsome, plausible, visionary fellows who seem born to rule over woman-kind, and was fully disposed to magnify his office. Miss Dorcas worshiped him with a faith which none of his numerous failures abated. The cupboards and closets of the house were full of the remains of inventions which, he had demonstrated by figures in the face of facts, ought to have produced millions, and never did produce anything but waste of money. She was sure that he was the original inventor of the principle of the sewing-machine; and how it happened that he never perfected the thing, and that somebody else stole in be-fore him and got it all, Miss Dorcas regarded as one of the inscrutable mysteries of Providence.

Poor Dick Vanderheyden was one of those perma-nent waiters at the world's pool, like the impotent man in the gospel. When the angel of success came down and troubled the waters, there was always another who stepped in before him and got the benefit.

Yet there was one thing that never left him to the last, and that was a sweet-tempered, sunny hopefulness, in which, through years when the family fortune had been growing beautifully less in his hands, Dick was still making arrangements which were to bring in wonderful results, till one night a sudden hemorrhage from the lungs settled all his earthly accounts in an hour, and left Miss Dorcas and Mrs. Betsey without a male relative in the world.

One of the last moves of brother Dick had been to take all the sisters' United States stock and invest it for them in the Squantum and Patuxet Manufacturing Company, where, he confidently assured them, it would in time bring them an income of fifty per cent.

For four years after his death, however, only a moderate dividend was declared by the company, but always with brilliant promises for the future; the fifty per cent., like the "good time coming" in the song, was a thing to look forward to, as the end of many little retrenchments and economies; and now suddenly comes this letter, announcing to them an indefinite suspension of their income.

Mrs. Betsey could scarcely be made to believe it.

"Why, they've got all our money; are they going to keep it, and not pay us anything?"

"That seems to be their intention," said Miss Dorcas grimly.

"But, Dorcas, I wouldn't have it so. I'd rather have our money back again in United States stock."

"So had I."

"Well, if you write and ask them for it, and tell them that you *must* have it, and can't get along without, won't they send it back to you?"

"No, they won't think of such a thing. They never do business that way."

"Won't? Why, I never heard of such folks. Why, there's no justice in it."

"You don't understand these things, Betsey; nor I, very well. All I know is, that Dick took our money and bought stock with it, and we are stockholders of this company."

" And what is being a stockholder?"

" As far as I can perceive, it is this : when old women like you and me are stockholders, it means that a company of men take our money and use it for their own purposes, and pay us what they like, when it comes convenient; and when it's not convenient, they don't pay us at all. It is borrowing people's money, without paying interest."

" Why, that is horrid. Why, it's the most unjust thing I ever heard of," said Mrs. Betsey. " Do n't you think so, Dorcas ?"

" Well, it seems so to me ; but women never understand business. Dick used to say so. The fact is, old women have no business anywhere," said Miss Dorcas bitterly. " It's time we were out of the world."

" I'm sure I have n't wanted to live so very much," said Mrs. Betsey, tremulously. " I do n't want to die, but I had quite as lieve *be* dead."

" Come, Betsey, don't let us talk that way," said Miss Dorcas. " We sha'n't gain anything by flying in the face of Providence."

" But, Dorcas, I do n't think it can be quite as bad as you think. People could n't be so bad, if they knew just how much we wanted our money. Why, we haven't anything to go on—only think ! The company has been making money, you say ?"

" Oh, yes, never so large profits as this year ; but, instead of paying the stockholders, they have voted to put up a new mill and enlarge the business."

" Who voted so ?"

" The stockholders themselves. As far as I can learn, that means one or two men who have bought all the stock, and now can do what they like."

" But could n't *you* go to the stockholders' meeting and vote ?"

"What good would it do, if I have but ten votes, where each of these men has five hundred? They have money enough.· They don't need this income to live on, and so they use it, as they say, to make the property more valuable; and perhaps, Betsey, when we are both dead, it will pay fifty per cent. to somebody, just as Dick always said it would."

"But," said Mrs. Betsey, "of what use will that be to us, when what we want is something to live on now? Why, we can't get along without income, Dorcas, do'nt you see?"

"I think I do," said Miss Dorcas, grimly.

"Why, why, what shall we do?"

"Well, we can sell the house, I suppose."

"Sell the house!" said poor little Mrs. Betsey, aghast at the thought; "and where could we go? and what should we do with all our things? I'd rather die, and done with it; and if we got any money and put it into anything, people would just take it and use it, and not pay us income; or else it would all go just as my money did that Dick put into that Aurora bank. That was going to make our everlasting fortune. There was no end to the talk about what it would do—and all of a sudden the bank burst up, and my money was all gone —never gave me back a cent! and *I* should like to know where it went to. Somebody had that ten thousand dollars of mine, but it wasn't me. No, we wo n't sell the house; it's all we've got left, and as long as it's here we've got a right to be *somewhere*. We can stay here and starve, I suppose!—you and I and Jack."

Jack, perceiving by his mistress's tones that something was the matter, here jumped into her lap and kissed her.

"Yes, you poor doggie," said Mrs. Betsey, crying; "we'll all starve together. How much money have you got left, Dorcas?"

Miss Dorcas drew out an old porte-monnaie and opened it.

"Twenty dollars."

"Oh, go 'way, Miss Dorcas; ye do n't know what a lot I's got stowed away in my old tea-pot!" chuckled a voice from behind the scenes, and Dinah's woolly head and brilliant ivories appeared at the slide of the china-closet, where she had been an unabashed and interested listener to the conversation.

"Dinah, I'm surprised," said Miss Dorcas, with dignity.

"Well, y' can be surprised and git over it," said Dinah, rolling her portly figure into the conversation. "All I's got to say is, dere ain't no use for Mis' Betsey here to be worritin' and gettin' into a bad spell 'bout money, so long as I's got three hundred dollars laid up in my tea-pot. 'Tain't none o' your rags neither," said Dinah, who was strong on the specie question—" good bright silver dollars, and gold guineas, and eagles, I tucked away years ago, when your Pa was alive, and money was plenty. Look a-heah now!"—and Dinah emphasized her statement by rolling a handful of old gold guineas upon the table—"Dare now; see dar! Do n't catch me foolin' away no money wid no banks and no stockholders. I keeps pretty tight grip o'mine. Tell *you*, 'fore I'd let dem gemmen hab my money I'd braid it up in my har—and den I'd know where 'twas when I wanted it."

"Dinah, you dear old soul," said Miss Dorcas, with tears in her eyes, " you do n't think we'd live on your money?"

"Dun no why you should n't, as well as me live on yourn," said Dinah. "It's all in de family, and turn about's fair play. Why, good land! Miss Dorcas, I jest lotted on savin't up for de family. You can use mine and give it back agin when dat ar good time comes Massa Dick was allers a-tellin' about."

Mrs. Betsey fell into Dinah's arms, and cried on her shoulder, declaring that she could n't take a cent of her money, and that they were all ruined, and fell into what Dinah used to call one of her "bad spells." So she swept her up in her arms forthwith and carried her up-stairs and put her to bed, amid furious dissentient bark-ings from Jack, who seemed to consider it his duty to express an opinion in the matter.

"Dar now, ye aggrevatin' critter, lie down and shet up," she said to Jack, as she lifted him on to the bed and saw him cuddle down in Mrs. Betsey's arms and lay his rough cheek against hers.

Dinah remembered, years before, her young mistress lying weak and faint on that same spot, and how there had been the soft head of a baby lying where Jack's rough head was now nestling, and her heart swelled within her.

"Now, then," she said, pouring out some drops and giving them to her, "you jest hush up and go to sleep, honey. Miss Dorcas and I, we'll fix up this 'ere. It 'll all come straight—now you'll see it will. Why, de Lord ain't gwine to let you starve. Never see de righteous forsaken. Jest go to sleep, honey, and it 'll be all right when you wake up."

Meanwhile, Miss Dorcas had gone across the way to consult with Eva. The opening of the friendship on the opposite side of the way had been a relief to her from the desolateness and loneliness of her life circle, and she had come to that degree of friendly reliance that she felt she could state her dilemma and ask advice.

"I don't see any way but I must come to selling the house at last," said Miss Dorcas; "but I don't know how to set about it; and if we have to leave, at our age, life won't seem worth having. I'm afraid it would kill Betsey."

"Dear Miss Dorcas, we can't afford to lose you," said Eva. "You don't know what a comfort it is to have you over there, so nice and handy—why, it would be forlorn to have you go; it would break us all up!"

"You are kind to say so," said Miss Dorcas; "but I can't help feeling that the gain of our being there is all on one side."

"But, dear Miss Dorcas, why need you move? See here. A bright thought strikes me. Your house is so large! Why could n't you rent half of it? You really do n't need it all; and I'm sure it could easily be arranged for two families. Do think of that, please."

"If it could be done—if anybody would want it!" said Miss Dorcas.

"Oh, just let us go over this minute and see," said Eva, as she threw a light cloud of worsted over her head, and seizing Miss Dorcas by the arm, crossed back with her, talking cheerfully.

"Here you have it, nice as possible. Your front parlor—you never sit there; and it's only a care to have a room you don't use. And then this great empty office back here—a dining-room all ready! and there is a back shed that could have a cooking-stove, and be fitted into a kitchen. Why, the thing is perfect; and there's your income, without moving a peg! See what it is to have real estate!"

"You are very sanguine," said Miss Dorcas, looking a little brightened herself. "I have often thought myself that the house is a great deal larger than we need; but I am quite helpless about such matters. We are so out of the world. I know nothing of business; real estate agents are my horror; and I have no man to advise me."

"Oh, Miss Dorcas, wait now till I consult Harry. I'm sure something nice could be arranged."

"I dare say," said Miss Dorcas, "if these rooms were in a fashionable quarter we might let them; but the world has long since left our house in the rear."

"Never mind that," said Eva. "You see *we* don't mind fashion, and there may be neighbors as good as we, of the same mind."

Eva already had one of her visions in her head; but of this she did not speak to Miss Dorcas till she had matured it.

She knew Jim Fellows had been for weeks on the keen chase after apartments, and that none yet had presented themselves as altogether eligible. Alice had insisted on an economical beginning, and the utmost prudence as to price; and the result had been, what is usual in such cases, that all the rooms that would *do* at all were too dear.

Eva saw at once in this suite of rooms, right across the way from them, the very thing they were in search of. The rooms were large and sunny, with a quaint, old-fashioned air of by-gone gentility that made them attractive; and her artist imagination at once went into the work of brightening up their tarnished and dusky respectability with a nice little modern addition of pictures and flowers, and new bits of furniture here and there.

Just as she returned from her survey, she found Jim in her own parlor, with a thriving pot of ivy.

"Well, here's one for our parlor window, when we find one," said he. "I'm a boy that gets things when I see them. Now you don't often see an ivy so thrifty as this, and I've brought it to you to take care of till I find the room!"

"Jim," said Eva, "I believe just what you want is to

be found right across the way from us, so that we can talk across from your windows to ours."

"What! the old Vanderheyden house? Thunder!" said Jim.

Now, Jim was one of the class of boys who make free use of "thunder" in conversation, without meaning to express anything more by it than a state of slight surprise.

"What's up now?" he added. "I should as soon expect Queen Victoria to rent Buckingham Palace as that the old ladies across the way would come to letting rooms!"

"Necessity has no law, Jim." And then Eva told him Miss Dorcas's misfortune.

"Poor old girls!" said Jim. "I do declare it's too thundering bad. I'll go right over and rent the rooms; and I'll pay up square, too, and no mistake."

"Shall I go with you?"

"Oh, you just leave that to me. Two are all that are needed in a bargain."

In a few minutes, Jim was at his ease in front of Miss Dorcas, saying :

"Miss Dorcas, the fact is, I want to hire a suite of rooms. You see, I'm going to have a wife before long, and nothing will suit her so well as this neighborhood. Now, if you will only rent us half of your house, we shall behave so beautifully that you never will be sorry you took us in."

Miss Dorcas apologized for the rooms and furniture. They were old, she knew—not in modern style—but such as they were, would he just go through them? and Jim made the course with her. And the short of the matter was, that the bargain was soon struck.

Jim stated frankly the sum he felt able to pay for apartments ; to Miss Dorcas the sum seemed ample

U

enough to relieve all her embarrassments, and in an hour he returned to the other side, having completed the arrangement.

"There, now,—we're anchored, I think. The old folks and Aunt Maria have been wanting me to marry on and live with them in the old hive, but Jim does n't put his foot into that trap, if he knows it. My wife and I must have our own establishment, if it's only in two rooms. Now it's all settled, if Allie likes it, and I know she will. By George, it's a lucky hit! That parlor will brighten up capitally."

"You know, old furniture is all the rage now," said Eva, "and you can buy things here and there as you want."

"Yes," said Jim; "you know I did buy a pair of brass andirons when I was going to ask Allie to have me, and they'll be just the things for the fireplace over there. Miss Dorcas apologized for the want of those that belonged there by saying that her brother had taken them to pieces to try some experiments in brass polishing, and never found time to put them together again, and so parts of them got lost. I told her it was a special providence that I happened to have the very pair that were needed there; and there's a splendid sunny window for the ivies on the south corner!"

"That old furniture is lovely," said Eva. "It's like a dark, rich background to a picture. All your little bright modern things will show so well over it."

"Well, I'm going to bring Allie down to go over it, this minute," said Jim, who was not of the class that allow the grass to grow under their feet.

Meanwhile, when little Mrs. Betsey came down to dinner, she found the storm over, and clear, shining after rain.

"What, Mr. Fellows!" she exclaimed; "that dear,

good young man that was so kind to Jack! Why, Dorcas, what a providence! I'm sure it'll be a mercy to have a man in the house once more!"

"Why, I'm sure," said Miss Dorcas, "your great fear that you wake me up every night about, is that there *is* a man in the house!"

"Oh, well," said Mrs. Betsey, laughing cheerfully; "you know what I mean. I mean the right kind of a man. I've thought that those dreadful burglars and creatures that break into houses where there's old silver must find us out—because, Dorcas, really, that hat that we keep on the entry table is so big and dusty, and so different from what they wear now, they must know that no man wears a hat like that. I've always told Dinah that—she knows I have, more than twenty times."

A snicker from the adjacent china-closet, where Dinah was listening, confirmed this statement.

"Why, it's such a nice thing. Why, there's no end to it," said Mrs. Betsey, whose cheerfulness increased with reflection. "A real *live* man in the house!—and a young man, too!—and such a nice one; and *dear* Miss Alice—why, only think, bringing all her wedding clothes to the house, and I don't doubt she'll show them all to me—and it'll be so nice for Jack! won't it, Jack?"

Jack barked his assent vigorously, and a second explosive chuckle from the china closet betrayed Dinah's profound sympathy. The faithful creature was rolling and boiling in waves of triumphant merriment behind the scenes. The conversation of her mistresses in fact appeared to be a daily source of amusement to her, and Miss Dorcas was forced to wink at this espionage, in consideration of Dinah's limited sources of entertainment, and generally pretended not to know that she was there.

On the present occasion, Dinah's contribution to the

interview was too evident to be ignored, but Miss Dorcas listened to it with indulgence. A good prospect of
regular income does, after all, strengthen one's faith in
Providence, and dispose one to be easily satisfied with
one's fellows.

CHAPTER L.

DEAR MOTHER: You've no idea how things have gone on within a short time. I have been *so* excited and *so* busy, and kept in such a state of constant consultation, for this past week, that I have had no time to keep up my bulletins to you.

Well, dear mother, it is at last concluded that we are to have two weddings on one day, the second week after Easter, when Alice is to be married to Jim Fellows, and Angie to Mr. St. John.

Easter comes this year about the latest that it ever does, so that we may hope for sunny spring weather, and at least a few crocuses and hyacinths in the borders, as good omens for the future. I wish you could choose this time to make your long-promised visit and see how gay and festive we all are. Just now, every one is overwhelmed with business, and the days go off very fast.

Aunt Maria is in her glory, as generalissimo of the forces and dictator of all things. It is for just such crises that she was born; she has now fairly enough to manage to keep her contented with everybody, and everybody contented with her—which, by-the-bye, is not always the case in her history.

It is decreed that the wedding is to be a morning one, in Mr. St. John's little chapel; and that, after the reception at mamma's, Jim will start with Alice to visit his family friends, and Angie and St. John will go immediately on the steamer to sail for Europe, where they will spend the summer in traveling and be back again in the

autumn.   Meanwhile, they have engaged a house in that
part of the city where their mission work lies, and of
course, like ours, it is on an unfashionable street—a
thing which grieves Aunt Maria, who takes every occasion to say that Mr. St. John, being a man of independent fortune, is entitled to live genteelly.   I am glad,
because they are within an easy distance of us, which
will be nice.   Aunt Maria and mamma are to see to
getting the house all ready for them to go into when they
return.

Bolton is going over with them, to visit Paris!   The
fact is, since I opened communication between him and
Caroline, her letters to me have grown short and infre-
quent, and her letters to him long and constant, and the
effect on him has been magical.   I have never seen him
in such good spirits.   Those turns of morbid depression
that he used to have, seem to be fading away gradually.
He has been with us so much that I feel almost as if he
were a member of our family, and I cannot but feel that
our home has been a shelter and a strength to him.
What would it be to have a happy one of his own?   I
am sure he deserves it, if ever kindness, unselfishness,
and true nobleness of heart deserved it: and I am sure
that Caroline is wise enough and strong enough to give
him just the support that he needs.

Then there's Alice's engagement to Jim.   I have long
foreseen to what her friendship for him would grow, and
though she had many hesitations, yet *now* she is perfectly happy in it; and only think how nice it is!   They
are to take half the old Vanderheyden house, opposite
to us, so that we can see the lights of each other's hearths
across from each other's windows.

Mother, does n't it seem as if our bright, cosy, happy,
free-and-easy home was throwing out as many side-shoots
as a lilac bush?

. Just think; in easy vicinity, we shall have Jim and
Alice, Angie and St. John, and, as I believe, Bolton and
Caroline. We shall be a guild of householders, who hold
the same traditions, walk by the same rule, and mind
the same things. . Won't it be lovely? What nice
"droppings in" and visitings and tea-drinkings and con-
sultings we shall have! And it is not merely having
good times either; but, Mother, the more I think of it,
the more I think the making of bright, happy *homes* is
the best way of helping on the world that has been discovered yet. A *home* is a thing that can't be for one's
own self alone—at least the kind of home we are thinking of; it reaches out on all sides and helps and shelters
and comforts others. Even my little experiment of a
few months ago shows me *that ;* and I know that
Angie's and St. John's home will be even more so than
ours. Angie was born to be a rector's wife; to have a
kind word and a smile and a good deed for everybody,
to love everybody dearly, and keep everybody bright and
in good spirits. It is amazing to see the change she has
wrought in St. John. He was fast getting into a sort of
stringent, morbid asceticism; now he is so gracious, so
genial, and so entertaining,—he is like a rock, in June, all
bursting out with anemones and columbines in every
rift.

As to Jim and Alice, you ought to see how happy
they are in consulting me about the arrangements of
their future home in the Vanderheyden house. And the
best of it is, to see how perfectly delighted the two old
ladies are to have them there. You must know that
there was a sudden failure in Miss Dorcas's income
which would have made it necessary to sell the house
had it not been for just this arrangement. But they are
as gracious and kind about it as if they were about to
receive guests; and every improvement and every addi-

tional touch of brightness to the rooms seems to please them as much as if they were going to be married themselves.

Miss Dorcas said to me that our coming to live in their neighborhood had been the greatest blessing to them that ever had happened for years—that it had opened a new life to them.

As to Maggie, dear Mother, she is becoming a real comfort to me. I do think that all the poor girl's sorrows and sufferings have not been in vain, and that she is now a true and humble Christian.

She has been very useful in this sudden hurry of work that has fallen upon us, and seems really delighted to be so. In our group of families, Maggie will always find friends. Angie wants her to come and live with them when they begin housekeeping, and I think I shall let her go.

I shall never forget the dreadful things I saw the night I went after her. They have sunk deep into my heart; and I hope, Mother, I see more clearly the deepest and noblest purpose of life, so as never again to forget it.

But, meantime, a thousand little cares break and fritter themselves on my heart, like waves on a rock. Everybody is running to me, every hour. I am consulter and sympathizer and adviser, from the shape of a bow and the positions of trimming up to the profoundest questions of casuistry. They all talk to me, and I divide my heart among them all, and so the days fly by with frightful rapidity, and I fear I shall get little time to write, so pray come and see for yourself

Your loving

Eva.

CHAPTER LI

IT is said that Queen Elizabeth could converse in five languages, and dictate to three secretaries at once, in different tongues, with the greatest ease and composure.

Perhaps it might have been so—let us not quarrel with her laurels; it only shows what women can do if they set about it, and is not a whit more remarkable than Aunt Maria's triumphant management of all the details of two weddings at one time.

That estimable individual has not, we fear, always appeared to advantage in this history, and it is due to her now to say that nobody that saw her proceedings could help feeling the beauty of the right person in the right place.

Many a person is held to be a pest and a nuisance because there isn't enough to be done to use up his capabilities. Aunt Maria had a passion for superintending and directing, and all that was wanting to bring things right was an occasion when a great deal of superintendence and direction was wanting.

The double wedding in the family just fulfilled all the conditions. It opened a field to her that everybody was more than thankful to have her occupy.

Lovers, we all know, are, *ex-officio*, ranked among the incapables; and if, while they were mooning round in the fairy-land of sentiment, some good, strong, active, practical head were not at work upon the details of real life, nothing would be on time at the wedding. Now, if this be true of one wedding, how much more of two! So Aunt Maria stepped at once into command by acclama-

tion and addressed herself to her work as a strong man
to run a race; and while Angie and St. John spent bliss-
ful hours in the back parlor, and Jim and Alice monop-
olized the library, Aunt Maria flew all over New York,
and arranged about all the towels and table-cloths and
napkins and doilies, down to the very dish-cloths. She
overlooked armies of sewing women, milliners and
mantua-makers—the most slippery of all mortal creatures—and drove them all up to have each her quota in
time. She, with Mrs. Van Arsdel, made lists of people
to be invited, and busied herself with getting samples
and terms from fancy stationers for the wedding cards.
She planned in advance all the details of the wedding
feast, and engaged the cake and fruit and ice-cream.

Nor did she forget the social and society exigencies
of the crisis.

She found time, dressed in her best, to take Mrs. Van
Arsdel in full panoply to return the call of Mrs. Dr.
Gracey, who had come, promptly and properly, with the
doctor, to recognize Miss Angelique and felicitate about
the engagement of their nephew.

She arranged for a dinner-party to be given by Mrs.
Van Arsdel, where the doctor and his lady were to be
received into family alliance, and testimonies of high
consideration accorded to them. Aunt Maria took occasion, in private converse with Mrs. Dr. Gracey, to
assure her of her very great esteem and respect for Mr.
St. John, and her perfect conviction that he was on the
right road now, and that, though he might possibly burn
a few more candles in his chapel, yet, when he came
fully under family influences, they would gradually be
snuffed out,—intimating that she intended to be aunt, not
only to Arthur, but to his chapel and his mission-work.

The extraordinary and serene meekness with which
that young divine left every question of form and eti-

quette to her management, and the sort of dazed humility with which he listened to all her rulings about the
arrangements of the wedding-day, had inspired in Aunt
Maria's mind such hopes of his docility as led to these
very sanguine anticipations.

It is true that, when it came to the question of rent-
ing a house, she found him quietly but unalterably set
on a small and modest little mansion in the unfashionable neighborhood where his work lay.

"Arthur is going on with his mission," said Angelique, "and I'm going to help him, and we must live
where we can do most good"—a reason to which Aunt
Maria was just now too busy to reply, but she satisfied
herself by discussing at length the wedding affairs with
Mrs. Dr. Gracey.

"Of course, Mrs. Gracey," she said, "we all feel that
if dear Dr. Gracey is to conduct the wedding services,
everything will be in the good old way; there 'll be
nothing objectionable or unusual."

"Oh, you may rely on that, Mrs. Wouvermans," replied the lady. "The doctor is not the man to run
after novelties; he's a good old-fashioned Episcopalian.
Though he always has been very indulgent to Arthur, he
thinks, as our dear bishop does, that if young men are
left to themselves, and not fretted by opposition, they
will gradually outgrow these things."

"Precisely so," said Aunt Maria; "just what I have
always thought. For my part I always said that it was
safe to trust the bishop."

Did Aunt Maria believe this? She certainly appeared
to. She sincerely supposed that this was what she
always had thought and said, and quite forgot the times
when she used to wonder "what our bishop could be
thinking of, to let things go so."

It was one blessed facility of this remarkable woman

that she generally came to the full conviction of the axiom that "whatever is, is right," and took up and patronized anything that would succeed in spite of her best efforts to prevent it.

So, in announcing the double wedding to her fashionable acquaintance, she placed everything, as the popular saying is, best foot foremost.

Mr. Fellows was a young man of fine talents, great industry and elegant manners, a great favorite in society, and likely to take the highest rank in his profession. Alice had refused richer offers—she might perhaps have done better in a worldly point of view, but it was purely a love match, &c., &c. And Mr. St. John, a young man of fine family and independent fortune, who might command all the elegancies of life, was going to live in a distant and obscure quarter, to labor in his work. These facts brought forth, of course, bursts of sympathy and congratulation, and Aunt Maria went off on the top of the wave.

Eva had but done her aunt justice when she told her mother that Aunt Maria would be all the more amiable for the firm stand which the young wife had taken against any interference with her family matters. It was so. Aunt Maria was as balmy to Eva as if that discussion had never taken place, though it must be admitted that Eva was a very difficult person to keep up a long quarrel with.

But just at this hour, when the whole family were at her feet, when it was her voice that decided every question, when she knew where everything was and was to be, and when everything was to be done, she was too well pleased to be unamiable. She was the spirit of the whole affair, and she plumed herself joyously when all the callers at the house said to Mrs. Van Arsdel, " Dear me! what would you do, if it were not for your sister?"

Verily she had her reward.

CHAPTER LII

EVA'S CONSULTATIONS.

"NOW see here," said Jim, coming in upon Eva as she sat alone in her parlor, "I've got something on my mind I want to talk with you about. You see, Alice and I are to be married at the same time with Angie and St. John."

"Yes, I see it."

"Well, now, what I want to say is, that I really hope there won't be anything longer and harder and more circumlocutory to be got through with on the occasion than just what's in the prayer-book, for that's all I can stand. I can't stand prayer-book with the variations, now I really can't."

"Well, Jim, what makes you think there will be prayer-book with the variations?"

"Oh, well, I attended a ritualistic wedding once, and there was such an amount of processing and chanting, and ancient and modern improvements, that it was just like a show. There were the press reporters elbowing and pushing to get the best places to write it up for the papers, and, for my part, I think it's in confounded bad taste, and I couldn't stand it; you know, now, I'm a nervous fellow, and if *I've* got to take part in the exercises, they'll have to 'draw it mild,' or Allie and I will have to secede and take it by ourselves. I *could n't* go such a thing as that wedding; I never should come out alive."

"Well, Jim, I don't believe there's any reason for apprehension. In the first place, the ceremony, as to its mode and form, always is supposed to be conducted according to the preferences of the bride's family, and we all of us should be opposed to anything which would draw remark and comment, as being singular and unusual on such an occasion."

"I'm glad to hear that," said Jim.

"And then, Jim, Mr. St. John's uncle, Dr. Gracey, is to perform the ceremony, and he is one of the most respected of the conservative Episcopal clergymen in New York; and it is entirely out of the question to suppose that he would take part in anything of the sort you fear, or which would excite comment as an innovation. Then, again, I think Mr. St. John himself has so much natural refinement and just taste that he would not wish his own wedding to become a theme for gossip and a gazing stock for the curious."

"Well, I did n't know about St. John; I was a little afraid we should be obliged to do something or other, because they did it in the catacombs, or the Middle Ages, or in Edward the Sixth's time, or some such dodge. I thought I'd just make sure."

"Well, I think Mr. St. John has gone as far in those directions as he ever will go. He has been living alone up to this winter. He has formed his ideas by himself in solitude. Now he will have another half to himself; he will see in part through the eyes, and feel through the heart, of a sensible and discreet woman—for Angie is that. The society he has met at our house in such men as Dr. Campbell and others, has enlarged his horizon,— given him new points of vision,—so that I think the too great tendencies he may have had in certain directions have been insensibly checked."

"I wish they may," said Jim, "for he is a good fellow, and so much like one of the primitive Christians that I really want him to get all the credit that belongs to him."

"Oh, well, you'll see, Jim. When a man is so sincere and good, and labors with a good wife to help him, you'll see the difference. But here comes little Mrs. Betsey, Jim. I promised to get her up a cap for the occasion."

"Well, I'm off; only be sure you make matters secure about the ceremony," and off went Jim, and in came little Mrs. Betsey.

"It's so good of you, dear Mrs. Henderson, to undertake to make me presentable. You know Dorcas hasn't the least interest in these things. Dorcas is *so* independent, she never cares what the fashion is. Now, *she* isn't doing a thing to get ready. She's just going in that satin gown that she had made twenty years ago, with a great lace collar as big as a platter; and she sits there just as easy, reading 'Pope's Essay on Man,' and here I'm all in a worry; but I can't help it. I like to look a little like other folks, you know. I don't want people to think I'm a queer old woman."

"Certainly, it's the most natural thing in the world," said Eva, as she stepped into the little adjoining workroom, and brought out a filmy cap, trimmed with the most delicate shade of rosy lilac ribbons. "There!" she said, settling it on Mrs. Betsey's head, and tying a bow under her chin, "if anybody says you're not a beauty in this, I'd like to ask them why?"

"I know it's silly at my age, but I do like pretty things," said Mrs. Betsey, looking at herself with approbation in the glass, "and all the more that it's so very kind of you, dear Mrs. Henderson."

"Me? Oh, I like to do it. I'm a born milliner," said Eva.

"And now I want to ask a favor. Do you think it would *do* for us to take our Dinah to church to see the ceremony. I don't know anybody that could enjoy it more, and Dinah has so few pleasures."

"Why, certainly. Dinah! my faithful adviser and help in time of need? Why, *of course*, give my compliments to her, and tell her I shall depend on seeing her there."

"Dinah is so delighted at the thought that your sister and Mr. Fellows are coming to live with us, she is busy cleaning their rooms, and does it with a will. You know Mr. Fellows has just that gay, pleasant sort of way that delights all the servants, and she says your sister is such a beauty!"

"Well, be sure and tell Dinah to come to the wedding, and she shall have a slice of the cake to dream on."

"I think I shall feel *so* much safer when we have a *man* in the house," continued Mrs. Betsey. "You see we have so much silver, and so many things of that kind, and Dorcas frightens me to death, because she will have the basket lugged up into our room at night. I tell her if she'd *only* set it outside in the entry, then if the burglars came they could just go off with it, without stopping to murder us; but if it was in our room, why, of course, they would. The fact is, I have got so nervous about burglars that I am up and down two or three times a night."

"But you have Jack to take care of you."

"Jack is a good watch dog—he's very alert; but the trouble is, he barks just as loud when there isn't anything going on as when there is. Night after night, that dog has started us both up with such a report, and I'd go all over the house and find nothing there. Sometimes I think he hears people trying the doors or windows. Altogether, I think Jack frightens me more than he helps, though I know he does it all for the best, and I tell Dorcas so when he wakes her up. You know experienced people always do say that a small dog is the very safest thing you can have; but when Mr. Fellows comes

I shall really sleep peaceably. And now, Mrs. Henderson, you do n't think that light mauve silk of mine will be too young-looking for me?"

"No, indeed," said Eva. "Why should n't we all look as young as we can?"

"I have n't worn it for more than thirty years; but the silk is good as ever, and your little dress-maker has made it over with an over-skirt, and Dinah is delighted with it, and says it makes me look ten years younger!"

"Oh! well I must come over and see it on you."

"Would you care?" said Mrs. Betsey, delighted. "How good you are; and then I'll show you the toilette cushions I've been making for the dear young ladies; and Dorcas is going to give each of them a pair of real old India vases that have been in the family ever since we can remember."

"Why, you'll be robbing yourselves."

"No, indeed; it would be robbing ourselves not to give something, after all the kindness you've shown us."

And Eva went over to the neighboring house with Mrs. Betsey; and entered into all the nice little toilette details with her; and delighted Dinah with an invitation in person; and took a sympathizing view of Dinah's new bonnet and shawl, which she pronounced entirely adequate to the occasion; and thus went along, sewing little seeds of pleasure to make her neighbors happier—seeds which were to come up in kind thoughts and actions on their part by and by.

CHAPTER LIII

WEDDING PRESENTS.

ST. JOHN and Angie were together, one evening, in the room that had been devoted to the reception of the wedding presents. This room had been Aunt Maria's pride and joy, and already it had assumed quite the appearance of a bazar, for the family connections of the Van Arsdels was large, and numbered many among the richer classes. Arthur's uncle, Dr. Gracey, and the family connections through him were also people in prosperous worldly circumstances, and remarkably well pleased with the marriage; and so there had been a great abundance of valuable gifts. The door-bell for the last week or two had been ringing incessantly, and Aunt Maria had eagerly seized the parcels from the servant and borne them to the depository, and fixed their stations with the cards of the givers conspicuously displayed.

Of course the reader knows that there were the usual amount of berry-spoons, and pie-knives, and crumb-scrapers; of tea-spoons and coffee-spoons; of silver tea-services; of bracelets and chains and studs and brooches and shawl-pins and cashmere shawls and laces. Nobody could deny that everything was arranged so as to make the very most of it.

Angie was showing the things to St. John, in one of those interminable interviews in which engaged people find so much to tell each other.

"Really, Arthur," she said, "it is almost too much. Everybody is giving to me, just at a time when I am so

happy that I need it less than ever I did in my life.
I can't help feeling as if it was more than my share."

Of course Arthur did n't think so; he was in that
mood that he could n't think anything on land or sea was
too much to be given to Angie.

" And look here," she said, pointing him to a stand
which displayed a show of needle-books and pincushions,
and small matters of that kind, " just look here—even
the little girls of my sewing-class must give me something. That needle-book, little Lottie Price made. Where
she got the silk I do n't know, but it's quite touching.
See how nicely she's done it! It makes me almost cry
to have poor people want to make me presents."

" Why should we deny *them* that pleasure—the greatest and purest in the world?" said St. John. " It is more
blessed to give than to receive."

" Well, then, Arthur, I'll tell you what I was thinking
of. I would n't dare tell it to anybody else, for they'd
think perhaps I was making believe to be better than I
was; but I was thinking it would make my wedding
brighter to give gifts to poor, desolate people who really
need them than to have all this heaped upon me."

Then Arthur told her how, in some distant ages of
faith and simplicity, Christian weddings were always
celebrated by gifts to the poor.

" Now, for example," said Angie, "that poor, little,
pale dress-maker that Aunt Maria found for me,—she has
worked day and night over my things, and I can't help
wanting to do something to brighten her up. She has
nothing but hard work and no holidays; no lover to
come and give her pretty things, and take her to Europe;
and then she has a sick mother to take care of—only
think. Now, she told me, one day, she was trying to
save enough to get a sewing-machine."

" Very well," said Arthur, "if you want to give her

one, we'll go and look one out to-morrow and send it to
her, with a card for the ceremony, so there will be one
glad heart."

"Arthur, you—"

But what Angie said to Arthur, and how she reward-
ed him, belongs to the literature of Eden—it cannot be
exactly translated.

Then they conferred about different poor families,
whose wants and troubles and sorrows were known to
those two, and a wedding gift was devised to be sent to
each of them; and there are people who may believe
that the devising and executing of these last deeds of
love gave Angie and St. John more pleasure than all the
silver and jewelry in the wedding bazar.

"I have reserved a place for our Sunday-school to
be present at the ceremony," said Arthur; "and there is
to be a nice little collation laid for them in my study;
and we must go in there a few minutes after the ceremony, and show ourselves to them, and bid them good-
by before we go to your mother's."

"Arthur, that is exactly what I was thinking of. I
believe we think the same things always. Now, I want
to say another thing. You wanted to know what piece
of jewelry you should get for my wedding present."

"Well, darling?"

"Well, I have told Aunt Maria and mamma and all
of them that your wedding gift to me was something I
meant to keep to myself; that I would not have it put
on the table, or shown, or talked about. I did this, in the
first place, as a matter of taste. It seems to me that a marriage gift ought to be something sacred between us two."

"Like the white stone with the new name that no
man knoweth save him that receiveth it," said St. John.

"Yes; just like that. Well, then, Arthur, get me only
a plain locket with your hair in it, and give all the rest

of the money to these uses we talked about, and I will count it my present. It will be a pledge to me that I shall not be a hindrance to you in your work, but a help; that you will do more and not less good for having me for your wife."

What was said in reply to this was again in the super-angelic dialect, and untranslatable; but these two children of the kingdom understood it gladly, for they were, in all the higher and nobler impulses, of one heart and one soul.

"As to the ceremony, Arthur," said Angie, "you know how very loving and kind your uncle has been to us. He has been like a real father; and since he is to perform it, I hope there will be nothing introduced that would be embarrassing to him or make unnecessary talk and comment. Just the plain, usual service of the Prayer-book will be enough, will it not?"

"Just as you say, my darling; this, undoubtedly, is your province."

"I think," said Angie, "that there are many things in themselves beautiful and symbolic, and that might be full of interest to natures like yours and mine, that had better be left alone if they offend the prejudices of others, especially of dear and honored friends."

"I do n't know but you are right, Angie; at any rate, our wedding, so far as that is concerned, shall have nothing in it to give offense to any one."

"Sometimes I think," said Angie, "we please God by giving up, for love's sake, little things we would like to do in his service, more than by worship."

"Well, dear, that principle has a long reach. We will talk more about it by and by; but now, good-night!—or your mother will be scolding you again for sitting up late. Somehow, the time does slip away so when we get to talking."

CHAPTER LIV.

MARRIED AND A'.

WELL, the day of days came at last, and a fairer May morning never brightened the spire of old Trinity or woke the sparrows of the park. Even the dingy back garden of the Vanderheyden house had bubbled out in golden crocus and one or two struggling hyacinths, and the old lilacs by the chamber windows were putting forth their first dusky, sweet-scented buds. In about half a dozen houses, everybody was up early, with heads full of wedding dresses, and wedding fusses, and wedding cake. Aunt Maria, like a sergeant of police, was on hand, as wide awake and as fully possessed of the case as it was possible for mortal woman to be. She was everywhere,—seeing to everything, reproving, rebuking, exhorting, and pushing matters into line generally.

This was her hour of glory, and she was mistress of the situation. Mrs. Van Arsdel was sweet and loving, bewildered and tearful; and wandered hither and thither doing little bits of things and remorselessly snubbed by her energetic sister, who, after pushing her out of the way several times, finally issued the order: "Nellie, I do wish you'd go to your room and keep quiet. I understand what I want, and you don't."

The two brides, each in their respective dressing-rooms, were receiving those attentions which belong to the central figures of the tableau.

Marie, the only remaining unmarried sister, who had been spending the winter in Philadelphia, had charge, as dressing-maid, of one bride, and Eva of the other. There was the usual amount of catastrophes—laces that broke in critical moments, when somebody had to be sent tearing out distractedly for another; gloves that split across the back on trying; coiffures that came abominably late, after keeping everybody waiting, and then had to be pulled to pieces and made all over; in short, no one item of the delightful jumble of confusions, incident to a wedding, was missing.

The little chapel was dressed with flowers, and was a bower of sweetness; and, as St. John had planned, there was space reserved for the Sunday-school children and the regular attendants of the mission.

Besides those, there was a goodly select show of what Aunt Maria looked upon as the choice jewels of rank and fashion.

Dr. Gracey performed the double ceremony with great dignity and solemnity; but the reporters, who fought for good places to see the show, and Miss Gusher and Miss Vapors, were disappointed. There was only the plain old Church of England service—neither less nor more.

Mrs. Van Arsdel, and other soft-hearted ladies, in different degrees of family connection, did the proper amount of tender weeping upon their best laced pocket handkerchiefs; and everybody said the brides looked *so* lovely.

Miss Dorcas and Mrs. Betsey had excellent situations to see the whole, and Dinah, standing right behind them, broke out into ejaculations of smothered rapture, from time to time, in Mrs. Betsey's ear. Dinah was so boiling over with delight that, but for this tolerated escape-valve, there might have been some explosion.

Just as the ceremonies had closed, Mrs. Betsey heard Dinah whispering hoarsely:

"Good Lor'! if dar ain't Jack!"

And sure enough, Jack was there in the church, sitting up as composedly as a vestryman, and apparently enjoying the spectacle. When one of the ushers approached to take him out, he raised himself on his haunches and waved his paws with affability.

Jim caught sight of him just as the wedded party were turning from the altar to leave the church, and the sight was altogether too much for his risibility.

The fact was that Jack had been the subject of great discussion and an elaborate locking up that morning. But divining an intention on the part of his mistresses to go somewhere, he had determined not to be left. So he had leaped out of a window upon a back shed, and thence to the ground, and had followed the coach at discreet distance, and so was "in at the death."

Well, courteous reader, a marriage is by common consent the end of a story, and we have given you two. "We and Our Neighbors," therefore, are ready to receive your congratulations.

THE END.